Clarissa Hedgestone

and the

Blood Moon

Clarissa Hedgestone
and the
Blood Moon

BY

C. JILL HEFTE

A HUMAN FAIRY TALE® PUBLICATIONS
© 2019 C. Jill Hefte

FOR MOTHER AND FATHER

"In the end, there is only love."
—Miriam Dorothy Hefte

"There is evil in the world."
—Vern Glen Hefte

CONTENTS

Clarissa Hedgestone

and the

Blood Moon

Human Fairies

A long time ago, human-sized fairies lived on Earth with humans and mer people. This is the story of one of them—Clarissa Hedgestone.

Rumbling Clouds and Dark Gloom

The Human Fairy King was dead.

The creeks ran crimson with the blood of Human Fairies killed while fighting their first civil war. Strife between the son and daughter of deceased King Glendorf had divided the noble houses of the land, tearing apart every Human Fairy family as the royal siblings grappled to see who would rule.

As Human Fairies lived for over three hundred years, King Glendorf's reign had been long, and he had been fair and just. However, his rule had been unique in one important regard— prior to his coronation, the throne had always been occupied by a female. Glendorf's mother, Queen Tatiana, had borne no female children. As the only heir, Glendorf took the throne by default and became the first male Human Fairy monarch. The period of his sovereignty broke the time-honored tradition of rule through feminine wisdom and magic.

Flanyanna, the elder of the two warring children, was King Glendorf's only child with his first wife, Queen Aliafora, who died giving birth to her. Her half-brother and bitter rival, Markolous, was born to the king's second wife, Casafala.

Glendorf, at the strenuous urging of Casafala, had initially named Markolous to succeed him. However, troubling deficiencies in his son's character plagued Glendorf, eventually forcing him to change his mind. Over the violent objections of Queen Casafala, Glendorf decreed on his deathbed that Flanyanna would be crowned upon his demise. Therefore, the precedence of a female Human Fairy ruler was reestablished. Flanyanna was quickly crowned after Glendorf's passing, and she was the reigning Queen when Markolous gathered his rebel forces to challenge her.

Markolous gained support for his rebellion, as many in the kingdom had grown accustomed to the Human Fairy on the throne wearing the breeches and stiff black boots of a male. They balked at the idea of once again seeing a lady in petticoats occupying that lofty perch. The lavish gifts and trade and landholding privileges Markolous promised those who supported him undoubtedly encouraged their objections to a female ruler.

As the wind blew back the combatants' long, flowing hair, the clearly visible tattoos on their necks identified the noble house to which their families were traditionally pledged. They had proudly borne these markings since birth.

The uniforms of both armies were similar—high necks, double-breasted leather jackets that flared at the hips, and leather pants. Geometric, astronomical symbols in different colored threads identified the Human Fairy house to which they were affiliated.

Those wearing the white uniforms of the daughter, Flanyanna, bore the astrological symbol of Virgo, the virgin. Those wearing the black uniforms of the son, Markolous, bore the astrological symbol of Scorpio, instant death by a venomous sting.

The noble houses no longer presented a united front to the Human Fairy world. Cousin fought cousin. Brothers and sisters crossed swords with deadly intent. All harmony had disappeared.

The fighting surged on a plain bordering the Lost Forest, whose ancient trees, brought by the original Human Fairy immigrants, stood in silent witness to the conflict. The queen's white forces fought valiantly with their slashing swords but were unable to regain lost ground. Countless arrows raining down from the troops wearing the black scorpion insignia obscured the sun, casting a shadow on the battlefield. Queen Flanyanna's troops were forced back against the ancient rowan trees of the Lost Forest.

On a hilltop above the plain, Queen Flanyanna keenly observed the combat unfolding below her. A fierce tempest battered her body and whipped the green grass beneath her horse's hooves back and forth. It reflected the violent mood of the battle that ebbed and flowed below her. In the sky above her, a constable of ravens circled above the warring combatants. These were no ordinary ravens. They were the feared and misunderstood Shadow Fairies. Shadow Fairies disguised themselves as ravens when they entered the Human Fairy world. Their entire existence was of etheric bodies, light and malleable. Human Fairies were physical beings with the limitations of their heavy mortal bodies.

The Shadow Fairies were there because of the carnage of the battle. Human Fairies suffered no diseases, and they could only die a premature death from a traumatic or violent act. If they did not complete their incarnation of three hundred years, they would enter the Shadow Fairy world and become Shadow Fairies. There, they waited out the remainder of their incarnation before they could be reborn back as Human Fairies. Many Human Fairies joined the Shadow Fairy world that day.

Radiating a noble prowess, Flanyanna's supple body tensed and contracted as she leaned forward on her winged white charger, Arasthenes. Her hand tightly gripped the hilt of the rose crystal sword at her side that had been handed down to her from her father. Except for her ears that were pointed at the top, she looked like a Human on Earth.

Arasthenes was a flying horse, a Namdalarian, ancestor to the Andalusian breed of horse first bred in Spain. These marvelous, airborne animals chose to come along with the Human Fairy settlers from Earth centuries ago. Their ability to glide through the skies emigrated with them and left only earth-bound horses for Humans.

Flanyanna moved as one with the magnificent beast under her wind-whipped skirt. Both hers and Arasthenes' ears listened keenly to the sounds of the conflict below them.

Although it was far from the truth, the gossip in the taverns was that Flanyanna loved to mount her charger more than she did her husband. Her early, and as yet undisclosed, pregnancy attested to the inaccuracy of these rumors.

The proper moment to announce the impending arrival of a new heir to the throne was a point of fierce debate between Flanyanna and her husband, Petronero. Petronero wanted to shout the glad tidings far and wide, while Flanyanna feared that knowledge of her pregnancy would incite Markolous to redouble his efforts to usurp her.

Over a simple, flowing white satin gown, trimmed with white fox fur at her neck and wrists, she wore brilliant, burnished armor. The armor and her slender boyish torso, effectively concealed her pregnancy. The braided yellow, white, and rose gold threads of Flanyanna's royal crown that her brother coveted so fiercely covered the back of her head like a helmet. Her long, ink-black hair fell over the mail that protected her feminine shoulders.

Below Flanyanna's strong, slender nose, her Cupid's bow lips pursed. Above deep, almond eyes, her distinct black brow furrowed in concentration, creasing her translucent, unblemished skin. Her brow shot up in sympathy for her weary army. The early action had not gone well for her forces. She steadied Arasthenes with a firm stroke to his withers, effortlessly adjusting in the saddle as the horse rustled and shifted his wings, ready and eager to join in the fray.

Entrenched below the hill, a portion of Queen Flanyanna's forces in their tattered and blood-stained uniforms strove mightily to hold back Markolous' troops who sought to breach the Human Fairy barricade they formed and capture the queen.

Feeling Flanyanna's unease, Arasthenes belched steam from his nostrils. In her agitation, she yanked at his reins, something she had never done before.

"Where's my sister?" she cried out in frustration.

It was not just her half-sister's wise counsel she missed. She sorely needed the balm of her sister's powerful presence. It had supported her as long as she could remember. Flanyanna not only had a connection by blood with her half-sister, they also had a special bond in spirit.

Flanyanna's half-sister was the eldest child to King Glendorf on their planet, Kokakina. Born out of wedlock to his mistress, Lunamilla, she was illegitimate and consequently disqualified from consideration for the throne unless the king acknowledged her, something he never did. The question of succession had always been a choice between Flanyanna or Markolous.

Nonetheless, through Lunamilla, Flanyanna's half-sister was a descendant of the most magically powerful line on Kokakina. The Pink Fairies. The Human Fairy seers. The magical power of most Human Fairies had diminished after immigration to Kokakina, but the Pink Fairy line maintained its full magic because their heart-centered nature retained a true connection to Earth.

Flanyanna's Pink Fairy sister was the one with the greatest ability to interpret the messages provided by the Rose Crystal, the prime talisman brought to Kokakina from the heart of Earth. She had the deepest access to the heart-centered counsel it had provided since time immemorial. Despite that, it was worn by Flanyanna of the ruling White Fairies, known for their inner knowingness and wisdom.

A white-clad, chestnut-haired, chiseled rider riding a white Namdalarian dashed up the hill through the combatants, swerving around straining warriors to reach his queen.

Flanyanna immediately recognized her husband and breathed a sigh of relief.

"Petronero! Where have you been?" she said.

"The tide of the battle goes against us. We must retreat now," Petronero said as he rode up, his white uniform and breastplate drenched in blood. He looked deeply into his wife's eyes, but only saw the haughty regard of his sovereign.

"I will not retreat," Flanyanna said.

Petronero reached out and grabbed Arasthenes' reins. "Stop this madness. You shouldn't even be riding in your condition."

"Petronero—what are you doing?" Flanyanna asked, pulling on her reins, and trying to regain her regal composure. "Don't presume to tell me what to do—husband. You may be my consort, but need I remind you I am your queen?"

Before Petronero could respond, Augustino, the stout, silver-haired captain of the queen's guard raced up the hill to Flanyanna on his bay Namdalarian. The horse's black mane and tail sailed in the wind. Its reddish hair and black lower legs were matted with sweat, mud, and blood.

"Your Majesty," he said, lifting his blood-covered sword across his breastplate in salute.

"Petronero says we need to retreat." Not looking at Petronero, Flanyanna regarded Augustino intently, her cheeks flushing. "What say you, Augustino?"

"Ma'am, we stay and fight," Augustino said without hesitation.

"I tell you we will not prevail today," Petronero countered. "We must retreat now, or all is lost."

"Nonsense," Augustino scoffed, gesturing down the hill. "Our fortifications are holding. Look—our troops are gathering here at the base of the hill, my Queen. We'll soon be in a position to counterattack—we must press on."

"You see?" Flanyanna responded, finally turning back to her husband, her decision made. "I won't pull back until I've seen my brother's head on a stake!" Her breathing quickened, and her heart raced. She must stop her only brother who threatened her rightful rule.

"I say stop this insanity—this is no time to be a petulant child," Petronero said, neither swayed by Augustino's argument nor Flanyanna's determination. "You must withdraw now to avoid defeat. Your brother has yet to commit all his vile forces. If we retreat now, we can regroup and reengage when the advantage is unquestionably ours."

Petronero and Augustino locked eyes, vying for their queen's favor. Ignoring the tension between her two male advisors, Flanyanna looked toward the battlefield. She was gratified to see her faithful supporters' efforts were finally succeeding. Markolous' troops were pulling back.

"There will be no safe place on Kokakina if I don't defeat my brother today." She choked out the words, fearing for her unborn child.

Barely had she spoken when a rotten, rancid stench spread over the battlefield. A horde of Human Fairy-sized creatures wearing black uniforms and bearing a strong resemblance to pigs, with snouts ending in cartilaginous discs, ran on all fours from the woods behind Flanyanna's white army and charged into the fray. Except for their tails, which were naked and red, their odious bodies were covered in coarse gray and brown hair.

"Peccaries!" Flanyanna said indignantly.

"Why not?" Petronero asked. "They're stupid creatures who can be bought! He's brought these reinforcements in for only one purpose—to defeat you!"

The pig-like creatures stood on their hind legs and battered the queen's soldiers with their spears and their sharp, serrated teeth.

"This is preposterous!" Flanyanna turned to Augustino for his confirmation. "Markolous can't be serious?"

Augustino nodded in agreement. "Don't worry Ma'am. The Peccaries are stupid creatures and pose no threat we can't handle."

All three watched as a particularly large Peccarey slashed one of Flanyanna's white soldiers with his needle-sharp canine teeth, before turning on and slicing open another's belly.

"Stupid or not—" Petronero said, his eyes taking in the disembowelment, "—these giant swine are fierce and tenacious fighters and pose a great danger to your monarchy. Their teeth are long and sharp and are deadly weapons that can impale our soldiers' flesh." He turned his Namdalarian toward the bloody combat to engage and eliminate the hulking Peccarey before it harmed any more white-clad troops. "I'll save what troops I can to fight at another time."

"Petronero!" Flanyanna cried. "I command that you stop—this instant!"

He ignored her order and galloped on. He paused only to skewer the massive Peccarey through its ribcage with a mighty thrust of his clear crystal sword before disappearing in the melee. As she watched Petronero pull his sword out of the Peccarey's convulsing torso and gallop back into the fracas, Flanyanna was besieged by doubts. Had she made the right decision to stay and continue the fight? The only thing she knew for sure was that every fiber in her being desired to keep the throne.

Her breath coming in short heavy gasps, she turned back to Augustino. "Bring up the reserves."

Her eyes held his for a moment, communicating what she could not say aloud in front of her guards—she was afraid all would be lost.

Augustino saluted, turned his Namdalarian around, and raced down the backside of the hill to a different part of the Lost Forest where the remainder of Flanyanna's army waited in reserve.

The Enchanted Mouse

In another part of the forest that bordered the raging battle, Flanyanna's reserve forces waited in a grove of rowan trees. Wild horses, deer, coyotes, and huge wolves who had been transported from Earth long ago with the first Human Fairy immigrants had gathered to fight for their queen. A large ten-point buck stood in the front. Clinging to the buck's magnificent rack of antlers, a small gray field mouse keenly watched the combat.

"We must find Flan and protect her." The mouse's urgent statement to the buck came out in the clear, refined tones of a well-bred, upper class Human Fairy.

The voice was not the only remarkable thing about this simple field mouse. Its every move displayed a confident, poised air of command. Its darting, jade-green eyes missed nothing. Human

Fairies endowed with the most magical powers without fail had jade-green eyes and all the other magical beasts deferred to the mouse.

Despite an outward appearance of calmness, the mouse was shaken. It had not realized how strong an opponent Markolous would be. It was stunned at the forces Markolous had amassed.

Intently focused on their leader and waiting for the command to do battle, the wildlife did not sense the Human Fairies in black who crept up behind them with flaming torches. These interlopers used the torches to light the rowan trees. Ravenous flames flared up, engulfing the tree sentinels brought from Earth. The flames hungrily raced towards the unsuspecting, enchanted creatures.

"RUN!" screamed the little mouse.

The intense heat searing their fur, the wild beasts responded to their leader's command and dashed towards the battlefield. A flaming rowan limb from a burning tree cracked and fell, just missing the buck and the mouse as they led the way.

Without warning, a net dropped from the sky, entrapping all of the magical animals. Wasting not a moment, the jade-green eyed mouse used its tiny sharp teeth to gnaw furiously at the net's weft and warp to free them.

The black forces landed on their winged Namdalarians and encircled the ensnared creatures. They wrapped sisal cords attached to the net around the encircling rowans and backed off waiting for the fire to advance and incinerate the terrified animals.

Inside the net the captive beasts thrashed wildly trying to break free as the lapping flames approached. The smoke from the burning timber filled their nostrils and black soot and intense, suffocating heat closed their throats. Their eyes stung sharply.

The foul stench polluted the clean air as the forest fire burned in close and singed some of the creatures' flesh.

Even in the heat of the battle and her concern over the deadly threat posed by Markolous, the mouse's heartfelt connection made saving its friends the most important thing as it furiously worked the cords binding them.

"Stop! We don't have time. Use your third eye," the buck yelled.

Realizing he was right, the gray field mouse steadied its gaze on the net. In the middle of its forehead, a precise pink laser beamed out and cut a hole in the net's fabric. The buck pushed his antlers into the hole and thrust his way out, the mouse holding on tightly. The other frenzied animals followed suit. Straining against the tear, they ripped it wide open and escaped in the nick of time, just before the fire's fierce kiss incinerated them.

The stench of the burning flesh of their comrades filled the nostrils of Flanyanna's terrified four-legged troops as they ran for their lives. They stampeded pell-mell onto the battlefield, fleeing the flames. Their hooves and paws pounded maniacally as they ran through the fighting soldiers, knocking down and trampling the warriors in their path.

"Look—the queen!" The buck pointed his nose with its large sensitive nostrils up to the hilltop where Queen Flanyanna sat on Arasthenes.

Just as he spoke, a volley of crystal-clear arrows with serrated heads rained down. The arrows' razor-sharp points penetrated the armor of Flanyanna's soldiers.

"Flan...she's in danger. We must hurry," the mouse said.

With the mouse on his antlers, the buck bounded through the battlefield.

No sooner had the words left the mouse's mouth, a horrific ringing sound caused it to look up. An encroaching cloak of darkness rumbled across the bright blue sky. The ominous din of the looming blackness struck fear into the hearts of what was left of Flanyanna's white-clad army.

With swords and shields, Human Fairy-sized insects hovered above the battlefield. Grotesque and eerie wings extended far beyond their metallic, black-hued bodies. Their hollow abdomens resonated with a pounding, discordant boom. A strong, armor-like plate extended down to protect their vulnerable midsections. They swooped down in a blade-like formation, using tar-black projections as daggers to pierce the white troops still standing in front of the queen's hill.

"TETTIGARDS!" one of Queen Flanyanna's bodyguards cried as he and the three other members of the squad circled tightly around their queen.

Flanyanna reflexively covered her pointed ears from the abominable noise. She knew very well the danger the swarm posed for her army.

At one time these creatures had been cicadas, harmless insects that came with the Human Fairies when they migrated to Kokakina from Earth. Over the centuries, these benign herbivores fed on the nectar of the Rosa Centifolia, a high vibration thorny plant brought from Earth that had transformative powers. In doing so, the insects also ingested blood left when Human Fairy gardeners accidentally pricked their fingers on the plants' thorns. The remarkable combination of Human Fairy blood mixed with the plants' potent nectar fostered an astounding evolution on them.

The cicadas became altered creatures called Tettigards and were not part of the unified matrix of the heart connection that came from Earth. They were now carnivorous. Human Fairy blood became their preferred food, and many Human Fairies met their doom at the hands of the mutated cicadas.

The Tettigards created more penetrating projections that rained down onto the battlefield. Manes of black hair framed bulging, compound eyes that stared balefully at their prey as they hit the despoiled meadow. Dangerous individually, their massed, concentrated efforts were devastating to Flanyanna's troops.

Unlike Human Fairies, the giant insects had no magical abilities, but they had evolved sentient intelligence. The creatures moved almost like Human Fairies, but with an extra pair of arms. The claws of their top four legs had adapted and now possessed fiendishly strong grasping and slashing abilities. Both their swords and their sharp appendages were deadly weapons.

The Tettigards relentlessly slaughtered the queen's soldiers whose eardrums ruptured from the insects' high-pitched wailing. The soldiers bled profusely from their ears and staggered on the battlefield.

The Tettigards had an extra set of three small eyes in the shape of an inverted triangle on their foreheads between their two prominent eyes. This triangle of eyes could detect the slightest movement. Playing dead would not fool these savage predators. A ghastly Tettigard saw the shallow breathing of a wounded white-clad Human Fairy soldier lying in the meadow. The Tettigard's rostrum pierced his flesh and drained his blood, sucking hard as the warrior writhed in agony.

A female Human Fairy soldier came up behind the Tettigard warrior, cut off its head and bent down to pull the rostrum out of her comrade's lifeless body. She did not notice a nearby Tettigard flying over with her rough, saw-edged stinger protruding out of her abdomen. The jagged edged appendage impaled the female Human Fairy who fell to her knees and collapsed face down into the bloody mud.

Although over the centuries, Human Fairies had learned to fear the Tettigards, Flanyanna had not realized the catastrophic danger these bloodthirsty aberrations posed for their entire existence—until now.

Watching the Tettigards pulverize her dying army, she remembered something that had occurred in her brother's youth. A swarm of Tettigards had attacked him one day when they were out playing. If their nanny, Bessalina, had not intervened to pull him away, he would never have survived. No Human Fairy had ever before survived a Tettigard swarming.

After that incident, Markolous became vicious and cruel, a bully to the core. Flanyanna had always wondered if her brother had become tainted by these monstrous creatures. But no one, including Flanyanna, dared to speak of this abhorrent event, or the drastic change in his personality for the worse afterwards. All feared retribution from his mother Queen Casafala. Casafala was extremely protective of her son.

"Your Majesty," shouted the squad leader of her guards above the thunderous roar, "your brother has formed an alliance with these abominable flying mutants."

"I fear my brother's ambition to be the Human Fairy King may destroy us all," Flanyanna said.

On a coal-black Namdalarian, Markolous flew through the Tettigard swarm. The giant insects parted to make way for him, and the afternoon sunlight shined through, reflecting off his high metallic silver boots. On his back he carried a carved onyx bow and a quiver of arrows with unusual tips meant for murder. They were formed from clear crystal three inches long, serrated along their sides, and balanced to perfection. Their points were more than needle-sharp. A surgical scalpel would be like a dull, mistreated ax in comparison to these deadly projectiles.

Markolous took his bow off his back and an arrow from his quiver. He ran his finger along the edge of the arrowhead before notching it and aiming it down towards his sister on the hill overlooking the battle. The adjustments the arrow made seemed to be coming from the arrow itself. It was almost as if it knew where to go on its own. Markolous loosened his deadly shaft.

The arrow shot true and was on course to strike Flanyanna and pierce her heart. Arasthenes jumped to the side at the last moment, and the arrow hit the spot where they had been standing. If her charger had not reacted so swiftly, her brother's arrow would have met its mark, and she would surely be dead.

Now afoot, the green-eyed mouse zigged and zagged through the straining, shouting, and cursing combatants. Spotting a gross Peccarey gripping a serrated-edged sword, the mouse stopped dead in its tracks. One of Flanyanna's soldiers in her blood-stained, white uniform was down on the ground, beneath the raised blade.

Another pink laser beam shot out of the mouse's third eye—the focus of power of Human Fairies who still were still magically endowed. The ensorcelled beam lifted the Peccarey off its feet and slammed it with a terrific thud into a burning tree. Now on fire, the squealing pig ran off on all fours, just missing the green-eyed mouse.

Markolous' winged black stallion, Calamtheus, landed on top of two white-clad foot soldiers, crushing them under his hooves. The shadowed, usurping prince raised his sword high over a Human Fairy warrior and sliced into his back. Malice gleamed from Markolous' hate-filled eyes as he scanned the battlefield for another victim. Choosing one, he jerked violently on Calamtheus' bridle and shoved his crystal sword into a soldier's ribcage. The grinding crunch of cracked crystalline ribs accompanied his thrust. Blood from the soldier's ruptured lungs spewed out of his mouth. Staggering, he tumbled into the dirt.

Grunting in satisfaction, Markolous pulled the sword from the dying soldier's body and looked about.

A flat, metallic voice cried out, "Behind you—"

Markolous jerked on the bridle. As he turned his Namdalarian around, a flashing sword that would have impaled him swooshed past, missing him by a hairbreadth. He turned back and, with one savage blow, slew the Human Fairy soldier who had dared swing her sword at him.

Suddenly, a Hokkaido wolf, full-grown and powerful, jumped onto Markolous' back, knocking him off his horse. Markolous wrestled with the lean, muscled wolf that easily weighed 200 pounds. These wolves had a long-standing relationship with Human Fairies as protectors of the Human Fairy way of life. The wolf's long claws scratched him, his teeth ready to rip out Markolous' throat.

A Tettigard flew up and slit the wolf's throat with his hook-like appendage. The mate to the Hokkaido wolf jumped for the Tettigard's back. Her huge jaws gaped open, showing her fangs.

"Tithoreus—your back—" Markolous shouted out.

The giant insect turned just in time and thrust his clawed arm into the wolf's belly, killing her instantly.

Markolous drew his sword back and, with a savage blow, separated the head of a male Human Fairy soldier from his body. The decapitated head barreled down the meadow's incline toward the green-eyed mouse.

The mouse nimbly jumped out the path of the tumbling head. Pulling its wisp of a tail out of the way, it cast its small gray body into the air and landed on Markolous' silver-armored leg as he remounted his Namdalarian unaware that the small creature now clung to his boot. Once Markolous was on his horse, the mouse scampered to the cinch of the saddle and began to gnaw away at it in a frenzy.

Demoralized and overwhelmed from the relentless attacks of Markolous' Peccarey and Tettigard reinforcements, the queen's army lost heart and broke ranks. No match for their cruel, implacable foe, the outnumbered Human Fairy knights and enchanted creatures fell back in disarray. The end was near.

Third Eye Duel

Queen Flanyanna watched in disbelief as the soldiers of her Human Fairy army fled for their lives. Defeated and desolate, she slumped in her saddle. Clutching her sword to her side, she looked at the death surrounding her. Sweat dripped from her pale, sallow forehead. Arasthenes shifted tensely, tossing his long, alabaster mane and tail as he sensed her unease. Even as his head pitched up and down, his sapphire eyes remained level with the ground. The Human Fairy queen leaned to one side of Arasthenes and vomited. Her morning sickness could not be controlled.

Augustino rode back up the hill to rejoin his Human Fairy queen. "Your Majesty—" he reported, despondently, "—all our reserve legions have fled."

"My husband was right. I have miscalculated my brother's army. We should have withdrawn to fight another day...," she said to herself. Flanyanna wiped her brow with her gloved hand. "My brother must have promised the Tettigards plenty of Human Fairy blood...."

"Aye—and I fear this is only the first payment," Augustino said, his brow furrowing at the grim prospect.

Flanyanna was almost afraid to ask, but did so anyway. "Where is he—where's Petronero?"

Augustino paused before answering. "Ma'am—I have seen no sign of him since he returned to the fray."

"Then—I have lost even more." Flanyanna feared her husband was dead.

"Ma'am—I advised you poorly when I said to press the attack." Augustino bowed his head in shame. He feared that the Human Fairy world as he knew it had been lost.

"Augustino, I am the Human Fairy ruler," Flanyanna said. "I made the decision, not you."

Augustino leaned forward. "Ma'am—challenge your brother to a third eye duel."

Flanyanna adjusted herself uneasily in her saddle, knowing that she could lose her child if she fought Markolous with her third eye.

"You must kill your brother," Augustino said, unaware his sovereign was pregnant.

"I fear you are right—I must do away with my own brother."

"I would fight for you if I could," Augustino offered. "There's nothing else you can do to save your monarchy. Vanquish him, and his followers will lose the will to fight."

In their childhood King Glendorf had insisted that she and Markolous practice their swordplay together using their third eyes. She had bested him many times. She knew his strengths and weaknesses better than he did, but it never occurred to her that she might have to fight him to the death.

"How ironic that our play as children will decide if I live or die," she said.

"Remember to stay to his left," Augustino said, "that's his weak side."

Flanyanna nodded, remembering from her childhood that what he said was true.

"Ma'am…it's the only way to save Kokakina from your brother and the Tettigards."

Flanyanna looked down onto the battlefield. With her third eye she saw the ravens now diving down. A sole raven flew over a dead warrior's body. As it hovered, a ghostly specter drifted up from the corpse to meet the Shadow Fairy raven, and the two flew off together. Those who still had the power of the third eye could most easily see the Shadow Fairies collect the dead and take them to the Shadow Fairy world, though all Human Fairies could to a degree.

"I suppose the shadows would be better than oblivion," she said. She reached out and squeezed the hand of her captain of the guards. "I only hope I live to give birth—and my heir will have a protector as steadfast as you."

"Ma'am—I didn't know…." Dumbfounded, Augustino's eyes widened.

"It's all right, Augustino."

Augustino bowed to her and motioned to her bodyguards on their Namdalarians, who formed a square formation around their queen to protect her at all costs. He raised his sword to his chest in salute, honoring his sovereign, before turning to the royal herald, a young girl with golden hair, not more than fourteen years old, standing close by on the hill. "Sound the call for the Third Eye Duel," he commanded.

With a quick nod the girl plucked her crystal harp. The clear, clarion notes floated out over the meadow. The combatants on both sides stopped. All knew this call was a challenge to decide the fate of the battle by individual combat between the two royals, both of whom still possessed the power of their third eyes.

Flanyanna and Arasthenes flew upwards, closely followed by Augustino and her guards. She did not need to urge her flying horse on. The magnificent steed knew her intimately and understood what she wanted. He was an extension of her. Reaching the height of his flight's arc, the valiant Namdalarian dived down with his rider to meet their destiny.

Markolous beheld Flanyanna as she drew near on Arasthenes. He sensed the questioning eyes of his followers on him as they heard the harp's call. Would he accept the challenge?

His forces looked to win the battle, but he could not refuse individual third eye combat with his sister. He kicked his black beauty with a vengeance to rise into the air to duel with her.

The Tettigard who had slain the female Hokkaido wolf flew up next to Markolous.

"Sire, ignore this distraction—" he urged in his dispassionate, detached drone. "—don't expose yourself to the risk of defeat."

"Shut up, Tithoreus. Don't try to tell me what to do." Markolous yanked at Calamtheus' reins, casting a malevolent glare at the giant insect. He steadied his Namdalarian. "If I don't fight my sister, all will think me too weak to rule."

"Sire—"

"I said stay out of this!" Markolous interrupted him. "I know what I'm doing."

The Tettigard relented and backed away, bowing. "Sire."

Markolous raised his crystal sword high into the air and spurred his winged steed again, to take flight to meet Flanyanna in mid-air. Unknown to him, the small mouse still clung to his saddle's cinch, chewing away at it for all it was worth.

The delay of speaking with Tithoreus proved to be costly. Before he could get aloft, the queen and Arasthenes slammed into Markolous and his horse. The collision jarred Flanyanna, and she backed off to regain her balance. The two siblings locked their third eyes.

Knowing his masculine weight and strength would grant him the advantage if the fighting was in close quarters, Markolous charged straight forward at Flanyanna on his snorting black steed. He opened his third eye to bring forth a beam of laser light.

Without warning the leather cinch on his saddle gave way and it shot out from under him. With a stunned cry he fell off Calamtheus and rolled in the mud before slamming up against a dead Peccarey.

Freed of the weight of his cruel master, Calamtheus abandoned Markolous and flew off. Holding on tightly, the green-eyed mouse grasped the black horse's mane. Launching like an acrobat, the mouse vaulted from the fleeing animal. Pirouetting into space, it landed on the long, graceful white neck of Arasthenes.

Flanyanna moved closer to Markolous. Opening her third eye, she raised herself high in her saddle over him.

"I might have misjudged you, sister," Markolous snarled.

"Watch me, brother...I'll eat your heart and gain your magic...," she snarled back.

This was the ancient way the Human Fairies dealt with the power of their enemies. And though brother and sister, they were now mortal enemies and would fight until one of them was dead.

A blue-black laser beam shot out from Markolous' third eye and sliced through the air towards Flanyanna.

Flanyanna's body contorted, and she froze, her blood cold. "Brother—you dare to use the Black Hole Laser?" she asked.

In all the millennia of Human Fairy existence, only a few of the very darkest of wizards went to the Black Hole at the Milky Way galaxy's center to find the power to destroy others to oblivion. They only gained it by submitting themselves to the Lord of the Darkness, who lived in the Black Hole. In return for this power, they must provide the light of high beings for the Lord of the Darkness' insatiable appetite.

The Black Hole laser light had an instantaneous amplitude and phase that varied randomly with respect to time and space. Its chaotic nature wreaked havoc on any structure, including living bodies. It destroyed the chance of a Human Fairy it killed to join the Shadow Fairies. They would instead go into oblivion for all eternity.

With her third eye Flanyanna countered with a red laser while pulling Arasthenes back to escape. She knew the Black Hole laser had a short coherence length and could be nullified if she reacted quickly enough to form an effective counterattack. Her red laser's narrow spectrum of radiation batted aside Markolous' Black Hole laser beam and redirected it down on him. It focused a tight beam on his chest ready to cut his heart out. His black leather tunic began to smoke.

Flanyanna smelled the coppery, metallic odor of Markolous' iron-rich blood as it boiled and evaporated in a series of overlapping micro-explosions in his flesh.

"It's time to part ways…sister," Markolous ground his teeth in an effort to block out the pain of his injury.

Seeing their master was losing, a horde of Tettigards descended and gathered between the determined queen and her sibling foe. The chaotic melee ripped the brother and sister apart.

"The Tettigards have broken the rules of individual combat," Augustino shouted from where he sat on his horse to the side. He waved his hand and cried, "—protect the queen!"

He and the bodyguard contingent flew into the fracas. With their swords they slashed at the Tettigards in an effort to save their queen.

"Your Majesty—run for it!" Augustino cried.

Caught up in the heat of the duel, Flanyanna hesitated.

The enchanted mouse latched onto the queen's magical winged horse's silky alabaster mane. "Arasthenes, fly away—" it shrieked into the Namdalarian's ear.

Arasthenes snorted. He knew this voice very well. Although she was in enchanted mouse form, it was the unmistakable voice of the older half-sister of Flanyanna and Markolous.

Rising on two legs, Arasthenes spread his snowy white, feathered wings and lifted off, carrying away the queen and her sister.

"Follow your liege…," the queen's captain ordered. The guards disengaged from the Tettigards and their winged steeds flew after Arasthenes.

Some of the Tettigards twisted in mid-air to pursue the queen's party and feast on them as they retreated. They were blocked by an invisible barrier. Bouncing off the shield, the giant insects tumbled to the ground, shrieking in fury and pain.

The remaining Tettigards swirled in a defensive circle around their fallen leader. Intent on the kill, Augustino disregarded the danger they posed and drew his sword to kill Markolous and win the day for his sovereign.

The fierce warrior insects flew forward to challenge Augustino who cut off one of their heads. Another's sharp, pointed rostrum aimed at his chest to suck his blood, but Augustino's bay Namdalarian nimbly dodged and escaped.

The Tettigards mercilessly slammed into Augustino's body. For each one he killed, three more took its place. He slew many of the attacking Tettigards, but it was in vain. He was battling a swarm.

The queen's captain fell to the ground and disappeared under a host of Tettigards who feasted on his blood. He uttered not a sound.

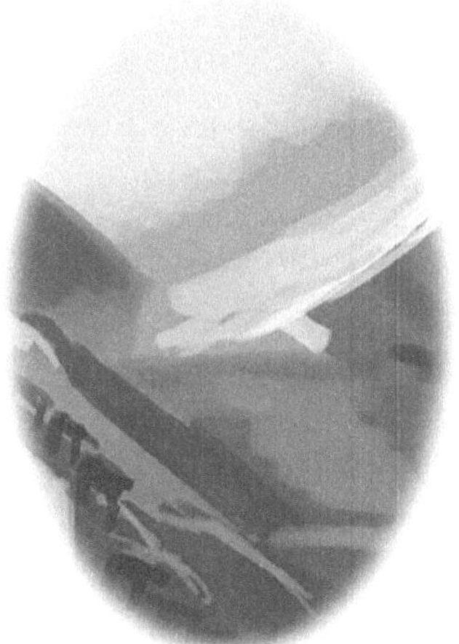

The Feydonian Pass

The Human Fairy queen, her enchanted sister, and her four bodyguards flew away from the battle and out over Kokakina, disappearing into clouds that were blowing in. Looking down through breaks in the cover, the panorama of what had been Flanyanna's kingdom receded from their sight.

Just ahead of them loomed the Lost Forest. Trees of all kinds, thickets of cedars, oaks, and cypress, permeated the landscape with a soft, rich, green color.

In front of the party, massive boulders covered with blue-green mosses dotted a meadow that ran up a slope to the edge of the forest. The boulders marked where the open area stopped and the trees began.

"Land, Arasthenes—" the mouse cried in the Namdalarian's ear, pointing toward the meadow and its rich, soft palate of aqua-marine mosses. Arasthenes obliged and tilted his feathered wings down, angling towards the open space. The other winged horses followed. They hit the ground and thundered across the lush terrain toward the waiting tree line and the protection the dense emerald forest offered. Their hooves churned up the blue moss under the ferns. It splattered up on them and cooled their sweating bodies.

The pervasively pungent yet soothing aroma of the dark red cedars enveloped the winged horses and their riders as they disappeared. There was no foul stench of death here. These trees had not been ravaged by war. With Arasthenes leading the party followed a trail deeper into the woods.

They came upon a tiny sunlit clearing. The crown of the trees overhead was sparse enough that sunlight could enter the woodland yet was dense enough that the royal party was protected from being seen from above.

"We'll rest here." Flanyanna called the party to a halt. She and her weary guards climbed off their exhausted Namdalarians. "My sister will warn us if anyone comes close."

The band sat down on blue-green lichen-covered boulders that were scattered about the woodland's edges and passed around a goatskin of water. The panting and sweating Namdalarians nibbled on the lichen spread on the gigantic stones.

"Thank you—" Flanyanna addressed the tiny mouse, who was nestled snuggly in the pocket of her half-sister's gown.

"Shhh," replied the tiny creature. "Flan, the forest is full of spies...." The mouse scouted the forest with both her jade-green eyes and her third eye, searching for Markolous' agents.

Flanyanna was comforted by this presence of the most powerful Human Fairy on Kokakina, her half-sister, or cousin, depending whose story you believed. Flanyanna was used to her older half-sister taking on different forms. She had done so since they were small children.

Flanyanna rigidly controlled her emotions. She knew better than anyone how much they had lost. Not only had she lost her throne, but she had also lost her captain, Augustino. "Where do we go from here, sister?" Flanyanna asked, not knowing if her husband was dead or alive. She patted Arasthenes and stared down at the tiny mouse in her pocket.

The mouse scampered up Flanyanna's arm onto her shoulder. "To the Faireye Manor—" she whispered in the queen's ear.

"Yes—I would like to see it...," Flanyanna smiled and replied, thinking it might be for the last time. The Faireye Manor was where the royal family spent its summers. It was on the White Cliffs by the Mara Sea and held fond childhood memories for both of them. It was as good a place as any to hide while waiting for the inevitable—her brother coming after her.

"We go to the Faireye Manor," the queen announced for all to hear. "We'll ride the Namdalarians on the ground. We'll be able to conceal ourselves better."

The shadows of the ancient trees that surrounded them comforted Flanyanna as she looked up into the branches of the aged timbers. The warmth of the sun filtering through their leaves flushed her cheeks.

Queen Flanyanna's four guards made a square escort formation around her as they mounted and rode under the trees' rich, canopy.

Framed by colorful wildflowers, a rambling, pristine stream flowed nearby. Flanyanna gazed into the water and beheld her reflection. She was shocked, for she had aged more in this one day than she had in the last twenty years. The cruelty of her younger brother plagued the queen's mind. She knew he would come after her and she feared for her unborn child.

"I don't know how my baby can possibly survive with our ruthless brother in power," she said, voicing her concern to the little mouse. Flanyanna touched her belly. She knew Markolous would kill anyone who could possibly be a rival to the throne—even her unborn baby. "Sister, how can my baby survive?"

The mouse did not respond, not wanting to believe Markolous was capable of killing his own sister and her child.

"Oh, yes—killing my child will be the first thing he'll want to do after he kills me," Flanyanna said, reading her sister's thoughts. "You mark my words, sister."

The enchanted mouse perched on the queen's armored shoulder, her jade-green eyes and magical senses keenly scouting their surroundings.

"Flan—don't talk like that—"

"Why not...you know it's true. He's a monster. Anyone who would sell himself to the Lord of the Darkness wouldn't hesitate to send my baby and me to oblivion...."

Entering thicker brush, the Namdalarians progressed single file. Two soldiers rode ahead of their fallen queen and two behind. The tall, dark, ghostly oaks and cedars were silent witnesses as Flanyanna, her bodyguards, and the little mouse retreated deeper into the Lost Forest, journeying toward royal family's summer mansion on the White Cliffs.

"Flan?" the little enchanted mouse asked.

"What?"

"Are you wearing the Rose Crystal necklace?"

Flanyanna nodded, touching her hand to her breastplate. Even though the Pink Fairies had their own Rose Crystals, the crystal of the queen's necklace was the most powerful because it came from the center of the Earth. Although Flanyanna, as queen, wore this most powerful totem of the Human Fairies, the Pink Fairy line was the most adept at reading it. Flanyanna's elder Pink Fairy sister had the greatest ability to read the Rose Crystal that was passed down from female to female in the royal line.

Lunamilla, the mother of Flanyanna's half-sister, was the most powerful Pink Fairy of her generation and had read the Rose Crystal for King Glendorf. She was also his mistress and Flanyanna's elder sister was their daughter.

At first, Glendorf was delighted when Lunamilla told him she was with child, but his interest waned when his queen became pregnant with Flanyanna a few months later.

Flanyanna was born two months after her sister. Although she had never been told that Lunamilla's daughter was her sister, Flanyanna always knew. From a young age they both knew their true relationship and that their destinies were intertwined.

"Pinky, I have lost," Flanyanna said, staring down at her sister's minuscule nose and whiskers poking out of her pocket and speaking the nickname given to her sister by their father. Flanyanna lowered her head, not wanting to show the humiliation and shame she felt in being defeated by Markolous.

"You have not lost." Pinky struggled to say the right thing to her sister.

"But I have. I have failed Kokakina and my people," Flanyanna said.

"Flan—you must listen carefully," Pinky said, looking up at Flanyanna from her pocket. "I have spent many days reading the

Rose Crystals. There's nothing you could have done differently. The prophecy is that your child is a girl—and the tradition of a matriarchal rule will be reclaimed by her."

"I don't understand—what are you saying?"

"Don't you see? Markolous won the battle."

"I know that…but you just told me your Rose Crystals said my child is the true heir to the throne."

"Yes—" Pinky paused, "—but the crystals said nothing about you winning the war."

The two sisters stared into each other's third eyes.

Pinky could only nod. There was no turning back to offer a different interpretation to the reading she had made. She was the seer of the land, and she had thought if Flanyanna's daughter was to be the heir to the throne, her half-sister would win the war. Pinky had withheld that her beloved half-sister was not in the vision. Flanyanna played no part in the prophecy. Pinky's prejudices and love for her twin-flame sister had clouded her reading. It had been an assumption and a faulty one that had cost her sister the throne. Now Pinky was concerned for her sister's safety.

"It's my fault…Flan. If I had only not misinterpreted the prophecy." Pinky had underestimated Markolous.

A very worried and puzzled look crossed Flanyanna's face.

The queen held back the flood of tears that threatened to overwhelm her. She stuffed her desolate feelings deep down in her belly, where her baby felt her sorrow. It was a loss the unborn princess would know and carry and not know why.

"What are you talking about, sister? Our brother sold himself to the Lord of the Darkness. Never before has the ruler entered into this evil pact. Markolous' alliance with the Lord of the Darkness will bring devastation and tragedy to my people."

The seemingly unlikely pair, a Human Fairy queen and a tiny mouse, traveled through the Lost Forest to their last place of happiness, the Faireye Manor by the Mara Sea where they played as children.

"Will I ever see my husband again?" Flanyanna asked.

For a moment, Pinky did not answer. For the first time ever, her confidence as the seer of the land had been shaken. "You will—you know that—we would both know if he was dead."

Magically endowed Human Fairies knew the moment someone close to them died.

They passed through more tall, slender evergreens with their dense branches radiating aliveness and freshness. It was a wild, untamed area of Kokakina, with a musty, spicy tang. Slowly, the Namdalarians maneuvered toward the entrance of a canyon that led through the coastal mountains, the Feydonians. It held the only pass to the bluffs overlooking the Mara Sea where the Faireye Manor was located.

A rock dislodged from above and tumbled down, echoing in the chasm. The mouse scampered up the breastplate that covered the queen's torso. She peered ahead keenly, checking out the terrain to make sure it was safe to proceed.

"It's nothing," Pinky said, seeing that the way was clear. She motioned that they should ride into the gorge.

Flanyanna fell silent. She adjusted herself on Arasthenes. Pinky slid down the side of one of the winged horse's front legs.

"Pinky, you're not leaving, are you?" Flanyanna whispered.

"I have to."

"It's Markolous, isn't it? You're going to see him, aren't you?"

"I'll see you in the spring—don't worry," Pinky promised evasively as she hopped on the ground. "You must get through the pass before nightfall."

"Why—is he near?" Flanyanna asked, looking down at her sister's small rodent body.

"No—he's not." Pinky wrinkled her nose and shook her whiskers. Flanyanna immediately felt comforted for she knew that her sister was using her magical powers to cast a spell that would protect her. The sky turned from sunny to gray as light snow began to fall and the temperature plunged to freezing. More than one Namdalarian snorted and stamped its feet, knowing that this change of weather was not of nature's doing.

Strangely, the snowfall had no effect on Flanyanna and her party. They were in a protective orb that Pinky's spell had created for them. Outside the orb, the snow was now falling quite heavily.

"This winter spell will close the pass—" Pinky said. "—if you're not through it, you'll be stuck on this side of the mountains where Markolous will be able to reach you."

The air in the upper Kokakinan atmosphere became denser in the winter months. If Human Fairies, Namdalarians, or Tettigards tried to fly high enough to cross over the mountains, their wings would freeze, and they would tumble to their deaths. Likewise, the air over the Mara Sea became more dense, making maritime passage unsafe during the winter as well. Ground travel through the pass was the only way to the Faireye Manor during the wintertime. When the pass was closed, there would be no way anyone could reach the ruling family's summer estate until the spring thaw. Pinky had effectively created isolation for Flanyanna, a temporary sanctuary to give birth to her child.

"I've always depended on you…," Flanyanna said. "I don't want to lose you." Pinky was going to see Markolous. Flanyanna feared he would harm Pinky even though she was not a direct threat to his accession to the throne. "Be careful. Our brother is capable of anything."

"I can take care of myself," Pinky scoffed, putting her tiny hands on her waist.

"If he doesn't know now, he will soon that you supported me."

"Yeah—yeah—okay."

"Promise me—you'll be careful."

"I will."

Pinky transformed into a stunning, ebony-colored raven with lustrous, blue-black, iridescent feathers. Her eyes sparkled as she bounded across the ground, gesturing with her beak. Since leaving Earth, only the most magical Human Fairies were able to transform into ravens like Shadow Fairies.

With light, two-footed hops, Pinky easily maneuvered her body with its heavy, Bowie knife-like beak and shaggy plumage around her throat.

"You always did look best in black…," Flanyanna teased her powerful and magical sister—wanting to believe that everything would be as it once was in the land.

The raven replied with a "Caw". Spreading her long wings to take flight, she soared, buoyant and graceful. Her elongated wingtips beat the air as she flipped over and glided over the riders upside down as if to say farewell before dissolving into the gray, misty ethers of her spell.

Chunks of snow and ice falling off the precipice and plummeting down the canyon towards their protective orb pulled

Flanyanna's and her bodyguards' attention away from Pinky's departure.

"RUN!" ordered Flanyanna over a thunderous roar. The snow had mixed with the freezing air to form a deadly powder avalanche. It was falling much faster than it appeared and in a heartbeat would be on top of them.

The horses needed no further encouragement. They ran out of the orb into the knee-deep snow. Stumbling and straining, they extended their legs to a full stride to escape being buried alive.

A ghostly vapor churned up by the snow billowed out of the far end of the pass. Phantom-like, the queen and her escort burst through it, barely escaping the snowslide that crashed down and sealed the passageway behind them.

Hot and sweaty from their narrow escape, the steaming Namdalarians' wet, perspiring flanks glistened with ice particles. The cavalcade resumed traveling down the snowy trail next to the steep wall of rock at an easy canter.

The storm clouds broke, and sunlight poured down. Flanyanna and her guards meandered along the narrow path that led down to the White Cliffs by the Mara Sea. The horses' feathered wings fluttered in the moist air coming in from the sea.

Flanyanna stopped abruptly.

The sun was moving down towards the horizon, its rays illuminating the craggy bluffs on which the Faireye Manor rested.

These cliffs butted into the sea and rose majestically above the crashing waves that wiped clean the pink quartz sands lying at their base. Inhaling the salty, ionized air, she relaxed as she had not in months.

They rode into the snow-covered meadow that lay before the Faireye Manor. The newly fallen snow glimmered in the late afternoon sunlight. The limbs of the flurry-laden trees that surrounded the heath bowed down to their queen as the sun cast a long shadow through their heavily burdened branches.

On the heath a herd of reindeer grazed. Nudging aside the snow, they munched on the tufts of frozen grass underneath. Two young bucks sparred, butting their antlers and practicing for the time when they would compete for the position of alpha male. The sugar-like powder floated up and diffused over their grayish-brown coats.

The combatants paused in their joust and stared at the intruders. They had never seen Human Fairies arrive in the wintertime.

Trudging through the fresh snow, the Namdalarians and their riders crossed a lichen-covered stone bridge that led to the Faireye Manor.

Flanyanna gazed through the sun's lengthening rays, out over the blue seascape of crystal-clear water. She felt a new purpose—to give birth to the baby growing in her womb who would someday rule Kokakina.

The Faireye Manor

The facade of the summer palace had weathered over the years to a bleached bone-white that reflected the setting sun's rays so fiercely that the riders were forced to squint to protect their eyes.

Constructed from locally quarried crystal, the builders placed the hand-chiseled blocks of the manor one on top of another, like the construction of Stonehenge on Earth. The windows, shuttered for winter, were painted the pale blue of the sky on a clear day.

The Faireye Manor was nestled on forty-two acres of forested land wedged between the foot of the Feydonian Mountains and the White Cliffs. It was divided into separate living areas for the queen and her family, their high status guests, and servants.

A misty ether rose from the snowfall that partially covered the gray pavers in front of the manor house and enveloped the queen's entourage as they passed through the rustic wooden gates that led into the courtyard. The gates were stoutly constructed using tongue and groove planks and strong mortise and tenon joints.

A small barn opposite the entrance also provided separate living quarters for the manor's garrison. Fallow bougainvillea trellised the outside walls of the picturesque manor.

One of the guards assisted Flanyanna to slip down from Arasthenes. Stroking his steaming nostrils, she felt Arasthenes' warmth flow through her body as she rubbed her cold cheek next to one of his brilliant blue eyes.

The stable boy, a lad no older than thirteen, crunched through the fresh snow towards them.

"Derrik, after you water him…," Flanyanna instructed using his name, "I want you to be sure to give him extra hay…."

"Yes, Your Majesty," the groom replied.

"And be sure to give him some garlic. He has inflammation in his front right leg," Flanyanna said, concerned for injuries Arasthenes incurred during the third eye duel.

"Yes, Ma'am." Derrik tugged his forelock to acknowledge his sovereign as he reached for Arasthenes' leather leads.

Flanyanna reluctantly released Arasthenes and watched the lad take her white charger and the guards' Namdalarians to the stable across from the manor.

"You're dismissed," she instructed her bodyguards.

The weary soldiers bowed to their liege and turned to follow their Namdalarians to their quarters next to the barn.

Alone, Flanyanna turned back toward the manor house. The early snowfall had turned the bougainvillea's leaves brown. Their deadness mirrored her bleak mood.

As she started towards the front door, she sensed something or someone watching her. She turned towards the gate. Two massive Hokkaido wolves crouched there, scrutinizing her every move.

They stood motionless, their piercing black eyes boring into her. Their presence put her at ease for they were the guardians.

Both wolves got to their feet and bowed. They stretched their front legs out and raised their hindquarters in the air, then bolted toward the bridge that led to the meadow. Just as quickly, they reversed their direction and ran back, panting with smiling faces. The wolves retraced to the bridge and ran back a second time.

The front door to the manor house burst open.

Still tying on her apron, Trista, a plump servant girl also thirteen ran out. Breathless and awestruck, she skidded to a stumbling halt in front of Flanyanna. Static electricity frizzed her hair. Self-consciously, she smoothed it back down along a severe middle part. Her chest heaved from her exertion.

This was the first time since Trista's early childhood when Flanyanna had agreed to accept her into the household that Trista had appeared before her sovereign and employer. The girl's parents had requested it as they could not afford to keep her. At only six years of age, Trista became a royal household servant.

Flanyanna's breastplate glimmered in the sun's late afternoon rays. The queen's armor left no doubt in Trista's mind that she was in the presence of her liege.

"Your Majesty—ummmm…," she giggled.

Flanyanna turned. The wolves were gone.

Trista awkwardly curtsied to her queen. Even though Trista had been at the Faireye Manor most of her life, her duties had kept her in the kitchen, where no direct contact with the royal family had occurred.

Without preamble Flanyanna graciously rewarded Trista with a kindly smile and touched her shoulder, indicating the overwhelmed girl could rise.

"Where's Bessalina?" Flanyanna asked.

The flustered girl's eyes bulged practically out of their sockets. She hadn't expected the queen to speak to her. Her vocal cords tightened, and she was speechless. Before Trista could stammer out a reply, an older, graying Human Fairy dressed in a long, brown, coarse wool dress and holding a wooden spoon in her hand waddled out the front door. A red crescent moon on her forehead over her third eye signified her connection to the royal house. This was Bessalina. Her family had served the royal household for thousands of years.

Bent from many years of hard labor since she was a child Bessalina placed her hands on her large waist to help straighten her back as she drew close.

Elated at seeing her mistress, she shuffled over to Flanyanna, her bare feet stepping through the cold, wet snow. Before becoming the cook, Bessalina had served as a nanny for Flanyanna, Pinky, and Markolous. She had dearly loved the children, like they were her own.

"Your Majesty—we weren't—expecting you," she stuttered. Afflicted with arthritis, she painfully curtsied, honoring her queen. She self-consciously slipped the over-sized wooden spoon, dripping with the evening stew, into her apron pocket.

As she straightened back up, she studied Flanyanna. Flanyanna stood before her in her tattered gown and battered royal armor etched with a spiral and three flying Ravens to the right—the personal insignia of the White Fairy queen.

"Oh—my dear girl—" Bessalina muttered breathlessly, still huffing and puffing. Flanyanna had arrived at the Faireye Manor unannounced. Bessalina harbored no doubt of what that meant. Markolous had won. "I hoped this day would never come. Are you all right?"

"Yes…Nanna. I'm fine."

Markolous had committed an unspeakable betrayal. He had taken his older sister's crown from her. Bessalina's greatest fear had become a reality—the fierce rivalry between the royal siblings she had witnessed since their childhood would destroy one of them.

Bessalina reached out her arms to soothe her surrogate daughter and encircled the deposed queen.

"I lost…." Flanyanna's eyes filled with tears as she felt the comfort that only her nanny's embrace could give her.

Bessalina's eyes widened in surprise. Flanyanna was pregnant! "Don't worry—I'll have something for you both to eat—soon," she said with a smile and yelled across the yard. "I'll have something for all of you to eat." One of the guards turned and waved to acknowledge her words.

"That no-good brother of yours…," Bessalina said to Flanyanna, her ample frame shaking with rage. "He was alway trying to beat you at everything, but don't worry, Ma'am. You're safe here—I can still handle Markolous."

"Wolves!" Trista screamed and pointed, interrupting Bessalina's reassurances. At the gate the two wolves had returned and were pacing back and forth, extremely agitated.

"Oh—hush—you ninny," Bessalina admonished her underling. "They're not going to hurt you." She pulled her spoon out and waved it at the patrolling beasts. "Shoo—go away."

The wolves didn't budge. They stared hard at Flanyanna. Then they jumped simultaneously over the low crossbuck fence into the meadow and receded into the distance.

Flanyanna watched them run towards the woods until they disappeared. The pounding surf crashing onto the beach below the White Cliffs broke into her musing. The roaring sound of the rushing, turbulent waves became the laughter of young children.

> *Flanyanna and Markolous run on the White Cliffs overlooking the calm Mara Sea.*
>
> *"I bet you can't fly to those islands." Markolous, seven years old, points to three islands some miles offshore.*
>
> *Markolous and Flanyanna had played 'life and death games' since he was five and she was six.*
>
> *"I bet I can!" retorts a slightly older Flanyanna.*
>
> *"Okay—I'll race you then," Markolous taunts as he sprints across the bluff. "The winner gets the other's sticky pudding for a whole week...."*
>
> *"That's not fair—" Flanyanna protests, "—you got a head start." Still, she rises to her brother's challenge and dashes after him along the White Cliffs.*
>
> *"Wait!" Pinky cries out, running after her half siblings. She wants to play too, but she sees the danger in their rash actions and fears for their safety. It was well known that the treacherous crosswinds created by the cliffs could snatch one of them, or both, and dash them on the rocks below.*
>
> *Unfurling her etheric wings, she takes flight to catch up with her brother and sister. Her pink iridescent wings shimmer in the sunlight as she flies across the top of the cliffs.*

Markolous and Flanyanna reach the end of the bluff.

They stop, glaring at each other.

"You go first—" Markolous says, "—I dare you."

"No—" Flanyanna replies, "—you go first."

"Stop! Both of you! You must stop!" Pinky swoops down from the sky. Her delicate, pink-tinged wings fold back and disappear. "You can't do this…you might be killed!"

"Be quiet—Pinky," Markolous snarls, his toes curling over the edge with his fitted leather boots. "Stay out of this—this has nothing to do with you. This is between Flanyanna and me."

Pinky feels like she's been physically slapped. She knows full well that even though she is their sister and the firstborn, she is the daughter of the king's mistress whom he never married. She had been born on the wrong side of the blanket and was not recognized by her own father to the court. Even though they had never been told, the immediate family knows of Pinky's true connection to them. The king chose to keep it from the public to appease Markolous' mother, his new queen.

Markolous unfurls his etheric wings, preparing to take off for the three islands.

"Okay—kill yourself. I don't care—" Pinky shouts back.

"We'll be fine." Intent on the game, Markolous dismisses her objections. "Are you coming or aren't you?" he asks Flanyanna.

"No—Flan, don't," Pinky says. "There's a storm coming—you'll be dashed on the rocks."

"There's no storm coming, Pinky," Markolous scoffs and turns pointing towards the calm ocean horizon. "You just made that up."

A fierce gale whips up, swiftly bringing in gray, stormy and dense cumulus clouds. The rough, white-capped sea churns into a vigorous froth, much like on the top of a mug of beer.

"Why'd you do that—" Markolous glares at Pinky. "—I was going to get her sticky pudding for a whole week until you butted in with your stupid magic trick."

"What'ta are you talking about…I didn't do any-thing," Pinky says, defending herself.

"Yes, you did—and you know it."

"No, I didn't, honest. It just happens sometimes—that's all."

Pinky's concern over the possibility of a storm had morphed into a spell that created one. Her powers of creation were great, and she was not yet in full con-trol of them.

Furious, Markolous' face turns a bright beet red, "You always side with our sister." Even at his young age, Markolous knows Flanyanna, not Pinky, is his rival for the throne.

"That's not true…she's not like you," Flanyanna taunts. "She's a Pink Fairy. She has a big heart—and you don't."

Without warning, Markolous pushes Flanyanna off the cliff. With a startled cry, Flanyanna falls headlong, in dire danger of dashing her head on the craggy boulders below.

Pinky jumps off the cliff. She opens her etheric wings and scoops up her sister just before she smashes onto the unforgiving, jagged, rocky beach.

With a secure hold on Flanyanna, Pinky deposits her safely on the empty, pink, sands.

"What did you do that for…I would have caught myself and landed on my own, just fine," Flanyanna says.

"I'm sorry, Flanyanna…I thought you were caught in the downdraft and couldn't get your wings open."

"How dare you talk to me like that—" Flanyanna's face smolders with humiliation and shame. She knows her half-sister's magical powers are greater than hers, and always will be. "—I would have landed just fine without your help."

Atop the cliff, Markolous throws down rocks, almost hitting them.

"Come on!" Flanyanna yells, forgetting her jealousy. She and Pinky run down the beach, the billions of Rose Crystal granules crunching under their feet.

A shiver went through Flanyanna's body. She realized she was chilled, a deep ache that went all the way down into her crystal bones. Her brother's victory on the battlefield had jarred up her haunting childhood memory of him pushing her off the cliff.

Flanyanna felt Bessalina's arm about her waist as the faithful servant beckoned her to come inside.

"Let's go inside by the fire," Bessalina said. "It's cold."

"Yes. Suddenly, I'm very tired," Flanyanna confessed. She looked deeply into Bessalina's caring eyes as she took her Nanna's arm. Her childhood summer home held more than good memories. It also held other, darker ones.

"Of course, you are…," Bessalina said, leading her farther towards the house and the warmth it offered. She did not want Flanyanna to sense the dread and anxiety she felt. "We don't want you to get a chill."

The floor of the Faireye Manor's entryway was made of dazzling crystal pieces, laid out like a jigsaw puzzle waiting to be put back together. Deep blue and purple prisms danced on the walls. Bessalina closed the front door behind her queen.

"Trista, go upstairs and build a fire in Her Majesty's bedchamber," she instructed.

Trista smiled and hurried upstairs. Her well worn black boots scuffled across each stairstep, tap-tapping up the staircase. At the top, she paused, blushing and giggling. She had forgotten to bow to her queen. Embarrassed, she looked down at Flanyanna and did another floundering curtsy before stomping down the open hallway.

"Ma'am, please forgive me. Trista's not yet well versed in the etiquette of the royal household. She's been helping in the kitchen all these years. I thought I'd have all winter to give her proper instruction," Bessalina said, flustered and embarrassed.

"How long has the girl been here?" Flanyanna inquired.

"Why, Ma'am—don't you remember Trista?" Bessalina's eyes widened in surprise. "She's been here since she was six years old.

You personally agreed to take her on. Her parents couldn't afford her upkeep."

"Oh—yes—of course. I remember now," Flanyanna said, recalling none of it.

"Ma'am…are you all right?" Bessalina asked, realizing the queen was not herself.

"It's just that—there's usually more servants." Flanyanna's voice became distracted.

"It's not surprising after all you've been through. Now don't worry. Trista is a good girl and truly wants to please you, Ma'am…," Bessalina said.

"Yes. I will enjoy having a young person in the house."

Bessalina let out a soft sigh, very much relieved that the queen was understanding about Trista. Changing the subject to what was really on her mind, she said, "All I can say—it's good the bairn is due in the spring."

"You know, then?" Flanyanna asked, "But, how?"

"Ma'am…you've never been able to keep any secrets from me," Bessalina said with a shy, yet crafty smile. She looked fondly at Flanyanna. "I always knew when your nappy needed changing—and you never told me."

"Bessalina…I've never been this tired."

"I understand, but wouldn't you like to sit by the kitchen fire to get warm, Ma'am? Let Trista warm up your cold bedchamber?" Bessalina asked, thinking it best if Flanyanna had some company. She was concerned about the melancholy that struck some pregnant Human Fairies, and even a queen was not immune.

"Nanna, if you don't mind, I'd like to stay here by myself for awhile."

"Of course, Ma'am. Since you have no further need of me, I'll return to my duties in the kitchen and prepare something for you and the guards to eat."

With a strained, but proper curtsy, Bessalina took her leave and turned towards the kitchen.

"Nanna," Flanyanna called out, "Where are your shoes?" With all the distractions, she had not realized until now that Bessalina was barefoot.

Bessalina paused, then turned back to her queen. "Ma'am— I'm saving them."

"Saving them? Saving them for what?"

"Ma'am—I'm saving them for when I need them," Bessalina answered, flustered. She started across the Great Hall to the kitchen.

Flanyanna's brow knitted in perplexity. "But—it's wintertime. You need to wear your shoes. You'll catch a cold."

Bessalina turned back before leaving the Great Hall to go to the kitchen. "It's the war—Ma'am. You've had to fight your brother for some time now."

"Well—what does that have to do with your shoes?" Flanyanna asked, upset that the nanny who had taken such good care of her as a child was going without shoes.

"Very well. If you must know, Ma'am, money that would have been available for household wages has gone to the war effort."

"You spent your own crystals to help me fight my brother?"

Bessalina shrugged her shoulders. "Your advisors let go of most of the staff some months ago. It never occurred to me that things would go the way they did."

"Oh—" Flanyanna said, starting to understand.

"I just thought I would have all winter to teach Trista her new duties outside the kitchen. I planned on surprising you in the spring with how well she was doing."

"I see…." Flanyanna knew the war effort had affected everyone, but she was touched by Bessalina's sacrifice on her behalf.

"Nanna—my mother's shoe size was about the same as yours," Flanyanna said. "I believe there are still some things of hers left upstairs in the attic—please go up there and get a pair of her slippers for yourself."

"I don't know what to say—Ma'am." Bessalina bowed her head in gratitude. She could see Flanyanna's arms were covered in goosebumps from the frigid air in the Great Hall. "I'll make you a cup of hot tea."

"I'll be along shortly," Flanyanna said. She walked from the Great Hall to the adjacent Banquet Hall. The plank benches and the massive aged timbered oak table had neither guests nor food to welcome her. The coldness of the crystal floor leeched through her riding boots. She rubbed her hands together and blew hot breath on her frozen fingertips. She felt a certain comfort in the family's Faireye Manor, remembering the many happy family dinners.

A beam of natural sunlight filtered down and caught Flanyanna in the eye. Startled, she looked up.

The ceiling was a stained glass crystal skylight depicting the entire celestial universe surrounding the Human Fairy world. The constellations and the astrological signs of their galaxy that had guided her people for millennia seemed somehow irrelevant to her now. For her whole life, she had been guided and instructed in the ways of their matriarchal society. Even her own father maintained the traditions, and it never occurred to her that their whole way of life could vanish. She averted her teary eyes from the magnificent dome, feeling guilty and full of shame for her failure.

Flanyanna's throat tightened. In a panic she abruptly turned and looked towards the kitchen. She no longer felt safe. The matriarchal society no longer existed for the Human Fairies. This possibility had not occurred to her when her father ruled. She had only known a secure life with him on the throne. But now that she had lost the throne to her brother, she understood that the long tradition of rule by females was gone.

The Faireye Manor of her childhood, even with its fond memories, would give her no comfort. Her brother ruled now, and she feared what was to come.

Abruptly, she walked toward the kitchen door. Her moist palm shaking, she extended her arm to open it. She reached out for the only kindness left to her, her nanny's offer to share her warm hearth and a cup of tea.

Flanyanna arose the next morning. She had tossed and turned all night, worrying about what the future held for her and her child. Having taken Bessalina's wool shawl from the kitchen the night before, she wrapped it around her shoulders, feeling some comfort from its embracing warmth.

Leaning in and pressing her forehead and hands up against the cold, leaded glass of the bedchamber window, she sat on the alcove's bench and peered out at the snow and ice-covered landscape.

A wintry breeze wafted through the barren trees in the garden, stirring up the drifted snow that covered the ground and the bushes. Drawing the shawl more tightly around her shoulders, she touched her growing belly. The trees' heavy, snow-laden limbs bowed down to the ground, their skeletal finger-like branches dancing in the wind.

"Petronero…," Flanyanna murmured her husband's name and traced it upon the glass with her finger.

Since they were children, Flanyanna and Petronero shared a passion for the winged horses of Kokakina, and it bound them together, first in friendship and then in love. They rode together in the Lost Forest as often as they could. Most avoided it because Shadow Fairies lived there, so Flanyanna's and Petronero's secret was protected. Her clandestine meetings with Petronero were the only times she had ever disobeyed her father. King Glendorf tried his best to talk her out of her infatuation, but nothing could change her heart.

She managed to avoid matrimony while her father lived. After his death and her coronation, the new queen defied the kingdom's ban on royals marrying commoners and quickly wed Petronero. The shock and outrage that many felt at her breaking with long-standing tradition fed into Markolous' challenge against her rule.

During the second year of Flanyanna's reign, drought came to the land. At first, no one gave the matter much thought. All were sure that the rains would come soon. They always did. Yet, years passed without rainfall. The people grew to know too well the rumblings in their empty stomachs. Many left the villages surrounding the palace in search of food. Some went to the frontier, never to return. In the local taverns gossip was that the Tettigards had devoured them. The Tettigards were becoming more of a menace to Human Fairies. Many blamed their queen for the bad times.

Word was spread by Markolous and his supporters that Flanyanna's marriage to a commoner had cursed the land and brought drought to Kokakina.

The snow flurries swirled in the garden, and Flanyanna sees a ghostly figure on a white Namdalarian.

"Petronero!" she cried, jumping up to her feet. She blinked, and the ghostly figure was gone. It was nothing but a figment of her imagination.

Slumping back down on the alcove bench, a deep melancholy came over Flanyanna. Her eyes fell on her empty bed. She had never felt so desolate and alone.

Moonstone Nettle Stew

Pinky's eyes popped open after a good night's sleep. She breathed deeply, filling her lungs with the pervasive rose scent that filled the air. The Rosa Centifolia fragrance had come alive during the night and could be smelled throughout the Lost Forest as the sun rose. While she slept, the scent of Rosa Centifolia connected Pinky to the etheric realm. She had come home to rest after leaving Flanyanna before going to see Markolous.

She rolled over on her simple, narrow cot and lifted her shimmering pink arms above her head to stretch her nubile body. Unlike her White Fairy sister who had pale white skin, Pinky's rose-tinged skin reflected her Pink Fairy lineage.

The spider-silk bed cover slipped down, revealing the rose tattoo that swirled around her body. Starting on her right arm it wrapped around her torso and onto her left thigh. Taking on a life of its own, the tattoo's intertwining leaves and petals pulsated and undulated. As Pinky flicked strands of her bubblegum pink and golden blonde hair forward, wild rainbow-colored sparks exploded throughout the tiny cottage.

Stretching again, she rose from her mattress tufted with nettles and wildflowers and her lower back twinged. She reached down and slipped sheepskin moccasins lying by her bed over her toes and rose stiffly, her body feeling the strain of yesterday's battle.

Pinky looked directly out of the narrow, leaded glass window into the morning sun and scanned the horizon. The glare of the bright sunlight stung her eyes and caused salty tears to stream down her face, but she did not turn away. The intense rays of the sun pouring into her eyes comforted her. She wanted to feel this physical sensation to distract herself from thoughts about going to see Markolous, the new ruler.

Feeling the morning chill through her slippers, she turned from the window and quickly went over to the cold hearth to stoke the coals. The flames cooperated and rose up from the embers. She placed the hand-wrought copper kettle on the crane and moved it over the blaze, grateful she did not have to go out for more wood. A firm, but very moist nose touched the back of her neck. "Stop that—" she complained half-heartedly, "—that tickles."

She turned and standing behind her was the handsome buck with a three-tiered chandelier of horns she had ridden during the battle. Warm, amber-colored eyes regarded her mischievously.

"Besides Elfman, your nose is cold—how many times do I have to tell you?"

As a child, Elfman was a Human Fairy and the son of the cook at the Crystal Palace when Pinky lived with her mother—the king's mistress—in an apartment in the palace. Pinky preferred to play with Elfman instead of with her half siblings. The two unlikely companions simply shared friendship without the rivalries and tensions of the royal family and the court.

King Glendorf allowed Pinky and her mother to live in the Crystal Palace as poor distant cousins. This deception infuriated Pinky's mother, who never stopped reminding Pinky that the king was her father, that she was the firstborn, and that she was better than her brother and sister because she was a Pink Fairy.

The king had fathered Pinky, Flanyanna and Markolous, each with a different mother. King Glendorf wanted an heir, and his wife, Queen Aliafora, appeared to be barren. When Lunamilla became pregnant with Pinky, he was delighted and promised to recognize the child as the legitimate heir to the throne. Shortly afterwards, Queen Aliafora became pregnant with Flanyanna but died giving birth to her. The king's grief was overpowering.

In his sorrow King Glendorf allowed Casafala, a cunning, devious, seductive female Human Fairy noble, to manipulate him into marrying her to give Flanyanna a mother. In doing so, he ignored Pinky's mother for whom he had a deep attachment and had promised to marry after a suitable mourning period.

Not one to tolerate a rival, Casafala quickly forced Lunamilla out of court. Lunamilla left in disgrace and went to live reclusively in the Lost Forest, where she raised Pinky. Consequently, Pinky grew up in the forest with all its magical animals, instead of learning the etiquette and intrigues of court life.

Casafala soon gave birth to Markolous. It was always her ambition that her child would inherit the throne. King Glendorf, who was overcome with joy, agreed to make him the heir.

Pinky enjoyed being with Elfman when she was at court. In the summer she went away with her royal siblings to the Faireye Manor, far away from the court with its intrigues and gossips, and while there they played together as equals. So, the fictitious relationship that she was a cousin never really bothered Pinky when she was a small child. She had her mother and Elfman, and, in the summer, her father and her siblings. But, as she got older and realized how being labeled a cousin rather than a sister isolated her from her only family, the charade began to hurt.

Over the years, Markolous became jealous of Elfman's relationship with Pinky, and the feeling only intensified as they entered their teenage years. He could not understand why Pinky preferred Elfman's, a commoner's, company to his. In his arrogance, it was incomprehensible that she could simply like someone else better than she liked him.

In puberty Markolous' feelings towards Pinky rose to the point that he declared that he would marry her someday. Pinky was horrified, but never said anything. She thought it was only an infatuation and he would get over it.

When Markolous turned sixteen and came into his mature magical powers, he turned Elfman into a buck. He incorrectly assumed that after he had done so Pinky would abandon Elfman and turn her affections towards him. Instead, his action alienated her and created a split between them.

Elfman's pink tongue reached into a basket on the kitchen table and grabbed a yellow mustard flower, stem and all.

"Stop that! I gathered those flowers from the meadow last night for our breakfast." Pinky reached for the flower, but he pulled his head away and swallowed it before she was able to get it out of his mouth.

"Hey!" Pinky snapped. "Why'd you do that?"

"Mmmmm—because—I'm hungry." He smiled disarmingly, his tongue jutting out.

Showing her true feelings, Pinky forgot about the flower and reached out to hug Elfman around his neck. His soft, gray-brown fur smelled of sweet sage. She relaxed into the wild strength and warmth of his body.

"You're always hungry." She touched her nose to his cold nose. Pinky's greatest regret was that she hadn't been able to undo Markolous' spell on Elfman. Each time she tried, her fear of losing him interfered with her enchantment and destroyed the spell. Gradually, she accepted that she could not bring him back to his Human Fairy form.

"Never mind...." She softened. "I can always go out and get more."

Not bothering to change into her clothes, Pinky picked up her straw basket and they went outside.

Wild purple lupine, yellow mustard, golden-orange poppies, and licorice danced in the wind in the meadow next to her cottage. The winter spell she had cast the day before to protect her sister had so far affected only the Feydonian mountain range and the coastline next to the Faireye Manor.

The reeds in the babbling stream undulated from the flowing current. Hitting rocks not completely submerged, the water gurgled as Pinky and Elfman walked along the bank.

"Try the licorice," Elfman suggested as he motioned with his head to the spidery green plant growing at the edge of the water. His long, pink tongue slipped out to grasp a stem, tasting its tangy sweetness. "It's especially delicious this morning—you know it's your favorite."

Pinky fell to her knees next to Elfman. "You're impossible!" she laughed pulling the licorice from Elfman's mouth.

"Heh—What?"

One of Pinky's favorite activities was to cook for Elfman. In that regard, Markolous' curse had not changed their relationship. "I'm making you your favorite—moonstone nettle stew." She put the final necessary ingredients in her woven basket.

"Yum—that is my favorite." Elfman smacked his lips.

When Pinky was a child, Elfman's father, to keep her entertained when her mother was away visiting the king, had taught her how to prepare moonstone nettle stew and other dishes. The recipe had been handed down from the best culinary wizards. It took many years for Pinky to master it. As with most Human Fairy cooking, it was all done by intuitive flare. One learned by observation, an encouraging word from the chef, a pinch of this, a dash of that and, of course—your own special magic.

Elfman followed her back to the cottage.

The Pink Fairy's modest cottage of rough logs blended in perfectly with the lush burgundy grasses, ivies, ferns, and Rosa Centifolia in the Lost Forest. Hanging over the cottage's slanted, thatched roof and flared eaves, the limbs of nearby oak trees canopied around it. They camouflaged Pinky's home, and only the keenest of eyes could make it out. The vegetation had grown up next to its walls, obscuring the dwelling's very existence.

Inside, Pinky put the black kettle on the crane over the hearth and tended to the fire. Elfman stretched out on the floor next to the outer hearth, closing his eyes to take a nap.

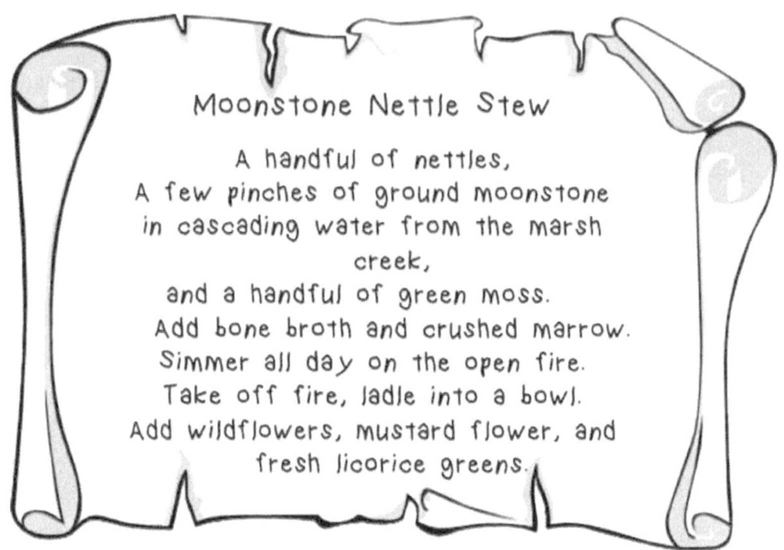

As Pinky stirred her brew, the pot swung from side to side over the fire. She lifted the wooden spoon to her lips and tasted it.

"A little more nettle…"

Pinky rubbed the herb into her palm. The scent drifted into her nostrils and filled the cottage with its healing properties as she dropped it in. She stirred her moonstone nettle stew in its cast iron pot, tasting it once more.

"And a little more moonstone," she said to herself. Cooking was always a way for her to forget about everything and then sense more clearly what was really going on.

Suddenly, she tensed. Someone was coming into her forest. She looked down at the sleeping Elfman and stepped over him to the front door.

She put on a long flowing brown and blue spider-silk skirt that flared from her narrow, slim waist and a matching top with a high neck hanging from a peg next to the front door.

Her hair was still tousled from the night's slumbers and she ran her fingers through it to tame it. Starting at the top, she pulled her long tresses back and braided them, tying the length at the nape of her neck.

The front door squeaked as she opened it. She looked over at the sleeping Elfman. She wanted not to awaken him. Putting on her three-quarter length coat made of animal hides—black, brown, and coral snake, arrayed in a crazy patchwork pattern, she slipped out.

She raced away from the cottage as quickly as she could, thinking it best to get as far away as possible, fearing the intruders would harm Elfman.

In the mist that had formed while she was inside, Pinky hurried across the bridge that spanned the stream. She ran through the blue-green forest of moss-covered white oaks towards the meadow. Once there, she gathered kindling in her arms.

Seeing Markolous' soldiers on their Namdalarians flying toward her cottage, she dashed back to intercept them. Crossing back over the ancient Stonehenge bridge covered in green algae, she took up a position next to her home.

The fluttering of winged horses broke the morning silence. Six horsemen swept out of the dense low fog, dropping below the trees and landing on the ground. Afoot, the horses stepped towards Pinky and encircled her.

She dropped the pile of twigs.

The winged horses slowly tightened their circle, closing in on her. "Pink Fairy?" the officer inquired.

Not acknowledging him and feigning indifference, she turned about and walked through the soldiers, back across the bridge and away from the cottage and Elfman.

The soldiers looked at each other, uncertain as to what they should do next.

Pinky picked up more twigs, and her animal skin coat slipped over her head as she bent to the ground. Entirely covered, she abruptly stood up. The coat's hood covered her head and face, and she looked like some wild beast.

Knowing her powers, one of the horsemen quailed. He turned his mount in a panic and rode frantically away.

"Steady—hold your positions," ordered the officer.

Suddenly, Pinky's head popped out of the fur hood, her pink and blond hair tousled and flowing wildly. "Get out of my forest—now—or I'll...."

"But you're ordered to come to the palace to read for the King...," the office interrupted. "You're the seer of the land and must obey his order."

"Unfortunately, I can't," Pinky retorted as she collected more twigs covered in the green and blue moss and bundled them together.

Brushing off her dirty hands, she looked like she was casting a spell.

"But—what'll I tell the king?"

"Tell the king—I will come when I—can."

The soldiers wrenched the reins of their Namdalarians, pulling back.

She walked farther from her cottage.

The officer could see his men were thoroughly intimidated by this slip of a girl who looked to be totally harmless. But knowing

Pinky was anything but, he took a deep breath and gathered his courage. "But the king will be very angry. You must come with us —now!" The leader pulled out his sword.

"I told you, I will not leave my forest today…," Pinky said, and continued to walk away further from her cottage and Elfman.

"Seize her!" the commander shouted.

The soldiers drew their swords and raised them over their heads, ready to charge her and take her by force.

Pinky flicked her arm in the direction of the nearest soldier, who flew from his horse and struck a tree with a resounding thump. "If you kill me—the new king will not get his reading— and he'll have your heads." She knew none of them would strike her down for fear of Markolous' wrath.

"Steady—he wants her alive," the captain ordered, trying to save face. "It's best for all of us if you just come with us now," he said.

Pinky calmly turned away from them.

Their ears flicking back and forth, the winged horses became extremely unsettled and fearful. They clamped their tails down, tucking them lower into their hindquarters and began to paw the ground. Their eyes darted from side to side.

All this did not go unnoticed by the captain. "But—what will I tell the king?" He just assumed that Pinky would not refuse such a command, but she did.

"I already told you—it's not a good day to read." Pinky looked up at the sky as if she was consulting the cosmos. "It's my job to tell the ruler his destiny. I need time to read my own Rose Crystals before I meet with the new king." She had missed something in her last reading and she did not want to make another costly mistake.

The officer stared at Pinky's back as she walked further into the meadow.

"Nothing has changed between those two...," he mumbled under his breath. "Very well. I'll tell him...."

"Good day, sir," she said curtly.

"Help him back on his horse," the office commanded, pointing to the soldier who'd flown off his Namdalarian and now lay dazed underneath the tree. A soldier promptly got off his mount and helped his stunned comrade, assisting the injured soldier to climb back on his steed.

Pinky watched the soldiers fly away. The enfolding mist swirling up from the stream grew more dense and cooler, hinting of cold weather to come. It drifted close, enveloping her as she walked back to her cottage.

In the evening, the crickets sang outside, incessantly talking. In the soft, indirect light inside the cottage, Pinky's pale rosy skin blended with her long, partly pink hair as she cleared the dishes from the table, and put them into a wooden bucket to wash. Elfman took great pleasure in watching the sparks from the fire leap out of the hearth. Pinky stomped on the firecracker coals, feeling the hot embers under her cold feet.

"What's wrong?" Elfman asked.

"Nothing's wrong." She evaded answering his question. She feared the answer would frighten him.

"Something is wrong—I saw you talking to the soldiers."

"Oh, that—it's nothing."

The fire crackled as Pinky fed it a new log.

"I think it's a good night to read the future," she announced, changing the subject as she lifted the pouch containing her Rose Crystals from the mantle. "Don't you?"

"Okay…fine." He lay his head down on his front hooves. "Don't tell me."

"Well—there's really nothing to tell," Pinky said. Her hands trembled as she opened the pouch.

"Then how come your hands are shaking?"

"Will you stop that! My hands aren't shaking. I'm just tired —that's all."

"Tired—or afraid?"

"Okay…I can't keep anything from you. I made a mistake. Okay?"

"Pink Fairies don't make mistakes."

"You think I don't know that? I misinterpreted the Rose Crystal prophecy—okay?"

"You did?" Elfman gulped.

"Yes, I did. Do you have to rub it in?"

"Well—what happened?"

"Very well, if you must know, I assumed that because Flanyanna's child would rule someday, Flanyanna would retain the throne." She pulled out the three Rose Crystals and they lit up in her hand.

"I see….Well, I can understand why you'd think that."

"That's the whole point! I'm not supposed to think! I'm supposed to feel with my heart."

"Oh—I didn't know you had a choice. I thought that's how you did things—always with your heart."

"Oh—please."

On the rough-hewn table, Pinky placed the three crystals that had been handed down in her family from generation to generation. Perfectly formed Rose Crystals. The crystals hummed and toned, speaking to their Pink Fairy.

She peered deeply into them. A moving nighttime skyscape of falling stars. Lifting her Rose Crystals, she hoped to see a way out. Her eyes rolling up in her head, she hovered over the singing crystals—the rose quartz that was not finite, but endless.

A storm brews at sea. Suddenly, one of the White Cliffs breaks off, crashing down into the brine.

In a meadow, all green and dense with magic, Pinky stands with her three Rose Crystals. Suddenly, her Rose Crystals crack, shatter, and cut her hands. Red blood trickles from her palms.

Underneath her, the meadow's ground shakes. A crevice opens in front of her. She jumps over it and runs to escape the ever-lengthening breach, but she falls. The breach devours her. Red blood seeps from the crack. It closes back up. She's gone.

The crystals turned dusky and silent.

Pinky opened her eyes. Putting her crystals back on the mantle, she gathered some brittle dead leaves to put on the fire. Her hands shook as she tried to control her emotions.

"It's Markolous—isn't it?" her buck asked, knowing her so well.

"No—no. That's not it. I have to do something—that's all."

"You're lying—I know it's Markolous—because you always get this way when it's him."

"All right—all right. I do have to go see Markolous—but it's only because I'm the seer of the land."

"No, Pinky—you were the seer of the land."

"Well, I've been ordered by Markolous to read for him."

"Don't do this. You fought for your sister—against him."

Sighing, she stroked the buck's back.

"Pinky, I can tell you're not listening. You mustn't have anything to do with him. He's dangerous."

"Don't you see? I need to talk to him for Flanyanna's sake—and for all of our sakes for that matter."

Elfman stood up, hoping she would listen to him. His three-tiered chandelier antlers hit the cottage ceiling. He looked straight into her jade-green eyes with his big amber-colored orbs. For a moment, they stared at each other, in love.

"Okay—have it your way. But I'm coming with you," he asserted.

"Okay. We'll both go in the morning. Let's try to get some sleep."

Pinky mused with her crystals most of the night while Elfman slept. In the amber glow of the rising sun, she got dressed. She put her long flowing riding skirt and the matching top back on. After putting on her masculine, high-top leather riding boots, she took down her patchwork animal skin coat from the wall peg.

She quietly slipped outside without awakening Elfman. Although she did not completely understand the crystals' message, she knew that the savior of Kokakina was Flanyanna's daughter, her niece, who wasn't even born yet. Regarding Pinky, the message from her crystals was very clear. Her own destiny was to save the princess from Markolous or die trying.

Pinky twisted, turned, morphed into a raven, and flew off into the brightening sky, leaving the sleeping Elfman behind.

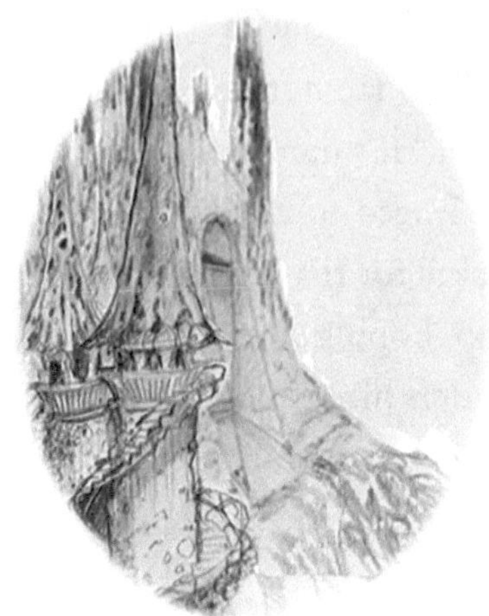

The Crystal Palace

Pinky, now a raven with brilliant jade-green eyes, soared through the misty maroon sky. Her quivering wings flashed in the dawn's beckoning light as she plunged down through a grove of evergreens whose needles were covered with a dusting of snow. The early winter her spell created had descended to the lowlands from the mountains overnight.

In front of the raven lay the Crystal Palace. The structure reflected the light and refracted it in prisms of psychedelic intensity. The Human Fairy architects who designed and engineered the Crystal Palace had done so using Stonehenge on Earth as a model. They channeled magic and creativity from the fourth dimension and higher. They well knew that in the fourth dimension, Stonehenge was not inert rock. It was a living crystalline structure that first absorbed and then projected solar energy. It was a device that could transport them through the galaxy and even to other dimensions.

Perched on a hilltop, the Crystal Palace's four slender towers spiraled upward into the stratosphere with three diamond-cut, sparkling crystal domes nestled below them. The royal citadel presented an opulent contrast to the simple village of the Human Fairy commoners nestled nearby.

The Crystal Palace's deep moat had proven to be impregnable to all Markolous' attempts to take Flanyanna's stronghold and home. But after his decisive victory over her, its garrison fled, leaving the castle to the victors without a fight. In triumph, Markolous rode across the moat and took possession of the abandoned fortress.

A partially attired female Human Fairy's body floated face down in the moat. Pinky's wings brushed the water's glassy surface as she swooped down to investigate. She shivered and thought maybe she should have brought Elfman after all.

Resuming her course, Pinky flew over the moss-covered rock bridge to the Crystal Palace's entrance. A shocking pink light beamed from her third eye. This third eye ray could be used to simply stun someone. The two sentinels at the front palace gate spasmed. Dropping their ebony and crystal spears, they buckled forward and fell to the ground.

Landing on the bridge, the raven hopped over the unconscious guards and slipped through the ornate gate into the large central courtyard with its opulent gardens.

Soft, thick spider-silk night drapes fluttered in the breeze that blew down the chimney in the room where Markolous slept in his sister's bed. He had ordered the chambermaid not to change the linens. He wanted to smell the sweet odor of Flanyanna's body that lingered on them.

A sudden pecking noise from above broke the morning's stillness and jolted Markolous awake. His eyes opened, but he could see nothing in the dark.

Snatching his silver dagger from under his goose down pillow, he flung aside the night drapes and jumped onto the cold crystal floor in his bare feet. Still hurting from the fall he experienced during the duel with Flanyanna, he winced as he landed. Scanning the bedchamber, he crouched low with his heart racing.

"Caw—caw."

Looking up to a narrow window high above on the chamber's wall, Markolous dragged a massive, hand-carved chair by the fireplace over and stepped up onto it. Rising up onto his toes, he peered cautiously out.

The intense jade-green eyes of the black raven stared back at him.

He jumped back. "Blasted—infuriating—interfering—female!"

Disgruntled, Markolous reached up and unhooked the latch. He flung the window open. Pinky had arrived in her time, not his. "You know you're quite capable of letting yourself in. You didn't need my help."

An ice-cold winter wind blew into the bedchamber. It carried in the enchanted raven who tumbled down past him onto the bedchamber floor.

"Thank you for fitting me into you calendar—" Markolous managed to say through his chattering teeth as he slammed the window shut. He jumped down from the chair and stared down at the bird sprawled on the rug. "Aren't you a little late for my reading? You were supposed to be here last night."

Before his eyes, the raven transformed back into Pinky, a petite, iridescent Human Fairy. The black feathers on her head morphed into her disheveled mop of long, flowing pink and blond hair.

"I needed to consult my crystals first." She lifted one of her sinuous arms, covered by the sleeve of her handmade patchwork coat. "Aren't you going to help me up?"

Markolous looked down at his half-sister. Although she was no threat to supplant him on his throne, she was the most magically powerful of the three children and therefore a power to be reckoned with.

"I notice there's been a change in the weather. I don't suppose you had anything to do with it?"

"That's very funny—brother—but why are you sleeping in our sister's bed?"

"Because it's my bed now."

Markolous cavalierly dismissed centuries of Human Fairy heritage—directly experiencing the messages of the Rose Crystals made females more qualified to be the monarch. He firmly believed his mother's constant message; it was his right to continue the patriarchal grip on the throne.

Pinky pulled down her skirt so that it covered the top portion of her masculine high-top boots. She spit out a few hairs and straightened her disarrayed locks. Giving her brother a hard look, she lifted herself up off of the floor unaided.

"Rosecenilla," Markolous said, deeply inhaling her scent.

"Don't you call me by that name," she responded lividly. She knew only too well that in private, her royal relatives often called her by the name her father had given her. The king had named her Rosecenilla to honor her Pink Fairy lineage on her mother's side. But the name was now used to remind her that she was only half a White Fairy. She had hoped that with her father's passing, the name would lose popularity, but it had not.

"Why? It's such a pretty name—for a very pretty Human Fairy. It fits you well," Markolous taunted.

"If you call me by my birth name one more time—I'll turn you into a buck." The roses and leaves of her tattoo quivered, flaring through her garment and betraying her outrage.

"Oh—we can't have that—two bucks. All right, let's not fight. I did win after all. I forgive you," he said.

Pinky scanned the bedchamber, remembering the body in the moat. She knew from the scent in the room that the dead girl had spent the night with him.

"Markolous—"

Even as a boy, Markolous had a fascination with the sweet fragrance of young female Human Fairies. He loved their scent. However, it did not turn out well for the ladies who caught his fancy. Many female bodies were found in the river and moat over the years. Despite their shock and horror upon learning that young Markolous was responsible, the king and queen hid his guilt.

"You and I would get along so much better if you would stop interfering in affairs of state," he said. "I always did like you, you know."

"Really? I never knew murdering females was an affair of the state." Pinky's eyes narrowed, and her full lips quivered.

Markolous touched her arm. "What strange material to wear for garments."

Pinky pulled her arm away from him and held it like a broken bird's wing. "I'll come straight to the point—our father proclaimed our sister to be his successor."

"I don't know why you remain so loyal to a father who portrayed you as a distant cousin rather than his own daughter...." He leaned in, whispering in her ear and smelling her again.

"And I don't know why a son would disrespect his father and not support his dying wish." Pinky pulled away again.

"I am the king—now."

Over the years, King Glendorf had reluctantly reached the conclusion that his only son was not fit to rule, but he never told Casafala his reservations. Her ambitions on her son's behalf were so strong that Glendorf never acted on his concerns until the end.

"Markolous, you know that's not true. Our father—on his deathbed—named Flanyanna to succeed him. She is his successor, not you."

"No, that was treachery on the part of our sister. You should know that better than anyone. She first stole the throne from you. You're the firstborn."

"That's not true and you know it. You know why I wasn't named. Father never married my mother." Pinky's old feelings of being lesser than her siblings stung her as she spoke.

"That's true. But—all my life I've been told—I would be king," Markolous responded.

"It was Father's dying wish that Flanyanna rule to continue the matriarchal way of life for Human Fairies," Pinky said.

"Our father was a patriarch on the throne these past three hundred years. I expect to rule just as long. No one else is nearly as qualified as I am."

It infuriated Markolous that so many believed that females had a natural right to occupy the highest seat. For him, for anyone to believe so was the same as saying that he was inferior.

"You need to give the throne back to Flanyanna."

"Really? Well, I'm not giving Flanyanna back the throne, cousin!" Markolous spat out Flanyanna's name like a curse, as if it left a bad taste in his mouth. "I'm not giving her anything!"

"You asked me to read the Rose Crystals for you. And—I did last night...," Pinky retorted.

"Aaaah, yes. My reading. You know perfectly well that the Rose Crystals can be altered by free will."

"I know you'd like to think so," Pinky said, sweat beginning to trickle down her back as she spoke.

Markolous stared at her footgear, men's riding boots, and decided to change the subject. "Aren't those my boots?" he asked, a fake smile plastered on his face.

Even though she had royal blood, Pinky could only afford serviceable, utilitarian footwear. She was the king's child who never had the chance to live at court as she grew up and wear the satin slippers customarily worn by courtly females. Soon after her birth, she became one of the family's secrets. The king could not undo the harm he had inflicted on her without causing significant problems in the realm.

"No, they're not your boots," she replied.

"Then whose boots are they?"

"If you must know—they're Elfman's."

"Oh, really? Well, I guess he doesn't need them anymore—does he?"

Though the timbre of his voice had matured as he grew, its disconnected quality gave Pinky chills. It was no different from how she remembered it so clearly from their childhood after the Tettigard swarming.

Markolous could not help but enjoy his half-sister's scent. After all, she was a Pink Fairy. Not only were they the most powerfully endowed in magic, they were also the most fragrant of all Human Fairies, and he did love the smell of a female Human Fairy.

"Let's have some breakfast, shall we?" Markolous said in a smooth, conciliatory tone. "I know you love quail eggs.…"

"I'm not hungry."

Without warning, he slipped the silver blade of his dagger under her throat's soft skin, slamming her up against the wall.

Pinky struggled to form her words as the blade pressed harder on her neck.

"Stop that," Pinky said, forming her words with difficulty with the knife's blade pressing on her neck. "I *really* don't like that…," she added, stunned he would turn on her so fast and remembering Elfman's warning. She held his gaze. The silver dagger broke out of his hand and flew across the room, crashing against the wall and dropping to the floor.

"Pinky, you always were so much more fun than Flanyanna."

"Brother, you must leave the Crystal Palace now," she said. "Flanyanna will understand and be compassionate."

"Oh, I'm sorry. I can't do that."

"Why not?"

"I crowned myself king yesterday—I live here now…," he said casually. "I did invite you, but apparently you had a more pressing engagement?"

Despite his casual, controlled demeanor, Pinky detected a smoldering undercurrent of anger.

"You did get the invitation to my coronation, yes?"

"No, your officer failed to mention that."

"Really? No matter," Markolous crooned, taking and kissing Pinky's hand. "I thought—what better queen could I have than you—dear cousin?"

"You're asking me to marry you?" Aghast, Pinky pulled her hand out of his grasp. "You're my brother."

"Exactly—and that's why it's so perfect—nobody knows. Everyone thinks you're my distant cousin."

"You can't be serious?"

"No one has to know about us being brother and sister. It will be our little secret. I think we'd be a good match to rule Kokakina—together," he said, taking her hand again and kissing it, sensually this time. He looked into her eyes and deeply inhaled her scent, the sweet high Rosa Centifolia scent.

Revolted, Pinky flinched and jerked her hand back. "You must abdicate. All will be forgotten and forgiven by our sister...."

"Unlikely—dear sister," Markolous responded, his cruel smile growing wider. "Flanyanna and I never forget, nor do we forgive. You should know that better than anyone."

"Markolous, the people will never willingly support you...," Pinky countered, shaking her head, now fearing the hopelessness of her mission to put Flanyanna back on the throne.

"Very well—then let them do so—unwillingly...," Markolous said with a malicious smile.

Pinky looked at her brother. "Goodbye Markolous. I won't be visiting you again." She turned to leave.

Markolous flipped his hair from his forehead and sauntered over to retrieve his dagger.

"You know, I thought you'd jump at the chance to be the Human Fairy Queen," he remarked casually, "Especially after what happened to your mother." He reached down to pick up the dagger.

With her magic, Pinky lifted the dagger from the floor just before Markolous grasped it. It somersaulted through the air, coming to rest in front of her.

"Keep my mother out of this...." Pinky took the blade and placed it in the waistband of her skirt. "Some would show compassion for you—if you would let them," she said.

"I suppose you mean—you?" Markolous laughed. "Don't insult my intelligence. You've made your choices very clear—and this marriage wasn't my idea. The advisors suggested it—imagine...," he scoffed, "the illegitimate daughter of the king, and they suggested it. Actually, I find you gross and distasteful."

Pinky's cheeks burned. Markolous' words seared open her raw wound of not ever having been accepted by her family.

Despite his words, Markolous was genuinely shocked. He had believed she would jump at the chance to be his queen. This was not the first time Pinky had refused him. He felt jilted and humiliated once again. He could not accept that she would dare to be anything but loyal and devoted to him.

"I never understood you—until now." Markolous' voice shook with rage.

The dagger in Pinky's waistband pressed into her belly. She feared she would have to pull it out and use it on him. He did not yet know about Flanyanna's child. If he did, he would want to kill Flanyanna before she gave birth.

"Goodbye—Markolous."

"I thought after all these years you would know how I really feel about you…," Markolous said.

"I would have given you even that if I thought it would make a difference," she said.

"Pinky, I learned a long time ago that only one Human Fairy will ever show concern for me. There is only one who will see that I get what I deserve, and that one person stands before you now, in his nightshirt," Markolous said.

"Then—I'm truly sorry for you," Pinky said, turning away.

Markolous balled his hand and struck a massive blow to her back between her shoulder blades where her etheric wings were located—a spot on Human Fairies that was particularly vulnerable. Pinky arched back in excruciating pain and collapsed to the floor, unconscious.

"Pity," he said, standing over her and looking down. "Loyalty is such an overrated virtue." Markolous stepped over her prostrate body. "Guards!"

The bedchamber door flung open. Tithoreus and the Human Fairy guards on duty in the hallway rushed in.

Tithoreus bent over Pinky.

"Sire—she breathes." He took Markolous' dagger from her waist and handed it to him.

"She—she tried to kill me with my own dagger…."

"Sire, what shall we do with her?"

"Take her to the dungeon—she's a traitor," Markolous said calmly.

The Human Fairy guards picked up Pinky's limp body and dragged her out the door and down the open hall.

"Sire, do you think this is wise—" Tithoreus asked. "I fear rebellion in the land. After all, she is your other sister…."

"Nonsense. Nobody even knows she's here. She came through the window as a raven—and she's only my cousin."

"But, what about the guards?" Tithoreus asked. "They know she was here...."

Markolous stared for a moment across the bedchamber and turned back to Tithoreus.

"You're right—kill them," Markolous replied, coldly. "Go now and do it quickly before they tell anyone."

"Sire—may my kind feast on their blood?"

"I don't care—do as you like. Just get rid of them." Markolous heard the echoing Human Fairy boots on the open, cold, Crystal Palace walkway dragging Pinky to the Tower of the Forgotten, a place from where no one ever returned.

The Poacher

A few weeks passed. At the Faireye Manor, there were no signs of the war waged in the past few years.

The rays of the rising sun filtered through the icy window into Flanyanna's bedroom. Having slept better than she had in years, she bounced out of bed, and as her feet touched the freezing cold crystal floor, she shivered. The fire had gone out during the night and she was wearing the summer nightclothes that were all she had available to her.

A frigid breeze blew down the chimney of the stone fireplace. Her sister's winter spell protected her from Markolous, but she missed the warm weather she had when she usually came to the Faireye Manor. She wrapped the fur-lined cloak that she wore in the battle around her light, intricate, lacy, cream-colored nightgown of spider-silk to keep warm. She rubbed her extending belly. Despite all the uncertainty, she would be a mother soon.

"Even a queen has to wait for the birth of her child," she said to herself with a smile.

Finding the boots she wore during the battle under the bed, she put them on. The summer slippers she kept at the manor would not keep her feet warm, but she was safe for now.

Flitting nimbly down the oakwood stairs like when she was a child, Flanyanna remembered the steps that creaked and skipped over them. Just as then, she wanted to be as quiet as possible so she would not disturb the sleeping household.

In the Great Hall one of the guards was on duty. She turned to go towards the kitchen hoping to find something to eat. Her pregnancy sometimes increased her appetite, and this morning she felt like eating.

The fire was banked with a few glowing embers. To her relief Bessalina and Trista had not yet come into the kitchen. She pulled off a chunk of bread from yesterday's round loaf still on the kitchen table. Unwrapping the cloth from the cheddar cheese sitting next to it, she cut herself a piece. With great gusto, she ate the simple breakfast, enjoying the solitude.

Something caught her eye. By the door leading outside used by the tradesmen and servants, a tattered straw peasant's hat worn in the fields hung on a hook.

"Trista must have found Petronero's hat in the hayloft while hunting for chicken eggs in the horse barn," she said to herself.

Flanyanna vividly remembered Petronero wearing it during one of their many happy summer visits, and he always kept it in the barn. Feeling a pang of loss, she impulsively placed it on her head. She did not know if she would ever see Petronero again and wearing his hat made her feel like a part of him was still with her.

She opened the kitchen's outside door and stepped into the frosty morning breeze. She audibly gasped as the brisk, outdoor air invaded and seared her lungs. The ground was covered in a soft white blanket of snow.

In the tranquility, Flanyanna gathered her cloak tightly around her neck. The white cloak streamed behind, contrasting sharply with her raven black hair, which cascaded freely from under Petronero's hat and down her back. She took great delight in crunching through the snow outside the Faireye Manor.

The wind picked up. Shuddering, she raised her cloak's hood over her tossed, uncombed hair and her husband's straw hat. She was grateful for the warmth that her battle cloak offered. She leaned her body forward, keeping her head down to protect herself from the icy wind. She broke the virgin snow under her feet as she strode behind the manor house towards a wooden gate and the path that led down to the beach.

Sensing she was not alone, she looked up. In front of her sat the two Hokkaido wolves who greeted her the day she came to the Faireye Manor. For a moment, she was startled and stepped back. Vaporous breath floated up from the wolves' black steaming noses. It was the only movement that emanated from their massive, powerful bodies. Motionless ears pointed in her direction, and wild, black eyes bored straight into her. Slowly, they rose up and began to walk towards her.

Flanyanna touched the Rose Crystal pendant around her neck. The stocky creatures sat down, now softly whining. As she opened the gate, the wolves rose, and, like playful puppies, followed her out onto the cliffs.

"Have it your way then." She made no attempt to get rid of them for she did enjoy their company.

In silence, Flanyanna and her new, four-legged friends walked across the pure white sediment cliffs overlooking the Mara Sea.

Finally, they stopped and stood still at the edge of the White Cliffs, looking out over the water. Tumbling gray and white clouds rolled above the blue-green ocean. The clouds kept breaking the sun's light and casting shadows on Flanyanna's face.

She knew the winter spell Pinky had cast would provide only temporary sanctuary for her and her coming child. It was only a matter of time before her brother would arrive to take his vengeance. Her only hope was that Pinky had been able to persuade Markolous to abdicate, but Flanyanna had not heard anything from her sister since her arrival at the Faireye Manor.

Flanyanna inhaled the frigid, salty sea air as the morning sun fell on her face.

She scanned the horizon. Deep feelings of loneliness and abandonment overcame her. She was a Human Fairy queen with no land to rule, soon to give birth to a child with possibly no father.

She looked back and the wolves were gone. Flanyanna looked down the sheer escarpment.

Standing at the edge of the white sediment cliffs, the wind tossed the deposed queen's hair straight up like sails on a ship in a storm at sea. In her despair her thoughts turned to flying with no particular destination. She longed to have her infant wings again and to unfurl them releasing herself into the skies. She remembered the freedom of flight, the sheer ecstasy offered by her tiny wings that never needed to rest in the etheric realm.

An unexpected burst of wind whipped the cape's hood off and snatched Petronero's hat from her head. Stretching her arms out, she desperately lunged to catch it almost falling off the edge of the cliff. She watched it sail away, far out over the rough, churning white surf, out to sea.

Below, a strange chameleon-like creature about her size with a large fishing net waded in the waves. He had a neck like a turtle's that protruded out of his body and then retracted back in. At that moment, his skin was deep blue to match the color of the water, to blend in so as not to alert his prey that he was fishing them for his dinner.

His eyes, red with black centers and surrounded by yellow, rotated separately, scanning the vast water for a fish or two. He wore thick, round spectacles that made his nose and his bulging eyes appear even larger.

The clothing he wore was of the fashion of the day, a sage green vest with a thin velvet collar, once owned by a Human Fairy but now worn by this creature. It had been beautifully altered and reconstructed, likely by his wife, to fit the peculiarities of his species. His sailor breeches made of rough brown wool were rolled up over his knobby knees as he waded in the water. A knee-length coat of rust-colored wool lay back on the sand, above the waterline.

Pulling the fishing net from the surf, he was gratified to see it contained various fish—struggling, flopping, and gasping. A peasant's straw hat was mixed in with his catch. Perplexed, he stuck his head out of the loose skin on his neck and glanced about, rotating his eyes out over the water, to his right, to his left, and finally upwards where his search bore fruit.

He saw a Human Fairy female on the lip of the White Cliffs, swaying back and forth. With her arms outstretched, her body appeared ready to plunge down off the precipice.

"Stop!" he cried out. "Don't jump!"

Startled, Flanyanna stepped back from the edge. She had not realized how close she was to tumbling off.

The creature wrestled with the waves, jumping, wading, and swimming back to the shore, pulling his fish and the hat back into the shallows.

"Tarragonian—you're poaching the queen's fish," Flanyanna yelled, infuriated that a lowly creature would dare pilfer her fish.

After the Tarragonian's home planet, Tarragon, was rendered uninhabitable by a devastating war that poisoned their environment, Human Fairies agreed to bring them to their planet. Once on Kokakina, the Tarragonians were used over the centuries as a source of cheap labor. Tarragonians had marvelous chameleon abilities that allowed them to take on the color and shape of things that caught their attention. They changed color to reflect their emotional state and to camouflage themselves. Also, they had a marvelous ability to change their physical appearance to blend in with others as needed.

"I have a family to feed," the Tarragonian shouted back over the crashing waves, turning bright red in his agitation, for he knew he was speaking to the deposed queen.

"Your color betrays you." Flanyanna could see that, knowing he was stealing her fish, he was in a highly emotional state. "I'll—I'll put you in the Tower of the Forgotten—" she yelled at him over the sound of the crashing waves on the beach. "You're familiar with the Tower of the Forgotten, aren't you?"

"Yes—I am quite familiar with the dungeon—Madam," he responded tersely. The Tarragonian calmed down and changed his color back to the cool blue of the Mara Sea as he pulled his catch closer to the beach.

"Don't you know who I am?" Flanyanna asked. "I'm your queen."

"There is no Human Fairy queen anymore," the Tarragonian spoke boldly for being a member of an outcast species. Removing the fish from his net, he placed them in a netted pouch on the beach.

"How dare you speak to me that way...," Flanyanna cried, miffed at his insufferable impertinence. She could see the Tarragonian pulling more fish out of the net, except this time, some of the flopping fish were in Petronero's hat.

"Stop—stop—that's my hat! I command you to bring me my hat!"

Reaching down, the Tarragonian pulled the fish out of the hat. Placing the fish in the bag, he hoisted the soddened, dripping hat up in the air, waving it at the queen.

"Is this the hat you're referring to—Madam?" he asked, not caring one bit about the hat. All he wanted was his poached loot to feed his hungry family.

"Of course it is, you insolent creature. What other hat is there?" she shrieked.

"Very well, Madam, I'll leave your hat on the beach for you— good day."

"How dare you. I don't want you to leave it on the beach. I command you to bring that hat to me this instant— Tarragonian—or I will call my guards and have your ugly head for poaching my fish! Do you hear me?"

"Aye. I hear you and I believe you. You'd have my head if you were still queen," he answered. "But you are no longer the queen. It's the king's fish now and he's not here." He reached down and gathered up his catch. "Now, if you'll excuse me, Madam, I have thirteen mouths at home to feed and I must dress the fish before they spoil."

"Such insolence—I demand to know your name!"

"My name is of no importance," the Tarragonian yelled back. Then, he muttered to himself, "I'm a lowly Tarragonian, as you can plainly see. Besides, I see no benefit to her knowing my name."

"Tarragonian—I asked you—what is your surname?" Flanyanna persisted haughtily.

"My surname is Tikkum. I'm Doc Tikkum and I have worked these many years for a paltry sum in your Tower of the Forgotten—taking care of the sick and dying," he blurted out, giving in and revealing both his name and his longtime resentment.

Although he did not allow himself to get involved in Human Fairy politics, everyone had been affected by the ravages of the civil war. Fortunately, for the moment at least, Doc Tikkum still had a job, as the physician for the dungeon's prisoners. 'Doc' was the title Tarragonians bestowed on their healers. Not only were Tarragonians chameleons, but some also had extraordinary healing gifts. Over the centuries, those who did were used as physicians in Human Fairy society. These fortunate Tarragonians were excused from slave labor, which was the lot of most Tarragonians. Doc Tikkum was one of these powerful shamans—when he wasn't poaching the queen's fish.

"How dare you speak to me like that!"

"You're right. My apologies. My poor salary all these years has nothing to do with you wanting to know my name."

"You speak well for a Tarragonian. Why aren't you a court healer?"

"Because, Madam, I chose the dungeon—to minister to the lost and forgotten, who need my help the most," Doc Tikkum said, turning a bright, beet red.

"Oh—I see. You supplement your poor salary ministering to the unsavory lot in the Tower of the Forgotten by stealing my fish?"

"Yes, Madam—I do. Now, with your permission—" Doc Tikkum gave her a courtly bow, "—I will take my leave."

"I cant believe this. You even admit that you've poached my fish before." Flanyanna was outraged at his arrogance and willingness to disregard the laws of the land.

"I have done so for many years to feed my family," he replied bluntly.

Flanyanna couldn't believe what she was hearing. "I demand that you bring me the hat and my fish!" With her last command, her vocal cords tightened, and her voice came out a strident, shrill croak.

"Very well—as you wish." Doc Tikkum relented. He put the bag containing the wet, flopping fish on his back and the straw hat on his head before effortlessly slithering up the forbidding cliffs. His ascent displayed the extraordinary climbing ability of his kind.

Upon the top of the cliffs, he dumped the day's catch in front of Flanyanna with the soggy hat still on his head.

"Your fish...Madam," he grumbled.

The overpowering stench of fish wafted into Flanyanna's nostrils. In her pregnant condition, it almost knocked her over. Determined to maintain her dignity, she willed herself to steady her balance.

"The hat. Give me that hat," she said, reaching out her hand.

Doc Tikkum took the drooping straw hat off of his head and offered it to her, being careful that there was no contact between them. Tarragonian shamans were required to always wear gloves when attending to Human Fairy patients. A commonly held belief in Human Fairy society was that the touch of a Tarragonian would contaminate a Human Fairy. Doc Tikkum was following the protocol of the times in not touching a Human Fairy when he had no gloves.

Snatching Petronero's hat from his green, clawed hand, she put it on her head. Like many of the educated Human Fairy upper class, she did not believe the tale about how the touch of a Tarragonian would contaminate you forever. To her, it was just an old custom.

For a moment, Doc Tikkum stared at her. "Madam—if I may say so—you need to take better care of yourself."

"I feel quite well—thank you very much," she said, sneezing. "I'm only reacting to the wretched odor of these fish."

He reached into his pocket and offered Flanyanna his water-logged handkerchief.

She took it and held it up to her nose, violently blowing into it. "Thank you." Flanyanna was an exiled queen talking to a poacher, but she somehow felt comforted by this lowly Tarragonian creature.

"You may keep it…," he said, "the handkerchief."

Flanyanna was mystified by his gentlemanly manner and kindness. "And you may keep the fish," she replied as she began to walk away.

"You must eat more for your child," Doc Tikkum called out after her as he picked up the fish.

Flanyanna stopped in her tracks and slowly turned. "What did you just say?"

"I've seen many in your condition," he replied, his voice rich with the calm, assured composure of an experienced and talented doctor. He had seen many pregnancies in numerous species.

"How do you know about—my condition?"

"Madam, I may be a Tarragonian, but it's the same signs for all species. I'm just observing what any healer can see."

"I only thought—I mean—your comprehension was not possible for a Tarragonian since you are not a healer of the court."

"Madam, your condition is the same for all species. And a pregnant Human Fairy in the dungeon is no different than one in the court. When it comes to procreation—there is no class distinction," he stated matter-of-factly.

"I can't believe I'm having a conversation with a Tarragonian like I would with a Human Fairy," she muttered to herself. She turned to walk back to the manor wearing her husband's hat.

"Your child is a girl," Doc Tikkum called out after her as he leaped down the incline, as only a Tarragonian could, to retrieve his coat. His supple clawed hands and feet molded around the rocky edges of the bluff, adjusting to adhere to the jagged surface.

"Wait! How do you know my child is a girl?" Flanyanna asked, leaning over the edge of the cliff.

Doc Tikkum paused and poked his head high out of his neck, looking back at Flanyanna. "I have delivered many children into the world."

"That doesn't answer my question. How do you know my child is a girl?"

"As I just told you...I have delivered many children. I know the sex of your child because you have a serenity about you that only happens when the baby is of your own sex. Like to like—as the saying goes—and your belly is high, which is the sign of a female child in all species."

"Oh...," she said, relieved that nothing had leaked out about her pregnancy since her exile at the Faireye Manor, and only Pinky and now the Tarragonian doctor knew about it. "I would appreciate that you tell no one about our meeting."

"I will tell no one—Madam."

"Also, please tell no one of my condition."

"I will not...Madam," he assured her. "No word of our meeting or your condition will ever reach the palace from me." With these words Doc Tikkum continued his descent down the White Cliffs moving effortlessly from one handhold to the next.

On the pink crystal beach, Doc Tikkum bent down to pick up his rust-colored coat. He slung it over his scaled back and slithered on all fours along the dry sand and back up the cliffside to get his fish and go home. His long forearms and forelegs allowed him to build up momentum and dramatically increase the size of his steps and the speed of his ascent in a short time.

Unlike the Human Fairies and their Namdalarians, for whom the sharp rocks and snow rendered the peaks of the Feydonian Mountains inaccessible, Doc Tikkum's superb climbing skills would allow him to handle that difficult terrain with the same ease he had exhibited when he scaled the White Cliffs. All others must wait until spring and go through the pass.

"I'm glad it's only your kind that can scale the cliffs and mountains with such ease," Flanyanna remarked, heartened that Pinky's spell to make the Feydonian pass inaccessible had confounded Markolous for the time being.

"Madam, you startled me." Doc Tikkum stood up, dropping his coat to the ground. "I thought you'd gone back to the manor." He stooped over to retrieve the coat.

"Well, I do need to get back. They're probably up now and wondering what happened to me...."

"Well—thank you for the fish." Doc Tikkum stuffed his clawed hands through his coat's sleeves and picked up the bag of fish, slinging it over his back. "I'd best be going. It's getting late. Good day to you, Madam."

"Please...walk with me for a while, sir."

Doc Tikkum paused, knowing that Flanyanna wanted something from him. He offered his hand to help her cross a rocky part of the cliff's top. "Madam?"

"I know this may seem odd—but—please, tell me one thing before you go...."

"Yes?"

"Is your life—" Flanyanna paused. "—you're a strange creature. You must know that. Your ability to morph into almost looking like a Human Fairy is truly remarkable."

"We are no different than any other species. We have adapted over time to survive."

"Yes, of course. How foolish of me to think you're magical."

"Madam?"

"Oh, nothing....You said that pregnancy has similarities in all creatures?"

"Yes, Madam."

"Is there something I could take to calm my symptoms?"

"Ah, I understand now. You want some kind of herbal potion?"

They walked back together on the path towards the back gate to the manor.

"I know I'm putting you in something of an awkward position, possibly a dangerous one," Flanyanna said. "I'm no longer the queen and you now work for my brother."

All in the land had heard of the war she had lost to Markolous. Doc Tikkum's gentle spirit chaffed at the harshness and injustice he witnessed every day in the Tower of the Forgotten under Markolous' reign. It was bad before, but now the cruelty was devastating. It was truly beyond the measure of the crimes committed, if any crime had been committed at all.

He knew Flanyanna's days were numbered, even if she survived the baby's delivery. He wanted to say something that would give her ease. After all, his calling was to offer well-being to the sick and comfort to the dying. She, not he, was the one in great peril.

"Your Majesty—" he said, showing his shifting allegiance to Flanyanna by using her royal title, "—even though I work for your brother, his cruelties inspire no loyalty."

"I am grateful that I have at least one loyal subject left in the realm."

"Ma'am—I do have something that will help you," Doc Tikkum said as they neared the Faireye Manor. He dropped the bag of fish onto the ground. Reaching into the brown burlap medical bag that he always carried across his chest, he took out a golden herb.

"What is it?" Flanyanna was curious.

Could it be he had just betrayed his true intention, to finish me off with a poisonous potion? Is he a loyal subject or a spy? Does he truly now favor me as he said, or is his allegiance still to my brother? she thought.

Flanyanna was raised to be among the highest gentry of the land, and even though this Tarragonian appeared to be among the highest of his kind, his kind was the lowest. He could have been paid handsomely by her brother to scale the Feydonian Mountains to assassinate her.

"This is—*Aetheleus*," Doc Tikkum disclosed offering it to her. *"Aetheleus?"* She took the dried herb.

"Yes, it's a healing herb known for its relaxing, calming effect," Doc Tikkum explained. "I gather it in the spring when it's most potent, approaching full bloom, and dry it all summer."

"But this is a Human Fairy herb."

"I use all herbal remedies and medicines that heal."

"Of course." Flanyanna smelled the golden herb. It did smell like the herb *Aetheleus*. Breathing its calming properties, she began to relax and felt a bit foolish that she thought it might be poisonous.

"Steep it and drink it three times a day," he instructed. "I must leave you now or my family will go hungry." Picking up the bag of fish, he threw it over his back again and dropped to all fours to travel quickly. "Remember, steep it well or it will be too bitter to drink."

She regarded the reptilian creature as he began to slither over the snow-covered heather.

"When my time comes, do you think I'll suffer much?" she called after him, betraying her anxiety about the delivery of her first child.

Doc Tikkum stopped and turned. "I don't know," he replied. "All deliveries are different."

"Will you help me when my time comes?"

Doc Tikkum stood up. "I will offer whatever help I can."

"Good then. Go quickly now before I change my mind and call my guards to beat you silly for stealing my fish," she teased. She grasped the healing herb tightly as she watched this strange creature leave her.

Doc Tikkum lowered himself down on all fours.

"Wait! I need to know one thing—are you happy?" she asked suddenly.

Doc Tikkum looked up. "Yes, Ma'am. I'm happy," he replied without hesitation.

The kitchen door to the Faireye Manor creaked open and Trista stepped out, her long black skirt clinging to her legs from the biting sea breeze. She ran to the gate that was open and banging in the wind. The long, flowing hair on her head blew with abandon, making her young, plain face attractive.

Doc Tikkum lowered his body down to the ground to conceal himself. His color turned to match the dark speckled pink rocks and the purple heather that led down to the Mara Sea.

"Your Majesty, it's too cold out here. Come back inside by the fire and have something warm to eat," Trista said, walking over to where Flanyanna stood on the White Cliffs and placing Bessalina's shawl around her white caped shoulders.

Flanyanna turned back to look into the morning light. She could see no sign of Doc Tikkum.

"Ma'am—is something wrong—did you see the wolves again?" Trista asked, fearing that the wolves were nearby.

"No, nothing's wrong, Trista. And I didn't see the wolves," Flanyanna fibbed to spare the girl's feelings.

Flanyanna and Trista walked back to Faireye Manor.

He could have done me great harm—or even done me in, and no one would ever have known, Flanyanna thought.

But she knew differently of Doc Tikkum now. She did not know why she trusted this alien creature, but she did.

"Trista—I am hungry. I'm starving in fact."

"Bessalina will be so happy, Ma'am," Trista said, giggling. She was delighted herself. Flanyanna had sometimes brooded, displaying a listless appetite. "She's going to make porridge with dried apples, apricots, and black walnuts to entice you to eat something."

"Well, then we must neither tarry nor disappoint, mustn't we?"

"No, Ma'am," Trista said, giggling again.

With Flanyanna and Trista almost to the manor, Doc Tikkum no longer felt the need to conceal himself. With his fish on his back, he continued on his way on all fours. He leaped rapidly across the brown-purple snow-covered heather. Hoping to be in time for dinner, he headed towards home and his family in the Tarragonian village.

The Evil Spell

Flanyanna hummed softly as she peered out the leaded triangular window in her bedchamber. She looked off towards the now empty, snow-covered cliffs where she had met the Tarragonian doctor. The crashing surf in the distance provided a percussive accompaniment to the tune in her head.

"Ma'am—your bath is ready," Trista said, rising from the freestanding copper tub with her elbows red from the hot water. Steam rose from the bathtub. Beads of condensation trickled on the natural crystal wall behind it.

Still humming, Flanyanna dipped her toes in the bathtub. "Oh, that feels good," she said as she slipped into the embracing warmth.

With a ceramic pitcher, Trista poured more steaming hot water into the tub.

"Trista—you needn't call me 'Ma'am', anymore."

"Then what should I call you, Ma'am?"

"Call me by my name—better yet—call me by my nickname."

"What is your nickname?"

"Flan—like the pudding."

The chambermaid's green eyes opened wide in surprise and lit up with a sparkle.

Oh—I love flan. It's my favorite."

"I'm famished," Flanyanna said. "Aren't you?" She immersed herself into the water.

Trista nodded. "Bessalina says I'm always hungry—because I'm still growing."

Flanyanna raised her head above the water. "Let's eat breakfast together—right here in my room," she said, inviting Trista to share her meal. She slowly arched her back and dropped her head beneath the water's surface once again. Trista grinned wide, from ear to ear, as she watched Flanyanna underneath the water.

"Your hair looks like black seaweed floating on top of the Mara Sea," Trista said.

Flanyanna looked up through the water, not hearing her. *That Tarragonian doctor has given me a strength I don't quite understand,* she thought

Suddenly, Flanyanna sat up. Breaking through the water's surface, she gasped for air and splashed the grinning girl.

"Well—go on," she said aloud to Trista. "Aren't you going to tell Bessalina it's time to make us breakfast? That porridge sounds yummy."

Wiping the hot water from her flushed face, Trista answered, "Yes, Ma'am. I mean, no, Ma'am. I mean...." Flustered, Trista accidentally dropped the scrub brush she was holding into the tub. The water splashed up and hit Flanyanna in the face.

Flanyanna was taken aback and looked at Trista—surprised. "You did that on purpose!" she said, thinking she might have taken her familiarity with Trista too far.

Terrified, Trista covered her mouth. "Oh no—Ma'am. I'm sorry. I didn't mean it. Really—it was an accident." She was certain she had committed an unforgivable breach of etiquette and would be severely reprimanded by Bessalina.

Flanyanna burst into side-splitting laughter. After a moment's hesitation, Trista joined in, much relieved that her sovereign, who was now her friend had forgiven her.

"Of course, it was…there was no harm done," Flanyanna said, taking the poor girl at her word. "Now, off you go to fetch our breakfast."

Needing no more prompting, Trista ran out the door. Flanyanna got out and wrapped a heavy linen towel with fringed edges around her. After drying herself, she slipped her lace, spider-silk nightgown over her head. Wiggling her cold toes on the icy crystal floor, she went to her dressing table. Picking up her abalone comb, she ran its teeth through her fine, wet dark locks. Pulling her hair from her face, she pinned it into a chignon at the back of her neck. Gazing into the silver glass, she noticed a change within herself. She felt different, calmer. She had always wondered what it would be like not to be privileged and not be controlled by the demands of the court.

When my time comes, I'll have Bessalina send Trista to the Tarragonian village. She could go there, an inconspicuous peasant girl. She could reach the Tarragonian village and Doc Tikkum's home without being noticed, Flanyanna thought.

"What am I thinking? She could get hurt or even killed," she said aloud to herself.

Flanyanna threw her cloak around her shoulders and looked at her reflection. She slipped into her white summer spider-silk slippers and went downstairs, not wanting to be alone.

In the afternoon Flanyanna curled up in Bessalina's rocking chair next to the kitchen fire. The motion of the chair soothed her as she snuggled under a patchwork quilt made of scraps of fabric from her family's clothing.

"This is good medicine you brought," Bessalina remarked, putting another tumbler with Doc Tikkum's hot brew on the outer hearth next to Flanyanna. Bessalina wore some red, satin slippers she had found in the attic that had belonged to Flanyanna's mother, Aliafora. Bessalina gently stroked Flanyanna's crown of hair, like a mother comforting her child.

Flanyanna drank the fresh brew and closed her eyes, relishing the hot liquid as it slid down her throat. She took hold of Bessalina's rough calloused hand, squeezing and kissing it. "You're always so good to me," she said, looking deeply into her nanny's eyes and saying nothing about Doc Tikkum.

Touched by her queen's and former charge's expression of love, Bessalina squeezed Flanyanna's soft pale fingers and held back her tears of joy and fear of losing her.

"Move closer to the fire to stay warm." The old cook's voice broke off. She pushed her rocking chair with Flanyanna in it closer to the warm hearth.

Flanyanna sipped her tea, enjoying the herb's robust, twiggy taste. Doc Tikkum's herbal concoction was handling her morning sickness. She smiled as she remembered the Tarragonian doctor's audacity admitting to the capital offense that he had poached her fish on many occasions. At least his hand would have been cut off for such a crime while she ruled.

Ashamed, Flanyanna stared into the fire as she ruminated about her past actions and policies as the Human Fairy queen. She felt the heat of the hot coals penetrate into her feet through her white silk slippers. She closed her eyes, drifting off, hoping her subjects would remember her kindly.

> *In the architectural garden in the back yard of the Faireye Manor, Flanyanna's hair tosses in the sea breeze and her white, rose-embroidered gown whips about her in the strong sea winds.*
>
> *She kneels and snips a Rosa Centifolia bud off of a rose bush, inhaling its sweet scent. This exotic rose only grows in this part of Kokakina. On Earth, it had grown in the area where the small town of Grasse, France is now located. As she places it into a rustic woven basket, she pricks her finger. Blood trickles down her hand and spots her white dress with red droplets. A dark shadow looms over her.*
>
> *Frightened, Flanyanna drops her knife and runs away towards the White Cliffs and the sea.*

"Your Majesty—wake up!" Bessalina shouted, fearful she was not getting through. The old cook stood behind her queen by the outer hearth in the kitchen shaking Flanyanna from her altered state. With her cheeks flushed from the fire, Flanyanna trembled in the rocking chair.

"Nanna."

"Ma'am, are you all right?"

"I pricked my finger. It bled on me," Flanyanna barely spoke, afraid she was cursing herself.

"It's not real, Ma'am. You know that. Markolous put an evil spell on you," Bessalina said, fuming.

Flanyanna nodded. "It was Markolous. He was there—I'm frightened." She clung to her nanny.

"He attacked you in your dream state. You're all right now—and that's what matters."

"But it was so real."

"Of course it was. Dreams are no different than our awakened state. But you woke up—that's all that matters."

"No—no—Nanna. I live in fear now…I'm afraid it will happen again."

"You must fight back against these weak creations."

"I can't help myself. So much has happened. What has become of my husband and my sister?"

Bessalina patted Flanyanna's back, wanting to give peace of mind to her sovereign who was more like her child. "Now, we can't have any more melancholy, can we?"

"But what if Pinky's winter spell doesn't work? What if Markolous gets here before my baby is born? What if…Petronero's dead?"

"Stop this. You must stop this."

"We haven't heard from him in months…."

"You'd know if he was dead."

"But—my sister. I haven't heard from her either. It's so unlike her."

"That's enough. Do you hear me?" Bessalina said firmly. "I don't know why I didn't think of this before. Of course, your vile brother attacks you in your dream state—in your female condition." She pulled Flanyanna's thick raven-black hair back. "Sit still." Bessalina took a dark brown, bark-like strand from one of the stalks hanging by the weathered outer hearth and weaved some of the *Aetheleus* into it.

"What's that?"

"I'm braiding an old peasant charm for your melancholy. The herb will protect you from harm. Markolous will not be able to invade your dreams anymore."

"I always loved it when you braided my hair when I was young."

"That's right."

Flanyanna breathed in the relaxing fragrance. "I do feel better. What is this strange plant?"

"It's the bark of the rowan tree from the Lost Forest."

"Of course," Flanyanna said. "How silly of me. My sister would have known...." Her voice trailed off.

Bessalina and Trista looked at each other and the old cook touched Flanyanna's shoulder. "Now, how about a good steaming hot cup of that tea?"

Flanyanna grasped the old cook's gnarled hand and kissed it. "I don't know what I'd do without you."

"There, there. You must be strong. I know you will—I raised you," Bessalina said.

Flanyanna nodded. "I will not weaken in my thoughts any-more—Nanna—I promise."

"That's right. Markolous' evil spells can't get to you if you're strong."

"I'm very sorry that I've been so melancholy."

"Now don't you worry. You're safe here at Faireye Manor. Trista and I will make sure he can't hurt you," Bessalina assured her.

The Winter Spell

Months passed. Early winter slipped into normal wintertime. The cold weather spell continued to work and the pass stayed closed. Markolous would have to wait until spring to come to the Faireye Manor. The peasant charm continued to protect Flanyanna when she slept.

Bessalina stirred the robust, cold weather soup simmering in the black, cast iron cauldron that hung over the open flame in the massive brick fireplace that extended the length of the kitchen. The charred, blackened bricks that made up the hearth were a testament to the many meals prepared there and shared among the royal family and the household staff.

At the kitchen table Trista finished chopping the sweet potatoes. Balancing the cut pieces on the worn, wooden cutting board, she carried them over to the fire and scraped them into the pot. Then, she sat down on the outer hearth to warm herself.

"You're faster than me," Flanyanna said. Still wearing her nightgown that hid her approaching motherhood, she dropped carrots, parsnips, celery root, turnips, rutabaga, and sweet potato into the soup. "It smells good," she said, leaning over and inhaling the aromatic steam.

"This stew will take the bite out of the cold winter air," Bessalina said as she dropped a clove of chopped garlic into the pot.

Flanyanna crumbled some sage in her fingertips. Savoring its zesty aroma, she started to place it in the cauldron.

"I wouldn't do that if I were you. You'll ruin the broth if you add more," Bessalina cautioned. "Besides—too much might upset your stomach with the babe growing inside you."

"You always know best." Flanyanna patted her expanding stomach and threw the rest of the sage into the fire. Quickly, the smoldering herb released a pungent, earthy scent that filled the kitchen.

"I remember my mother burning sage in the family cottage to purify it," Trista said, inhaling the distinct, familiar scent.

"Yes, my mother, too," Bessalina said as she stirred the thick combo with a large wooden spoon. "It's an ancient custom. I believe it dates back to our Earth ancestors."

"Yes—I remember you burning sage as well, Bessalina," Flanyanna said.

Bessalina nodded and flicked her fingers over the pot. "I cast a spell I know that speeds up the cooking process." Satisfied that her enchantment was successful, she said, "Go ahead taste it now, Ma'am."

She handed Flanyanna the wooden spoon. "Blow on it first or you'll burn your tongue," she warned.

Heeding Bessalina's words, Flanyanna blew on the steaming winter soup before tasting it. "It's perfect."

Bessalina blushed with pride at her sovereign's words. She tuned to Trista. "And what do you think you're doing… just sitting there?"

"I was cold—I was just gettin' warm by the fire," Trista said defensively.

The old cook pushed her aside and pulled another log from the wooden box next to the outer hearth, tossing it onto the crackling flames.

"I finished everythin' ya asked me to do—all the cuttin'."

"Then go fetch some water—now." Bessalina tidied her bun and took a brown ceramic bowl down from a shelf.

"I can't."

"What do you mean—you can't?"

"The water's frozen—and it's cold outside," Trista objected.

"Nonsense—what nonsense—you may use my shawl when you go out," Bessalina replied, ignoring Trista's objection.

Trista went to the back door. She grudgingly lifted Bessalina's shawl and wrapped it around her shoulders. "You'll be sorry if somethin' happens to me."

Bessalina shook her head in exasperation as she measured some flour and poured it into the bowl. "You don't really believe Derrik's story—do you?"

"It's true." Trista blanched, pausing before opening the door.

Bessalina shook her head. "Seriously, Trista, how could a wolf carry off the previous scullery maid?"

"Well, she was younger than me!"

"Bessalina, that's enough. You're scaring her," Flanyanna admonished.

"Hogwash, she's loving every minute of this nonsense."

"Well, maybe those wolves ate her on the spot," Trista said.

"You see? Sometimes, Trista, I think you have fairy dust between your ears." Bessalina shook her head another time, placing her hands on her hips. She stared at the flour in her bowl. A few ounces of it rose up and created a powdery white spiral. It swirled across the kitchen table and powdered Trista's face.

Bessalina plunked a wooden mallet into Trista's hand. "Here—use this to break the ice," she instructed.

Trista swung the mallet a few times before releasing the iron latch to go outside.

Bessalina laughed. "Any wild beast that tries to pounce on you will be very sorry indeed—and close the door behind you," she instructed Trista. "This is the only warm room in the house and I want to keep it that way."

Trista slammed the door shut as she went out. Flanyanna and Bessalina traded glances.

"Bessalina, I think you were too hard on the poor girl."

"Humph. If anything I've been too easy on her all these years. I treated her like she's my own."

At the table Bessalina placed more of Doc Tikkum's powdered root of *Aetheleus* in a crystal mortar. Taking up a pestle in her hand, she pulverized the herb. The medicinal smell that the smashed plant released infused the kitchen.

"There's something—Ma'am—I didn't want to say it in front of Trista," Bessalina said, raising the copper tea kettle from the fire pit and pouring hot water on top of the crushed *Aetheleus* in the crystal bowl.

"Yes? What is it?"

"It's our supplies, Ma'am. They're getting quite low."

"Why, that's very odd." Flanyanna was more confused than she was alarmed. "Didn't we leave you plenty of supplies for the winter?"

"Nah, that's not it....It's the guards, Ma'am."

"Of course, we have more mouths to feed."

"Nah—nah. That's not what I meant," Bessalina said. "They're stealing food and wine from the cellar. Why, I caught one of them this very morning. Oh, did I give him a tongue lashing."

"I-I don't know what to say? I mean—why would they do that? Don't we feed them enough?" Flanyanna asked.

"Um, of course, you don't understand. How could you? It's hard times ahead, Ma'am. Food and drink will be more valuable than crystals and gems," Bessalina said. "You mark my words."

The muscles in her stomach tightening up and the acid taste of vomit flowing into her mouth, Flanyanna put her hand on the mantle to steady herself.

"Drink this—now!" Bessalina urged, handing the crystal bowl with the tea to her. Bessalina's greatest fear was that Flanyanna would not be able to control her melancholy, and she would lose the baby.

"I can't. It smells too bad." Flanyanna put her hand over her mouth.

"Relax—just relax," Bessalina said. She touched the back of the girl she raised to be queen, who was no longer the land's sovereign.

"I don't know if I can," Flanyanna said.

"Now, now. You mustn't go there. You have to think about your babe," Bessalina remarked, wanting to bring Flanyanna back to the present.

She took off her apron and tied it around Flanyanna's growing waistline in an effort to distract her. "There now. Look at you. Now you look like a proper cook."

Trista slammed the door behind as she came back in. "She's not fat enough to be a proper cook," she said saucily, dumping the bucket of ice on the kitchen table. "Here's your ice."

Bessalina picked up one of the wooden spoons from the table and gave a smart rap to the top of Trista's head.

"Ouch! That hurt!" Trista yelped like a puppy as she covered her head with her hands.

"It's supposed to hurt." Bessalina wagged an admonishing finger. "You need to respect your elders and your betters! Now —the both of you—help me knead the bread." She motioned to Trista and Flanyanna to follow her to the wooden table in the center of the kitchen.

"May I have some of the leftover dough please—to eat?" Trista pleaded.

"On one condition...," Bessalina started to say but was dis-tracted by Flanyanna bolting towards the door leading "Ma'am, are you all right?" outside.

Not replying, Flanyanna struggled with the door's latch.

"You can't go out there. It's cold. You'll catch pneumonia." Bessalina thrust the mixing bowl into Trista's hands. "Give this to Flan to upchuck in." Bessalina caught movement out of the corner of her eye. Out the window, a shadowy figure on a horse stood at the kitchen door.

Suddenly, the door started to push open. Trista screamed.

Bessalina grabbed a big pot and gripped it over her head, ready to strike a mighty, fatal blow.

Petronero stood in the door frame. Wearing battle armor and covered all over in a dusting of snow, his infectious, boyish grin lit up the kitchen. He was sporting a scruffy beard and still wore the queen's white uniform under his armor. Behind him stood a white Namdalarian with a black crescent moon on his face. Petronero had raised him from a colt and named him Blackie.

"I know, Bessalina...the kitchen is the warmest room in the house...and you want keep it that way." Petronero closed the door behind him with his booted foot.

Flanyanna flung her arms around her husband's neck. He embraced her tightly and twirled her around. She felt the same happiness she'd felt when they had met all those times in secret in the Lost Forest. Now, she realized she did know the happiness that Doc Tikkum had mentioned to her. She had it all the time, but was too busy to notice.

"Oh—Master, you're alive...," Bessalina cried, dropping the copper pot to her side. "I can't believe my eyes." Letting go of the pot's handle to cover her mouth, the pot clanged onto the dark, hand-hewn wooden floor.

"Let me look at you...." Petronero placed his hand on his wife's stomach to feel the developing baby in her womb before walking over and giving Bessalina a big hug. "Bessalina—are you feeding her too much?"

"Oh, stop that! How did you ever get here, Master, with the pass blocked?" Bessalina asked, all flustered. She always had a soft spot for Petronero—and he'd taken full advantage all the years at Faireye Manor.

"You know us peasant boys," he answered with a twinkle in his eye.

"I knew it! You didn't take the pass, did you?"

Petronero shook his head.

"Thank goodness—it's still closed," Bessalina said, very relieved.

"But…how did you get here?" Flanyanna asked.

"We peasant boys do have our ways."

Bessalina's eyes widened. "Master—you didn't?"

Petronero grinned even more.

"You went through the Shadow Fairy cave, didn't you?" Bessalina asked.

"Did you see any Shadow Fairies?" Trista could not help but ask.

"I did…but I was able to hide from them."

"How many were there?"

"Be quiet, Trista," Bessalina admonished, making a sign of protection to ward off Shadow Fairies with her index finger and circling it around Petronero's head.

"You're lucky to be alive," she said to Petronero. "They'd have liked your company for sure."

Trista's brow furrowed in puzzlement. "How did you get your horse through the Shadow Fairy cave, Master? I thought Namdalarians wouldn't go near Shadow Fairies."

"Trista, would you stop asking questions and help Master remove his armor," Bessalina said.

"Bessalina, I don't mind," Petronero said to her. "Simply put…my horse trusts me."

"And…Markolous' horse doesn't trust him," Bessalina added with a wink.

Everyone laughed.

Petronero unbuckled his breastplate. Taking it off, he handed it to Trista. He breathed a sigh of relief. The warmth of the fire on his back, still blue from the cold, felt wonderful. "Oh—this feels good."

"Trista—go tell Derrik to come and come and get the Master's horse."

"Okay—but please don't say anythin' until I get back. I want to hear everythin'." Trista grabbed Bessalina's shawl and hurried out the back door.

"Are you sure you weren't followed?" Flanyanna asked.

"No. I wasn't. Tettigards are more afraid of Shadow Fairies than we are." Petronero sat down by the outer hearth, and Bessalina pulled off one of his boots.

Outside the window Derrik led Blackie to the barn with Trista following him.

"Have you any news of my sister?" Flanyanna asked. Petronero's countenance turned grave at this question.

"Markolous locked her up in the Tower of the Forgotten months ago. I fear she could be dead."

"My sister can't be dead! I'd know for sure if she was," Flanyanna said.

"Of course, I'm sure you're right," Petronero said to placate his pregnant wife. "I'm hungry. What smells so good...Bessalina?"

He turned to the hearth and the bubbling bone broth in the cast iron pot.

The Weeping Willow

After supper, Flanyanna and Petronero strolled hand-in-hand on the pale, pink beach. In the twilight Petronero spied a shell. Picking it up, he placed it up to Flanyanna's ear. In that moment she forgot the past and didn't fear the future. She only heard the eternal roar of the Mara Sea inside the shell.

Leaning into his wife, Petronero touched her cold cheek with his warm hand. She closed her eyes and felt safe, enjoying the feeling only Petronero had ever been able to give her.

"Why'd you think my sister is dead?" she asked, not sure she really wanted to know.

Petronero took her in his arms. He was afraid he could not form the words to tell her that Pinky had been tortured for months in the dungeon and her chances of survival were very slim. "Don't worry...," he said. "I'll take care of both you and the baby." He gently stroked her black hair with his hand.

Tears flooded Flanyanna's eyes. "Pinky's not dead—I know it."

"Then, I'm sure you're right."

They stood still for a moment in silence, looking out over the crashing waves.

"Before she left…she told me we're going to have a daughter."

"A daughter—we're going to have a daughter?"

"Yes…can't we all go away…and find someplace far off where no one knows us? We can live like ordinary people—Bessalina, Trista, and Pinky—they can come, too," Flanyanna said.

"And have our daughter live like a commoner?"

"We'll all be together…isn't that what matters?"

"To grow up and marry a farmer who offers her a thatched hut with a dirt floor?" Petronero shot back.

"It would be better than…"

"There can be no exile for us. You know that better than anyone. You know Markolous will hunt us down."

"Then—what are we going to do?"

"I didn't say this in front of Bessalina…."

"You do have a plan then? You always have a plan. I'm sorry I didn't listen to you at the battle."

"Never mind—I've been to the Còrcair Mountains. You still have loyal subjects. They're gathering there in growing numbers to fight your brother and bring back their queen."

Flanyanna's regal spine straightened and she looked like the queen she had been raised to be. Those loyal to her still fought and risked their lives for their queen and their way of life.

"Then there's still hope. I will reign again."

Petronero nodded.

"There's something else I need to tell you," Flanyanna said.

"What?"

"After we lost the battle...."

"Yeah?"

"The Rose Crystal prophecy foretold that our daughter will be the ruler of Kokakina."

Petronero's eyes widened. He knew that if the Rose Crystals predicted that their daughter would rule someday, it was destined. "Your supporters must hear of this—as soon as possible."

"Yes...," Flanyanna agreed, turning her head up and looking deeply into his eyes. "I didn't understand how I could lose to my brother—and have our child still reign, but it all makes sense now...we have supporters...we will win. We'll beat Markolous and his bloody Tettigards."

Petronero nuzzled her ear with his nose.

"Your nose feels like Arasthenes'," Flanyanna said with a giggle.

"Flanyanna, you're getting cold." Petronero took his leather jacket off and put it around her shoulders. "We don't want you to get a chill in your condition...." With a gleam in his eye, he took her hand. "Let's go back to the house."

In the softer, dry sand, Flanyanna felt an electrifying energy as he pulled her along to the pathway leading up to the Faireye Manor. Ecstatically, they ran up the path in the moon's cool light, feeling that all would be well, that she would regain the throne.

In that moment there was no queen. Even though she did, she enjoyed pretending she did not know where they were going. Every fiber in them desired to love each other.

Suddenly, a rattling sound broke their trance.

"Tettigards!" Flanyanna whispered, pushing herself up against the moist, sandy white cliff wall.

"Flanyanna, it can't be Tettigards. It's wintertime, remember? Nothing can fly over the mountains during the winter." Even so, Petronero leaned into the cliff's shadow with her to protect her.

"No. No. I tell you it's—Tettigards. They're looking for us," Flanyanna insisted, frantically. "Markolous has sent them—to kill our baby!"

"Flanyanna, calm yourself. He doesn't even know we're going to have a baby," Petronero said, cautiously peering over the top side of the White Cliffs. "Look!" He pointed toward the gate to the Faireye Manor. "It's the gate. We forgot to close it. It's only the gate."

Flanyanna peered over the top of the cliff. In the wind the gate swung back and forth on its iron hinges slapping into the fence. Not ready to sleep, the waning moon lingered on the horizon as the two Human Fairies ran back to the Faireye Manor closing the gate behind them.

Early the next morning a gray-winged dove flitted in and out of the bougainvillea that climbed the stone walls beneath the bedchamber. It sang to its mate as the sun rose.

The delicate rays of early morning sunlight filtered into Flanyanna's and Petronero's bedchamber. Flanyanna still slept. Petronero was dressed in a coarse linen shirt and wool under-breeches that Bessalina found for him in the attic. Looking out the window at the icicles that anchored onto the red tile roof, he feared that Pinky's magic spell would not last long enough for the birth of their child. He knew Markolous would stop at nothing to maintain his grip on the throne. He was simply thwarted from going after Flanyanna for the moment by the blocked pass.

Petronero knew he must get to his wife's surviving partisans gathered in the Còrcair Mountains and rally them with the news that there would be a legitimate heir to the throne and the Rose Crystal prophecy foretold she would rule Kokakina.

Petronero would willingly risk his life to protect his wife and child. He would leave Faireye Manor alone that morning to travel back through the Shadow Fairy cave to Flanyanna's supporters. He knew if he told her, Flanyanna would want to accompany him and rally her forces herself, but she was in no condition for such an arduous journey. *Pinky's magic winter spell will protect her while I'm away,* he thought. Looking down, he regarded his wife's swollen stomach. *I might never know my child.* He lowered his head and kissed her belly. *Your first kiss, my daughter—a father's kiss.*

Flanyanna stirred. Petronero quickly slipped out of the bed chamber before she woke up.

He knew this was their only chance. He must tell Flanyanna's supporters about the princess to bolster their spirits and wills.

Flanyanna woke with a start, feeling a violent kick inside her. "Petronero?" she said frantically.

She leaped out of bed. Without putting her cloak on, she ran down the Faireye Manor's oak staircase in her bare feet.

"Petronero!" she cried out, struggling to unlatch the bolt on the wooden front door. Her fingernails clawed at the iron clasp, finally pulling it open. She rushed outside.

"Petronero!" she cried out again, hearing a Namdalarian nickering and hooves striking the frozen ground.

Both Petronero and his mount were dressed for battle. They wore the suits of armor they had been wearing when they arrived.

Flanyanna's hands flew up to shield her eyes from the brightness of the sun's rays reflecting off Petronero's shining steel armor with its silver and gold embellishments.

She was livid.

Petronero's restless white stallion pawed the ground as Derrik held the reins for Petronero to mount.

"No—you can't leave—I forbid you!" Flanyanna spoke in the imperious tone Petronero knew so well.

Blackie reared up on his hind legs.

"Flanyanna—be quiet. Blackie's getting upset." Petronero reached out and took the reins from the lad.

"I don't care. I hope he runs away."

The stallion snorted, nostrils flaring. Roiling steam floated from them into the low morning mist.

"Flanyanna, you don't mean that. I must go—and I must go now." Petronero's tone was stern. He had not planned on seeing Flanyanna before he left.

"I said you can't go. I'll send one of my guards."

"Your loyal subjects need to hear about the Rose Crystal prophecy," he responded as he mounted, "and they need to hear it from me, not one of the guards. I'm going to the Còrcair Mountains to rally your troops. It's the only way."

"But you just got here."

"Don't make this harder than it already is."

"No wait. We have Pinky's winter spell. Surely we have more time before you have to leave."

"Our supporters must be heartened. I fear if we wait until spring their numbers will diminish and we won't have the strength we need," Petronero said.

"Then you must take me with you." She clutched his lower leg.

"It is too hard a journey. In your condition—we can't risk it." He pulled her hand from his high-top riding boot.

"I can ride as well as you," she insisted, defiantly positioning herself in front of his Namdalarian.

"Flanyanna—stop it. You know this is our only chance to stop your brother," Petronero said firmly. "You must remain for all our sakes and have our baby. I'll be back before the baby arrives."

Just then, Bessalina and Trista came out of the Faireye Manor in their nightclothes.

"Bessalina, take her back into the house," Petronero ordered.

"Yes, my lord."

"How could you? You selfish bastard," Flanyanna cried, her voice hysterical. "Don't you want to see our daughter being born?"

Bessalina put her arm around a cold Flanyanna and nudged her back towards the front door. "Ma'am, let's go sit by the fire."

"Let go of me," Flanyanna said, turning back to Petronero.

"I am your liege. I am the queen. I command that you wait for me." She removed herself from Bessalina's hold. "Boy, saddle my Namdalarian," she ordered Derrik as she ran into the house to get dressed.

The lad looked up at Petronero, confused.

"I'm sorry, Master. She is quite strong-willed just like her brother," Bessalina said.

"Bessalina, if I don't return..."

"Surely you don't mean that?"

"Do I have to listen to two hysterical females this morning?"

Bessalina lowered her head.

"After the baby is born—if I'm not back—you must leave this place. Do you understand?"

"Yes, sir."

"You must take Flanyanna and the princess and go to the Còrcair Mountains."

Bessalina gasped. "The Còrcair Mountains? Surely you don't mean that, Master?" She had heard many stories from the peddlers that the Còrcair Mountains were full of thieves and murderers. "Surely—we stay here until you get back."

"Do as I say, Bessalina. It's the only place she and the baby will be safe."

"What has happened to this family?" Bessalina shook her head

"Don't speak of this to your mistress, but Pinky is surely dead. She's been in the Tower of the Forgotten for many months, and, as you know, nobody survives that long once they're there."

"But she'll be very angry just the same. Can't you wait to say goodbye?"

"No, I must go now, before she returns and protests more. The remnants of the queen's army are the only ones left who can help us and our child to fulfill the Rose Crystal prophecy."

"She'll be determined to follow you."

"Then, if you must, tie her up."

"I'll probably have to do just that."

Petronero smiled. "Probably." Turning to Derrik, he said, "Lad, take the queen's Namdalarian out of the stable and ride him into the woods and don't come back until midday."

"Yes, my lord." The lad picked up Petronero's sword and lance and handed them to him. The sword's hilt was embedded with rose crystals and silver.

Derrik ran to the barn and Trista ran after him.

Petronero pulled on the reins, and Blackie sidestepped. Petronero steadied him, staring down at Bessalina.

"Take good care of her while I'm gone."

He rode around the side of the Faireye Manor. Blackie jumped over one of the snow-covered, manicured hedges and headed towards the path that led down to the beach and the Shadow Fairy cave.

"Don't worry—I'll take good care of her," Bessalina yelled.

As Petronero rode away, Bessalina wearily walked across the frozen snow in the courtyard. In her heart she wanted to see him again, but, in her gut, she knew different.

Looking over to the barn, she saw Derrik on Arasthenes, bare-back, and reaching down to lift Trista up behind him. "Oh no you don't! Trista! Come back into the house this instant! I'll need your help to restrain the queen."

"It's a good thing this winter keeps going on. Otherwise the new king would already be here," Derrik said.

"Don't say that," Trista said, slipping down from Arasthenes' back.

Derrik whispered softly in the Namdalarian's ear. Arasthenes nodded. They galloped out the gate over the stone bridge, through the pasture and into the woods.

Trista reluctantly walked back to the front door. She entered the Faireye Manor with Bessalina. They bolted the door behind them.

It had been some days since Petronero left. Flanyanna sat on a stone bench under a weeping willow tree in the garden. The sun's rays beamed through the spaces in the tree's limbs.

The old mossy stone bench felt hard and unforgiving. She stared blankly at the hand-hewn plank fence which barred the wild entanglements of nature from overrunning the manicured garden. Different species of birds—cardinals, red-breasted robins, sparrows, and doves—flitted in and out of handcrafted birdhouses scattered about the garden on whitewashed wooden poles.

A snowflake fell onto her face. A hawk circled high overhead.

Her heart pounding fast, she ran over to her birdhouses. She wanted to protect her birds. A dove darted out. Flapping its wings, it took flight and flew up into the azure sky.

"No!" Flanyanna gasped.

Among the cumulus vapors, her husband gallops on his Namdalarian towards her.

"Petronero," she cried out, running across the frozen landscape, keeping pace with the flying steed's flashing hooves in the roiling clouds. She reached the very end of the garden's fence and stopped. Panting, she scanned the sky far above.

In the rumbling clouds, Petronero and her supporters charge Markolous, his Tettigards, and his Peccaries on the arid plains at the foot of the Còrcair Mountains. Petronero rides up to challenge Markolous. The two Human Fairy males trade savage blows with Petronero's strength and skill gaining him the upper hand.

Just as he prepares to deliver the killing blow, Tithoreus flies up from behind and slams into his back, knocking him off balance. Taking advantage of this opportunity, Markolous severs Petronero's head with one fell swoop.

The hawk swiftly swooped down, attacking and savaging the dove with its razor-sharp talons. Flanyanna felt the claws of the hawk as they tore into the dove's neck, killing it instantly. A drop of blood fell from the sky and splattered on her cheek. It mixed with her tears.

She collapsed onto the ground. No longer the queen, she could not decree any creature's safety.

"No—No—No," she whispered, feeling the cold wind whip at her cape. The cape fluttered and snapped like a ship's sail in a storm at sea for royal Human Fairies could feel the death of a loved one the exact moment it happened.

A sole black raven swooped down from the skies over her head and cawed.

Her husband, Petronero, was dead. Now only the winter's snow banks remained between her and the wrath of her vengeful brother.

The Magic Compass

Several months passed. Hanging low over the Faireye Manor, the forgotten moon languished in the late night sky. Sensing the approaching sunrise, a blue heron glided up and out over the surf crashing onto the beach below the White Cliffs. On the Faireye Manor roof's overhang, icicles dripped down into the melting snow.

The winter thaw had begun.

For some time, since the master left, Trista had noticed more and more bruises on the queen's body when she helped her to dress in the mornings and undress in the evenings.

The blue-black blemishes now covered most of Flanyanna's pregnant torso. Noticing Trista's frightened, bewildered face, Flanyanna covered her stomach with her dressing gown.

"I'll dress myself this morning," she spoke sharply.

"Yes—Ma'am," Trista said. With a quick curtsy, she took the empty food tray from the curtained bed and escaped the queen's bedchamber. Salty, burning tears streamed down her face as her worn leather boot soles pattered down the long wooden staircase to the kitchen.

"I should've said somethin' about her bruises to Bessalina a long time ago—but I thought they'd go away." She answered her own question. "Now—what'ta' goin' to do?"

Before opening the kitchen door, Trista wiped her nose on the robin-egg blue apron that Bessalina had made for her many years ago. Even though it was too small for her now, she had been wearing it for the past few weeks because doing so gave her great comfort. Her stomach churning, she went into the kitchen.

"Well, how'd she do this morning?" Bessalina asked, looking up from some fresh dough she was flattening with a black crystal rolling pin on the wooden kitchen table.

"She ate everythin'."

"It's about time she appreciated my cooking," Bessalina groused, going over to the hearth. "Well, don't just stand there girl, go out to the barn and fetch the eggs from the haystack."

Trista loudly plopped the tray on the kitchen table and reached for the egg basket on the rough wooden shelf above the stone outer hearth.

"You've been acting strangely for some time now. Now what's wrong?" Bessalina asked, studying her protégé.

"I know—I should've told ya," Trista said.

Bessalina dried her sticky, wet hands on her worn, stained apron and went over to the outer hearth to stir a simmering pot.

"Sit down here next to the fire." She motioned to the sniveling girl.

Bessalina sat down, feeling the warmth of the fire on her ample buttocks. "Oh, does that feel good on my backside. This warmth soothes my aching bones." She knew something was wrong. "Now—what's bothering you?"

Trista sat down by Bessalina, her eyes downcast.

"What's this—what could possibly be so bad?" Bessalina asked, lifting Trista's chin to look into her eyes.

Trista averted her gaze.

Bessalina took Trista's hand and patted it like she was kneading raw dough.

Trista pulled her hand back. "It's not my fault, really," she blurted out.

"Oh, you clumsy girl." The old cook shook her head. "What did you break this time?"

"Nothin'. I didn't break anythin'—honest," Trista blubbered through her tears.

Bessalina pulled her frayed linen handkerchief from her apron pocket and gave it to the girl.

"Blow your nose."

As instructed, Trista blew into the handkerchief with a loud honk.

"Now tell me the truth. Did you break another dinner plate?"

Trista shook her head. "Promise you won't get mad at me?"

"I won't get mad at you," Bessalina said.

"It's the queen."

"What about her?"

"I don't know. That's just it—her body—it's covered with purple bruises."

A chill ran up Bessalina's spine, and she stood up, feeling cold air invade her whole body. *The bruising can only mean one thing,* she thought with a shiver.

"What is it? I thought she'd be all right. I'm sorry. I didn't want to bother you, is she all right?" Trista asked.

"It's the master. He's dead for sure." Bessalina prodded the fire with the cast iron poker and put on another log.

"Master's dead?" Trista repeated Bessalina's words in a very solemn, hushed tone. "But, you said he was coming back—and— if he's not coming back, what's going to happen to us?"

"We'll manage. We always do."

"But what about the babe?"

Bessalina looked into the flames for a moment. She hadn't told Trista about when Flanyanna had confided in her of her vision of Petronero's death in the garden.

She knew that Trista, living most her life cloistered at the Faireye Manor, hadn't learned what was common knowledge for most Human Fairies, the nature of the Shadow Fairies. "I've meant to tell you these past years, but there was so much else I needed to teach you—the master is a Shadow Fairy now."

"Markolous killed him, didn't he?" Trista asked.

"Yes, Markolous killed the master and I'm afraid he doesn't want to endure his Shadow Fairy banishment, alone."

"So, Master comes here to be with her?"

"Yes, but not exactly. He comes in the night to lie with her."

"But why does he hurt her?" Trista asked, trying to understand.

"Because she's resisting him."

"She wants to have her babe," Trista said, connecting the dots.

The flames flared up, blasting Bessalina's face. "That's right. He tempts her to go and live with him in the Shadow Fairy world."

"But—that's not right!"

"Loneliness drives us all to do unthinkable things," Bessalina said as she walked over to the window. She understood loneliness too well, having never married. She had only known service her whole life and had no children of her own. She placed her hand on her lower back, stiff from many years of hard labor since early childhood, and stared out the window noticing a stream of tiny water droplets falling from an icicle to the ground.

"I'm afraid the queen is torn between two worlds."

"No. That's not fair. He can't take her."

"She wants to go to the Shadow Fairy world to be with him."

"No! she must fight him."

"Oh, she fights him. That's why she has all those bruises, Trista. Don't you see? She also wants to stay here to give birth to her baby." Bessalina's heart sank with deep pangs of sadness, knowing there was nothing she could do to protect either her queen or the unborn child. "Their innocent child may never see the light of day." She lowered her head.

"No—no—the baby must be born. We must help her."

"I'm sorry, Trista. There's nothing I or you or anyone can do."

Going to the kitchen table, Bessalina picked up a carving knife and, with one blow, severed a wing off of a headless duck.

"How can you say that?"

"Because I know about Shadow Fairies. My aunt was taken to the Shadow Fairy world by her deceased husband. There's nothing we can do...."

"I don't believe you. There's got to be somethin' we can do?"

Bessalina chopped the other wing off of the duck with her knife's sharp edge. Red blood spilled onto the rough-hewn, wooden tabletop and splattered onto the floor. "I tell you—there's nothing we can do."

"You can't mean that," Trista cried out. "What's goin' to happen to us? The baby has to be born. Flan told me—she's going to be the ruler of Kokakina someday."

She stormed for the door and opened it.

"Where do you think you're going?"

"I'm goin' to tell the guards to come into the house and protect the queen and her baby from the master," Trista retorted, "and I don't care what ya say…."

"Very well. But you won't find them. They left in the night."

"They left us alone?"

Bessalina paused and wiped her hands on her already blood-stained apron.

"Yes…," Bessalina replied, "While you were with the queen this morning, I thought it strange that not one of them came to get their breakfast. So, I went to look for them in their quarters. They were gone—with all their belongings—gone!"

"What about Derrik?"

"He's gone, too."

Trista froze. "He wouldn't do that—he wouldn't do that."

"Well, I'm telling you girl. I went to the barn to find the guards—they and their Namdalarians are gone—and Derrik too."

"He left me?"

"They even stole the silver candelabras and utensils for the dining room table—those no-good, worthless scoundrels."

"He wouldn't do that," Trista said, defiantly.

Trista was so young and so innocent in the ways of the world. Bessalina knew she had overprotected her. The old cook reached over and brushed a few errant hairs from Trista's face.

"Child, sometimes things just don't work out the way you plan and you might as well learn now—the opposite sex—will disappoint."

"The queen lied to me," Trista accused.

"The queen did not lie to you."

"She did, too. She told me about the Rose Crystal prophecy, and that her baby would rule Kokakina—someday."

"That's not a lie!"

"Yes it is and you lied to me too."

"Child—I never—why would I lie to you?"

"You lied to me because everythin's falling apart. You said everythin' would be all right. Nothin's all right—nothin'!"

Trista had grown up to be a young woman before Bessalina's eyes. "All right, Trista. You're right. I haven't told you everything. The snow around the house has been melting for days. The pass will be open soon...."

"What happened to the winter spell?"

"Look around you—the thaw has begun. The queen's sister is dying or is already dead. In any case, it's obvious she can't hold the spell anymore."

"Well, I'm not afraid of Markolous or the Tettigards."

Bessalina tenderly kissed Trista on the third eye. "I've been thinking. It's time for you to go and visit your birth parents." Bessalina saw herself in Trista when she was that age. For some time now, Bessalina had not been sleeping well at night. She lay awake, wondering how she could keep everyone and everything she loved so dearly safe from Markolous.

"My birth parents? I hardly remember them."

"I know that and that's why a visit is in order. Now go and pack up your things."

"No. I don't want to...."

"Well, you have to. The queen doesn't want you here anymore."

"Thats not true! The queen likes me."

"Oh, for fairy sake! I don't want you here anymore. You have been nothing but trouble these past months." Bessalina did finally lie to her. Having Trista with her at the Faireye Manor gave her great joy.

"Very well...then...I'll go home to my real parents," Trista said, and a great relief passed through her until she saw the effort it took for her surrogate mother bend over and put a log on the fire. The flames immediately engulfed it.

"Good. Then it's finally settled," Bessalina said.

"I changed my mind."

"What's this?" Bessalina asked, feeling proud of her charge. She felt Trista spoke from her heart.

"I'm not leavin' you or the queen and that's final. I don't care what you say or do."

"What if I told you that I had a plan to swoop our queen and her baby away to safety. Would you leave then?"

"No. I want to stay with you. You're the only mother I've ever known. Besides, you're old now and you need me."

"I can take care of myself," Bessalina huffed.

"But you'll need help to fight Markolous?"

Bessalina laughed. "I used to change his nappy. I was his nanny too...."

She remembered intervening when the Tettigards attacked him. She covered him with her large torso until the guards chased the Tettigards away, taking some of the stinging bites herself to save his life. She nursed him back to health, sitting at his bedside day and night. Until then, no Human Fairy had ever survived a Tettigard swarming.

"I don't...how could he have anything to do with those unnatural creatures that nearly killed him? How could my boy grow up and consort with such monstrous beings? The boy I raised and loved?" she asked in reflection.

Trista took hold of the old cook's gnarled hand. Her fingers tightened on the only mother she knew.

"Trista, you must pack your things. I don't know what Markolous would do to you."

"I'm not coming back—am I?" Trista feared she would never see her adopted mother again.

"I don't know. But I do know we'll see each other again."

Trista held back her tears. "We will see each other again?"

"Of course we will. I'm sure of it."

Trista stood still for a moment. "I don't really remember my parents much. I just remember you and this place." She put her arms around Bessalina and hugged her.

"They'll be so glad to see you. You're a young lady now."

"You're sure you'll be okay?"

"I'll be fine. Now listen carefully. You know the old path on the White Cliffs?"

Trista nodded. "You mean the path down to the beach?"

"That's right. Follow it down to the beach—to the very end. There's a cave..."

"You mean the Shadow Fairy cave? I'm goin' through the Shadow Fairy cave?"

"You'll be fine, just fine. You're a brave girl. You'll be all right." Bessalina smiled, covering up her apprehension. She feared the Shadow Fairies, but she feared Markolous and his troops more, for Trista was—after all—coming of age. "Now go—before I change my mind and have you break the ice to get some water to do the breakfast dishes," Bessalina said gruffly.

Trista stood still for a moment. "I just know you and this place." She put her arms around Bessalina and hugged her.

Bessalina ruffled the girl's hair, trying to be as brave as possible though her heart ached. She already missed the young girl.

"But there's no ice to break this morning," Trista added. The spell was broken.

"Hurry—and gather up your things. Take only what you can carry along the path," Bessalina instructed, "and not a thing better be out of place in my pantry."

Without another word, Trista hurried to the tiny pantry where she had slept since she was a small child.

At the kitchen door, the open sea wind whipped at Bessalina and Trista's skirts. "You can see the path from here." Bessalina looked toward the narrow path on the White Cliffs that led to the beach below.

"Bessalina," Trista said.

The plaintive tone in her voice wrenched at the old cook's heart. Bessalina smiled to hide her sadness and hold back her tears. She wanted what might be Trista's last memory of her to be a happy one. She handed the girl a folded cheesecloth holding some bread, pork, and cheese.

Trista removed the leather satchel with her meager belongings from her back and put the cheesecloth bundle inside.

"I have something else for you." Bessalina handed Trista a small pouch with some crystal fairy money from one of her apron pockets. "It's not much."

"What is it?"

"It's a bit of money. I've been saving it up," Bessalina said.

"You bought no shoes to save money for me?"

"Take it—it's for you. You must accept my gift or..."

"It's bad luck for a lifetime, right?" Trista asked.

"That's right," Bessalina whispered. "Don't talk to strangers and don't let anyone know you have any money. It's best to hide it in your underdrawers."

With a nod of understanding, Trista lifted her black skirt and hid the pouch in her white muslin bloomers. "There—no one will ever find 'em there."

"And here's your letter of recommendation." With a flick of her wrist, Bessalina conjured a letter bearing the stamp of the royal household and it floated into Trista's waiting hand. "I thought your parents might want to see how well you've done here at the queen's household."

Trista threw her arms forward and hugged the only mother she could remember.

Bessalina held onto her, maybe for the last time, but finally released her.

"I want you to have something—that was mine." Bessalina pulled a needle on a thread from her apron pocket and allowed it to dangle below her hand. She focused on it fiercely for a moment, and it began to lean predominately in one direction.

"What is it?"

"It's a magic compass to keep always and remember your dear Nanna," Bessalina answered, her eyes twinkling with her tears.

"Oh—thank you. It's the best present ever!" Trista cupped her left hand to receive the compass.

"Remember, it will always bend to the north when you hold the end of the thread and let it drop down. Keep it pointing to your right with the mountains at your back, and you'll be going in the right direction." The cook patted and kissed her surrogate daughter's cheek. No mother could love her child more. "Go on. If you don't leave now, you might not get through the Shadow Fairy cave to the village before dark." The snow was melting fast and she wanted to be sure the girl was far gone before Markolous showed up with his soldiers.

Trista hurried along the White Cliffs. Between the patches of melting snow, she followed the barely visible, long-neglected footpath that led down to the beach where the royal children once played. She looked back at the old cook one more time and waved.

Bessalina watched one of her surrogate children vanish in the sea of purple heather still covered by snow. "I love you," she whispered. With tears flooding her eyes, Bessalina wiped them on her dirty apron. She hurried as best she could across the courtyard to the barn and opened the large, hand-hewn wooded door. It was a struggle, for she suddenly felt very old and tired.

Arasthenes

A young lad shyly entered the Faireye Manor foyer. He wore a knitted green wool cap pulled down low over his eyes and a thick scarf bunched around his neck. Under his brown leather jacket, his flax colored peasant tunic had a hood that was pulled up over the cap. Matching leather britches and wool hose covered his legs. Scruffy knee-high boots with turned down cuffs scuffed along the crystal entryway.

"What'ta think?" Flanyanna asked, imitating a lower class accent. She twirled in front of Bessalina. Her hood fell back and, her hat fell down to the floor. Her raven black hair escaped, cascading down about her shoulders.

"You look like a—very fat peasant boy—my queen," Bessalina said with a curtsy.

"I know. I couldn't button Derrick's britches all the way up. Poor boy...."

"Whatever do you mean—poor boy? Umph—he deserted you!"

"I don't think so, Nanna. I think my guards took him against his will. I mean, why would he leave all his clothes?"

"Well, I'm glad we have his clothes for you to wear, Ma'am. Are you ready to go?"

"I want to say goodbye to Arasthenes."

"Very well, Ma'am, but hurry. The snow is melting fast."

Flanyanna nodded and ran to the Faireye Manor barn.

The worn, rusty hinges on the barn door creaked open. Flanyanna entered quietly, pulling the hood tightly around her neck.

"How do you like my new outfit?"

Arasthenes jerked his head up and nodded. His nostrils flared. He sensed Markolous' approach.

"I know—there, there—my beauty. I don't like it either, but we'll be together again." Flanyanna stroked his nose. "I have something for you." Pulling a carrot from her leather jacket's pocket, she offered it to his eager mouth. She stroked the side of his neck as he chewed on it.

Arasthenes settled down at her soft spoken words and gentle strokes on his flank. Many Human Fairies had learned cruelty on Earth and were harsh with their animals. Flanyanna could not bear the thought of Arasthenes getting into the wrong hands. She did not want to leave her flying horse behind, but she feared what Markolous would do to her sweet Namdalarian if he got hold of him.

Searching in the straw near the horse stall, she found the three-legged milking stool. Standing on it, she slipped on his bridle and lifted herself up on him by holding onto the crest of his neck. She straddled his broad back, feeling his fine, smooth mane between her fingertips. Stroking him, she could feel his muscular strength, and it gave her courage to do what she must do. They left the barn.

Flanyanna listened to the hollow echo of Arasthenes' hooves clicking on the cobblestone pavers as they walked across the Faireye Manor courtyard. She whispered in his ear, and her stallion trotted off. After crossing the bridge, he jumped over the crossbuck fence and cantered toward the forest that lay between the manor and the mountains. They galloped across the meadow, through the now melting snow, a brisk wind at their back.

At the edge of the woods, Flanyanna slid off Arasthenes' back and onto a fallen oak tree. Her cheeks and forehead flushed a pinkish red. She smelled his musty scent. Flanyanna lovingly stroked his back, not wanting to let him go.

Arasthenes found a bit of grass sticking out from a patch of snow at the edge of the meadow. Bending down, he nibbled at the green shoots.

"I'm going to leave for a little while." Flanyanna removed his bridle. "It's better this way. Next spring, after the princess is born, I'll come and find you. We'll teach her how to ride."

She hugged Arasthenes neck and kissed his forehead.

"Go on...." She nudged him, holding the bridle in her hands. Arasthenes did not budge.

"Arasthenes...," she scolded in a gentle tone. "I told you I'll be back in the spring for you. Now go on."

He looked into her eyes, and she looked into his. He nuzzled her. "Stop that. I want you to go," she said, her voice choking up. He licked her face with his scratchy tongue, wanting more carrot. Then, he pushed her and went to the pocket of her jacket looking for more treats.

"Stop that—do you hear me? I want you to go," Flanyanna cried. She slapped his rump. "Run Arasthenes—run far away— get away from here."

Arasthenes jerked his head up as the raw feeling of freedom coursed through his body. Looking into the dark forest, he some- how knew it was time to leave his mistress. He raised himself high over her on his two back feet and, coming back down, bolted into the woods.

She watched him gallop away from her until he disappeared. A cloud passed over the sun, casting a shadow on the meadow. Flanyanna felt a chill descend on her heart. "Markolous," she whispered, for he was very near. Not having the time go back and to say goodbye to Bessalina, she ran across the now patchwork brown and white meadow towards the White Cliffs and the path.

A few hours passed. The eerie silence was broken by the rus- tling sound of a dozen Namdalarians straining to control their wingspans as they landed in front of the Faireye Manor.

Markolous and his Human Fairy soldiers waited tensely on their restless steeds. The silver ornamentation of their black leather gloves flashed in the sunlight as they cast their eyes about. The calm quiet surrounding the royal family's summer home was unnerving.

"No one seems to be here," Markolous said.

"Sire—it could be a trap," Tithoreus said in his metallic, monotone voice.

Inside, Bessalina cringed from the loud knocking and gasped, pulling back from Flanyanna's bedchamber window.

"Markolous," she said to herself.

Slowly she walked down the winding staircase, listening to each step's creaky groan. "This could well be the last door I ever answer."

As she reached the Faireye Manor front door, she smoothed the severe middle part of her speckled gray-brown hair.

"Open up in the name of the king...."

Bessalina reached for the latch.

Hearing the door unlock, Tithoreus stepped back with his sword raised.

"Umph—Markolous—but, you're no king," Bessalina said, her imposing figure filling the doorway.

"Bessalina...I see you haven't changed," Markolous said.

"Tettigard, you filthy swine—get away from the queen's manor," Bessalina said with a disgusted look at Tithoreus. Although she feared the mutated creatures, she stood her ground, voicing deep disdain, for they preyed on her species.

"Enough—where is she—old cook?" Markolous demanded, voicing no respect for the nanny that had taken care of him all his childhood and even saved his life from the Tettigards.

"Marko—and you haven't changed one bit either—you're still an ungrateful little brat," she said, calling him by his childhood nickname. The name she had given him when he was a lad. She had nicknamed all the royal children. Flanyanna was

Flan for she loved her pudding, and Rosecenilla was named Pinky by their father and it just stuck.

An amused chuckle ran through the grinning soldiers as they sat on their Namdalarians. They were not used to such familiarity towards the new king.

"I asked you a question—old cook."

"Is that the way to treat your old nanny?" Bessalina asked. "I changed his nappy when he was a baby," she said to everyone.

Everyone laughed.

"Sire—this could be a trap," Tithoreus said again.

"Why, you don't even have a stink—and that's not natural," Bessalina said, sniffing at Tithoreus.

Markolous' face reddened with anger. He slid down off Calamtheus' sweating back, his body rigid with tension.

"Old fairy woman are you deaf?" he shouted. "Get out of my way!"

Bessalina placed her hands squarely on her hips, barricading the front door. "You're unnatural. There, I said it. It's what everyone has always thought about you but was afraid to say, because of your mother's bullying."

Markolous pushed Bessalina and she fell to the ground. "Search the place." He motioned to his soldiers.

"Search if you want, but you'll not find her here, She left this morning with her guards," Bessalina said as she raised her head and pointed towards the forest, which was in the opposite direction of the White Cliffs.

Markolous and Tithoreus looked at each other.

"You mean the queen's guards?" Markolous asked.

"Of course I mean the queen's guards. Who do you think I mean?" she snapped.

"You mean—" Markolous pointed to the back of his entourage. The queen's guards were tethered to Markolous' soldiers' Namdalarians. "—she wasn't with them when we caught them."

The soldiers laughed again.

"The stars were aligned for madness the night you were conceived," Bessalina said, unfazed at being caught in her lie.

"Get her out of the way," Markolous ordered Tithoreus, waving his hand in a dismissive gesture.

Bessalina felt perspiration trickle down her back.

Tithoreus grasped Bessalina with his claws, lifting her up. She fainted and fell to the ground. The soldiers stepped over her prostrate figure and entered the Faireye Manor.

Markolous jerked savagely on Calamtheus' reins as he mounted. Bessalina turned and lifted her head up, pushing her body up from the stone stoop. "You were never good with Namdalarians, were you?" she chided him. "Not like Petronero. Now he was the finest with the flying horses."

"I've had just about enough of you," Markolous said.

"You were always envious of him. Envious of your sister, Flan, too. It's really sad—isn't it? I mean you just weren't as good."

Tithoreus came out the front door of the Faireye Manor. "Your sister's not in the house, Sire."

"You and your soldiers won't be around to finish your lifetimes. She has loyal troops in the Còrcair Mountains who will destroy you. You'll soon all be Shadow Fairies—or worse—gone to oblivion—but—I suspect the Lord of the Darkness won't have you—*you don't have enough light!*"

Markolous glared at her and raised his sword to lop off her head.

"Go ahead. Kill me. My three hundred years is almost done. I'm tired—and I'm especially tired of the likes of you. I'd like nothing better than to haunt you from the shadows for the rest of my incarnation," Bessalina said and shut her eyes—bracing herself for the fatal blow.

At that moment a Human Fairy soldier ran around the side of the Faireye Manor.

"Sire, a Human Fairy has been spotted down on the beach, running away from the manor."

Markolous dropped his sword down to his side.

"All this killing because you can't forgive your sister for being better than you," Bessalina said.

Markolous looked at Bessalina.

"I'll deal with you later."

"Are we taking her with us?" Tithoreus asked, gesturing to Bessalina.

"No. She'll only slow us down."

Without another word Markolous trotted around the Faireye Manor to the path that led to the pink quartz beach. Tithoreus and his command followed along behind him. Markolous stood up in his stirrups. The wind gusted and tossed his hair. Markolous looked down, scanning the rose quartz beach.

"Sire—look." Tithoreus pointed to the end of the bluff where the path led down to the beach.

A pair of Hokkaido wolves blocked the trail. They held themselves stiff and rigid, their tails tucked between their legs as they growled at Markolous and his troops. The wolves lowered their bodies down to the ground ready to pounce.

"Trying to get around them to descend to the beach will be very dangerous. The cliff's a sheer drop," Tithoreus said, knowing that to continue would cause an altercation with these fierce beasts who guarded the Human Fairy way.

"There's another trail. We'll take it down to the beach," Markolous said.

The male wolf dug into the ground with his front paws like a bull. He pointed his muzzle straight up and howled.

"Good idea!" Tithoreus said.

Markolous and his soldiers turned around.

Her chest burning, Flanyanna stopped running on the wet sand to catch her breath. Bending painfully forward, she felt a strong twinge in her side. The sharp decaying odor of the rust-colored seaweed covering the sand filled her lungs with each inhalation making her feel nauseous. As she stood back up, only the endless clamor of the tumbling, cascading waves crashing on the shore greeted her. Except for her the beach was empty of life.

The eternal balm of the Mara Sea seeped into her soothing her troubled mind. The pink, crystal sand beneath her feet felt cold. The chill penetrated deeply up her legs, into her crystal bones. The wind picked up to a wailing pitch. Swirling sand flew up, stinging her eyes and blinding her. She grabbed her hood and held it tight around her head.

If I had only listened to Petronero, so many things would be different now. I wouldn't be here dressed as a boy. Petronero would still be alive to see our first child being born. I would have won the war and still be queen, she thought to herself.

In front of her on the desolate beach, a dim, fuzzy light came towards her. As it drew nearer, Flanyanna could make out a Human Fairy female in a long, flowing cotton candy pink gown floating just above the beach.

"Pinky—Pinky!"

The insubstantial figure beckoned to her.

"You're alive—you're still alive," Flanyanna rejoiced. She stumbled toward the female Human Fairy.

The ethereal being swirled around Flanyanna.

"You're not Pinky. Get away from me," Flanyanna cried out.

Frightened, she backed into the turbulent surf. A wild wave crashed over her and pulled her out to sea. She struggled and gasped for air, but the recoiling waves pushed her down.

Yielding, she released herself into the agitated surf. At the mercy of the seething waves, her hapless body miraculously rolled back onto the beach. Her head was face down in the sand. Gagging and choking, she coughed the bile out of her lungs.

A warm, rough tongue licked her face and revived her. She rolled over on her back. A large female wolf stood over her. The she-wolf turned and ran toward a crevice in the white limestone cliff, barking. She turned to look back at Flanyanna.

"You want me to come with you?" Flanyanna asked. She staggered to her feet and stumbled towards the cave. She quickened her steps in the hard sand as she approached the mouth of the cave. She turned and looked. No one—not even the mysterious specter. She ducked inside.

Footprint in the Sand

With her fingertips pressed against the damp cave wall, Flanyanna cautiously walked deeper into the dark cavern.

"The she-wolf brought me to the Shadow Fairy cave," she whispered.

Her trembling fingers gathered some dry driftwood and withered brown seaweed scattered about the cave. With her third eye she focused a beam of white light on the pile of debris. It soon glowed and flamed, radiating heat. Her teeth chattering, she rubbed her cold hands together. She moved closer to the meager flames. Shivering, she rocked herself back and forth to stave off the chill and the loneliness that threatened to overwhelm her.

In the dim firelight two tunnels lay before her, but she was not sure which one to take. No one had said anything about two tunnels, nor which one led through the mountains.

"I must find my way, like Petronero, to the other side of the mountain where my troops wait," she said to comfort herself.

Inhaling some of the smoke as it rose up, she coughed. Realizing the smoke was drifting out of the grotto and would betray where she was, she jumped up and kicked over the flames to extinguish them.

Still hacking she leaned her hand against the cave wall. With her fingertips she felt water flowing from a crack located there. Aware that she was very thirsty, she stuck her tongue out to drink and was relieved to find that it was fresh spring water. Eagerly, she cupped her hands drinking long and hard.

Finally, having satisfied her thirst, she remembered the life inside her and curled into a fetal position to conserve what warmth she could. She needed to rest before going further. The cool dampness in the grotto had chilled her to the bone, but her thoughts were no longer on her discomfort. Her eyelids drooped. The splashing sound of the water falling into the cave's pool became children's voices.

The White Cliffs tower above the pure, pink crystal beach. In their bare feet, Markolous, six years old, and Flanyanna, seven, dig with sticks in the sand. Nearby, Bessalina watches over the royal children.

"Catch me—catch me if you can," Markolous says and throws sand in Flanyanna's face.

Flanyanna turns her head to protect her eyes.

"You stop that! Don't be bothering your older sister," Bessalina scolds Markolous.

Flanyanna throws sand back at her brother and runs away down the beach. Markolous races after her, scooping up more sand to retaliate.

"Stop this—both of you. Look at you. You're getting yourselves all dirty again, and there's no time to change before dinner."

Markolous dashes past Flanyanna. He reaches the rocky buttress at the end of the beach and raises his hands triumphantly high over his head. Sticking out his tongue, he cries, triumphantly, "I won—I won!"

"Did—not—did—not!" Flanyanna gasps out, pausing between each word.

"Did too!" Markolous retorts.

The sound of crashing waves on the rocks drowns out his words.

"Look—a cave," Flanyanna shouts. She points to a barely visible opening above the turbulent waves smashing into the boulders, above the shoreline.

The children scramble over the rocky barrier deposited by the Mara Sea in front of the cavern. Exploring the cave is far more interesting than another sibling argument.

"Wait—don't go in there." They hear Bessalina's alarmed warning. "Come back—come back this instant!"

The children disobey and enter the crevice hidden in the cliff. Boldly, Markolous moves forward, disappearing into the darkness.

Suddenly, Flanyanna hears the sound of splashing water. "Markolous?" she screams.

"It's a pool. I fell into it," Markolous exclaims, laughing despite his soaked clothing.

Flanyanna cautiously reaches her hand out and follows the damp wall into the cave's interior. Slowly, her eyes adjust. Reaching her brother, she dips her hand into the underground pool. Markolous strips off his wet shirt.

"You better not," she says.

Ignoring her, he jumps into the pool with a splash. A moment later, his head pops out.

"It's freezing cold," he yells.

Not wanting to miss out on anything or let her brother get the better of her, Flanyanna sheds her clothing and follows him into the freezing water. She comes up to the pool's surface, gasping for air.

"Children—where are you? Come back right now," Bessalina wheezes out as she lumbers into the cave. "Get out of that water or I'll give you both a royal thrashing you won't forget."

Flanyanna immediately gets out of the water, even though she knows Bessalina never follows through on her threats of corporal punishment and covers herself, giggling.

"Oh—if anything had happened to you...," Bessalina trails off, shuddering and immediately enfolds Flanyanna's wet body in her ample bosom. "Where's your brother?"

Markolous' head pops out of the water.

"Get out of the water," Bessalina screams.

"Nanna, there's an underground cave down there."

"Get out of the water!"

"But you don't understand…I found a secret hiding place under the pool. You can even stand in it. You can breathe in it." Very reluctantly, Markolous swims towards the edge of the pool.

Bessalina grabs his arm and pulls him out of the water. "I don't care if you found a whole new world."

"Ow—that hurts!" he screeches.

"Splendid. I finally got your attention." She turns back to Flanyanna. "Come along."

Bessalina drags the struggling, naked prince toward the entrance of the cave and calls back, "Flan, bring his clothes."

Picking up Markolous' clothing, Flanyanna dutifully follows her nanny out of the cave.

In the sunlight Markolous dresses himself and pushes his sister. She falls and cuts her knee on the rocks.

Bessalina whacks him on the side of his head.

"All you care about is her…," he mutters.

They scale down the craggy terrain to the beach.

Without warning a deafening roar of flapping wings assaulted Flanyanna's eardrums. Her eyes popped open, and she stared into the darkness. There were Shadow Fairies in the cave with her.

Without pausing to think, she inhaled deeply and dove into the intensely cold pool. She feared Petronero would be among them and she knew she could not resist the temptation to go to the Shadow Fairy world to be with him. She propelled herself down into the dark abyss. The congress of ravens flew directly over the pool and exited through the mouth of the cave.

If her childhood memory served her right, she would find the secret hiding place Markolous had mentioned. She would have a way to escape and save herself and her unborn child from her evil brother and her Shadow Fairy husband.

Using her third eye to light the way, Flanyanna swam deep down into the underground pool. Her lungs soon craved oxygen, but she forced herself to disregard her discomfort as she stroked through the darkness seeking the hidden cavern.

Just when she thought her lungs would burst, the light from Flanyanna's third eye revealed a wall leading upwards. She exploded up through the tunnel that seemed to go on forever and finally broke through to the surface. Gasping and choking, she wearily pulled herself out of the frigid water and collapsed on the tiny floor of the secret underground cave.

She spat out brackish water. Inhaling the cave's dank air, she lay on a narrow shelf with high stone walls that shot up into the darkness.

Markolous and his band trod down another path to the beach. Tethered to the soldiers' Namdalarians, the captured, bound royal guards followed behind. The Namdalarians' folded wings nestled against their bodies and rustled in the ocean's breeze. The soldiers walked alongside their unsteady steeds. They dared not fly down for, like everyone else, they knew about the White Cliffs' unpredictable and dangerous air currents.

"Spread out and find her," Tithoreus ordered once they hit the beach.

The Human Fairy soldiers fell silent as they complied. No one dared not to follow the order. Though they considered Tettigards to be lesser than them, they followed the command out of fear of the new king's wrath.

The horses' hooves slipped in the soft, loose, dry sand. The party maneuvered down onto the firmer wet sand near the waterline, hunting for the mysterious figure seen on the beach.

One of the soldiers spied an impression in the sand next to a half-buried boulder. He dismounted and bent down to examine it more closely—a footprint! Glancing about he saw that the incoming tide had washed away any other footprints. The boulder had protected and preserved this one in the crystal sands. He vigorously waved his hand to get the others' attention. "Over here!" he shouted.

Markolous furiously kicked Calamtheus in his ribs. The winged horse flared his nostrils and grunted as they galloped over to the soldier. Markolous slid off. Crouching down, he studied the imprint in the powdered rose quartz sand as the other soldiers rode up.

"This is too small to be a male's footprint, Sire. It's either that of a boy or a female," the soldier said.

"It's got to be hers...," Markolous said.

"But Sire, could it be left by that stable boy who ran off into the night when we captured the guards?"

"I don't think so. He couldn't possibly get to the beach on foot that quickly."

"Sire, maybe he can still fly?"

The sky undulated with a dark, ominous pitch, a throbbing curtain that covered the sun's bright light. A deafening roar of flapping wings assaulted the soldiers' eardrums.

"Shadow Fairies!" one of the soldiers yelled.

"Petronero," Markolous cried out.

A single raven dive bombed Markolous. Hordes of ravens descended upon them, attacking the soldiers, pecking at their eyes.

"The Namdalarians," Tithoreus shouted.

"Cover their eyes!" Markolous screamed. "The ravens will blind them."

Tithoreus ripped off his tunic, revealing his exoskeleton chest. Dodging the attacking birds, he tied the material around Calamtheus' eyes.

"Cover all the Namdalarians' eyes," Tithoreus yelled to the soldiers.

He twisted and contorted, flapping his membranous wings to protect himself from the Shadow Fairies. The soldiers ripped off their shirts and wrapped them around their mounts' heads—all the while dodging the beaks of the attacking birds.

At last, the constable of ravens flew away leaving Markolous and his soldiers with their mounts alone on the rose quartz beach. A cutting wind needled Markolous' face as he impatiently scanned the invisible horizon. The encroaching darkness prevented further search.

"We'll have to wait until morning," he said.

The soldiers threw blankets down on the sand and prepared for bed. Their Namdalarians were picketed nearby.

Flecks of gold floated high in the liquid midnight sky. The captured guards huddled together—in the cold—while the soldiers sat close to the fire. One played an old tune from Earth on a handmade whistle, and the others joined in.

> ♪   Merlinetta, aye Merlinetta,   ♪
> She lies with me in the meadow,
> She lies with me on the moor,
> But in the morning, she's gone,
> For her own true love hath come,
> Preferring her Magic rather than me.
> Merlinetta, aye Merlinetta
> ♪

In the still, starry night, they laughed and passed a goat udder filled with red wine. The soldiers drained the rubbery tits while a few brave souls danced a jig—challenged each other—and jumped across the crackling and popping fire.

The morning sky was clearly visible through the hole at the top of the underground cave's shaft. The beam of light that shot down woke Flanyanna from her sleep. The light meant the chamber had another way out. Her pulse quickened and she put back on the boots she had taken off the night before.

Rising from the cave's crystal floor, she opened her etheric wings. They smacked the sides of the underground cavern. Her wingspan was too wide for the narrow shaft. She tumbled backward, hitting her left shoulder against the bottom of the shaft. Grabbing her shoulder blade in pain, Flanyanna moaned. She rolled over on her side, lifted herself up, and pulled her etheric wings back into her body. They returned to their resting position—in the fourth dimension—undamaged. They would not help her efforts to escape this coffin.

Gripping the crystal stone wall's rough-textured surface, she used the protrusions and fissures to pull herself up the escarpment. She laboriously clawed her way up the crag, climbing to freedom. Suddenly, her right foot slipped off the moist surface and her already injured body slammed hard against the crystal rock. Searing, throbbing pain coursed through her side as a dislodged rock crashed to floor of the cave. She gritted her teeth. Digging her now broken and dirty fingernails into the rocky wall, she resumed her climb.

Feeling her belly move, she paused for a moment to rest. Looking down at the swell of her belly, she whispered, "Don't worry, we'll get to the Còrcair Mountains soon. You know nothing about them. That's where the rebels are." She grabbed another rock. This one held.

With her last bit of her strength and no further incident, she scaled the remaining portion of the precipice. Pulling herself out from what she feared would be her tomb, she stood atop the White Cliffs, overlooking the vast, blue-green Mara Sea. The ocean wind whipped at her tattered tunic and jacket. After being underground so many hours, the bright sunlight blinded her eyes. She shaded them and looked out over the endless shoreline. Licking her parched lips, she deeply inhaled the salty sea air.

The Feydonian Mountains flowed down to the Mara Sea and the pink crystal beach below the White Cliffs. She was a Human Fairy, queen of a kingdom she so dearly loved that had no place for her. Like the rock that had fallen into the cave she was now dislocated from her world.

She fell to her knees. She had not gotten to the other side of the Feydonians where her loyal partisans had gathered in the Còrcair Mountains.

"I can't go back," she said, for she feared her brother was too near. "Don't worry, my little princess," she said to her protruding belly. "We'll punish those who try to steal our kingdom."

She patted her stomach and walked in the direction of the Còrcair Mountains. She was filled with a fierce determination to rally her supporters, to give birth to her child and to regain her throne.

The Secret Cavern

The following morning the soldiers searched the beach's enclaves and rugged rocks in the bright sunlight. Two of them climbed the boulders at the end of the beach's shoreline.

"I smell smoke," one of them said.

"It's coming from over there," responded the other, indicating the fissure in the cliff wall where Flanyanna had disappeared the night before.

"Come on," said the first one.

They stood in front of the cave's entrance and looked into the darkness.

"I'm not going in there," said the second soldier.

"Why not?"

"It's a Shadow Fairy cave, you dummy." The second soldier started down the rocks to the beach.

"Oh, no you don't. You're coming with me, or I'll tell—*the Insect*," threatened the first soldier.

Reluctantly, the second soldier, now lower down on the jumble of boulders, turned around and came back. He feared the appetite of the king's new Tettigard captain for Human Fairy blood more than he feared Shadow Fairies. Together, the two soldiers walked into the darkness of the cave's interior.

"See. She's not here. Let's go," said the second soldier, feeling queasy.

"Wait…." The first soldier kicked at some flickering debris.

The algae and seaweed of Flanyanna's fire instantly reignited and lit up the cave's interior. "Shadow Fairies don't need fire to keep warm."

The second soldier squinted his eyes and, aided by the dim light of the fire, looked deeper into the cave. "Hey, look. This cave has two tunnels in it."

The first soldier walked towards the pool without answering his companion and bent down. In the campfire's flickering light, he saw something in the sand on the cavern's floor.

"Look! Footprints!" he said.

"We need to tell the others," exclaimed the second. They dashed out of the cave.

Shortly afterwards, Markolous and his soldiers, carrying torches made from driftwood and algae, entered the Shadow Fairy cavern.

The flaming torches bathed the interior of the grotto in a shifting pattern of dark and light. The first soldier pointed his torch to the footprints in the damp sand that led toward the pool not toward one of the tunnels.

"Sire, here. The prints look like the ones of the lad we saw on the beach."

Markolous crouched down and closely examined them. "Or they're my sister's...."

"Sire, Petronero must have led your sister to the cave and has taken her to the Shadow Fairy world," Tithoreus said. "That's why they attacked us yesterday."

"Shut up. I need to think," Markolous snapped, observing the footprints going over to the pool, but not coming back. "Somehow, it just doesn't add up."

"What do you mean, Sire?" Tithoreus queried.

Markolous turned abruptly to his captain. "Could you stop your linear insect thinking for a moment?"

Tithoreus bowed and backed away.

"Give me that torch," Markolous said. His heart pumping with adrenalin, he grabbed the torch out of the first soldier's hand. He stood at the pool's edge and waved the torch over its surface.

"I've been here before, when I was a young boy." He thrust the torch back at the soldier and pulled off one of his polished, black riding boots.

"Sire," Tithoreus asked, "I don't understand?"

"What's not to understand?" Markolous retorted as he took off his other boot and stripped off his jacket and shirt. "There's a hidden cave down there and I'm going to find it."

Slipping into the water and treading for a moment, he called to Tithoreus, "Well, what are you waiting for? Come on."

Markolous took a deep breath and plunged down into the pool's abyss. Tithoreus pulled off his footgear, his uniform jacket and his shirt, then dove into the water after him.

"Yuck, he's ugly," muttered the second soldier.

"Shhh—" cautioned the first soldier. "Do you want to get us killed?"

As he swam, Markolous cast the light of his third eye into the darkness looking for the entrance to the hidden cave. Finally, he pulled himself into a vaguely familiar narrow opening. Using his muscular arms and legs, he traced the contours of the submerged passageway.

Tithoreus swam upside down, following the light from Markolous' third eye. Like many other traits his kind had acquired during their evolution on Kokakina, he now had lungs and could hold his breath as well as Markolous. His back legs propelled him through the water while his middle pair of appendages steered his body.

From above a diffused light shined down through the water.

Almost out of oxygen, Markolous burst through the water's surface, coughing and gasping for air. Tithoreus shot out of the water behind him.

Markolous pulled himself from the pool. Spotting a crystal rock lying on the cave's narrow ledge, he picked it up. It was the one Flanyanna had dislodged during her ascent. His magic allowed him to sense that the rock had been touched by his sister.

Out of the pool, Tithoreus shook his wings like a dog shaking water off of its back. "What is it, Sire?"

Markolous looked up. His face was bathed by the light from above. "She's been here, all right—come on—let's go."

Tithoreus looked up towards the light. "Sire, I think it's best we go back and get the others. She might have met the rebels here."

Markolous was no fool. He was very aware that many did not accept him as the new ruler. Some even openly viewed him as a traitor who deserved to die for stealing the throne. He had killed Petronero and many of the rebels, but he knew the remaining rebels would still pose a grave danger to him especially with his sister leading them. He and Tithoreus dove back into the water to go back to the others.

Wanting to put distance between her and her brother, Flanyanna traveled all night and made it over the Feydonian Mountains.

Now in the Lost Forest, she wearily trudged through the low-lying shrouding mist that covered the terrain. Far off above, in the distance, she saw the lofty Còrcair Mountains where her supporters waited for her. The mountains' peaks rose above heavy, coiling dark gray clouds. The clouds moved in fast ready to explode.

A loud rumbling noise rolled over her. Pins and needles of cold, driving rain suddenly poured down. Shielding her face, she lowered her head and marched on.

In the curtain of rain, the Namdalarians labored single file along the steep, treacherous path that led up the White Cliffs from the beach.

A coyote scout, over five feet long from nose to tail and weighing over sixty pounds, ran up in front of Calamtheus.

Markolous jerked at his Namdalarian's reins, causing the winged horse to stumble. His coal-black eyes rolled and his nostrils flared in outrage from this unkind treatment by his cruel master.

"She's alone, in the Lost Forest," the coyote reported. He had located the opening where Flanyanna had escaped and tracked her all day.

Panting, the coyote's beady eyes turned. His sharply pointed ears stood straight up. He swung the narrow snout above his jutting fangs back in the direction of the Lost Forest.

"Take me to her and you will be handsomely rewarded." They followed the coyote whose eyes gleamed greedily at the prospect of a great prize.

"We must capture her before she reaches her followers," Markolous said to Tithoreus as they climbed the steep hill in the rain.

The storm had subsided and gauzy clouds lay splattered across the lavender sky. Drenched from the deluge, Flanyanna shivered. Her raven-black hair blew in the stormy wind, as she redoubled her efforts in the morning chill.

"I will get to my supporters. I will! The Rose Crystal prophecy said my child will rule someday," she said to keep herself going. In front of her, a rushing creek filled with water from the newly melted snow and the rain flowed through a deep ravine. Thirsty, she knelt and cupped her dirty hands, sipping the cool, refreshing water. Tilting her head back, she breathed deeply and detected delicious aromas, ones she knew very well.

"Mustard flowers and licorice," she said. Her stomach rumbled. She had not realized how hungry she was. She had eaten nothing during the two days since she had left the Faireye Manor.

Ravenous, she followed the wafting fragrances. She climbed the rocky embankment that led towards the herbal blossoms that were delicacies to Human Fairies. Peering over the steep, rocky incline, she saw a field of wild, yellow mustard flowers and dark green licorice. The plants seemed to have sprung up overnight. She did not want to think her sister dead, but spring was exploding around her.

She crawled over the rocks and knelt down. Plucking a mustard flower up by its roots, she wolfed it down. Then, she pulled at a licorice root and chewed on it with gusto. She basked in the sensation of the sweet, anise flavor filling her mouth.

A Namdalarian snorted.

She rose to her feet and her body stiffened. A sisal net flew out from behind one of the boulders next to her. Entangled in its mesh, Flanyanna collapsed onto all fours. Through the sisal netting, she saw Markolous and his troops emerge from their hiding spots behind the huge boulders in the meadow.

Flanyanna wanted to summon her magical powers to fight him, but she restrained the impulse. She knew any kind of magic would imperil her unborn child.

"Ready for a little fun, boys?" Markolous grinned.

His soldiers leered. They understood his meaning very well.

"Sire, what if something happens to her?" Tithoreus asked, placing his claw on Markolous' forearm.

"She looks well enough...."

"But what of the Lord of the Darkness?" Tithoreus asked.

Markolous jerked his arm out of Tithoreus' grasp. "Oh, let them have their fun."

"Sire, she must die by fire," Tithoreus said, his claws clenching. He was fearful that Markolous' hatred would have him kill her now, which would render her useless for the promise to the Lord of the Darkness.

"Stay out of this!" Markolous said. He wanted her to feel what he had felt all those years—lesser than.

He lifted the net from his sister. "Take her!" he yelled.

A soldier grabbed Flanyanna and tossed her to another, like a sack of potatoes.

She wanted to transform herself into a raven and fly away. She was one of the few White Fairies who, like the Pink Fairies, could still transform themselves into other forms. But, she knew that to do so would endanger her child.

A stout, Human Fairy soldier with a full, red beard grasped Flanyanna's waist. "Well, aren't we a plump miss?" Turning to the others, he said, "Why, she's no different than a scullery maid."

"Let's have a kiss," yelled one of the other soldiers.

"Aye!"

"Aye—give her a kiss."

The red bearded soldier smiled at Flanyanna, revealing his rotting, scummy yellow teeth. Breathing heavily, he bent forward to plant a kiss on her mouth. Revolted, Flanyanna turned her head and kneed him in the groin. In excruciating pain he rolled back onto the ground.

The other soldiers roared with laughter.

"What's the matter, Fregroid?"

"Can't you handle your females?"

"We want to see a proper kiss!"

A short, dark, elf-like Human Fairy pulled out his long knife and carefully circled the queen.

The other soldiers raised up their swords. "Take her—take her—take her!" they chanted.

The elf-like soldier reached out his blade and slowly cut the buttons from Flanyanna's peasant boy tunic. She pulled back from his violating touch. His approving comrades let out hoots and howls to encourage him.

"It isn't every day we get to play with a queen, even if she's a fallen one," the elf-like soldier gloated. He reached down and lightly ran the knife up her calf and her thigh to the juncture of her britches. Just as it reached the top of her groin, he raised his head up in his lechery. "Why—this is no boy!"

Everyone laughed, again.

Without hesitation Flanyanna took two of her fingers and poked him in the eyes. He screamed in agony, and his knife fell from his grasp to the ground. Without missing a beat, she scooped down and snatched it up. Her tormentors backed off.

"It appears, sister, my soldiers are afraid of you." Undeterred, Markolous focused on the knife. It flew into his hand, and he slipped it into his belt. His followers cheered raucously. They raised their crystal encrusted blades high above their heads as they voiced their approval of their powerful leader.

"Markolous! Markolous!"

The soldiers rhythmically slapped the flats of their swords against their thighs in anticipation of a fight to the death between the two royal, sorcerer siblings.

"You can't kill me!" Flanyanna spoke in defiance, but she knew he was king and could do whatever he wanted.

"Kill you? I'm not going to kill you. I'm just going to scare you a little," Markolous snarled. His eyes burned with hatred. Despite his words, every fiber of his being wanted to do away his sister—now.

Markolous walked away, and Tithoreus rushed after him. "Sire, you must stop this. She's pregnant!"

"Shut up! I know what I'm doing," Markolous sneered.

Flanyanna kicked one of the soldiers in the head. He fell backwards, unconscious. Two soldiers attacked her from the back.

She flipped one to the ground, twisting his arm out of his socket. He writhed in pain, rolling in the dirt. Two other soldiers crept up behind her. One leaped onto her back and the other grabbed her legs. They forced her to the ground.

"You must stop this! They'll kill her!" Tithoreus said. "They're killers. That's what they're trained to do."

"Oh, let them have their fun," Markolous said, ever so calmly.

"You may be king, but you can't defy the traditions of your people," Tithoreus said. "You can't let them rape and kill a pregnant female especially your sister, who was once the queen."

"I can do whatever I please."

"No one, not even these soldiers who will rape and kill her will follow you if you do—

"—You must publicly try her, condemn her, and burn her—as a witch."

Tithoreus' words sank in. As much as Markolous wanted to shame and humiliate Flanyanna right now, his hunger for her death could not be fulfilled at that moment.

"Tell them to back off. I beg you, Sire. This will come to no good."

"And what about her child?"

"Sire, the child will only be more light for our master."

Markolous went over and yanked the soldiers off his sister.

"That's enough. The fun's over."

They pulled back, knowing the king had changed his mind.

Reaching over with his free hand, Markolous jerked the dynamic, glowing Rose Crystal from Flanyanna's neck.

"I believe this is mine now—sister." Markolous placed the amulet around his neck. The vibrant glow of the Rose Crystal turned dark, a lifeless and meaningless bauble in the hands of a male Human Fairy, even if he was the king. "I will try you for witchcraft, and you will be burned until you are nothing but ash."

Once Human Fairies were seared to ash, they could never come back. There would be no time in the Shadow Fairy world and no reincarnation. This was the ultimate cruelty that one Human Fairy could show to another for the Lord of the Darkness fed upon their light and they would be obliterated for all eternity.

"Tie her on a horse next to me," Markolous ordered.

"But, Sire, we have no extra horse," Tithoreus said.

"Then let her walk. She led us on a merry chase on those feet. Let her dance on them to the dungeon."

Two soldiers dragged her over and tethered her to Calamtheus. Markolous rode on his black stallion. Looking down from his winged steed, he enjoyed Flanyanna's humiliation as she staggered and stumbled along at the brisk pace he set. Tithoreus' wings beat a horizontal figure eight in the air, keeping him aloft behind her.

Triumphantly, the party marched back to the crystal palace. Throughout the countryside, word traveled fast. The deposed queen had been captured.

The Tower of the Forgotten

A gray ether's cloying dampness clung to and shrouded everything, living and otherwise. The Crystal Palace's four towers spiraled into the foreboding sky. The grotesque gargoyles guarding its entrance suddenly left their stone perches and flew up, circling over the palace like vultures.

From far and wide Human Fairies traveled to the Crystal Palace to witness this unprecedented event, the trial of a royal Human Fairy. Never had a ruling monarch been deposed and tried by her successor. The occasion would provide a story to be told and retold to children and grandchildren for many years.

Trials in Kokakinan society were open to all with no regard for social status. Those not able to gain entrance to the Throne Room where the trial would take place jammed into every niche of the palace courtyard and town. There were so many spectators that the sheer mass of Human Fairies completely covered the red-tiled roofs of the villagers' cottages. All hoped to catch a glimpse of their fallen queen.

"Has she arrived yet?" A stout farmer shouted. He stood in the sardine-packed cobblestone square, looking up to an open window on the second floor of the palace.

"No, I don't see her," a mason yelled. He leaned precariously out of the crystal casement, holding a pottery jug of elderberry wine wrapped in dried woven twigs supplied by the new king.

Markolous, in his efforts to manipulate the masses, provided liquor to all who wished to have it. Many in the crowd had taken him up on his offer and now stumbled about in a drunken daze.

"Here she comes," the mason said with his bird's-eye view from the arched, exterior window the wine slurring his words. He pointed with a finger and then guzzled more wine.

Flanyanna dragged her heavy chains through the crowd, toward the staircase that led into the Crystal Palace. Her former subjects parted in the congested courtyard as if hypnotized. Markolous could have brought her through the interior open hallways, but he chose to humiliate her by having her walk through the streets like a common beggar boy.

"Guilty! She's Guilty!" someone in the crowd screamed.

This accusation jolted the crowd out of their self-induced intoxicated trance. Even in their inebriated state, they were aware that their queen would be paying with her life for the cheap spirits they imbibed so freely. Some huddled together, talking only in hushed tones for fear of retribution. They were shocked by Markolous' cruelty as Flanyanna labored up the exterior crystal staircase to the Throne Room from where she once ruled.

Inside, representatives from all classes of Kokakinan society—common laborers, merchants, farmers, seamstresses, and servants—rubbed elbows with Human Fairy nobility.

A mural of the night sky covered the ceiling above the masses. In the center of the ceiling's transparent crystal dome, ten concentric circles created a bullseye. An image of the moon dominated the innermost circle. The twelve Zodiac signs decorated the two circles surrounding the moon—a testament to the revered Zodiac created on Earth and brought to Kokakina in ancient times. Gold flecks, representing the stars of the galaxy, were scattered on and reflected down the walls. The constellations spilling across the walls made everyone feel as though they could still fly, like before, when their ancestors were on Earth.

Next to the throne, the silver-haired and grey-cloaked court justice keeper, Hermanicles, held a tall, thick staff. For centuries, Human Fairies had carved enchanted staffs from the wood of magical rowan trees brought from Earth. The clear quartz crystal mounted on top of his rowan staff identified him as a master scholar of Human Fairy traditions. Its magic turned away harm and evil influences, deflecting misfortune and the evil eye.

"Order! Order in the court," Hermanicles said, pounding his staff on the floor.

A crystal gong floating in mid-air sounded a sharp note that vibrated in the crowd's pointed ears. Its clear tone announced the arrival of a Human Fairy of great importance.

Markolous entered the Throne Room wearing the now dark queen's necklace around his neck. He was accompanied by

Tithoreus. Everyone was aware that Tettigards were a prominent part of the new regime, but having that knowledge did not make them more comfortable with seeing a Tettigard accompanying their monarch into the Throne Room.

"Sire, with all due respect, do you really think it's wise to bring a Tettigard into the Throne Room?" Hermanicles asked.

"These Tettigards are our trusted allies," Markolous said.

Hermanicles looked over to the other advisors, hoping they would support him. They looked away and said nothing, for fear of losing their property, or their heads. "Sire, his kind has preyed on Human Fairies for centuries." Hermanicles forged on bravely, alone.

"That's in the past. We need to forgive and acknowledge their contribution to my rightful ascension to the throne," Markolous replied.

"Sire, they drink our blood," Hermanicles protested.

Markolous waved his hand dismissively. "They have agreed to refrain from attacking any of my subjects. We live in peace now," he countered.

The Human Fairies in the crowd whispered and mumbled among themselves.

Hermanicles bowed, saying no more, for fear he would follow Flanyanna and be the next prominent Human Fairy to be incarcerated in the Tower of the Forgotten.

Markolous sat down on the throne. Covered with feminine imagery—carved birds, butterflies, flowers, and sylphs—it was a stark reminder of Kokakina's matriarchal heritage.

"Proceed with the trial," Markolous said.

Standing next to Markolous, Tithoreus flexed his muscles, and locked the sticky pads on the end of his feet to hold himself still. He fixed his compound eyes on a cook located in the crowd.

"She's a sorceress," the cook stuttered remembering why she had the coins in her apron pocket she so nervously fingered. They were given to her to be a shill and denounce the queen.

"She ate while we starved," screamed a fat merchant's wife.

"Burn her! Burn the witch," shouted a village prostitute.

"Silence! Silence! You shall all be removed if you are not silent," Hermanicles shouted, pounding his rowan staff onto the floor.

Markolous smiled and gestured to him to proceed. His agents had done an excellent job of recruiting false witnesses to discredit Flanyanna.

"Bring forth the prisoner!" Hermanicles cried out. He struck upon the floor once more with his staff.

Just as he did so, a red vapor floated out of the moon in the center of the ceiling and drifted down. The crowd moved back in a hush. The vapor descended and coalesced, materializing into an attractive, androgynous Human Fairy with golden-brown hair dressed in a plush velvet robe. In the Human Fairy's hand a pentacle crystal secured by a burnished gold wire topped off a rowan staff. The crystal glimmered softly like a moonbeam.

"Merlinetta," Markolous managed to say, taken aback.

Merlinetta was related to the royal family and was the most powerful Human Fairy who had ever lived. Her mastery of magic had allowed her phenomenal longevity. Some even said she was immortal. She had been alive at the time of the cataclysmic event that prompted the Human Fairy migration from Earth to Kokakina and was one of many Human Fairies who chose to remain behind on Earth to protect the mother planet.

She brushed off tiny particles of celestial stardust, which floated over and covered Markolous, causing him to sneeze.

She was the youngest of nine sisters. Those who came into power on patriarchal Earth spread the story that she was actually nine different beings to weaken public perception of her power. Eventually, all Humans on Earth came to believe that she was nine separate females—not one.

To counteract this falsehood and function as the most powerful magical being on Earth, she impersonated a male. She infiltrated the highest echelons of patriarchal society to perform her mission to fight the forces that denigrated the feminine Earth power, the Gaia, the ancestral mother of all life.

"To what do we owe this unexpected pleasure?" an irritated Markolous asked still brushing the stardust off of his rich, black suede doublet.

"My name is Merlin now," Merlinetta replied. She took off her robe and dropped it, revealing tight, tan britches and a flowing, brown tunic—attire usually worn by a male Human Fairy. She carried a crystal encrusted sword about her waist.

"Merlin, may we proceed with the trial?" Markolous asked.

"Why, by all means. That's why I'm here. To make sure that we honor the ancient Human Fairy laws brought from Earth."

"Right."

The floating gong sounded again.

"Make way for the prisoner!" Hermanicles cried out.

With no ceremony, Flanyanna was dragged into the Throne Room by Peccarey guards. Their bestial strength allowed them to manhandle her slight form. The odious stench that accompanied the creatures caused many of the Human Fairies in attendance to hold their noses or cover them with their spider-silk handkerchiefs. Human Fairies were not accustomed to this foul odor. Until Markolous recruited them for his army, Peccaries were only as guards in the Tower of the Forgotten dungeon. A Peccarey poked Flanyanna in her back with his crude spear.

"Merlinetta," Flanyanna said, very glad to see her distant cousin.

"Flanyanna."

Markolous gave one of the porcine guards a curt nod.

Adjusting the grip on his spear, the guard struck Flanyanna across the back of her legs forcing her to fall to her knees. The crowd was aghast. Never before had Peccaries dared to touch a member of the royal family let alone assault her.

"Your Majesty?" Merlin interrupted, stepping forward, tight lipped at the abuse heaped on Flanyanna.

"Yes, what is it?"

"The prisoner has the right to counsel," Merlin said. She turned to Flanyanna. "Flanyanna, I offer you my services."

"I accept," Flanyanna answered, rising painfully to her feet.

"What are the charges?" Merlin asked. A pair of reading spectacles appeared and settled on her nose. A scroll floated out of Hermanicles' hand and uncoiled in front of her.

"The charge is witchcraft?" Merlin asked, looking over the top of her glasses at Markolous. "Can't somebody ever come up with something a little more original when they fear the powerful female essence?"

Suddenly, a heckler in the back shouted, "Burn her!" Nodding imperceptibly, Merlin motioned toward the door with her staff. She thrust it at the heckler, and the portly farmer was swept off his feet. He gave a startled cry as he hung suspended in mid-air above everyone's heads. The doors to the Throne Room opened and the heckler shot out of them.

"The next time anyone speaks out of turn, I'll ask Merlin to make of thee a squealing pig," Hermanicles said.

Everyone fell into a subdued silence.

Hermanicles turned back to Flanyanna. "You are charged with witchcraft. How do you plead?"

"I plead not guilty."

"The queen pleads not guilty," a lad screamed out a side window. In the courtyard the crowd cheered, the sound reverberating off the walls of the Crystal Palace. They were going to have the show they had hoped for.

Merlin pointed her rowan staff and everyone near her stepped back. In front of Merlin, a long, wooden table with spherical legs appeared and settled gracefully on the crystal floor. She pointed her staff at the table. A rotating golden globe and a very large book, the Book of Magic and Shadows, bound in burnished leather materialized and floated onto it. The book opened and flipped its pages, abruptly stopping at page ten thousand and thirty-three. Merlin walked over and regarded the open page.

A dropped pin would have made more noise than what was heard at that moment.

"Under Human Fairy law, page ten thousand and thirty-three, those accused of witchcraft have the right to be judged by the Rose Crystal," she declared. Letting her gaze settle on Markolous, she added, "and none may deny that right."

Markolous grimaced through his clenched teeth. He had not counted on Merlin being present to force him to play by the rules. His intention in this, as in all situations, was to play by his rules, not by the laws of the land. He could have manipulated the courtroom and called his sister a liar because he was the king, but he could never call the Rose Crystal a liar. Its impartial truths were subject to no one's will. Relying on the Rose Crystal in matters of law was how Human Fairies were protected from persecution by those in power—on Kokakina as on Earth. It was how fair justice had been implemented for centuries.

Merlin smiled, knowing she had outfoxed him.

Turning to Flanyanna, Hermanicles asked, "Do you agree to be judged by the Rose Crystals?"

"Yes, I do," Flanyanna replied without hesitation.

"Will you accept their judgment?"

"Yes, I will."

Merlin lifted a duplicate to the queen's necklace from around her neck. On it, a pink Rose Crystal amulet was mounted in a gold setting that displayed jeweled zodiac symbols. This Rose Crystal was a twin to the queen's pendant that now hung dully and lifelessly around Markolous's neck. Except that one was male in its essence and the other female, the two were replicas. Only the most gifted could discern the difference.

The onlookers mumbled and whispered among themselves at the introduction of the second Rose Crystal amulet, one they had never seen before. But none doubted its authenticity. Human Fairy folklore spoke of the paired rose crystals on Earth. All the other crystals the Human Fairies possessed were subordinate to these two most powerful and magical crystals.

"May I please have the queen's necklace?" Merlin asked Markolous.

Markolous did not want to comply, but he did, handing the queen's necklace to her. It immediately came alive in her hand. The light momentarily blinded those close to her as she took off her own necklace and intertwined the two crystal necklaces. They swung together, back and forth below her right hand's fingers and then she flipped them to her left hand.

A blue aura burst forth from Merlin's male Rose Crystal and a pink aura from the queen's female Rose Crystal. The auras expanded throughout the Throne Room, engulfing everyone.

A profound hush settled on the room, for all could see this was enchantment to tell about in enthralled wonder. The walls and ceiling faded away through time and space. A turbulent, dark cloud hovered over the palace courtroom and transformed into a horrific battle.

> *Markolous led an army of Peccaries and Tettigards. Opposing him were magical creatures from the Lost Forest and Human Fairies in tattered clothing. All those opposing Markolous carried makeshift weapons—clubs, pitchforks, and a few rusty swords. Their leader was an unknown female Human Fairy with long, flowing, red hair. The redheaded Human Fairy rode a white Namdalarian stallion that looked like Arasthenes.*
>
> *The redhead brandished a rose crystal sword as she urged her troops on against Markolous and his army. The sword was Flanyanna's—or was it Merlin's?*

Markolous exploded up from his seat, on what had been, before his father's time, the Human Fairy queen's throne. "Enough. I've had enough of this ridiculous soothsaying—

"—This vision of the future is a—meaningless, theatrical—conjuring act," he fumed.

The vision disappeared. A restless mumble coursed through the Throne Room.

"Beware, Markolous, the Rose Crystals have shown you the future," Merlin said. She took the entwined Rose Crystals and dangled them in front of Flanyanna. "Is she guilty of evil witchcraft?"

The entwined Rose Crystal necklaces in Merlin's hand answered 'no' by swinging from side to side and coming to a stop pointing away from Flanyanna.

"She has been found 'NOT GUILTY' of evil witchcraft," Hermanicles intoned.

"Father chose me," Flanyanna screamed in her elation.

Even though Merlin was the most powerful and revered Human Fairy alive, she couldn't change the deadly sibling rivalry between a brother and a sister. Markolous looked at his sister, not moving a muscle. Tithoreus leaned and whispered in his ear. Only Markolous' strained, ragged breathing broke the silence.

"You dare to challenge your king?"

Flanyanna's own words condemned her, for it was Human Fairy law that the ruler was not to be challenged. If any Human Fairy challenged the ruler, they could be burned for treason. The infallible counsel of the Rose Crystals that guided all decisions of earlier monarchs made it unnecessary to question the ruler's decisions until now, when Markolous chose to ignore them.

"I've seen enough of your treachery. As the rightful king of the Human Fairies, named by our father, I sentence you to death by burning. It is the way and law of the Human Fairies."

In desperation, Flanyanna looked at Merlin.

Merlin lowered her head in defeat knowing that Flanyanna's rash words had condemned her. Merlin had prepared herself to help Flanyanna be found innocent of evil witchcraft, but when Flanyanna spoke against her brother, who was now king, she had doomed herself—for treason.

"By His Majesty's judgment, the deposed queen has been found 'GUILTY' of treason," intoned Hermanicles. "It is the law." He turned to Flanyanna. "For your crime of treason, you will be burned alive at the stake tomorrow morning."

"I'm sorry, but there is no more I can do for you. Under our laws, you have committed treason. Plead your belly now and save your child," Merlin whispered into Flanyanna's ear, knowing Markolous must let her live until the child was born.

"I plead my belly!" Flanyanna screamed for all to hear.

"She speaks the truth. She is with child. You must let the child live. It is the law," Merlin said loudly for all to hear.

The audience broke out into a loud clamor. According to ancient Human Fairy tradition, a pregnant female must be allowed to give birth to her innocent child before being executed.

A Human Fairy commoner ran to a window overlooking the courtyard and bellowed, "The queen is with child."

A Peccarey guard roughly yanked him away.

"Quiet! Be quiet or I'll incarcerate all of you," Hermanicles called out and stamped his magical staff.

A few hoping to be the first to spread the news ran out the Throne Room before the Peccaries secured the now closing doors. Confined, the rest became silent.

"Markolous, you cannot take an innocent's life. Flanyanna must be allowed to give birth. The child will not suffer for the mother's deeds," Merlin said.

All inside the courtroom could hear the uproar of the crowd in the courtyard as it heard the tidings from the ones who had escaped.

"Thank you. I heard you the first time," Markolous said.

"Sire, listen to the crowd outside. There'll be rebellion if you don't comply with your laws," Tithoreus whispered. His giant insect body stiffened, and he slowly pulled back away from the throne and the king.

Markolous' body stiffened as well with his poisonous contempt, but he resigned himself to the inevitable. He must wait to burn his sister. To do otherwise would strengthen the opposition against him. He nodded to Hermanicles.

Hermanicles stamped his magic staff three times on the crystal floor. "The defendant will be allowed to give birth to her child," he proclaimed. He looked at Flanyanna. "You will then be taken to a place of execution. For your crime of treason you will be burned alive at the stake."

Everyone went silent. Death by burning meant she would not be able to reincarnate at all. She would disappear from the face of the universe for all eternity like she never existed at all.

Hermanicles gestured to the Peccarey guards who dragged Flanyanna towards the doors.

The silence erupted into chaos. The doors opened, and everyone rushed towards them. They pushed and shoved each other to get out. They wanted to share with their families and friends the news that the queen would have the chance to give birth and would then be burned alive for treason.

In the madness the Peccarey guards pushed and pulled Flanyanna out the Throne Room door.

"Yes, take her away. She irritates me," Markolous said to himself.

For a moment the Throne Room was filled with a deafening and haunting silence for everyone had left except…Merlin swung her staff above her head and the heavy volume on the table flashed briefly in a bright light. The judgment was sealed and recorded in the Human Fairy records. She had fulfilled the prophecy. Her work was complete. The unborn child would have the right to live. She would be safe for the time being. The table, the book, and the globe 'poofed' away in a cloud of blue smoke.

"I'll be watching you, Markolous," Merlin warned, turning toward him before vanishing in a red vapor exactly like the one that announced her arrival.

With no reply, Markolous rose from the throne chair and left the now vacant Throne Room.

Outside the Throne Room, Flanyanna and her guards were pushed and jostled by the crowd of Human Fairies. The crowd shouted and gestured with no respect for their deposed queen for she had been found guilty of treason. She and the Peccaries were swallowed up by the mob as they paraded down the alley to the Tower of the Forgotten dungeon.

Flanyanna stumbled in the press and a green clawed hand took hold of her arm. The Tarragonian who had poached her fish at the Faireye Manor was standing over her shielding her from the onslaught of the mob. Flanyanna stared into Doc Tikkum's calm, gentle eyes. The compassion and strength she saw dispelled the fear and panic that were overwhelming her.

He reached out his other hand to her. "Your Majesty, take my hands."

She took his Tarragonian hands, and he lifted her up over the frenzied crowd. The crowd pulled back fearing they would be forever tainted by the touch of a Tarragonian. The Peccarey guards—now having enough breathing space—took back up their formation around the deposed and condemned queen.

Doc Tikkum, Flanyanna, and the Peccarey guards walked down the now empty alleyway to the Tower of the Forgotten as everyone dispersed and went home.

The Village Square

As time passed, news of Flanyanna's capture spread like wildfire throughout the land. All of Kokakina heard about the trial of their now beloved Human Fairy queen imprisoned in the Tower of the Forgotten—a place from where no one ever returned. She would be burned at the stake after the birth of her child. All trembled at what this unprecedented event would mean for the land.

Many hoped the rumors they heard in the taverns were true, that the rebels in the Còrcair Mountains were preparing to free the deposed queen. Markolous' spies told him large numbers of his subjects were leaving to join the rebels. In hopes of crushing all opposition, Markolous issued the following decree:

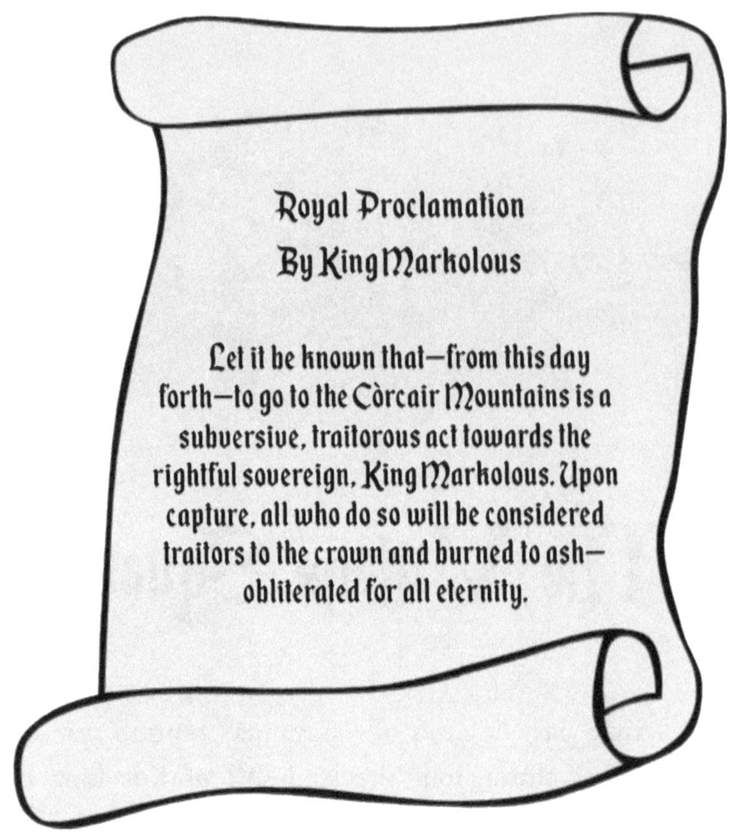

In one of the village's narrow alleyways, a disheveled female beggar passed the king's proclamation where it was tacked onto the side of a building. Her wrinkled face, once beautiful, now sagged and drooped. Her feet shuffled painfully across the hard, uneven cobblestone surface. Reaching the end of the lane, she entered the busy village square.

The shouts of vendors hawking their wares greeted her. Seeing the beggar, some villagers paused in their shopping, and other Human Fairies simply ran away.

"Hot meat pies. Get your delicious, hot meat pies here," a young lad yelled. A wooden box overflowing with the enticing pastries was strapped across his chest.

Freshly baked breads and pastries on a baker's cart behind the boy drew the beggar like a magnet. Seeing her approach, the baker covered his goods with his muffin-top stomach. Across from the baker's cart, the skinny keeper of a millinery shop facing the square and a plump matron gossiped in front of the shopkeeper's establishment.

"Isn't that...," the skinny shopkeeper spoke quietly, pointing at the beggar.

"I'll be right back," the well-endowed female interrupted and bustled over to the beleaguered, middle-aged baker standing in front of his cart.

"Get away from my cart, you filthy old hag." She heard him say as she approached.

The hag stretched a bony, disfigured finger out in front of her, pointed at the baker and began a spell...

"May you, your children and your children's
children be cursed for eternity..."

"What's this? Where's your charity, husband?" the matron asked, smiling at the dirty old beggar and leaning into her spouse's ear. "You idiot," she whispered. "Can't you see she's touched by the Shadow Fairy world?"

"Huh?"

The baker's wife reached for a loaf of fresh rosemary bread, still warm from their stone oven, and offered it to her.

"Please, forgive my husband. He has a bit of indigestion this morning," she said shooting the perplexed baker an angry look.

With a scathing glance at the now nervous baker, the old beggar snatched the loaf from the baker's wife and hobbled across the square wolfing down her meal.

"Why'd you do that? We can hardly pay our mortgage or our taxes?" the baker complained.

"You old fart..."

"Old fart, is it—you're the one who's giving our bread away."

"My mother was right about you. I should have listened to her. Don't you know who that is?

"That's the Dungeon Witch," she answered her own question.

"That's the Dungeon Witch?" His eyes widened.

"She has the power to curse our family for all eternity." His wife poked the baker in his doughy stomach. "And you almost got our bloodline blighted forever over a measly loaf of bread," she said, shaking her head in exasperation. They watched the Dungeon Witch disappear into an alley.

Slipping into the recessed doorway of a red tile roofed building, the Dungeon Witch looked around. No one was watching. She tugged her left earlobe and her body transformed into that of a small gray field mouse. The mouse scampered across the moat to the Tower of the Forgotten—unnoticed by the gargoyles guarding the entrance.

At the massive dungeon gate, the Peccarey guard on duty squealed and stomped his foot to squash the tiny creature. The magical mouse darted back and forth to dodge his flailing hooves and squeezed under the wooden door to the dungeon.

Anguished screams reverberated off of the crystal walls as the little rodent scurried down the wet, puddled crystal corridor. She covered her ears with her tiny paws to block out the wails of the forgotten prisoners.

Going deep into the dungeon, to the very bowels of the Crystal Palace, she peered into each cell. A filthy, calloused hand with grimy broken fingernails thrust through one cell's bars and snatched her up ready to swallow her whole. Contorting her body, the mouse slipped from the prisoner's grasp and dashed on down the corridor. The prisoner's hand pulled back into the dark cell.

The mouse ran to the moving staircase and quickly scurried down the escalating steps. Reaching the bottom, she sampled the air and turned left. It looked like she knew the dungeon very well. That she had been there before. At each cell, she stopped and put her nose down to the bottom of the cell door and sniffed. Reaching the last cell, she smelled the scent she was looking for. "Well, finally…." She pancaked herself flat and squirmed through the small space under the door.

The rodent's eyes adjusted to the dimness. In front of her, Pinky dangled, suspended four feet above the cell's floor. Her wrists and ankles were tautly bound and chained with iron links to the stone walls.

Changing back into her Human Fairy form, the Dungeon Witch raised one bristling, white eyebrow and stared at Pinky. "Oh, you look terrible!"

Pinky slowly raised her head. "Who's there?" she croaked.

"How long has he had you strung up like this? Tsk—tsk," the Dungeon Witch asked, shaking her head.

Pinky's head motioned toward a wooden bucket in the corner. "Water. Please, may I have some water?" she said through her parched, bleeding lips.

Walking over to the bucket, the Dungeon Witch filled the wooden carved ladle there and lifted it to her lips—sipping a small amount. Immediately, she spat out the stagnant, foul water.

"You can't drink this. It tastes like mud. It's poison."

"Just give me some wa—ter."

"Oh," the Dungeon Witch said, shaking her head in disapproval. "—I see nothing much has changed here."

"Please, give me a drink of water."

"Certainly." The Dungeon Witch flicked her hand with a flourish above the filthy water, across and down then one circle to the right, one circle to the left. The clouded, muddy water became clear.

"Here you go, poor child."

Pinky slurped it down long and hard. "How did you get into my cell?" she asked, her thirst was satiated.

"Don't be silly…the usual way, dearie…magic!"

Pinky's head dropped down.

The Dungeon Witch deftly grabbed her by the hair and pulled her head back up. "N-N-No, you don't. Don't fall asleep on me."

"You could be a spy for Markolous," Pinky said, slurring her words.

"Poppycock! Here, have another sip."

Pinky shook her head.

"Oh, come on now. I know you're still thirsty. Drink up." The Dungeon Witch refilled the ladle.

Pinky drank the dram the Dungeon Witch put to her mouth.

"There. There. That's a good girl," the Dungeon Witch said, taking down the cup from Pinky's lips. "I'll bet this is the first enchanted elixir you had in a long time."

"Yes…yes it is—and it's really good! Who are you?" Pinky knew that, despite her appearance, this old Human Fairy was a powerful magical being.

"Not now. I'll tell you later, after we get out of here," the Dungeon Witch said, studying Pinky's cuffs and chains. "Kinky. I'd say your brother's kinky," she cackled.

She raised her first two, crooked, bent fingers. Using her other hand to force open a third crooked, bent ring finger, she pointed them at Pinky.

Instantly, Pinky was released from her bondage and floated like a feather to the floor where she collapsed in a heap. She lifted her head up to look at her rescuer.

"I remember my mother—a long time ago a lost friend—no a long lost relative," she said.

"Don't worry. The elixir will be taking effect soon and you'll be as good as new."

"You are…I know I should know you," Pinky said.

"Ummmm…I suppose," the Dungeon Witch said.

"Ca—Calis—you're Calisandra, aren't you?"

"How strange…."

"How so?"

"Well, I haven't been called that name since before you were born."

"Help me up," Pinky said.

Calisandra reached out her hand and helped her stand up. "You know, I think your brother has it in for us females."

"You said…brother?"

"Yeah, Markolous, your brother."

"My mother knows you?" Pinky asked. "Is that good or bad?"

"Oh, oh, it's good. We used to be...friends...girlfriends... before you were born. A long time ago. We used to have so much fun putting spells on our boyfriends. They didn't know which way was up."

"That's really strange. I didn't know my mother had any friends."

"Well, perhaps we were m-m-more than friends."

"So, you're a relative?"

"Well, in manner of speaking, yes."

"That's great! I didn't know I had any relatives on my mother's side."

Pinky went to the cell door and peered out, squinting her eyes to see into the corridor's darkness. "Excuse me. Do you know how long have I been in here?"

"Oh, for quite some time. Nobody's out there," Calisandra said. She could tell Pinky was contemplating a spell. "Dearie, I wouldn't try that if I were you...."

Ignoring Calisandra's warning, Pinky flicked her wrist—three times—and transformed herself into a tiny field mouse. The spell only worked for a moment before backfiring, throwing the tiny mouse up against the cell's wall. Pinky's body returned to her Human Fairy form, but she now had a gigantic mouse head.

"Tsk, tsk. I tried to tell you." The Dungeon Witch shook her head and reached out to help Pinky rise.

"I'm all right."

"Oh, of course. What was I thinking? You're just like your mother and look where it got her. A little hovel in the Lost Forest and look where it's gotten you." Calisandra cast her eyes around the dismal confines of the cell.

"I'm nothing like my mother."

"Oh, yes…I think you most definitely are. You're pretty, you're smart, you're magical, and you're the perfect Pink Fairy—just like your mother."

Pinky staggered back to the cell door. Clutching the bars, she leaned her large mouse head forward to look out into the corridor. It was all one big blur.

"You know, I was there when you were born. Oh, yes, I was.…"

"Would it be all right if we discussed my birth later?"

"Your father, the king? He doted on you. After all, you were his firstborn."

"Did my mother send you?"

"What? Of course not! We haven't spoken in years!"

"Oh, I see."

"Yes, she could have been the queen of the Human Fairies."

Pinky shook her head. "I don't get it. Why do you care so much?"

"Your mother was the worst game player at court."

"I know that. So?"

"Well, I don't know. Heartbreak just does something to you, dearie," Calisandra said in exasperation. "Sometimes you have to choose to do something you don't want to because the alternative is worse—a lot worse."

"And that's why you're here?"

Calisandra nodded.

"All right. Just keep my mother out of this."

"As you wish."

Pinky closed her eyes for a minute and rested her head against the bars. "As we are here together sharing a cell, how's my sister doing?"

Calisandra tossed the ladle back into the bucket with a splash. "Oh dear. A lot has happened since you've been locked up in here and I can see you know nothing about it."

"What do you mean?" Pinky asked, her eyes widening, now worried for her sister's safety. Her own predicament was a testament to what Markolous was capable of doing. She no longer had any illusions as to the extent of his cruelty.

"You really don't know do you. Your sister is right here in the Tower of the Forgotten—just—it's spring now."

Pinky looked down the blurry hallway. "What of Petronero?"

"He is one of many who lost their lives in the Còrcair Mountains trying to regain your sister's throne. Your brother has done worse than anyone ever imagined, and everyone lives in fear now."

"I don't understand? Why didn't anybody else try to help her?"

"Well, actually, I tried to help her," Calisandra replied. "I met her at the Shadow Fairy cave on the beach near the Faireye Manor, but she'd have nothing to do with me."

"Well, you probably frightened her."

"No, I don't think so. If you must know, I looked like a beautiful, young Pink Fairy, just like you—little Miss High and Mighty."

"You're telling me you impersonated me?"

"Let's get something straight, dearie. I'm trying to help you, okay?"

"I think you're trying to help yourself," Pinky said.

"And what's wrong with that? At least I have the decency to help you unlike someone we both know." Calisandra sized up Pinky with her third eye.

"And you think because I'm in this place…well, I'm not interested," Pinky said, refusing to acknowledge how bad her situation was.

"Look, I understand how you feel. I've felt the same way. If I can be frank, you're in no position to help Flanyanna."

"I just need a little time to rest that's all. I'll be all right—soon enough."

"You can't even turn yourself into a mouse and that's the oldest trick in the Book of Magic and Shadows."

"Can you get me out of here?"

"Yes. I know this place like the back of my very veiny hand."

"Okay. Let's go."

"Well…in exchange for a small fee."

"NO. The answer is no."

"Oh, that's too bad. I guess taking help from those of a lower station is beneath all of you royal Human Fairies?"

Pinky turned away from the bars and looked to her. "Let's get something straight. I'm not going to take your place in the Shadows."

Calisandra smiled, for Pinky had spoken out loud what she did not want to create—which was very bad magic.

Very angry, Pinky swayed, off-balance from her large mouse head and her emotions that she squelched deep inside.

"Very well, if you must know, I did have business dealings with the Shadow Fairies some years ago—I admit it," Calisandra said, matter-of-factly.

"What are you talking about…business dealings? You sold your heart to the Shadow Fairies, and I'll never do that."

"Oh…you make it sound so—tawdry," Calisandra retorted, remembering she said the very same thing before accepting.

Again, Calisandra smiled benignly, for Pinky had spoken aloud what she did not want a second time, creating more momentum for its creation. As a powerful Human Fairy, Pinky's words could invoke what she said into reality.

"You know, you're very spunky, just like I was until...." Calisandra stopped in mid-sentence, letting her hands drop to her sides. "We need to speak in private." Calisandra invoked her third eye and leaned into Pinky's third eye to have a private conversation with her that could not be overheard either by spies or by seers using their crystals.

"I didn't have the magical power—and you don't have the magical power—either. If you don't let the Shadow Fairies help you get out of this cell, your sister is doomed to walk in oblivion forever. Markolous would have already killed her if it wasn't for our laws that protect her until the baby is born—then, after she's had her baby—she'll be light for the Lord of the Darkness."

Pinky responded with her third eye for she also did not want to say something aloud that could be heard by a third party. *"Very well—what is the deal—exactly?"* she asked.

"You will take my place and be the heart connection between the Human Fairies and the Shadow Fairies." Calisandra leaned in. *"So, do we have a deal?"*

"Somehow, wandering between two worlds, neither a Human Fairy nor a Shadow Fairy, doesn't have all that much of an appeal—if you know what I mean."

"Okay. Very well. Have it your way, but I need to show you Kokakina's future under Markolous' rule."

"Thank you, but I have my own Rose Crystals."

"Yes, but you don't have the time to get them," Calisandra snapped aloud.

Pinky hesitated but realized she really did need Calisandra's help to get out of the dungeon. She said, "Okay, but can you fix this first?" She pointed to her giant mouse head.

"Of course." Calisandra waved her hand counterclockwise. Flicking her fingers towards Pinky's head, it changed back to its Human Fairy form. "Take my hand. You must see what Kokakina's future will be under Markolous," she said.

Calisandra lifted her other hand and made a full circle. A glowing orb floated in front of them. Their etheric bodies left their physical ones and stepped into it.

Two Magic Mice

The orb of light that held the etheric bodies of Pinky and Calisandra floated over a crystal wall covered in exotic bougainvillea of purple, pink, red, and orange.

The picture-perfect Human Fairy village next to the Crystal Palace lay before them. The sky-blue shutters and handmade red tile roofs of the villagers' cottages basked in the sunlight. In the village square, Pinky and Calisandra materialized, unseen by the throngs of carefree, dancing Human Fairies, spinning and cavorting around a maypole, celebrating springtime. Vendors sold, and circulating customers bought in the marketplace. Drunken Human Fairies weaved in and out of the vendors' stalls. The sound of noisy, carefree children chasing each other around the square filled the air.

"Kidney pies! Get your tasty kidney pies!" shouted the young lad again wandering through the crowd selling the baker's pastries. His

*voice reverberated off of the black walnut timbers of the buildings'
walls. Strapped across his chest, his wooden box full of pies dwarfed
him.*

"It's just as I remember it!" Pinky said.

"Yes—this is now!"

*"Boy, over here. A kidney pie over here," Pinky called out, realiz-
ing how hungry she was. She bent down to smell the enticing aroma
when he passed.*

*"He can't hear you," Calisandra said, "and you can't smell the
pies."*

*Not to be deterred, Pinky reached out to take a pie. She bit
into it. A look of shocked surprise crossed her face. "I can't taste it
—not at all!"*

*Calisandra nodded her head in understanding. "We're in
the Shadow Fairy world now. Shadow Fairies can see and hear
life, but they can't smell or taste the Human Fairy world. They're
very aware of life but they're not part of it."*

*"Yes—I see—it must be a very lonely existence for them until they
come back," Pinky said.*

*"Rosemary. I've got fresh rosemary, thyme, and, acorn
thistle." A young girl's thin, sweet voice floated through the
crowd. Holding her herbs in her spindly arms, she sought to catch
shoppers' attention. Wearing a torn, dirty dress, she sat on the curb
at the corner of the square. Her shoulders slumped with exhaustion.
Her long legs, bowed from of working long hours from a young
age, were folded beneath her.*

*Suddenly, the crowd opened up. Markolous' soldiers, led
by Tithoreus, galloped into the center of the square with a cart
full of logs. The frightened villagers backed off, going inside and
closing their doors and shutters. Tithoreus' sticky fingers latched
onto a stout Human Fairy wearing a blacksmith's leather apron.*

"Unload this cart," Tithoreus ordered. He put his boot into the unfortunate laborer's backside.

"He can't do that!" Pinky said, aghast.

"They're preparing for your sister's burning."

The blacksmith pulled the logs from the cart and dropped them on the ground.

"Stack them upright, you lazy fool—around the center pole." Tithoreus seized a simple farmer, hiding behind a merchant's cart, by the scruff of the neck and dragged him to the center of the square. "Put logs around the other pyres. The traitor queen is to have company in oblivion."

"I didn't want to believe you earlier. I didn't want to believe he would actually go through with it!" Pinky said, slumping against a nearby cart.

"Markolous prepares to feed her light to the Lord of the Darkness —come. I have more to show you—Kokakina's future after the queen is gone."

Reentering the orb, their etheric bodies traveled to the future.

Pinky and Calisandra settled on the ground and left the orb. Around them, the Lost Forest's rich evergreens and purple foliage had all but been destroyed by fire. The magical forest, once full of life, was nothing more than blackened, burnt, and charred stumps where the magical trees once stood.

"I can't bear to look at it," Pinky said.

"Markolous set fire to the Lost Forest."

"But why—why would he do such a horrible thing?"

"Because the magical creatures who lived here rose up against him."

"Where are the animals now?" Pinky asked, afraid to know the answer....

"They're all dead. If your brother is not stopped, this is what is to come."

"I've seen enough."

"I have one more thing to show you of what will happen if Markolous is not stopped," Calisandra said.

The orb traveled to another time in the future.

Pinky and Calisandra looked down on the village.

"It looks deserted," Pinky said.

"Many have fled Markolous' cruelty. The rest are slaves now."

They stepped from the orb, outside of the Human Fairy village, where in the fields, half-starved Human Fairies of all ages toiled. Tettigards flew up and down the rows. One stopped and lifted a small boy no more than three years old from his mother who was working in the fields. Flying over to a wooden cart, he placed the toddler into it. In the cart, an aged man, old beyond his years, sat on the cart's wooden bench, holding a two-year old in his lap.

An old female Human Fairy, bent over and toiling in the field, lifted a bundle of wheat far too heavy for her. She stumbled and fell. The Tettigard flew down over her. He cracked his whip made from the hides of the magical creatures that once lived in the Lost Forest across her legs.

"Get up, you worthless hag, and get into the cart." The Tettigard whipped her as she struggled to rise. But she did not cry out.

"Bessalina! Bessalina!" Pinky cried, recognizing the poor wretch as the giant insect grabbed Bessalina with his sticky arm appendages and dragged her towards the cart. "Stop!"

"You can't help her."

"I beg you—show me no more."

"It's not just Flanyanna who'll go to oblivion if Markolous has his way…."

"What do you mean?"

"Your half-brother sold the life force—the light—of all creatures on Kokakina to the Lord of the Darkness to gain the throne."

"You mean…?"

"Every Human Fairy and all magical creatures will be doomed to live in darkness for eternity…. The rose crystals chose you, but you already know that, don't you?"

"Yes. At first I thought it was about making sure Flanyanna maintained her rule. I've known for sometime it was about her daughter, but I didn't want to…"

"Believe it?"

"Yes. I pushed it away."

"Until now?"

"Yes."

"Yes," Pinky repeated, sobbing for the loss of everything she held dear.

After a bit, she regained some composure and said, "I've seen enough. Take me back."

Their etheric bodies returned to the dungeon cell. Calisandra spied a spider crawling up the wall. Slapping her hand down fast, she snatched the bug and popped it into her mouth. Her eyes squinted as she smacked her lips, munching on her snack.

"Now, you understand why you must take the Shadow Fairies' deal." Calisandra's voice dripped with the fatigue of almost three hundred years of wandering between the two worlds.

"If I take—" Pinky asked through her third eye, feeling sick to her stomach. *"—the Shadow Fairies' offer, they'll intervene?"*

"Yes," Calisandra said through her third eye.

"And what of my sister?"

"She'll live out the rest of her incarnation as a Shadow Fairy and return to the Human Fairy world. It's the only way you can save her from the Lord of the Darkness and oblivion."

"And the baby, the princess?"

"Tonight is the Blood Moon," Calisandra replied.

"Tonight, the princess will be born on the Blood Moon?"

"Exactly. If you take the deal, the Shadow Fairies will rise up and help you save her. They're offering you their allegiance."

"Markolous will surely kill the princess, too," Pinky still spoke through her third eye. She still hesitated. "Deals with Shadow Fairies never work out the way you want them to," she said aloud. Her eyes darted around the cell. She was desperate to find a way to get out without help from her new cellmate.

"We don't have much more time," Calisandra said.

"It's just that the Rose Crystal prophecy didn't tell me..."

"Foolish girl. Look at me. I'm old and decrepit. My three hundred years are almost done. It's too late for me even though our bloodline resonates most fully with the heart matrix that lives in the Rose Crystal and connects us all to the Human Fairy world— even to our mother planet, Earth."

"The Shadow Fairies need a new heart, a young Pink Fairy heart?" Pinky asked with her third eye.

Calisandra nodded.

Pinky stood still, for a moment that seemed like an eternity.

"I'll accept the Shadow Fairy offer with a few conditions."

"There are no conditions with the Shadow Fairies."

"There are always conditions," Pinky stated with her third eye.

Pinky's mother had learned the hard way about conditions. She had mistakenly trusted Pinky's father, the king. The fine print in the documents she had signed after the king married Markolous' mother had contained conditions that disowned her own child, Pinky.

Calisandra stood still, mumbling to herself, then said, *"All right, what are your conditions?"*

"That I maintain all my magical powers."

"Agreed."

"And..."

"I thought you said you had one condition?"

"No, I said conditions."

"Very well! What is your other condition?"

"The Shadow Fairies don't take my heart now."

"Impossible!"

"Let me finish. They wait until after the princess is safely away," Pinky said with her third eye. She had no idea how to keep the princess safe after her birth, or where to hide her for sixteen years until she came into her magical powers to lead the fight to become the new ruler of Kokakina. Pinky only knew she needed more time.

Calisandra's eyes drifted up as she went into a trance. After a moment she looked back at Pinky and spat out a piece of leftover spider shell. *"All right. They agreed."*

"Not to take my heart yet?"

"Shhhh…yes."

Pinky sighed in relief.

"You've got three days. The time starts when the princess is born," Calisandra said aloud.

"Okay. I agree to those terms."

Pinky had gained three extra days to find a way to save the princess from Markolous, who would surely kill her.

"We have a deal then?"

Pinky nodded in agreement, then flinched as Calisandra briefly touched Pinky's third eye with her right hand.

Taking Pinky's right hand, Calisandra placed it on her own third eye. "Hold your other hand over your third eye," she said.

"Is this really necessary?"

"Now give me your hands and turn your palms up!" Calisandra said smoothly. "This is standard protocol."

She took Pinky's hands into her gnarled ones and turned them palms up. She peered intently at Pinky's hands, reading her life line. Calisandra's body stiffened, and she shot Pinky a sharp look. For a moment, Pinky pulled her hands away, fearing Calisandra saw something that might block her from saving the princess.

"What? What is it?"

"Nothing—I'm just admiring your young soft hands. I use to have soft hands a long time ago. Now don't be afraid," Calisandra said, taking Pinky's right wrist and flipping it over.

She bent down and punctured Pinky's flesh with her fang-like canines. Pinky's eyelids fluttered.

"Let it in. Let in the Shadow Fairy world. Let the Shadow Fairy world in," Calisandra droned hypnotically.

Pinky's warm, red blood dripped onto the cell's floor. She looked down at the bleeding wound and swayed woozily. Her blood felt cold as it coursed through her veins. She shivered and surrendered to her fate.

"Oh, come on. It's really not so bad to live as a Human Fairy but tied to the Shadow Fairy world—I should know. I've done it for almost three hundred years," Calisandra cajoled.

"Three hundred years is a long time to wander, especially without my heart," Pinky fretted. For the first time in her life, she was terrified of what the future would bring her. This was uncharted territory. Why had the Rose Crystals not revealed to her that she was to wander Kokakina without her heart? Her body tensed and convulsed, processing all her feelings.

"Aren't you almost done?" Trepidation and anxiety tightened Pinky's voice. The princess was being born this very night, and she needed to get going.

"Patience!" Calisandra wrapped the torn petticoat around the wound on Pinky's wrist three times.

"Ouch—that hurts!" Pinky blanched from the tight binding.

"It's supposed to hurt," Calisandra crooned. She circled around Pinky clockwise, then counterclockwise. "You're a Human Fairy who lives in the Human Fairy world, but you do the bidding of the Shadow Fairy world. Above and Below. Light and Dark. Good and Evil in all dimensions, galaxies, and portals."

Calisandra repeated the incantation three times.

"There now, that wasn't so bad now, was it?"

"I don't know—I'll tell you later."

"Now, let's see here." Calisandra looked at the empty chains. She raised her arm. Suddenly, a purple ether emanated from her hands and encircled Pinky.

"What is this part?"

"Shhhh. We need a replacement for you, dearie." Calisandra spread her hands, and the purple ether traveled to the spot where Pinky had been suspended and swirled around. She nodded her head, and an exact replica of Pinky hung above the floor, suspended in mid-air. The facsimile moaned.

"Perfect, if I do so say myself," Calisandra said.

"That's good, really good," Pinky said. Her captors would not know the difference until she and Calisandra were long gone.

"Well, that's high praise coming from you."

Pinky wanted to ask Calisandra many questions about how her mother was before she became the late king's mistress. Now was not the right time.

"It's…I mean, nice to meet a relative on my mother's side."

"I suppose you want to know about your mother before she was the late king's mistress?"

"Of course, you read my thoughts."

"Naturally…."

"S-o-o-o—you must already know—I want to see my sister."

"Oh, no, that's not possible. It's in the opposite direction."

"I don't care about that. I still want to see her."

"But what if we get caught, then what?" Calisandra said.

"I'll take that chance," Pinky said. Seeing Calisandra was still hesitating, she added, "I won't leave the dungeon until I have."

"Okay. Have it your way—just like your mother—but I'm not going with you."

"I don't know what cell she's in." Pinky knew she had to get to Flanyanna and figure out a way to get the princess out of the dungeon after she was born. She now spoke through her third eye again, just in case anyone was viewing with their crystals. *"Look— you have to go with me, I can't go alone. It'll be too dangerous if I do. I don't know the way. Besides, in three days, I'll be the new connec-*

tion between the Shadow Fairy world and the Human Fairy world. Too much is at stake for you, Calisandra. I'm your replacement."

"Very well," Calisandra said, making no further protest. She did not want to lose her replacement. "I don't like this. It's highly irregular, but I'll go with you."

She knew that the bond Pinky had with Flanyanna was no different than the one she had with her sister, Lunamilla. She softened, remembering her younger sister when they were children. "It is hard to let go of someone when you don't want to, isn't it?"

Yes, I knew you'd understand."

"All right. I'll show you the way," Calisandra said. "But, you have to promise me that you'll leave right after seeing her."

"Okay, I promise."

"And remember," Calisandra said with a hard look at Pinky, "nothing is what it appears to be."

She pointed her finger at Pinky and then spun it around to point to herself. They morphed into small field mice on the dirty, straw laden floor.

"Follow me," the mouse that was Calisandra instructed.

Squeezing under the cell's door, they escaped and scampered down the corridor, deeper into the Tower of the Forgotten.

A single candle barely lit the confined space of Flanyanna's cramped, dirty cell. As she lay on the straw cot in the corner, her back seized suddenly in a strong contraction.

The mice entered the cell.

"Pinky? I knew you would come," she whispered.

"Flan." Pinky transformed back into herself and knelt by her sister's cot.

Calisandra stood back in the shadows not wanting her presence to complicate things.

"I'm so glad you're here," Flanyanna said, and her swollen stomach contracted again. "You'll be the first to see the princess."

"She needs a doctor," Pinky said to Calisandra.

Calisandra went to the cell door fearing the guards. "I'm sorry, but we can't intervene. If the guards see us, it'll endanger the baby."

"Pinky, who's with you?"

"It's a long story, but she's my aunt, on my mother's side."

"I didn't know your mother had a sister."

"Until tonight, I didn't either."

"Pinky, we have to go now," Calisandra said.

"No. I'm not going until a doctor comes."

"Don't worry about that. I've already made arrangements, Doc Tikkum," Flanyanna gasped as another contraction came.

"Doc Tikkum? Who's Doc Tikkum?" Pinky did not know a Doc Tikkum.

"He's a wonderful Tarragonian healer. He cares for all the prisoners in the Tower of the Forgotten. He promised he would be here for me when my time came."

"But he's a healer for the dungeon. Surely you would like a court healer?"

Flanyanna started to breathe more heavily. She shook her head and strongly grasped Pinky's arm. Her words came out in fits and starts. "Get—me—Doc—Tikkum."

"All right. I'll go get him. Where does he live?" Pinky asked.

"He lives by the stone bridge that goes over the stream that separates the two villages."

"Just keep breathing deeply."

"Pinky, you've never had a child! What are you talking about?"

"I know that. I know that, but deep breathing is always good."

"Pinky, we have to go now," Calisandra said again. She raised her arm over her head and transformed back into a mouse.

Don't worry, Flan. I'll be right back soon with the doctor," Pinky said. Raising her arm, she tugged her left earlobe, and also became a mouse. She had gotten her magical powers back. The Shadow Fairies had kept their promise.

The two mice scurried under the cell door, leaving Flanyanna.

The Queen's Necklace

Pinky's betrayal and refusal to read Flanyanna's Rose Crystal necklace for Markolous had forced him to search far and wide for another female Human Fairy seer. He found her among the Blue Fairies, a nomadic people who wandered across an obscure part of Kokakina. Although not part of the direct royal line, the Blue Fairies produced powerful prophetesses. From a very young age they studied the cosmos and developed their divining powers.

Immediately after sending Pinky to the Tower of the Forgotten, Markolous sent an envoy to the Blue Fairies to engage in negotiations for the hand of Evila, the very gifted daughter of the lord of the Blue Fairies. It was believed that, after Pinky, she was the most powerful prophetess in the land. Starting as a child, Evila had spent her nights studying the messages in the stars. She was adept at reading Rose Crystals which meant she could read the queen's necklace.

Markolous did not want to admit it, but there was no denying that a talented female Human Fairy was needed to read the queen's necklace. As much as he feared, hated, and envied feminine power, he needed a female to access the Rose Crystal necklace and foretell the future.

In the Throne Room of the Crystal Palace, the heads of the noble families, the king's advisors, and the king's spies feasted at a long dining table waiting to meet Markolous' betrothed. They sat on benches upholstered with rich, spider-silk velvet, gorging themselves on quail, mutton pies, and copious quantities of dark cherry wine. But, behind the pomp and grandeur they displayed, those present at the banquet feared their privileged stations in life were jeopardized. Everyone at court was disturbed by the recent changes that Markolous had enacted, especially his intention to burn a former monarch and his introduction of Tettigards into the fabric of Human Fairy society. Things that had never happened before were now part and parcel of their everyday lives.

Markolous surveyed his courtiers as they all stuffed their faces with good dry and sweet wines and exotic delicacies of red walnuts, purple plump figs and medjool dates.

"I knew nothing would come from his majesty's offer of marriage to that ungrateful upstart cousin of his…," commented one august counselor. He, like all the advisors, was cloaked in a long, spider-silk robe, the borders decorated with astrological signs that identified his importance and station in society.

"So did I. I said so right from the beginning," replied his self-important colleague.

"Strange—no one has seen her lately in court," the first advisor remarked.

The two looked at each other. They nodded sagely, but said no more. Pinky's present whereabouts were a mystery and these counselors were world-wise enough to know when questions should not be asked.

At the head of the table, Markolous surveyed his courtiers with contempt. "Look at them. They're all worthless," he said, leaning back in his chair.

"Sire, Evila of the Blue Fairy line, your future bride and the new seer, is here," Tithoreus said.

"Where? I don't see her!" Perking up, Markolous scanned the crowd, hoping to catch a glimpse of his new seer and betrothed. He hadn't seen her in years. He had been told she had grown to be an alluring beauty, and he loved beauty almost as much as he loved—power.

"Why, Sire, she waits out in the hall. She's waiting for you to introduce her to court."

"Well, I see. Very good. Well, don't just stand there. Bring her in. I want to see her."

At that moment, the crystal gong floating near the door that announced the entrances of Markolous and Flanyanna at the trial sounded. Someone of importance was coming.

The advisors glanced at each other, their eyes filling with anticipation for the entrance of Markolous' betrothed.

Unnoticed by anyone, a black raven flew in an open window and settled on a rafter, high above the festivities.

Markolous stood up. Taking their cue from the king, everyone else rose as well to meet the Human Fairy who would be their new queen.

An ancient Human Fairy with a long, gray beard, bent over from living almost three hundred years, hobbled forward. He wore a purple and burgundy robe embedded with crystals. He cleared his throat. "Your Majesty, Princess Evila, the Blue Fairy, our future queen and, the new soothsayer of the land." He ceremoniously struck the floor with his magical rowan and crystal staff.

A strange clicking and clacking sound could be heard. Those of lesser social status who were in attendance, but not seated, stepped aside for the Blue Fairy to enter.

Evila teetered and tottered in on gold and blue satin platforms. Her delicate, gauzy gown was a symphony of complementary shades of sky blue that floated seamlessly in the air. The gown's silky chiffon fabric flowed with sublime grace.

She is pleasing to the eye..., Markolous thought.

On her head, an oversized ornate bird's nest hat swayed unsteadily. Its overall shape was like what on Earth became known as a top hat. It was covered with peacock and duck feathers, and miniature blue roses. A silver birdcage veil with a striking lime-green band covered the bride's face. Suddenly, she stumbled.

Everyone gasped, thinking how difficult it must be to balance on those shoes.

Markolous scrutinized his exotic cousin as she stood unsteadily before him. She bowed, and losing her balance, tripped again.

"Cousin," she said.

She reached for him and kissed him on his third eye without removing her veil. Recoiling from the very scratchy kiss, Markolous turned away from her and looked at Tithoreus.

"She's drunk," he said, softly.

Tithoreus leaned in. "Her nervousness at the prospect of meeting you, her king and future husband, must have prompted her to fortify her nerves with a drink."

"*One* drink?" Markolous asked skeptically, his eyebrows rising up practically to his hairline.

Evila swayed back and forth before Markolous. He was quite prepared to dismiss any protests that she was not of noble enough birth, but he had not counted on her showing up to their betrothal party besotted.

"Welcome to my court, dear cousin," he said and bowed to her. Then, there was a long awkward pause where no one said anything. Tithoreus leaned in so only Markolous could hear him. "Sire, ask her about her journey."

"Your journey here…I fear you had an arduous time," Markolous said.

"The desert winds were beastly," Evila said. She burped and curtsied. Her bird hat fell forward, covering her eyes.

There was a rumbling in the Throne Room, the sound of a raven cackling.

Evila's hat toppled down over her brow. Giggling, she pushed it up and stumbled off to the side. Regaining her balance, the Blue Fairy held her hat in place with one hand.

"Excuse me." She bowed and smiled.

Markolous snapped his fingers, and the steward came forward. "Help her remove that ridiculous hat."

Evila motioned to the steward to stop. She waved her hand over her hat and it disappeared. The crowd applauded, more in relief of having a distraction from the awkwardness of Evila's drunken state than for the magical act itself. Evila sought to regain her composure as she fixed her tousled blue-black hair.

"Your Majesty, with all due respect, may I suggest you let Princess Evila try on the queen's necklace?" an advisor said with an ingratiating smile at the new queen-to-be.

Evila's eyes glinted greedily. She coveted the queen's necklace since she was a child. "Oh yes, Sire. Please, let me try it on."

She had envisioned that one day she would wear the queen's necklace around her neck. The other children, even the adults, had laughed when she told them she would someday wear the necklace and be queen. And now, after all these years, she would prove then wrong and have her wish.

High above on one of the wooden rafters, the raven fluffed its feathers in a huff.

How dare she! That Blue Fairy interloper reaching out for my necklace! it squawked silently to itself.

"Yes, give her the necklace," Markolous said, snapping his fingers. He needed someone who could read the Rose Crystals and he wanted to make sure Evila could to do so before they wed.

A page came forward with a red satin pillow on which rested the Rose Crystal necklace that Markolous had taken from Flanyanna. Markolous lifted it up. Evila smiled. Lowering her head, he placed it around her neck. Instantly, it lit up to the approving applause of everyone present.

"The necklace looks beautiful on you, and it's perfect for *my* queen," Markolous quipped. He was delighted and relieved. She was truly a seer; her line still had magical powers.

Her glassy, inebriated eyes took in the luxurious surroundings, the gold, velvet, and gems that decorated the Throne Room.

"I could get used to this lifestyle...," she whispered ever so softly to herself.

"How about a glass of—how about some grapes?" Markolous asked, indicating that she should sit next to him. He motioned to a servant to attend to Evila. Leaning into the servant, he whispered, "Don't let her have anything more to drink. Give her some grapes instead."

"But, Sire, what if she asks for more wine?" the servant asked.

"Just give her grapes. Can't you see she's already drunk?"

As instructed, the servant picked up a large platter of purple, green and red grapes as Evila sank into the exquisite, goose down stuffed chair next to her betrothed. With her tapered fingers and long, baby-blue lacquered nails, she popped a few grapes from a platter the servant offered into her mouth. She squeezed them with her cuspids and their pulp oozed throughout her mouth. She picked up a napkin and delicately wiped away the juice dripping down from the corner of her mouth while smiling into Markolous' eyes.

"These grapes are very sweet." She was very aware that Markolous intended to burn the former Human Fairy queen, his sister. From a very young age, Evila had been taught to view life politically and had learned to take a philosophical view of the grim things that could happen. Human Fairy nobility and those who sought to improve their position often engaged in gruesome and cruel acts to gain and keep power. It was just the way things were.

"Will our cousin, Pinky, dine with us tonight?"

"No. She wanted to stay home," Markolous said, offering a disarming smile, believing Pinky was still in his dungeon.

"She does relish nature and the forest animals in preference to the royal court and its—complexities," Evila observed.

This conversation was all part of the power game. Evila's view, colored by her new position, allowed her to choose to forget the misfortunes of her female cousins, Markolous' sisters—Flanyanna and Pinky.

"Let's not talk about our cousin tonight." Markolous studied Evila's alabaster face. Smiling, he revealed his own well-defined cuspids, reducing Pinky to being a distant cousin, not his sister.

Satisfied that Pinky was no longer a threat to her ambitions, Evila popped another grape into her mouth as she fingered the Rose Crystal necklace around her neck.

She inhaled Markolous' strong, masculine scent, a mixture of pine, frankincense, porcini, and something wild. A tingling feeling of excitement and danger filled her senses. It was puzzling. She had studied the aromatic essences of Kokakina since childhood, but had never smelled this scent before and could not place it. She found it to be alien, but very exciting.

She smiled back and popped another grape into her mouth, crushing it and relishing the flavor. She understood this chess game very well. It was well known that Pinky had turned Markolous down many years ago for Elfman.

Foolish cousin. To have the opportunity to be queen and reject it. Markolous must marry to produce an heir and he needs a seer who can read the Rose Crystal, she thought.

Markolous leaned in close over her torso to smell her scent of ginger and jasmine and unclasped the necklace.

"You're not the queen yet, my dear...," he said.

In his hand, the necklace immediately darkened. He handed the queen's necklace back to the page.

"Take this back to my chamber, for now...."

With an elegant bow, the page took the necklace and placed it back on the pillow. He ran across the floor as fast as his young legs could carry him and out of the Throne Room to do the king's bidding.

The raven took off from its perch on the rafters and followed closely behind. But at that very moment, the court musicians and dancers entered the Throne Room and blocked the raven's exit. It frantically fluttered above the door—waiting for another chance.

Grasping Evila's hand, Markolous rose to his feet. Taking the cue, she rose to stand beside him. He addressed the room. "Today, I would like to announce my betrothal to Evila, princess of the Blue Fairies, soon to be my queen. Let the dances begin!"

The royal crowd cheered its approval.

The court musicians broke into an elegant gavotte, and dancers took their places around a maypole that descended from the ceiling. Colorful ribbons swirled about it and pirouetted into the dancers' hands.

Unnoticed in the uproar, the raven finally flew out through the door.

Streamers floated and intertwined as the dancers capered about the pole. The cords created a complex pattern, tying and untying themselves as the dancers' nimble feet skipped across the crystal floor. Other Human Fairies climbed up on trapezes, vaulting through the air. The airborne dancers soared from one end of the Throne Room's domed ceiling to the other.

"Come and dance with me!" Markolous bellowed to Evila over the music, reaching for her hand.

"Your Majesty, I'm not wearing dancing shoes."

"It's expected that we dance together. It's our custom."

"I don't know the court dances. I only know the folk dances of my people."

"Foolish girl. Take my hand. Everyone's watching us."

The small hairs on the back of Evila's neck rose. Perspiration droplets trickled down her back. She sensed that something was not quite right, that she was in grave danger. She should have paid more attention to the stories about the female Human Fairies whose bodies were found in the river and moat.

But after a moment, she dismissed her reservations. She would never again have this opportunity, to marry the king and wear the queen's necklace. Since she was a child, these were the things she wanted above all. She slipped off her platform shoes and extended her hand to Markolous.

The stately strains of the gavotte gave way to a lively tune that drowned out her disquieting thoughts.

"Can you polka?" Markolous asked.

Evila nodded, feeling a red-hot flush infuse her body as Markolous took hold of her feminine hand in his masculine one. Joining the frolicking crowd, they danced their way across the crowded floor. Then, they polkaed around the maypole staring with lust into each other's eyes.

The music filled the room as she twirled with her betrothed—and they even somersaulted together through the air, to everyone's delight.

Surely, things will turn out better for me than it did for them, she thought, thinking of Flanyanna and Pinky.

Passion is fleeting. Still, she'll be a source of great entertainment for as long as the novelty lasts, Markolous thought as he lifted Evila high up in the air—*or as long as she lasts.*

Looking down the crossing hallways and trying to catch up with the servant with the Rose Crystal necklace, the raven zigged and zagged down an open stone corridor of the Crystal Palace.

Before it, on her hands and knees, a wisp of a maid with pale blue lips scrubbed the hallway's frigid, inlaid crystal floor. As the servant girl placed her natural bristle brush in the bucket, she heard fluttering wings. Looking up, she saw a mass of blue-black feathers hurtling towards her. Sharp black talons loomed so closely before her eyes that she was looking at them cross-eyed. Thoroughly alarmed, she shrieked and fell to the floor.

Seeing her, the now squawking bird frantically flapped its wings to arrest its flight and avoid the prostrate housemaid. Only partially successful, it splashed into the bucket, spewing suds everywhere. Drenched from head to toe, the girl raised herself up on her elbows and found herself eye to eye with the raven.

Doused in lathery water, the very unhappy, dripping-wet black bird addressed her. "Excuse me, dearie, can you direct me to the king's bedchamber?"

The maid was aware that some of the royalty were magically endowed and could shapeshift, but this was the first time she had ever been in the presence of one. Thoroughly rattled, the servant girl dropped her face onto the cold stone floor and pointed an unsteady finger to her left. No sooner had she pointed, the page carrying the now empty pillow that had held the necklace turned the corner on his return to the Throne Room.

"Thank you, dearie." The raven shook off the soapy residue and a few sodden feathers fell to the floor. It wobbled down the hallway towards the king's bedchamber.

The maid furrowed her brow, relieved no harm had come to her. She rose to her hands and knees and wiped her wet hands on her apron. She knew the bird had to be an enchanted Human Fairy—the enchantment concealing its true identity.

"I wonder who just asked me for directions?" She looked about. No one else had seen the bird, not even that snotty page who never looked at her. Shrugging, she dropped her scrubbing brush back into the remaining, lathered water.

"I'll not stick my nose into the new king's business...," she admonished herself as she bent back down to her labors. "There are fates far worse than cleaning floors." Everyone in the household was talking about what happened to Markolous' sister, the former queen.

Stationed outside the king's bedchamber, two Tettigard guards stood at attention, blankly staring forward. They wore black, billowy pants and black leather, double breasted, sleeveless vests that showed off each one's two pairs of muscular insect biceps.

Unseen, the raven stood below them. It cocked its head, first to the left and then to the right. The guards' bodies stiffened. Their eyes turned glassy and their heads drooped down.

The raven pushed open the bedchamber door with its black beak and entered the king's bedchamber. Once inside, the bird transformed into a very old Human Fairy who closed the door behind her with fingers that were still raven claws.

This was Lunamilla, Pinky's mother. Her long life had involved numerous instances of shapeshifting into the raven form. She had done so enough times that this raven form was bleeding permanently into her Human Fairy form and her hands were now always bird claws.

Her forehead bore a tattoo of a spiral with three arched black birds over her third eye. Her glistening green eyes that darted bird-like about had no brows to frame them. With charcoal black tattoos encircling them, they looked like two orbiting planets. Her lips were stained with the pigment of purple lumen flowers found in the Lost Forest's meadows. The potato sack dress she wore was of coarse, cocoa-brown muslin and fell straight from her shoulders. Two rows of brown and black feathers trimmed her shoulders and drooped down wrapping around her hips.

For a brief moment, she leaned forward. Putting her ear to the door, she listened intently. Nothing. Wasting no time, she looked around the room. Sensing there was something under the bed, she crouched down and looked. Reaching under, she pulled out a pair of female bloomers. After examining them for a moment, she threw them back with a disgusted sigh. Disturbed by the movement of her arm, six gold bracelets on it, gifts from the late king honoring the births of their children, jangled in harmony.

Again, she scanned the bedchamber with her clairvoyant third eye. She was drawn to a leather-bound trunk in the corner. Taking a moment to study the double strands of various ornamental crystals on the trunk's hinges, she wobbled over and jostled the lock with one of her claws.

"Now this has possibilities." She smacked her lips. It was securely fastened. With a twirl of a left hand clawed finger, she invoked a spell that released the latch.

"I haven't lost my touch."

Lifting up the trunk's lid, she rummaged through the box's contents but didn't find what she was looking for. "It's got to be here somewhere," she muttered. Disgruntled, she let the lid drop back down.

She plopped down on the bed and tapped her claws on the spider-silk bedspread beneath her. Bouncing a bit, she felt the quality and luxurious softness of the densely woven fabric. She stroked the fine spider threads. "Oh—yes—yes," she ruminated. She stretched out her arms in sublime pleasure. Her dark green eyes blinked a few times in disbelief. Above her head, Flanyanna's glowing Rose Crystal necklace dangled from the bed's canopy.

"The queen's necklace—you were here all the time," she gleefully cackled. It was what she desired most when she was younger. Still chortling, she rose unsteadily to her feet. Reaching her right claw fingers toward the necklace, she snagged it before losing her balance and toppling back down. She rolled off the bed onto the floor, holding her prize close to her heart.

"I found you. I knew you wouldn't hide from me. You should have been mine."

Happy to have a female Human Fairy imbued with magical talent holding it, the queen's necklace glowed and grew brighter.

"Never you mind. Don't worry. You're in good hands now."

She caressed the amulet. A purple ether emanated from her right hand and encircled it. Pointing her right clawed fingers, the ether swirled and traveled up to the spot where the queen's necklace had been inside the bed's canopy. With a quick nod of her head, the ether coalesced, and an exact replica of the necklace hung above the floor, suspended in mid-air, creating a fake just as Calisandra had created for Pinky in Pinky's cell.

Changing back to her raven form, she picked up the dropped real queen's necklace in her beak and flew out the open window above the four poster king's bed.

Out over the quaint village, the raven flew toward the Lost Forest. In the distance, the Còrcair Mountains provided silent witness. The black bird disappeared with the queen's necklace into the gathering darkness.

Knock at the Door

Waiting for the Blood Moon eclipse, crickets chirped beneath the star-studded night sky. The creek that separated the Human Fairy village from the Tarragonian village rippled over the water-smoothed rocks lying on its bottom, a gentle, hypnotic sound. Smoke ribboned from the stone chimneys of the Tarragonians' cottages. Their village was called Happy Hollow—a strange name for a place that was anything but happy.

Just as Flanyanna had told Pinky, Doc Tikkum's cottage was at the edge of the Tarragonian village closest to the stone bridge that led to the Human Fairy village. His home was dark except for a sliver of silver smoke that rose up out of the chimney and drifted into the midnight sky. It was one of the few houses in the village that was more than one story. The extra height was necessary to accommodate the cupboard beds for Doc Tikkum's family that climbed up the cottage walls. Doc Tikkum took great pride in designing and building these thirteen bunk beds for his family, one for each of his children and the one he shared with his wife.

Tucked into their cupboard beds, the twelve Tikkum children were fast asleep. Mother Tikkum's snoring and occasional short snorts were the only sounds breaking the silence.

Pounding at the door broke the restful tranquility and startled Doc Tikkum awake. Disoriented, he abruptly sat up and smacked his head on the exposed low-beamed ceiling above his sleeping loft. Though he was often woken up at odd hours during the night, being jarred from a deep sleep was always a shock.

"After all these years you'd think I'd have learned by now not to sit up so quickly," he groggily moaned, talking to himself and rubbing his bruised head as he pulled the quilted blanket off his clawed feet. "It's funny and I don't know why, but everyone always needs me in the middle of the night."

A lump developed in the center of his forehead, making him look more like a dragon than a mutant lizard.

Still half asleep, his wife rolled over and mumbled, "It's the queen's time to have her baby." Her eye popped wide open. "Don't answer the door—I'm frightened."

"Now, Mother."

Mother Tikkum could not contain her worry for their safety with her husband going out at all hours of the night. It was well known since Markolous took over that he encouraged Human Fairies to abuse Tarragonians. "We're being targeted and scape-goated even more than before he came into power," she fretted.

Doc Tikkum patted her shoulder. "Now, stop your worrying. Just stay in bed and I'll be back before the family is up."

"Oh, that's just it. What if you don't come home? What will become of us?" Trembling, she pulled the covers up over her mouth.

"Now, now. Let's not talk like that. All will be well," Doc Tikkum said. He had lived with his wife for thirty years and knew how to console and comfort her fears and anxieties.

"I wonder who they sent. It's not a stinking Peccarey. My nose would tell me if it was."

Now wide awake, Mother Tikkum sniffed the air with her long, wide nose that turned slightly to the right. It usually gave her an answer to the caller's identity before they opened the door.

Doc Tikkum crawled down the wall, his grasping toes balancing and supporting him all the way.

Another loud knock at the door.

"Hurry! Answer the door before they wake up all the children," Mother Tikkum said.

At the outer hearth Doc Tikkum gathered his warm, freshly hand washed clothes from where Mother Tikkum had hung them up to dry.

"If you don't mind, I'd like to put my pants on first, Mother."

"Shhhh. Don't talk so loud—the children."

"All right," he whispered.

Doc Tikkum stood on the cold, dried mud floor and fastened the last button on his heavy wool britches as he went to the front door.

"No, wait! Husband, look out the window first."

"Why, Mother? There is no cause for alarm."

"But, what if it's a Tettigard?" she whispered. "They're everywhere now.

"Tettigards don't eat Tarragonians," he whispered back. "You know that."

Even though his words relieved her, Mother Tikkum still worried. She plopped back down on her straw pillow covered in coarse natural muslin, hoping the caller in the night would not awaken any of their twelve children.

Doc Tikkum slipped his linen shirt on over his head. With its rather large bump, his head now definitely had a dragon appearance.

"This floor is unusually cold this morning," he whispered.

"What's this? Complaining about cold feet when our queen is about to give birth in that deplorable Tower of the Forgotten dungeon? Umph—and you're complaining about cold feet."

"You're right, Mother."

Mother Tikkum raised herself up and looked down.

"You look strange? Whatever happened to your head?" Even as she voiced her concern, she somehow felt his appearance, although different, was quite becoming on him. "Your shirt is untucked," she added as an afterthought.

"Thank you, Mother, you're a good wife."

Doc Tikkum pushed his shirt down into his trousers.

"Hurry! Answer the door."

He peered out the leaded glass paned arched window.

"Who is it? Tell me who it is? Who did they send to fetch you to delivery the queen's baby?" Mother Tikkum asked.

"I don't know. It's strange."

"What do you mean?"

"I mean, I don't see anyone." Doc Tikkum opened the front door and looked outside. "Hello? Is anybody there?" Being a creature of science, he was perplexed. Seeing nothing, he added, "Maybe it was just the wind."

"Wind? What wind?" Mother Tikkum asked. "I don't hear any wind." In her anxiety, her color changed from blue to yellow. "My nerves. My poor nerves."

"Since the children are still asleep, let's just go back to bed," Doc Tikkum suggested.

"Sleep? I can't sleep now," Mother Tikkum said. Feeling safe to come downstairs, she lifted the crazy quilt off of her ample figure. "I'll make us a good pot of hot tea. Just think— in a few hours, you could be delivering the queen's baby."

"Very well. I'll have to get up anyway to make the rounds at the dungeon."

Mother Tikkum huffed and puffed her way down the wall in her muslin nightgown, using the suction pads that she, like all Tarragonians, had on the bottom of their feet.

Doc Tikkum looked out the door again. Nothing. "Strange, very strange," he said, stepping outside to peer into the darkness.

Mother Tikkum stood behind him and looked out too. She squinted her upper lids, almost closing them. Her eyes were hazel, the yellow-brown of an acorn. They were soft and gentle, Human-like. The dark folds around her eyelids lightened in the middle, contrasting her dark irises.

"I distinctly heard a knock at our door," she insisted.

"Well, so did I. But I don't see anybody. Do you?"

"Brrrr—it's cold—just shut the door."

"Yes, it is rather nippy for a summer night. It must be because of the Blood Moon."

Mother Tikkum's round lizard eyes contracted momentarily, then they widened in surprise and alarm as a raven hopped into her house. Suspicion radiated from her depths and her tongue jutted out. She tried to speak, but only "Ahhhh" came out.

"Mother? What is it?" Not having seen the bird, Doc Tikkum didn't understand his wife's distress. He closed the door. "I'll put the kettle on for our tea."

He turned to see Mother Tikkum's eyes bulge and her body turn beet red. With an audible moan she fainted dead away to the dirt floor.

"Mother?" His goose-egged forehead furrowing in concern as he stooped down to lift up his wife.

"You're needed at the Tower of the Forgotten. Queen Flanyanna is ready to deliver her baby." The raven had morphed into Pinky.

Startled, Doc Tikkum jumped up and bumped the back of his head. This time on the front door.

"Ouch!" he groaned. "Not again."

Stepping over Mother Tikkum, Pinky checked out the window. Turning to Doc Tikkum, she asked, "Are you all right?"

"Yes—I hit—never mind." He knelt over his wife.

"We must hurry!" Pinky said.

Mother Tikkum moaned, starting to come back to her senses.

"I can't just leave her. My wife has a nervous condition," the good doctor explained to their unexpected guest.

He helped his wife move unsteadily over to her rocker by the outer hearth.

"Are you the Pink Fairy who lives in the Lost Forest?" a young child's voice asked. The second youngest Tikkum, the youngest who could talk, Tither, surrounded by her still sleeping siblings, peered out from her cupboard bed.

"Yes, I'm one of the Pink Fairies who live in the woods," Pinky answered. She looked up at Tither as the tiny tot slithered down the wall between the cupboard beds.

Tither sized Pinky up. Pink was Tither's favorite color and, she knew Pinky was the most powerful Human Fairy on Kokakina. "If you're so powerful, how come you're not going to deliver the princess?" Tither asked.

"Well, I could, but the queen asked for your father," Pinky said. She looked at Tither briefly and then turned her gaze to Doc Tikkum who shrugged his shoulders apologetically.

"Sorry. She's very young and I fear I have spoiled her."

"It's okay. Can we go now?" Pinky asked.

"You don't look all that powerful. You look pink," Tither said.

"Don't talk to our guest that way, Tither," Doc Tikkum admonished.

Seeing that his wife was breathing easily in her favorite rocking chair, Doc Tikkum said, "I'll get my bag."

"A black bird," Mother Tikkum muttered, her eyes closed.

"Tither...," Doc Tikkum started to say.

"Don't worry, Daddy. I'll take care of Mommy."

"Tither, put the tea kettle on," he instructed.

"Okay, Daddy."

Tither checked the kettle for water. Satisfied there was enough, she placed it on the metal crane and pushed it out over the fire.

"You best add a log...."

"Yes, Daddy." She put another log on the fire and sat down on the warm outer hearth near her mother. Her blue color changed to orange as she warmed up.

Doc Tikkum turned back to Pinky. "You know, I examined the queen only yesterday morning, and it looked to me her time isn't for some days now."

"It's her time, all right."

"How do you know?"

"The Blood Moon is tonight, and the princess will be born on the Blood Moon," Pinky said.

Doc Tikkum nodded his head in understanding. He lifted his medicine bag from the wooden peg next to the door and looked back at his comfortable home and family.

"Take good care of Mother."

Tither nodded. "Daddy?"

"Yes, Tither?"

"Will the princess be born in the Tower of the Forgotten?"

Doc Tikkum nodded solemnly to her.

"But, what will happen to her?" Tither asked.

"I don't know, child."

"You can't just leave her in the dungeon. Won't she die there?"

"Tither, you just take care of your mother and I'll take care of the princess."

He winked at her and she giggled.

He walked outside and closed the door behind him and Pinky. Tither peered out one of the leaded glass small windows as the rest of her siblings slept undisturbed. Her round blue eyes grew as big as saucers as Pinky turned back into a raven and flew off into the night.

"Magic," Tither whispered to herself. The raven circled high in the bright, full moonlight. Slithering along the dirt road and across the stone bridge, Doc Tikkum followed the enchanted raven, melting into the darkness.

Doc Tikkum slipped across the moat that led to the Tower of the Forgotten. *How strange. I, a Tarragonian, will attend to the needs of the deposed Human Fairy queen. Only a few months ago, I would have been imprisoned for touching her since I am not a physician of the court. I guess that's how inequities are. They just don't make any sense,* he thought.

The raven hovered next to Doc Tikkum. "I'll meet you inside," Pinky whispered.

"Wait! Where inside?" Doc Tikkum asked frantically.

"Who's there? Identify yourself," the metallic voice of a Tettigard cried out.

At the entrance of the dungeon, a patrolling Tettigard watchman raised up his insect arm. A blackened, steel lantern dangled at the end of a pole he carried. The watchman thrust his lantern towards Doc Tikkum face. The candle inside the lantern shined brightly through its translucent horn panels. In the light, Doc Tikkum's blue-green skin turned red to match the candle's flame.

Out of the corner of his eye, he saw a mouse squeezing under the dungeon door.

Doc Tikkum quickly turned away from the dungeon's gate and faced the sentinel. He wanted to make sure the sentinel did not to notice or suspect anything, for he knew that the mouse was Pinky in her enchanted form.

"You there, Tarragonian, state your business."

Even though he recognized Doc Tikkum and was accustomed to seeing him coming at all hours of the day and night to treat the prisoners in the dungeon, the Tettigard still had to ask. Protocol was protocol and, he was the night watchman. The candle hissed in the lantern from the evening mist.

"I'm Doc Tikkum, the Tarragonian physician to the prisoners of the Tower of the Forgotten. I've come to do my nightly rounds." His voice faltered. Although they did not prey on Tarragonians, Tettigards were an unfriendly species and he was not comfortable around them.

He thought it best not to mention Flanyanna's name, or that the deposed queen was giving birth that very night. She had been treated like any other prisoner of the Tower of the Forgotten and given no special privileges these past months.

"Nightly rounds?" asked the Tettigard.

"Just let me in or you'll answer to the king," Doc Tikkum blustered. Even though he appeared calm on the outside, he shook to his very core.

The giant insect stared blankly at Doc Tikkum for what seemed like an eternity before deciding it was best not to risk the king's displeasure by refusing the Tarragonian doctor admission to the dungeon. He turned and pounded on the thick, wooden door encased in the vertical iron bars of the ponderous dungeon gate with his strong clawed appendage.

After a few moments a small portal in the massive door opened. A hairy snout poked out and snorted.

"Oink."

"Open the door. The Tarragonian doctor is here for his nightly rounds to attend to the prisoners."

The Peccarey smelled Doc Tikkum's familiar, cool, marshy odor. "Oink."

Doc Tikkum braced himself for the grinding sound of the dungeon door opening. The rough-hewn door's red metal hinges protested loudly as they creaked open. Years of moisture from the palace's living crystal walls dripping down onto them had badly corroded them.

He entered and the Peccarey guard closed the worn door with its very rusty hinges behind him.

The prisoners never see the light of day once they enter here, Doc Tikkum thought.

Standing there, waiting for the guard to lock the door to the outside, Doc Tikkum shuddered, fearing he might become the next prisoner of this forgotten, dreadful place. His already green-blue body turned completely blue from the chill as he was assaulted by the frigid cold inside the crystal dungeon. Fortunately for him, he was able to leave every day, but the warm-blooded prisoners under his care knew no end to the cold, dreary dampness and dangerous mold that constantly afflicted them.

"Oink," the creature escorting him grunted. Sensing Doc Tikkum's unease, the guard's feral nose turned towards him and sniffed.

"Indigestion from supper—spider leg soup. I, I fear I'm going to be sick," Doc Tikkum explained.

Adjusting the medical pouch on his back, Doc Tikkum turned his head aside not wanting to inhale the beast's foul, rotten-egg body odor. He felt his supper climbing up his throat.

The Peccarey snuffled. "T's way—Tar'gon," he grunted, garbling out his poor speech like he was swallowing mud. Taking a torch from a rusty red metal bracket on the wall, he started down the corridor on two legs.

By the light of the single moss torch carried by the Peccarey guard, they crept down into the wet crystal stone hole buried underneath the palace.

Maybe my little Tither is right. I wonder if the queen and her baby will live out the night? Doc Tikkum couldn't help thinking.

He adjusted the medical pouch on his back and glanced about to see if the magical mouse was nearby. She was nowhere in sight. The moving crystal spiraling staircase carried them into the depths of the dungeon. Doc Tikkum felt motion sickness rising up in him from the action of the escalator.

He looked up the dungeon's funnel shaft. He glimpsed a full yellow moon above him and felt relief, for it was not yet a full red Blood Moon. He breathed deeply to inhale the last bit of fresh air he would get for the duration of his work in the dungeon that night.

"T's way—Tar'gon," the guard repeated in the guttural Peccarey dialect that Doc Tikkum had come to understand over the years.

The Peccarey swung the torch in the direction of a passage in the wet crystal rock beneath the palace that led away from the queen's cell.

Doc Tikkum panicked.

This isn't the way to the queen's cell! he thought. He looked about—no Pinky.

The guard's hoof scraped across the crystal stone in the corridor.

Fearing he might arouse suspicion if he said anything, Doc Tikkum mutely followed him. It was the custom that the guards would identify those in most need of his care. Maybe that was the reason for this detour.

Frantically, Doc Tikkum looked about again for Pinky or a mouse or a raven, but she was nowhere to be seen.

There are so many tunnels and dead ends. It could take me hours to find the way back to the queen to deliver her baby, he thought.

"How much farther?" he asked. Breathing heavily, he looked down the dark and mysterious narrow passageway. He did not recognize this part of the dungeon, and he thought he knew every inch of it. He rummaged in his medical bag and found a very sharp bone scalpel. Studying the tunnel wall, he scratched an 'X' on it to mark the way back.

They approached the end of the corridor's steep and slippery incline. Moss and mold grew on the now dripping wet stone floors. The Peccarey stopped to rest in front of a dark cell at the end. He pointed his spear at the cell. "T's 'ell."

Using his own torch, he lit a dark one on the wall next to the cell. Unlocking the cell door, he handed the freshly lit torch to Doc Tikkum and proceeded back up the passageway.

"Wait! You're not leaving me here, are you? I don't know how to get out," Doc Tikkum shouted. Somehow, the Peccarey's awful smell was suddenly less offensive. He was not sure if he could find his way back despite the marks he had left on the walls, let alone find Flanyanna's cell.

"Oink," The Peccarey snorted, in the dim light. "There's only 'ne 'ay in and 'ne 'ay out, and 't's t'e same 'ay," he jabbered in his dialect. With no further comment, the guard put his torch in his teeth and dropped on all fours. Moving fast for all his ungainly bulk, he rapidly faded into the darkness and vanished.

"Wait," Doc Tikkum called after him, but his echo was the only reply.

"Wait," he repeated forlornly, shivering.

The chill of the crystal rock seemed to intensify his fear and anxiety. The cell's door opened on its own. The musty smell of mildew blew out and assaulted Doc Tikkum's nose.

"This is all—very strange." He suspected that this unexpected detour had something to do with meeting up with Pinky, or even a spell's illusion. Clutching his medical bag over his shoulder in his left hand, he held the lit moss torch high over his head in his right. He cautiously inched his way into the smelly and dark cell.

"Pinky—Pinky—are you in here?"

A soft moan.

He lifted the torch up higher. Another barely audible moan.

Raising his torch even further, Doc Tikkum inched into the darkened cell with its stale, stagnant, and very wet air.

"Hello? I'm here. Is anybody here?" he called out.

He squinted his eyes to see better. Behind him, the cell door slammed shut, startling him. He looked down. In the dim torch-light, a young female Human Fairy writhed on the ground. From the color of her skin, he could see she was a White Fairy. Suddenly, her breathing stopped, and her blue-green eyes glassed over. A tiny newborn lay on the cold and damp, dungeon floor next to her. Doc Tikkum's eyes opened wide.

She gave birth before dying! he thought.

He could see the infant was a girl. The baby's physical wings fluttered.

"Oh, she lives!"

The tiny infant instinctively but unsuccessfully attempted to wrap her wings about her to create a cocoon to keep herself warm. Doc Tikkum was quite familiar with this action, for all Human Fairy babies did it upon birth. Dropping the torch, Doc Tikkum scooped up the infant in an attempt to keep her warm. He loved all babies.

"Over here! Behind you." He heard a soft cawing come from the darkness of the cell.

Holding the infant in his one arm, Doc Tikkum reached down to scoop up the torch with the other one. Whirling around, he spied the raven standing on a narrow ledge up on one of the cell walls behind him.

"Pinky. It's a girl, a White Fairy baby."

"Shhhh! The walls can hear you. Hurry, we don't have much time," Pinky whispered.

"But, I thought you told me that I was here to deliver the queen's baby?" he asked.

Before Pinky could reply, the baby's color changed to a ghastly ash gray. Doc Tikkum dropped the torch and bent to resuscitate her.

"It's no use," Pinky said. "This child was born sickly and had no chance to survive through the night."

"Then, why am I here?"

"You must put the dead baby in your medical bag."

"I'm not to leave her with her mother?" Doc Tikkum asked, hesitating. He felt it would be the right thing to do.

"No, do as I say."

With no further questions, he did as he was told. Out of respect, he gently rewrapped the baby's wings like she attempted to do on her own and placed the dead infant in his medical bag.

"Now, you must cover the mother up. No one can know she already gave birth or there will be another mother and child lost this night."

"What'ta ya done?"

"I haven't done anything. The Rose Crystal prophecy foretold this child's death this tonight."

Full of doubts, Doc Tikkum covered the young mother's body in the filthy blanket that was beneath her. The enchanted raven examined the covered dead female and was satisfied that Doc Tikkum had successfully hidden that she had already delivered her baby.

"You're going to switch the babies, aren't you?" Doc Tikkum asked in alarm. "That's how you're going to save the princess from Markolous."

"We must save the princess," Pinky said. "Once Flanyanna gives birth—you must switch the babies." She knew what she was asking him to do would be dangerous, but it was the only way the princess could be rescued.

"You're asking me to commit treason. You do know that?" Doc Tikkum blurted out. The ramifications of what Pinky wanted him to do appalled him. He was terrified of what this action meant for him and his family.

"You're the only one that can get to the queen unnoticed, you do know that?" Pinky repeated his question back to him.

Pinky knew it was true, he knew it was true, and soon, Doc Tikkum feared, everyone would know it was true. "I'm sorry, but I can't do that. I have a family. I will deliver the baby, but you'll have to be the one to do the switch and get her out...."

"Very well," retorted the raven. "This way." The enchanted raven skittered toward the cell's door.

"Even if Flanyanna's baby survives the filth and dirt of this dreadful place, what will you do with her? How do you intend to keep her safe?" Doc Tikkum asked.

Before Pinky could answer, the sound of heavy footsteps reverberated down the hallway. With a puff the raven disappeared just before the guard stuck his snouted face inside the cell.

"'Re u 'bout don' 'ere?" he asked.

Doc Tikkum turned to the Peccarey, relieved there would be no questions about the presence of a bird in this cell, deep underground.

"There's nothing more I can do here. She died without giving birth to her child. I lost them both," Doc Tikkum said. His lizard tongue had lied. He was one step closer to committing treason and the light bundle in the satchel on his back seemed to grow much heavier with each word he uttered.

The Peccarey sniffed the air and stiffened. He smelled death.

"Take me to the deposed queen now. There's another baby that needs delivering this night," Doc Tikkum said.

The Peccarey stared at him and turned his head.

"Come on! I'm in a hurry. I'm not familiar with this part of the Tower of the Forgotten. I'm here on the king's orders," Doc Tikkum said.

The Peccarey dropped on all fours and clambered down the narrow passageway. Doc Tikkum slithered closely behind, the dead infant in his medical bag. They stepped on the moving spiral staircase that delved down into the abyss of the Tower of the Forgotten, the most feared place in the land. He looked up the breathing tunnel. The yellow moon was turning red. Doc Tikkum felt his blue reptilian skin shivering.

Droplets fell from the whispering rock crystals, striking him as he passed along the weeping corridor that led to the queen's cell. Burrowing down, they descended into the very pit of the Tower of the Forgotten where Flanyanna's brother had imprisoned her. Buried in the depths of the crystal rock, the queen labored.

Doc Tikkum's long lizard tongue licked his parched, dry lips. He could taste the wall's salty tears in the dripping crystal water. The crystals mirrored his fear for his family, himself, and what would happen to all of Kokakina after this night.

I wonder if I'll get out of here alive tonight? he thought. Suddenly, the flickering of a torch broke the darkness.

Adjusting the dead infant on his back, Doc Tikkum slithered towards the quivering light by the queen's cell.

Born in a Dungeon

Burning torches flared on both sides of the heavy, locked door that led into Flanyanna's cell. The light illuminated the dozing Peccarey guards stationed on each side of the cell's entrance.

Following his own Peccarey guard, Doc Tikkum hurried down the narrow hallway. Suddenly, the walls in the dungeon corridor echoed the scream of a tortured prisoner. Doc Tikkum adjusted his medical bag holding the dead baby on his back.

In front of the sleeping guards, the Peccarey escorting Doc Tikkum stopped and kicked them in their stomachs with one of his hooves.

"Oink th' 'or," he squealed.

Startled and blinking, the odoriferous beasts roused themselves and stood stiffly upright on their back hooves. In front of them, lit by the bright red torches, stood the Tarragonian.

The hairy beasts snorted and jumped back. They feared his touch would change their color forever. The prisoners in the Tower of the Forgotten were among the few who did not fear the touch of the Tarragonian healer. They were already outcasts and were quite willing to forego their prejudices to be treated by him. Unfortunately, their experience did not change this widely held false belief, for they were all trapped in the dungeon and had no contact with the outside world.

"You heard him. Open the door," Doc Tikkum curtly repeated the order.

The hair on the neck of the Peccarey with the cell's key bristled straight up. He fumbled under his uniform's vest to retrieve a circular key chain with many dangling skeleton keys. Jostled against each other, the skeleton keys let out a discordant clank. The guard inserted one into the lock and, with a click, the door opened. The grating sound of the cell door opening echoed off the dungeon wall and reverberated throughout the underground tunnel.

Doc Tikkum entered the crypt-like cell. Gently, he placed his medicine bag onto the dungeon's hard crystal floor as his eyes adjusted to the light of a single candle that also provided the cell's only source of heat.

He overheard one of the guards outside the cell mutter in his dialect, "She 'on't 'ast t' ni'gt."

"Be quiet. She can hear you. Have you no respect?" Doc Tikkum scolded the offender.

In the corner on a dirty, decomposing straw cot, he glimpsed a silhouetted, writhing figure. Flanyanna breathed heavily between her contractions.

These accommodations are not fit for any delivery—let that alone a royal princess, he thought.

He moved towards a narrow ledge that protruded from the wet, crystal wall. On it sat a beeswax candle in a crude bone holder. After his previous visit to attend to Flanyanna, he had left it there. He lifted the meager light source and felt its heat on his cold hands.

"Your Majesty," was all he said.

The candle hissed and spat. Flanyanna moaned, her lips quivering as her labor contractions deepened with each breath.

"Doc Tikkum," was all she said.

He turned towards the guards and ordered, "Bring me hot water and clean rags."

"W're 'posed t' 'ay 'ere 'til t' bab' born," the guard with the keys said with a gulp, revealing his rotting, yellow teeth.

"If the king is unhappy with how this business ends tonight, he'll skin you both alive."

Doc Tikkum drew himself up on his back legs to his full and impressive height, nearly hitting the crystal cell's ceiling. "I told you to go get me some hot water and clean rags—now." His temper rising, he turned a brighter red. His Tarragonian tongue darted out of his mouth. The fury inside him was so strong smoke hurled out of his nostrils and flowed onto the Peccaries. "Now, go, I say—or I'll touch thee!"

Coughing from the smoke, the dimwitted brutes dropped their spears and ran down the dingy hallway with the walls reverberating Doc Tikkum's words.

"Or I'll touch thee!"

Resuming his calm demeanor, he lowered himself down beside the queen, placing the candle on the floor. In the flickering candlelight he saw Flanyanna's belly contract.

Remembering the last several contractions, he could see the timing between them was shortening. He stroked her forehead.

"Is my sister with you?" Flanyanna asked.

He shook his head.

"Psst! I'm here—up here!"

Looking up at the cell's breathing tower, Doc Tikkum saw a tiny inconspicuous field mouse sitting on a narrow, chiseled rim of the shaft. If not for her brilliant jade-green eyes, one would never know she was not just an ordinary mouse.

"Pinky, I knew you would be here," Flanyanna said.

Even though he was not particularly pleased with the green-eyed mouse, Doc Tikkum was relieved that Pinky was there.

"My sister has a way of just showing up in her own time and in her own way," Flanyanna said.

"Yes, I've noticed that...." He glared up at the mouse.

The mouse shrugged her shoulders.

"You need to breathe deeper, Ma'am," Doc Tikkum said.

Flanyanna smiled at the mouse. "I'm so glad you're here, sister."

"Yes, I'm glad you're here too," Doc Tikkum said. "And maybe you could help?" he added, looking up at Pinky.

The little mouse obligingly threw herself off of the ledge into the air. Doc Tikkum unrolled his tongue and caught her just before she crashed onto the floor.

"Be careful. We don't want to lose you now, do we?" he said.

"Shhhh—remember, the walls can hear us," Pinky whispered. Scrambling over to her sister, Pinky touched Flanyanna's hand with her minuscule paw and changed back into herself.

Flanyanna pushed anew, feeling another contraction.

"Where are those idiot guards with the hot water and rags?" Doc Tikkum fumed. He was painfully aware that under these filthy conditions, the chances of the queen's survival were slim, not even fifty-fifty. With his shirt sleeve Doc Tikkum wiped away the cool perspiration gathering on Flanyanna's forehead and said, "Breathe deeply. Keep pushing. It'll be over soon, and you'll have a perfect babe in your arms."

Doc Tikkum stroked her head like she was an ill child of his. Flanyanna felt the contractions deep inside as she contorted on the cold, hard crystal cell floor—the stony part, the hard and unforgiving rock that was now her only sanctuary.

Doc Tikkum heard clambering hooves echo in the tunnel hallway coming towards them.

"Quickly, hide!" he whispered to Pinky.

Pinky dashed into the shadows disappearing from sight. The cell door's lock clanged and clicked and the door opened. The guard entered with a burlap bag and a wooden bucket of water that he dropped on the floor splashing Doc Tikkum. The water that struck his face was cold.

"You moron—I said, hot water!"

More hot smoke swirled from his nostrils and rose up the breathing shaft.

"Oooooink!" the Peccarey squealed in terror. He ran out of the cell.

Doc Tikkum followed him.

"Oooooink! Oooooink!"

Scrambling hooves against the hard crystal pavement echoed in the corridor as both guards scampered away escaping down the darkened dungeon corridor.

"Stupid beasts."

Doc Tikkum snatched one of the torches from the wall and his hands turned red from its flame. Going back into the cell, he thrust the torch in the bucket. The water hissed and steam rose. Touching the water with his finger, he was satisfied with the temperature. "Now—this is hot water," he said proudly.

Opening the burlap bag, he was glad to see the rags were clean. He dipped one in the hot water.

The mouse scurried up the wall to the ledge that had held the candle. Her lip quivered. She knew she would have no children of her own. It was the price she paid, the sacrifice she made to save what she loved—her sister, her magical animals, and Kokakina.

Flanyanna's legs fluttered like butterfly's wings as the labor contractions grew more intense. A stream of red moonbeams funneled down the tower's shaft and filled the tiny cell with a magical rosy glow. The Blood Moon prophesy by the beloved Rose Crystals was upon them.

"It's time," the mouse squeaked.

"Ma'am, let's bring your child into the world, shall we?" Doc Tikkum said. "Push—push harder." He spoke with the authority of a doctor who had delivered many babies.

He bent down to assist the queen in her final stages of labor. The underground chiseled rock crystal cell was bathed in the red moonlight. They could all feel the magic of creation.

"I see her head—keep pushing," Doc Tikkum said. After delivering all types of baby creatures, he was relieved to see her tiny head come first, which was right and proper.

Without even a whimper, the new baby left the safety of her mother's womb and drew her first breath, silhouetted in the red of the Blood Moon. Doc Tikkum knew all babies were beautiful, but the tiny princess took his breath away. He was deeply humbled by the universe's ability to produce life out of nothing.

"She's beautiful—" a tearful Aunt Pinky gushed bending down to get a better look at the newborn.

"She has all her fingers and toes?" Flanyanna asked.

"Of course, she's perfect, just like her mother. She's a healthy, beautiful, baby girl," Doc Tikkum whispered. Tying and cutting the umbilical cord, he gently lifted the infant to the bucket and washed her in the warm water, careful not to tear her fragile physical wings. The physical wings would fall off after a time, leaving her etheric wings intact. They all watched as the princess wrapped her wings around herself like a cocoon to keep warm just like the deceased Human Fairy baby attempted to do.

"She is healthy, isn't she?" Flanyanna asked in a whisper.

"Yes." Doc Tikkum turned back to Flanyanna. He washed off her red stained thighs with water from the bucket and one of the clean rags. He set aside the afterbirth next to his medical bag and covered it with some of the rags.

The last of the Blood Moon's rays left the cell.

"Let me hold her," Flanyanna whispered. She reached out her trembling hands.

In the glow of the yellow moon, Flanyanna cradled her infant. The newborn suckled from her mother's engorged breast.

"I think she looks just like Petronero," Flanyanna whispered, fearing the talking walls might hear. She could see her husband and feel his zest for life in their child. She flushed with happiness.

In the distance stomping hooves echoed down the hallway.

"It's the guards," Pinky said.

"What'ta we gonna do?" Doc Tikkum asked.

Flanyanna clutched her now sleeping child.

"Quick—your bag!" Pinky whispered.

"But, I thought you were going to take her," Doc Tikkum whispered, intently.

"No. I mean take out the—" Pinky whispered and gestured to the bag where the dead baby was concealed.

Doc Tikkum was terrified the walls would reveal what he was about to do. He squatted next to his medical bag and took out the deceased baby.

"Bathe her. There can be no trace of her mother's scent," Pinky whispered.

Doc Tikkum lifted the deceased infant over to the water bucket and bathed her in the still warm water to remove the scent of her natural mother.

The echo of the hooves was closer.

"Now, you must rub her in the princess' afterbirth—hurry!" Pinky murmured. "The scent has to be right. It has to be the white rose's fragrance. She must smell like a royal White Fairy or all is lost."

Flanyanna held her baby tightly to her bosom.

Doc Tikkum gently coated the impostor with the aftermath of the princess' delivery.

The jangling of the keys was heard outside the door.

"Hide the princess in your bag," Pinky whispered transforming back into the mouse.

"But, what if she cries?" Doc Tikkum asked, not sure it was such a good idea.

"Shhhh!" whispered the mouse.

Doc Tikkum fumbled at the closure of his medical bag and could not get it open.

"Put her in the bag!"

"I can't...can't get it open...there isn't enough time." Doc Tikkum bent over Flanyanna. "Put her up under your dress."

Flanyanna bent over the newest royal Human Fairy who had already lost her title, but hopefully, would not lose her life this night. She tucked her baby into her stained, bloody skirt.

Aloud, Doc Tikkum whispered, "Please keep her quiet—her life depends upon it."

The cell door exploded open. The mouse scampered across the cell floor, crawled up Doc Tikkum's pant leg, and hid inside his vest pocket. The Peccarey guard stuck his inquisitive dribbling snout in the cell. Sniffing the air, his nose wrinkled, for he smelled both birth and death.

Not sure the baby was concealed yet, Doc Tikkum slowly rose and blocked the guard's view of Flanyanna and the princess. "Tell the king his sister's baby was stillborn." He spoke his treason loudly and with conviction.

"Tell the king his sister's baby was stillborn," echoed the walls.

He walked over to the door and slammed it shut, in hopes of hiding his treason. The cell door swung open again, and the slavering nose poked in again.

"'irl or 'oy?"

Doc Tikkum leaned into the beast's snout. His chameleon face, still red from the Blood Moon, took on aspects of the Peccarey's face. "It's a girl!"

"It's a girl!" the walls echoed back Doc Tikkum's words.

He pushed the door closed in the Peccarey's face. Seeing the change in Doc Tikkum's face, the terrified guard fell back, hitting the back of his head on the opposite wall. Very dizzy, he ran down the hallway on all fours zigging and zagging.

"Flan, we-we must take her now," Pinky whispered from Doc Tikkum's pocket. Still in her mouse form, she climbed up onto Doc Tikkum's shoulder.

Doc Tikkum looked at her. "Wait a minute—what t'ya mean—we?"

"I need you to get her out of the dungeon. I thought you understood that?" Pinky whispered.

"Now, wait a minute—that is most definitely treason," he whispered back, very agitated.

"If you don't do it, all is lost," the magical mouse spoke softly in his ear.

"Stop this, both of you. Stop arguing." Flanyanna adjusted the sleeping princess lying in her lap.

"Surely you can do a magic spell or something and get her out?" Doc Tikkum asked, speaking ever so softly to Pinky still in his vest pocket.

"No, I can't."

"Why not?"

"Because she still has her physical wings. I can't perform magic on her until she has her etheric wings. It's too dangerous."

"Well, it's dangerous if you don't...."

"You don't understand."

"No, I guess I don't."

"She's not quite in our dimension yet. She's—how do I say this—she's still too Human and not enough Fairy. She'll die if I perform magic on her."

Then, the mouse ran down Doc Tikkum's back. She scurried over to Flanyanna with her sleeping newborn and stared into the deposed queen's third eye.

"I want you to promise you'll take care of my daughter and be her mother," Flanyanna told Pinky through her third eye.

"Flanyanna, you're her mother," Pinky responded in the same way.

"Say you will be her mother."

"Of course, I will."

Pinky knew better than anybody that the child would be an orphan, but she felt it would be unkind to burden her sister with how she had sold her heart to save Flanyanna and the princess from the Lord of the Darkness.

Doc Tikkum heard every word and said nothing for he knew these would be their final moments together.

"I'm afraid, Pinky," Flanyanna whispered.

Before replying, Pinky transformed back into her Human Fairy form and embraced her sister.

"Don't worry. I promise I won't let Markolous take you to the Black Hole," she whispered back so the walls could not hear.

"Take good care of her," Flanyanna said through her third eye.

"I will."

Pinky held her sister tightly for the last time and could say nothing more.

The hearing of Tarragonians was more keen than Human Fairies and Doc Tikkum heard hooves and heavy boots coming towards them. He went to his medical bag and bending down pulled out the baby spider-silk blanket made by Mother Tikkum. She had made it for the princess knowing that the Tower of the Forgotten was a damp and chilly place. But, he would not be giving it to the princess. He wrapped Mother Tikkum's baby blanket around the impostor and offered her to Flanyanna.

"I'm sorry, Ma'am, your baby—did not survive," he said. He put his hand on Flanyanna's shoulder. Knowing it was the baby's only chance for survival, he hoped she would give the princess to him.

"Ma'am, your baby did not survive," he repeated loudly.

"Ma'am, your baby did not survive," echoed the talking walls.

"Flan, you must...," Pinky whispered.

Flanyanna clutched her very alive baby knowing she had precious little time left with her. She did not want to give up her child, but she had no other choice if she wanted her to live.

"I'm sorry...," Doc Tikkum said loudly so the talking walls would have no trouble hearing him.

"I'm sorry...," echoed the walls.

Doc Tikkum gently lay the dead Human Fairy baby, wrapped in Mother Tikkum's handmade baby blanket, next to Flanyanna. He wanted to give her every possible moment to hold her baby, but he was afraid of what would happen if she did not release her and he could not bear to take the child away by force.

"There is nothing I can do—I'm no longer queen," Flanyanna sobbed.

She released one hand from cradling her daughter, and touched the dead infant's head, caressing the child's golden locks of hair. Tears streamed down Flanyanna's cheeks flushed from giving birth.

"I'll grieve her for her own sake," she whispered softly.

Flanyanna's sorrow at relinquishing her own child would mourn the death of another innocent newborn who died that night and gave her child a chance to live.

She returned her hand to under her own baby's soft back. The infant's small, warm body would soon be gone from her arms forever, and she wanted to remember her. She made the sign of the Human Fairy blessing on the princess' forehead. She touched the princess' third eye, once with her index finger. Two taps with a cupped hand were followed by three flicks.

"May you be safe and protected from all evil and darkness on your life's journey, my little darling," she whispered.

Flanyanna kissed her child's third eye. The kiss activated intuitive powers that each generation passed on to the next one.

Feeling her pain, Pinky and Doc Tikkum lowered their heads.

Flanyanna turned to Doc Tikkum and offered him her baby. "Take her now or I'll be foolish and ask my brother for mercy."

Doc Tikkum held out his arms and gently received the princess in his green hands.

Having left her mother's warmth, the infant folded her tiny physical wings about her, wrapping herself in a protective cocoon to self-care until she was held once again by her mother—or so she thought.

"I can't do this. I can't take her from her mother. There's got to be another way," Doc Tikkum whispered. He looked down at the helpless infant in his green hands, wrapped in her own wings to keep warm—waiting to be held once more by her mother.

Pinky shook her head.

"Markolous will let neither the mother nor the child live," she whispered.

Doc Tikkum felt like a fist had been thrust into his gut. He cradled the princess. She opened up her wing cocoon just enough to show her face and she gurgled and smiled at him.

"Please forgive me, little one," he whispered. He placed the tiny winged stowaway in his coarse, burlap medical bag. She enclosed herself back up in her little cocoon.

Doc Tikkum closed the flap, knowing any sound she made would mean death to all of them, but there was no other choice.

"I have no way to repay you," Flanyanna spoke softly, knowing that he risked not only himself but also his family.

Doc Tikkum lifted his medical bag and was surprised by how light it felt.

"Ma'am, you'll always be my Human Fairy queen," he said.

"And you'll always be my poacher," she replied tenderly. Flanyanna placed her hand first on his left shoulder and then, raising it over his head, placed it on his right.

Shocked and humbled, Doc Tikkum bowed to his queen. She had just bestowed upon him, a Tarragonian, membership in the Privy Order, an honor received by very few Human Fairies. He had just been knighted.

"Please—let me see her one more time," Flanyanna said through her third eye to her sister.

Doc Tikkum looked at Pinky. "Surely—we must risk it," he said.

The two sisters looked at each other, surprised.

He hears what we're saying? Pinky thought to herself.

"We must grant to her last request," Doc Tikkum said. He opened the flap and showed the sleeping princess to her mother. The child was blissfully unaware of the great peril any second might bring. Sensing her mother's presence, she opened her tiny wings.

"Please forgive me, dear beautiful, darling daughter," Queen Flanyanna whispered, ever so softly.

An inner calmness came over the princess as her mother touched her little fingers to say goodbye. The little princess cooed and basked in her mother's love.

"Go now. Take her to safety." Her mother's spirit melted into the bag with the baby.

The echoes of approaching Peccarey hooves and Human Fairy soldiers' boots intruded loudly, echoing on the walls.

Doc Tikkum's heart leaped up into his throat. "I'm so sorry —I must take her—now," he whispered.

Flanyanna let go of the tiny fingers.

He looked out the cell, clutching his open medical bag with the princess in it.

"It's Markolous!" Pinky said.

"If I've been unkind, please forgive me." Flanyanna needed to say the words she had held it back too long. It was time to tell her sister, who loved her more than anyone. "I was jealous of you."

"Stop, please." Pinky hugged and kissed her sister one more time. "It doesn't matter. I love you. That's all that matters."

Flanyanna took the dead baby in her arms. Its lifeless body was a devastating contrast to her daughter's bursting vitality.

She struggled to rise with the dead infant in her arms.

"Your Majesty?" Doc Tikkum asked, helping her to her feet.

"I want to meet my brother standing."

Doc Tikkum so wanted to leave before Markolous came, but he was afraid of what would happen to her.

"I'll be back...," Doc Tikkum said.

Despite her dirty attire, Flanyanna stood tall with her prowess and dignity, for her demeanor was still that of a queen.

"Go now or my brother will...." Flanyanna did not finish her sentence for fear of speaking into reality her newborn's death.

"I'll be in the crowd. Look into my third eye. All will be well...I promise you," Pinky told her.

Pinky returned to her enchanted mouse form and shot herself into the bag alongside the princess.

Doc Tikkum closed and secured the flap over Pinky and the princess. He placed the bag across his shoulder and pushed open the door to the cell with his shoulder.

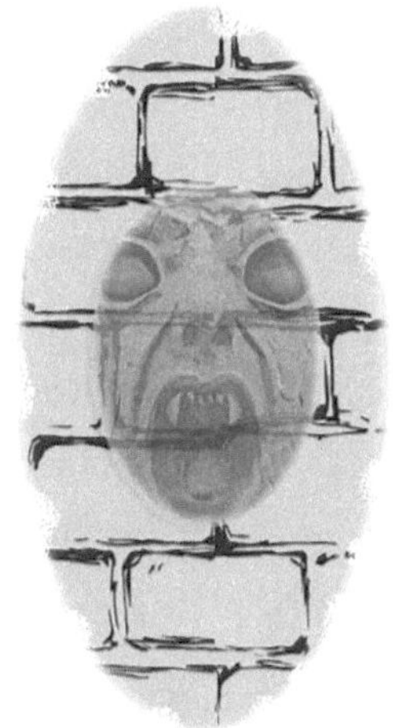

The Talking Walls

Markolous stormed into the cell. Tithoreus and the guards in their black leather uniforms burst in behind him. The medical bag stirred a bit and then settled down on Doc Tikkum's back.

Markolous and his entourage had eyes only for the infant in Flanyanna's arms.

"Your Majesty, the baby was delivered stillborn. My work here is done," Doc Tikkum said with a bow. He escaped out the cell door with the stowaways.

Let me see the child," Markolous said.

Flanyanna did not move.

"I said, let me see the child." Markolous motioned to a Human Fairy guard.

Uneasily, the guard moved in and wrenched the baby from Flanyanna's unyielding arms. He handed the lifeless infant to Markolous.

Flanyanna turned and hid her third eye, not wanting to give away that her baby and her sister were escaping down the corridor with the good doctor.

Markolous raised the infant corpse to his nose. He inhaled the white Rosa Centifolia aroma of his own royal Human Fairy line. After a moment's inspection he looked up and smiled. "The baby is dead," he said. The deception had worked.

He pulled out his silver dagger, studded with crystal stones, from the sheath on his belt. In one swift movement, he drove it into the baby's chest. The moment he defiled the infant, Flanyanna felt the dagger plunge deeply into her womb. Pulling the red, bleeding heart out, he ate it in front of her and dropped the baby's remains to the floor.

She dropped to the floor and crawled to the desecrated baby. Picking her up, she cradled the baby in her arms. She buried her head into the infant and rocked her making sure Markolous never saw her third eye.

"What's this? Oh, come on, sister. We've done this for centuries, eating our enemies' hearts to get their power."

Markolous wiped his bloody mouth with his black leather glove. Puzzled and curious, he looked about the cell.

"Has anybody besides the Tarragonian doctor been here?"

The Peccarey guard shook his head.

"You can't even feel the magic of the one whose heart you have stolen and you call yourself the ruler of a magical land?" Flanyanna screamed from where she crouched over the desecrated baby, still hiding her third eye.

Markolous turned towards his sister.

"And you call yourself the ruler of a magical land," the walls echoed Flanyanna's words.

Markolous walked over to Flanyanna. Looking down at her, he raised his dagger.

"Sire, stop. Don't kill her. Remember the Lord of the Darkness. She must die by fire," Tithoreus warned.

"Remember the Lord of the Darkness. She must die by fire," the talking walls echoed.

Markolous slowly lowered his dagger.

"Sister, tomorrow, I'll be rid of you forever." He motioned to Tithoreus. "Give it to her."

He left the cell.

Tithoreus held a red spider-silk satin dress in his insect claws. "You are to wear this tomorrow," he said and dropped it to the floor in front of her.

He and the guards left the cell.

Flanyanna cradled and rocked the dead infant. The talking walls went silent.

Doc Tikkum hurried down the dungeon tunnel with Pinky and the princess in his medical bag. A Peccarey guard led the way back up the dimly lit crystal corridor to the moving staircase. The only light came from the Peccarey's lantern that he carried in one of his fore hooves. Breathing heavily, more from fear than exertion, Doc Tikkum followed the guard up the Tower of the Forgotten's spiraling staircase, hoping they could get out of the dungeon before being discovered.

"Burp!"

The Peccarey guard stopped dead in his tracks. Slowly he turned and stared at Doc Tikkum.

"Excuse me," Doc Tikkum muttered, covering his mouth.

"Argh," the Peccarey grunted. He resumed climbing up the moving staircase.

Very much relieved that there was good reason why the Peccarey species was not known for its intellect, Doc Tikkum adjusted the burlap bag on his burly shoulder. They were very close to getting out, and he was prepared to make a run for it.

"Burp!"

The walls echoed. "Burp!"

The smelly beast stopped and turned around again, sniffing the air to find where the burps were coming from. The repetitive echo ricocheted off the crystal walls and disguised the first burp's location.

"Indigestion from a piece of mutton from my supper," Doc Tikkum explained, holding his stomach with one hand.

He braced himself for a fight with the bristly beast for he feared the baby would burp again and reveal where she was.

"Argh—shut up, 'all!" the Peccarey barked, not realizing the talking wall had disclosed to him that the princess still lived and was escaping.

The walls went silent.

Pleased with himself for his cleverness, the Peccarey looked at Doc Tikkum who smiled disarmingly and rubbed his stomach.

The guard opened the Tower of the Forgotten dungeon's gate. As always, it creaked and moaned on its rusty hinges as it swung open.

"Good night," Doc Tikkum said.

"Argh!" bleated the Peccarey, who closed the dungeon gate. It groaned one more time.

The now brilliant full moon bathed Doc Tikkum's face as he fled over the dungeon moat into the night.

"That was a close call," the little mouse said, climbing out of the satchel, leaving the princess behind. Her nose wrinkled, sniffing the pale scent of scarlet bougainvillea in the moist, night air.

"Yes—it was." Doc Tikkum looked up and marveled. His feelings were mixed. He felt relief that he had escaped with his precious cargo safely in his medical bag but he also felt deep remorse leaving the queen behind to confront her brother alone.

"The Blood Moon has passed—the eclipse is over," Pinky said.

"I had forgotten all about it," he said, surprised he had not remembered. He normally made note of such things for he was a creature of science and enjoyed studying the celestial bodies.

The little mouse looked at the full shiny yellow moon in wonderment. "The princess was born on the Blood Moon."

"Yes, I know that."

"Well, what you don't know is that in our Human Fairy folklore—that's a very good sign."

"Is it now?" Doc Tikkum asked. He was a bit bewildered and disoriented for the proceedings of this child's birth had hardly been easy.

"It means the princess will to do great things."

They entered the village square.

Loud, drunken voices and the clanging of ale mugs filtered down from the Jolly Fairy Tavern. Even though the hour was late, some Human Fairies were out and about, wanting to celebrate the rare Blood Moon.

"Poor thing didn't have a chance."

"Stillborn, you say?"

Hearing the buzz of gossip floating through the air, Doc Tikkum stopped under the Jolly Fairy Tavern's swinging sign and he and the tiny mouse listened.

"Dead at birth!"

"Her own brother can't wait to burn her at the stake!"

"Tomorrow, ye say?"

"That Markolous didn't waste any time makin' himself the new ruler of Kokakina."

"A sly one, he is—"

"Best keep that to yourself."

A few muffled laughs came out of the open tavern windows.

Doc Tikkum was keenly aware that the infant's safety depended on him and Pinky, for they were the only ones who knew that she still lived. "It's just as well that tales of the princess' death are being spread," he said.

"Yes, it is. But I fear—" Pinky replied.

"—that Markolous will find out the baby lives," Doc Tikkum finished her sentence.

"Yes."

He walked on the hollow-sounding cobblestone street towards the Tarragonian village hoping no one would stop him. Making sure nobody was following them, Doc Tikkum headed back to Happy Hollow.

The moon drifted into a shadow. The cobblestones changed to a rocky dirt road. In the darkness, they left the road at the stone bridge and disappeared down the slope. Doc Tikkum could feel the cold night air on his back. On many nights he had returned home alone along this path listening to the meandering stream and night crickets.

"Why are you leaving the road?" Pinky asked.

"Because it's late. Many Human Fairies come out at night and make a sport of beating Tarragonians."

"Good idea. We'll be less conspicuous on the path than on the road," Pinky replied, feeling remorse that some of her kind were so cruel to the Tarragonians.

They disappeared into a patch of swaying cattails. The moist scent of the stream's mountain water refreshed Doc Tikkum. He still shuddered, worrying about what would happen to him and his family for helping to save the princess.

They followed along the creek and the cattails until they reached a grove of oak trees. A dilapidated hut of wood, mud, and twigs stood in the distance—Doc Tikkum's house. With the burlap medical bag and its precious cargo over his back, Doc Tikkum slunk up the creek embankment, relieved he was almost home. He could feel the princess' warmth. He put the satchel down.

"Well, this is where I leave you," Doc Tikkum said as he opened up his medical bag. The magical mouse scampered out.

"I didn't tell you earlier, but the princess has to stay with you."

"What? I can't take her. I've got to think about my family."

"I'm sorry—but, your home is the safest place for her right at the moment. Besides no one would ever suspect finding a Human Fairy baby let alone a princess in Happy Hollow."

Pinky turned into a raven and flew up onto a tree's low branch.

"Wait! I-I can't take her. Please...," Doc Tikkum said. He stretched his neck, extending it up towards the bird. She lifted one wing to silence him.

"It's only for a little while. I have to go to my cottage in the Lost Forest and get a potion. I want you to give it to Flanyanna in the morning."

Pinky did not want to tell Doc Tikkum about her fear that the first thing Markolous would do when he found out about the deception would be to go to her cottage. The raven rose up.

"And what about my family and their safety?"

"There just won't be enough time if I take her. Besides, Markolous won't think of searching Tarragonian homes...."

"Not yet anyway...," Doc Tikkum grumbled as he watched Pinky become a small receding dot and disappear.

A twig snapped under Doc Tikkum's tail startling him. In the late night quiet, he stood still, frozen like a statue, and turned green to match the trees. He peered into the night to see if anyone was lurking about. A deep stillness told him he was alone and safe with the princess.

"Well, I guess there is nothing to fear for now. Everyone thinks you're dead," he said to the infant as he picked her back up.

He offered his green scaly finger to the princess' tiny hand. She clutched it and opened her eyes. She gazed up at him and love filled his heart.

You don't even know who your mother is, he thought, "And what am I going to tell Mother...," he said out loud to himself, having no idea how he was going to explain the princess to his wife. "Dear sweet mother of my twelve children, what's one more mouth to feed?" he rehearsed.

Doc Tikkum finished climbing up the slope from the stream bed towards his cottage. Entering through the woven twig gate, he yawned and realized he was very tired. His clawed fingers reached for the door latch. He was comforted to hear the familiar creak of the front door hinge that Mother Tikkum was always scolding him to oil. He quietly closed it behind him and barricaded it with the large, wooden bar there for that purpose.

Happy Hollow

Placing the satchel with the princess on the bench by the dining table, Doc Tikkum listened to the soothing sound of his wife's snoring. He jutted out his tongue with anticipation. *I wonder if Mother has any grasshopper stew left from last night's supper?* he thought.

"Father?"

Up the wall, little Tither's head peered over the edge of her cupboard bed. She saw her father's satchel move.

"What did you bring us?"

"Shhhh—you'll wake up the others."

Doc Tikkum looked out the window and drew shut the simple linen curtains Mother Tikkum had made for their home.

"Have you something in your bag?" Tither asked.

"Go back to sleep. I'll show you later."

Eleven more little green and blue Tarragonian heads popped out over the sides of their beds. With enthusiastic and excited cries all Doc Tikkum's children somersaulted down the cottage walls to welcome him home. Once on the cold, hard, dirt floor, they leapfrogged around their father. Clamoring and shrieking, they reached for his medical bag that he now held high over his head.

Avoiding the innocent, grasping green-blue clawed fingers, he held the burlap bag tightly. His actions only encouraged the children to leapfrog up and down even more, reaching for the moving bag.

In her cupboard bed, Mother Tikkum rolled over on the straw mattress she shared with her husband. Her bleary eyes blinked. A doctor's wife of many years, she had experienced homecomings at all hours of the day and night.

"Be quiet—my nerves. How many times do I have to tell you—I can't take all this racket."

She covered her ears with her straw pillow. She rolled out of her spider-silk blanket and straw-filled bed and slipped down the wall. Her feet touched the cold floor, sending shivers up her spine. "Now that the whole household is in an uproar, how did it go?" she asked.

Not answering, Doc Tikkum went back to the front window and looked out again. This scrutiny did not go unnoticed by the mother of his children.

"Husband, is something wrong? I'm asking you about the queen's delivery. Are she and the baby all right?"

"Mother, Father's bag is moving! Oh, Father, please. What did you bring us?" Tither licked her lips, beside herself.

All the children had high expectations, as their father had delighted them with sweets, fairy tales, and kindnesses since they were born.

"Is it something good to eat, Father?" Tither asked.

"I didn't know they had good things to eat in the Tower of the Forgotten," Mother Tikkum said suspiciously.

"Grasshoppers? Did you bring us grasshoppers?" another child asked.

The children howled in anticipation, bounding up and down the walls and across the floor.

A whimper escaped from the bag.

"It's a puppy. I've always wanted a puppy," Beaticella, his oldest daughter, said.

"Father has brought us a present from the Tower of the Forgotten," Abra, the eldest son, said. He puffed out his chest and raised his head high to add a bit more height to his adolescent frame, the instinctive response of a Tarragonian male to ward off predators. Everyone laughed.

"A present…from the dungeon?" Mother Tikkum asked, raising her eyebrows.

Everyone focused their attention on the animated sack that was now wiggling and squirming above their father's head.

"Father," she said, "there are no presents from the Tower of the Forgotten."

"Now, Mother…it's only for a little while."

"It *is* a puppy," shrieked Beaticella.

"I'll not have it," Mother Tikkum said. She pointed to the bag with her large wooden spoon she picked up from the outer hearth. Her voice was drowned out by the joyful cries of her children. "Quiet. I must have quiet." She put the cast iron pot with the remains of their supper over the fire and threw another log on the coals underneath. Her eyes narrowed as she regarded her husband. She shook her head in disbelief and studied the Tarragonian she knew better than he knew himself.

Doc Tikkum placed the satchel on the outer hearth to keep it warm.

"Frodora, bring me my chair," Doc Tikkum said to his second oldest daughter. "I have something to tell—all of you."

"Husband, this had better be good," Mother Tikkum said.

Young Frodora bound over to where her father's favorite chair was sitting. Hopping back over as fast as her legs could, she carried it back over and put it next to the outer hearth right beside her father's medical bag.

"Thank you, dear girl." With a big sigh, Doc Tikkum slowly lowered his weary body into his chair. Suddenly, an iridescent flying object burst out of the medical bag. It flew through the cottage to the ecstatic and joyful cries of the Tikkum children.

Mother Tikkum screamed.

"What is it, Father?" asked Frodora.

"It's a Human Fairy, dummy," answered Abra, in a superior tone.

"That's right. She's a Human Fairy. Look! She still has her physical wings which is the natural way of her species," Doc Tikkum said.

"It's the queen's baby, isn't it? I'll not keep the queen's baby here. I'll not be part of this, do you hear me?"

"That's not the Tikkum way."

"The Tikkums need to be around for there to be a Tikkum way," she exclaimed.

"Now, Mother."

"I think she's drunk!" Abra interrupted.

"She's not drunk She's just wobbly 'cause she's so young," Beaticella countered saucily.

"Children, she still lives in another dimension. That's why she acts the way she does," Doc Tikkum said. "She has yet to complete her transition to becoming a Human Fairy."

"What do you mean, Father?" Tither asked.

"I mean she's highly evolved, but she's confused because she's fallen into a lower vibration and now lives in a tiny body."

"What utter nonsense—you fill these children's heads with the most ridiculous ideas."

"Father, please, please, we must keep her," implored Tither.

"I'll do all my chores for the rest of forever," an ardent Aber, the second son, promised. He then looked puzzled when everyone laughed.

"You don't remember anything—you never do your chores— you're such a dreamer," Beaticella said.

"How could you—of all the numbskull, idiotic things—this one takes the pudding," Mother Tikkum moaned.

"Mother, I can explain. The Pinky Fairy will be here any minute to take her," Doc Tikkum said.

 "Oh, really, the Pink Fairy?" Now I've heard everything."

"Yes. She said she was coming to get the princess after…"

"You fool. If she were going to take this baby, she never would have left her. You must send her back immediately!"

"Mother, you know perfectly well what will happen to her if I take her back."

Not to mention what will happen to me, Doc Tikkum thought to himself, but wisely did not say aloud.

He unfurled his long, red tongue and snatched the teetering princess from her maiden flight. He offered her to his wife, who crossed her arms.

"I'll not take her in."

"Mother...."

Mother Tikkum ignored her husband and collapsed into her rocking chair next to the outer hearth.

Tither pulled on her father's britches.

"Thank you, Father," Tither whispered. "I promise to take good care of her."

"Doc Tikkum, don't you dare. I'm already all nerves and jitters with twelve children."

Doc Tikkum patted little Tither on her shoulder and said softly, "We'll see in the morning."

"I'll not have another child in this house." Mother Tikkum jumped up from her rocker and shook her finger at Doc Tikkum, but nothing could be heard in the uproar of the Tikkum children. The children had seen this argument before and knew their father had won.

"Be quiet now. You'll wake up the whole of Happy Hollow village," Doc Tikkum admonished, his lizard tongue flicking.

The children went silent, for it was not often their father raised his voice to them.

"Oh, just give her to me," Mother Tikkum relented. She held out her green reptilian arms to receive the princess.

"Father won—Father won—" Tither chanted.

All the other children followed suit.

"Father won—Father won—" screamed the other children at the top of their lungs.

"Would you be quiet—all of you," Doc Tikkum shouted. Sobered by his sharp tone, the children stopped their noise.

"Mother, you're the sweetest mother in all Kokakina," Doc Tikkum said, regarding his wife holding the princess. He flattered her unabashedly, but he truly believed what he spoke to his dear wife, who he loved so dearly.

"Don't you dare think for one moment that all these creamy, buttery words of yours are going to soften me up."

"Oh, I would never think that—Mother."

He smiled at his children and winked at Tither, who giggled.

"Frodora, get me the baby's goat udder," Mother Tikkum ordered.

Frodora went over to a cupboard and took out a goat udder containing nectar juice left over from feeding the youngest Tikkum.

"Children, now go to bed," Mother Tikkum said.

The children hesitated. They looked at their father.

"Father, the princess will be here tomorrow, won't she?" Tither whispered to him.

"We are *not* keeping a Human Fairy baby—and that's final," Mother Tikkum retorted.

"Children, no more noise. You know about your mother's nervous condition."

Doc Tikkum winked again at little Tither. She stifled another giggle, fully understanding what her father meant. The children leapfrogged up the wall. Jumping back into their cupboard beds, they settled down for the rest of the night.

The embers crackled in the hearth as Mother Tikkum rocked the princess in her arms. She enjoyed feeding the infant far more than she would admit to anyone, especially her husband.

She sniffed the air.

"The stew is ready to eat. You'll have to help yourself. I'm busy."

"Nothing would give me greater pleasure."

Doc Tikkum walked over and, with a wooden spoon scooped some stew into a ceramic bowl. Now realizing how hungry he was from his night's work, he gulped it down.

"Shhhh—don't make so much noise—you'll wake her up."

Doc Tikkum nodded.

"When you're done, get me the baby blanket I made for her. I'll make her a hammock with it over the outer hearth."

Finishing his food, he raised himself from the kitchen table bench and went over to the wooden pegs next to the front door. He took a thick, gray shawl from one of the pegs.

"I said the baby blanket I made for her," Mother Tikkum said. "What happened to it?"

"Uhhhh...."

"You left it behind, didn't you?"

"Mother, I did."

She sighed. Doc Tikkum finished wrapping the ends of the shawl on a low beam next to the outer hearth.

"How could you? Never mind. Fetch me a fresh tablecloth from the cupboard. We'll use that," Mother Tikkum said.

Cradling the infant, she rose, and wrapped the princess in a muslin tablecloth Doc Tikkum fetched for her.

"Look! She wraps her tiny wings around herself in a cocoon," Mother Tikkum marveled. They gently placed the princess in the jury-rigged hammock next to the fire. "There. She should be warm for the rest of the night even though she doesn't have the spider silk blanket I made her."

"We'll be up in a few hours. We'll start up the fire again to keep her warm, Mother." Doc Tikkum threw another log on the fire. It burst into a fierce blaze, turning him a deep red. The hot sap seeped out of the log, snapping and crackling in the heat.

He reached into a crock on the mantle and filled his black clay pipe with natural grasses from the marsh. With a piece of straw from the kindling pile, he lit the pipe and smoked a few puffs.

These were the very same grasses he mixed with sweet honey, comfrey, light sage, yarrow, plantain, and helichrysum to make the healing salves he used to soothe his patients' ailments.

"I fear the king will soon be eating Tarragonian legs."

"Don't worry, Mother. Everyone thinks the princess is dead."

"Such a dear little thing. Look at her. I fear she'll be the death of us all."

"There are only a few more hours before daybreak. I'm very tired. Let's go to bed."

"Let me tuck her in. It's a chilly tonight."

After she did so, they climbed up the wall to their double cupboard bed.

Mother Tikkum threw open the coverlet and slid into bed. "What's to become of her…?" she asked.

"Just love her like she's one of our own," Doc Tikkum said.

He crawled in next to her and blew out the candle attached to the wall sconce as he had done many nights after coming home from the Tower of the Forgotten.

"Brrrr—your feet are cold!"

Doc Tikkum rolled over to get out of the straw-thatched bed.

"Don't you dare get out of bed!"

"I was going to put another log…."

"The princess is closer to the fire. She's fine." She pulled the blanket over her head.

Doc Tikkum laid back down onto his straw bed and closed his very tired eyes.

"I know you need to put food on the table...."

Doc Tikkum started to snore.

"Especially now that there's another mouth to feed...."

Doc Tikkum snorted.

Mother Tikkum threw the blanket off of her head. "Doc Tikkum, you haven't heard a word I've said."

In his slumber Doc Tikkum puffed and snorted for he was fast asleep.

Mother Tikkum looked down at the hammock illuminated by the flames. Satisfied the princess was resting comfortably, she plumped up her straw pillow and made a cradle for her head with her fist.

"Well, I guess it doesn't really matter. One more mouth to feed. The poor child. I guess she has no place else to go. We'll manage, We always do. We'll just keep her in the house!" She pulled the cover back across her head and drifted off to sleep.

In the early morning stillness a knock at the door startled Mother Tikkum awake. To her surprise she was the only one who woke up. Doc Tikkum and all her children were still fast asleep, exhausted from the excitement of the previous night.

She climbed down the wall. At the outer hearth she peeked into the hammock. Wrapped in the shawl, like a mummy, the little princess, wide awake, gave Mother Tikkum a radiant smile.

Her shawl being used by the princess, Mother Tikkum put on Doc Tikkum's jacket that hung on one of the wooden pegs by the front door. She went to the front window and looked out. She was relieved, although puzzled when she didn't see anybody. "That's curious. I guess it was the wind."

There was another knock even louder.

"That isn't the wind," Mother Tikkum said to herself. Slowly, she opened the creaky door. "Oh, I wish he'd fix this door...."

Mother Tikkum looked about and saw no one.

Below her rather large, bare, green, clawed feet—an ebony raven hopped into the house without her noticing.

"Your door sounds like the door at the Tower of the Forgotten."

Mother Tikkum gasped and turned around.

Pinky, in her Human Fairy form, stood before her.

"Oh, you scared me half to death," Mother Tikkum said.

Drawing a deep breath to calm herself, she closed the door.

Pinky scanned the interior of the small cottage. The princess was not anywhere to be seen. "Where is she?" she asked, in alarm.

"Ummm, where's who?" Mother Tikkum deflected, shrugging her shoulders as perspiration broke out on her forehead.

"You know perfectly well who I mean. The princess your husband delivered this very Blood Moon night and brought home with him."

"That's ridiculous. A Human Fairy baby would stick out like a sore thumb in Happy Hollow," Mother Tikkum said, laughing nervously and jutting out her tongue. "Haven't you heard the sad news—the very sad news? The princess is dead. I suspect the whole land knows it by now, but you living deep in the Lost Forest, I suppose you haven't heard yet."

"Yes. That would be sad news," Pinky commented, her eyes narrowing.

"Yes, my husband told me last night, the sad news."

Pinky flipped one of the window curtains to the side and peeked out, just as Doc Tikkum had upon his arrival. "Where's your husband?" she asked, turning back to Mother Tikkum. "I need to give him something."

"I'm sorry. He's still asleep." Mother Tikkum flicked out her long, red tongue.

The most powerful Human Fairy in the entire land looked at her. Mother Tikkum's knees shook under her nightgown, but she did not fold. A substantial portion of the small room, including the princess, was hidden by Mother Tikkum's generous body. She had positioned herself in front of the princess who had now become one of her own.

"Mother Tikkum, step aside," Pinky said, moving closer to Mother Tikkum's formidable figure.

Not to be intimidated, Mother Tikkum puffed up her body, filling the small cottage even more. "I...I'll tell my husband."

With a poof, Pinky disappeared.

"Well, I guess I took care of her." Mother Tikkum brushed her hands together and placed them on her ample waist. When she turned around, she saw Pinky holding the princess in her arms.

"You sure a lot of trouble and you're not even grown up yet," Pinky told her niece.

"Actually, she's...no trouble at all," Mother Tikkum said. She took the baby princess and returned her to her hammock by the outer hearth. "If you have something to give to my husband you can give to me."

"Would you please wake up Doc Tikkum?" Pinky asked.

"I will not. He's fast asleep. Besides, nothing will wake him up. He's tired from the night's work."

Mother Tikkum motioned up to the loft bed where Doc Tikkum lay in a deep slumber.

"He's heartless, that new king! Did you know he cut my husband's pay in half? He doesn't even give him a living wage to feed our family," she said.

"Yes, there've been many changes for the worse in our land, I'm afraid," Pinky said. She returned her gaze back to Mother Tikkum and realized that she could trust her.

"Al right, I want you to promise to give him this...." Pinky took out a small leather pouch with thong ties from her belt around her waist and handed it to Mother Tikkum. "It's a potion to give to the queen." Pinky had no time to explain her plans to save Flanyanna from Markolous' diabolical scheming. She was surprised how warm Mother Tikkum's hand felt when it touched hers.

Taking it into her green clawed hand, Mother Tikkum admired the Pink Fairy's beautiful, long, tapered fingertips. "I see. It's some kind of medicine for her."

"Yes."

"Oh, of course, for the pain of the fire."

"Please give it to your husband. He's the only one who can give it to her before she leaves the dungeon."

"I will."

"But there's more. Flanyanna must take six drops when he first sees her," Pinky said. She paused, feeling the aching loss of her sister.

"She deserves far better than she's getting," Mother Tikkum said. "Six drops."

"Yes. But this is very important. She must take the rest right before she leaves the dungeon's gates."

"She has you to thank for this wee bit of mercy. You're a good sister for helping our queen," Mother Tikkum said. She grasped the latch of the front door. "I'll give the libation to my husband with your instructions. Six drops and..."

"...and the rest right before she leaves the dungeon's gates." Pinky finished her sentence.

Mother Tikkum opened the front door. "Will you be there?" she asked not wanting to say anything specifically about the burning. "I know your sister would want you there."

"Yes, tell your husband to meet me in front of her pyre after he gives her the sleeping drug."

"I will tell him. Six drops, the rest at the dungeon's gate and meet him in front of the queen's pyre."

"Yes."

"I'm sorry for the queen's fate," Mother Tikkum said. Even Tarragonians knew of the dire fate of oblivion that awaited Human Fairies who were burned alive and sacrificed to the Lord of the Darkness who lived in the Black Hole at the center of the galaxy.

"Yes. It's a cruel thing especially for a brother to do to his sister."

Pinky transformed into a raven and flew off.

Mother Tikkum closed the creaking door, holding the sleeping potion for the queen and very relieved Pinky hadn't taken the princess. But, she knew very well, after the queen's death the Human Fairy kingdom would in total chaos. She could only hope that they could hide the princess and keep her alive from her evil uncle.

The Burning Pyre

The scent of purple wisteria perfumed the early morning air as Doc Tikkum hastened through the empty streets in the Human Fairy village. He had escaped the Tower of the Forgotten with his precious cargo of the little princess and Pinky tucked safely in his medical bag a few scant hours ago.

He listened to his echoing footsteps on the hollow-sounding cobblestones and the rasping of his short breathing as he slithered through the gray mist. He shuddered. He couldn't help but worry about what was going to happen to him and his family for taking the princess in.

"I must get back to the dungeon with the sleeping potion before the queen awakens," he told himself in a mumble. "But, what if it's something else?"

Doc Tikkum felt slightly nauseous. Having not eaten any-thing, he had slipped quietly out the front door, managing not to awaken any of his children. Shivering from the chill, he drew his jacket lapels closer to his neck as he drew closer to the dungeon. He could not shake off the feeling that he might have seen his family for the last time.

Still mumbling, he said, "Could it be poison?" He looked up at the fog-laden sky. The cold air still slid down his neck. He remembered the significance of the princess being born on the Blood Moon. She was destined for greatness. The infant's safety depended on him and the Pink Fairy as they were the only ones besides his family who knew that she was alive and where she was hidden. He could only hope their secret would remain a secret.

As he slithered through the empty village square, he saw the five execution pyres waiting to be lit. The ropes twisted in the wind. The Tettigard guard posted in the square barely glanced at him. Very relieved, Doc Tikkum slipped into the alleyway that led towards the dungeon. He had trudged over this route on many mornings and nights, but, this time he dreaded the walk. He didn't want to be the one who had to administer the secret potion.

In his vest pocket he pressed the pouch containing the elixir for the queen. "Six drops right away—and the rest when we leave the dungeon," he chanted Pinky's instructions.

Pausing for a moment, he caught his breath. Part of him wanted to believe the elixir would simply numb Flanyanna to the pain of the burning, that she would just fall asleep. However, a nagging suspicion told him that the potion would kill her before the flames did, allowing her to go to the Shadow Fairy world.

"Well, that would be a blessing to be sure, as the alternative is eternal oblivion," he told himself. Still, it pained him. His oath was to heal, not to do harm. This task to euthanize the deposed queen, rather than to heal her, tormented him. Coming to a weathered, stone embankment buttressing the riverbank below the castle, he knew he was close to the dungeon's entrance. He again clutched the libation in his pocket as he walked across the bridge that spanned the dungeon's moat.

At the dungeon's entrance the patrolling Peccarey guard barred Doc Tikkum's way with his spear.

"What's your business, Tarragonian?"

"I'm here to attend to the prisoners of the Tower of the Forgotten," Doc Tikkum declared.

The Peccarey rapped on the gate. "The Tarragonian healer."

With shuffling noises another drooling, hairy Peccarey snout poked out.

Doc Tikkum averted his face, as he alway did. His ears picked up the jingle of some skeleton keys and the ponderous groaning sound the door made when opening. With a grunt the Peccarey guard pushed the door aside with his front hoof and let the green Tarragonian enter the confines of the dungeon.

As always, the decades' buildup of fecal matter, urine and vomit made Doc Tikkum gag as he slithered down the dark corridor.

He entered the queen's cell, his eyes adjusting to the dim light. The single candle on the crystal ledge above her cot had guttered out. A shadowy figure rose from a three-legged, wooden stool next to a single cot of dirty straw.

Flanyanna stood before him in an elegant red, satin, spider-silk dress. She was washed as was her hair, and she was beautiful. He seared her image in his memory.

"You're awake, Your Majesty," he remarked. "You look well, Ma'am."

"A gift from my brother."

Flanyanna twirled around in her finery as tears streamed down her face. "I've only known you for such a brief time, but you are the perfect being to hear my last words."

"Ma'am?"

"I've been up all night, contemplating my life."

"I didn't mean to intrude upon your reflection—would you like me to wait outside?"

"No. Your gentle, kind presence is always most welcome," she said, her voice trembling.

Doc Tikkum's throat tightened for he knew he must administer the libation.

"As you wish, Ma'am." Long ago, he had learned that the dying's greatest need was to know the living still cared for them.

"Would you like to sit, kind sir?" Flanyanna's voice broke again with emotion as she motioned to the three legged stool.

"Thank you, but I'll stand."

Flanyanna looked into the Tarragonian's eyes. A Kokakinan outcast, a social pariah.

"Well, where should I begin? I was the queen. I had powers of my own. I had free will. Let's see. I doubted the Rose Crystals prophecy. Oh, yes…I thought I was above it all."

"Don't you think that judgment's a bit harsh, Ma'am?"

"I don't think so. I made a mess of a good, loving marriage. I treated my own sister like she was a poor distant relative just because everyone else did and it suited the family's purposes. At times, I was arrogant and unkind to everyone because—actually, I don't know why."

"You've always had so much responsibility as queen."

"That's another thing. I'm not so sure I was such a great ruler to my subjects either. I could have made their lives so much better." She paused for a moment. "Oh, what's the point of going on like this? There's so little time."

"Ma'am, I am here to listen to whatever you need to say," was all Doc Tikkum said.

"Well then, I guess I should purge my hatred. I hated my own brother." Consumed with remorse, she turned away from him.

"It happens in families, Ma'am."

"But, if I had only accepted him for who he was. Pinky did! But I didn't. You see, I didn't think I had to! I competed with him and thought only of winning the throne and look where it's gotten me—in a dungeon wearing a red dress."

"Ma'am…."

"Shhhhh. How is…." Flanyanna did not finish, fearing the walls would hear her speak of her baby.

"Well, Ma'am."

Lumbering footsteps resounded in the corridor. The skeleton keys clanged.

Doc Tikkum pulled out the leather pouch that Pinky had given Mother Tikkum and removed the cork stopper.

"Here, quickly! You must drink six drops now. It's a sleeping potion from your sister," he whispered.

Without hesitation, Flanyanna tipped her head back, and Doc Tikkum squeezed six drops down her throat.

The door creaked open.

"It's 'me ta go," grunted the Peccarey guard.

The libation took immediate effect. Flanyanna's equilibrium was already failing her. Her body twitched and spasmed.

Doc Tikkum put the remaining potion back inside his vest pocket, wondering if he had the courage to administer the final dose. He did not know exactly what it was he was giving her—a sleeping potion—or poison to end her life.

"I realize now that the Human Fairy Rose Crystals from Earth are always right. I should have listened more to my sister." Her words slurring, Flanyanna faltered. "I could have made my life so much more simple...."

The door creaked open, and bright light from the torches in the hallway streamed in.

The Peccarey guard stuck his snout into the cell. "'et's go," he shouted.

"Hold on to me, Ma'am," Doc Tikkum whispered.

He steadied her with one hand and picked up his medical bag with the other.

"Why, you're not scaly at all." She felt his hand's surprising softness. She swayed back and forth, feeling the drug take effect. "Your skin is as smooth as mine."

"Ma'am, let me help you." He wrapped her arm around his thick Tarragonian body.

"Can you walk?" he asked.

"Yes, of course, I can."

"I mean—are you feeling okay to walk through the dungeon corridor?"

"Yes." She let go of him and stumbled as more of the drug got into her veins.

"Your Majesty, take my hand." Seeing that, despite her words, she needed help, he reached out his green, clawed fingers.

"Beautifully, I'm doing beautifully," was all she said as she fumbled for his clawed hand.

"Love or acts of kindness, perhaps they're the same thing—what do you think?" Speaking in a moment of lucidity, the Human Fairy queen took the Tarragonian's hand to steady herself.

"Yes, I think love and kindness are similar, perhaps they're the same."

"Do you dance, Doc Tikkum?" she asked, changing the subject.

"Me? No, I've got two left feet."

"Oh, that's too bad. I would have loved to have had one last dance."

"'ome on, 'ome on, 'et's go," the guard grumbled.

"I do look forward to seeing the sky again. Is it a blue day or a gray day?"

Flanyanna stumbled forward bracing herself on Doc Tikkum's arm grateful for his support. Her delicate, long, tapered fingers entwined Doc Tikkum's big green hand.

"It's a blue day, Ma'am. There was fog when I was coming here, but by the time we leave—it will be gone."

"Oh, I see. The morning mist. I will miss even it. Please call me Flanyanna. You must call me Flanyanna or better yet, call me Flan. I would like to hear it—the sound it makes. You know I used to fight with my bother over the sticky pudding."

"'ome on." The guard prodded the butt of his spear into Doc Tikkum's backside. They walked down the tunnel, Peccarey guards walking before and behind. The incessant moans and cries of the forgotten prisoners filled the dungeon corridors.

"To the queen," a prisoner's voice rang out.

"To the queen," the chiseled, crystal rock walls echoed back.

Then, the half-living rocky crystal went silent. A few salty crystal teardrops dripped down the wall. The crystal knew that its Human Fairy queen would soon be no more. Suddenly, the walls shuddered as if in an earthquake. The castle could no longer contain its anguish for its queen and the kingdom.

A jagged crack shot down the length of the Crystal Palace's front wall, throwing the dungeon's gate off-kilter. Doc Tikkum and Flanyanna slipped through the opening into the daylight.

The sparkling dew had not yet dried in the morning sun. Flanyanna's eyes strained and her vision blurred as they adjusted to the daylight. Surrounded by Tettigards, a wooden cart pulled by an ancient Namdalarian mare waited on the bridge next to the dungeon door. Tithoreus and his Tettigard soldiers turned towards Flanyanna.

A brisk wind was blowing. It snared Doc Tikkum's wool scarf and exposed his neck. *Even the wind mocks and taunts me*, he thought as he snatched at the scarf with his free hand.

"This way, Ma'am," Doc Tikkum said.

Flanyanna smiled and inhaled the fresh air she had thought she would never breathe again. "It is a blue day—just as you said, dear Tarragonian," she said.

Doc Tikkum guided her towards the cart where the four badly beaten royal Human Fairy guards slumped in their shame and dishonor. Upon seeing their queen they stood at attention despite being secured with heavy sisal ropes to the cart sides.

"Long live the queen," one of the royal guards shouted defiantly.

Tithoreus whipped the prisoner with his lash to silence him.

Still supporting Flanyanna by her waist, he saw that the guards and Tithoreus were not looking and pulled out the rest of Pinky's potion from his vest.

Very conflicted, Doc Tikkum still knew he would never forgive himself if Flanyanna went into oblivion because he did not give her the entire amount.

"Quick, Flan, no one is looking. Take the rest of Pinky's —sleeping potion," he whispered.

Shaking, Flanyanna held his hand on the bottle and tipped her head back, swallowing the rest of the contents.

"Tarragonian, stop! What are you doing there?" Tithoreus flew over screaming.

"You must promise me that you will be there for me. Please?" Flanyanna said.

Doc Tikkum nodded. "You want her to make it to the village square, don't you?" he roared at Tithoreus. Black smoke furled from out of his nostrils. He lifted Flanyanna into the center of the cart.

Choking and coughing, Tithoreus pulled back. "Beware Tarragonian—I'm watching you."

Suddenly, Tithoreus grabbed Doc Tikkum's shoulder and pulled him around. "Stay out of this. This is not your business."

"And I say this *is* my business, Tettigard."

"I've had just about enough of you, Tarragonian." Tithoreus shook his body, and a foamy froth exuded from his abdomen and shot into the air.

Doc Tikkum covered his eyes to protect them. If the slime had gotten into his eyes, it would have blinded him instantly.

"I'll take care of you later, Tarragonian." Tithoreus' body shook with anger. He motioned to the Human Fairy driver to go.

The driver slapped the mare's scarred flanks with the reins. "Walk on."

The groaning cart jolted forward and started across the stone bridge. Blurry-eyed and in a drugged stupor from the magic potion, Flanyanna looked down at Doc Tikkum.

Pulling off his hat, he dropped his head and knelt down to his queen for the last time.

The cart bumped forward over the moat, leaving behind the broken-hearted Tower of the Forgotten and Crystal Palace. It moved towards the Human Fairy village.

As he followed the cart, Doc Tikkum's clawed feet scraped against the unforgiving cobblestone pavers. His fear of Markolous changed to rage.

The queen was condemned for no other reason than she was in the way of a greedy, jealous, and angry brother. She will expire on the burning pyre because her death is the only way to appease Markolous' malice and hatred that, in the end, he was not chosen by his father, he thought.

Pulling down his wool cap upon his Tarragonian head while holding tightly onto the lapels of his coat, Doc Tikkum walked briskly behind the cart to the place of execution in the village square.

An upper floor cottage window opened. The smell of the previous night's Human Fairy excrement assaulted Doc Tikkum's nostrils. Knowing what to expect from his many trips through the Human Fairy village on his way to and from the Tower of the Forgotten, he nimbly leapfrogged across the crowded street of vendors and shoppers as a chamber pot expelled a dose of piss and more onto the street below.

A shopper screamed as the pot's contents splashed her.

Aghast, she beheld her soiled clothing and purchases.

"I'll have the magistrate on you!" the outraged Human Fairy screamed.

The indifferent resident slammed the window shut without replying.

Merchants and shoppers jostled in the square. The vendors were doing brisk business. Doc Tikkum searched the crowd for Pinky, but she was nowhere to be found. Mother Tikkum had instructed him that the square was where Pinky would meet him.

"Magic mushroom pies. Get your magic mushroom pies," a vendor cried out.

"Ale! Get your ale for the burning!" another hawker shouted.

Many Human Fairies passed the cart. Near the entrance to the square, Tithoreus paid out crystals from a pouch on his waist to villagers huddling there. As the cart passed, they ran up and jeered at the queen, spitting at her. One of the paid hecklers ran up particularly close to the cart and spat directly on her.

Suddenly, a red clawed hand reached out of the crowd, picked up the bold individual who had defiled the queen and threw him across the square. He landed against one of the buildings with a sickening splat and lay on the ground unmoving. The other hecklers ran off.

Her own species—how can they treat each other so atrociously? Doc Tikkum thought in disbelief, his chest heaving from his exertion.

Adjusting his vest over his protruding belly, Doc Tikkum shuffled his feet, not really wanting to go to the burning. But,

Mother Tikkum told him he was to meet Pinky there and he had promised Flanyanna he would attend.

The square was now filled, mostly with Human Fairies. Five wooden poles stood empty. Hungry piles of timber and twigs waited beneath them. The ropes jerked about waiting for the burning of a White Fairy.

Doc Tikkum felt sick. His eyes shot about looking for Pinky. Walking through the mostly drunken crowd, he positioned himself in front of the middle pyre where Flanyanna would be able to see him. He felt uneasy, for he was a Tarragonian. Not caring that he was a healer, most Human Fairies did not like for his kind to mingle in with them.

A simple farmer standing next to Doc Tikkum regarded him closely. "You're Doc Tikkum, yes?" he asked. "The Tarragonian healer?"

Doc Tikkum mutely nodded, staring at the pyre.

"You saved my boy a few years back. He cut his leg with a scythe. If you hadn't stopped the bleeding, we'd have lost him."

Doc Tikkum looked at the farmer.

"Yes, I remember your boy. How's he doing?"

"Fine. Just fine—thanks to you. You had to take your gloves off to stop the blood flow, and he never changed color at all," the farmer answered. "It's a silly lie, isn't it—that your kind's touch will change our skin color forever?"

Doc Tikkum nodded distractedly, seeing the cart come into the village square.

"He's got his own family now. We wouldn't have those little ones if it weren't for you."

He handed a jug of wine to Doc Tikkum, who shook his head.

"The wine's free," the farmer explained.

"Free liquor?"

"Well—yeah. It's available to all who have a gullet and desire to pour—compliments of King Markolous." The farmer threw back his head and drank.

"Nothing's free," Doc Tikkum said, grimly.

Suddenly very thirsty, he changed his mind and snatched the jug from the farmer—chugging long and hard—hoping the wine would give him the fortitude to honor his queen and be a silent witness of this cruel and unjust act. The red liquor stung his throat. Another farmer elbowed the farmer who had given Doc Tikkum the liquor jug.

"Hey? What's he doin' here?"

"It's okay. I know him. He saved my boy a few years back," the first farmer explained.

Doc Tikkum felt a tightness in his throat. He took another drink and handed the jug back to the farmer whose boy he had saved.

Will the libation be enough to save her from the fire? he thought turning to the waiting five pyres.

"Look, the executioner." The first farmer pointed to the tall timbered scaffolding behind the pyres.

Where's Pinky? Doc Tikkum swallowed hard looking around.

A hulking, bald-headed giant pushed through the crowd. His head rose a foot above everyone else's. His face, except for his eyes, nose, and mouth, was covered in a black leather mask. Gory tattoos showing different ways to torture and execute creatures covered his body.

"I know him," the farmer declared. Leaning into Doc Tikkum, he handed the jug back to him.

"I thought his identity was a secret?" Doc Tikkum asked. Taking the jug, he tilted back his head and drank deeply.

"It's hard to hide a giant, let alone those tattoos," the farmer laughed. He turned to the executioner and waved.

Out of the corner of his eye, Doc Tikkum spied a mouse scampering through the crowd towards him.

"Pinky. I didn't think you were going to make it!" Doc Tikkum said.

"What?" The farmer asked.

"Nothing." Doc Tikkum was very much relieved to see the jade eyed mouse. Without saying anything, the mouse used her tiny mouse hands and feet to scramble up his leg and slip into his vest pocket.

The burly executioner climbed the steps of the scaffolding amid the cheers of the drunk Human Fairies in the crowd.

"What took you so long?" Doc Tikkum asked in a whisper.

"I went to my mother's house."

"Your mother? I didn't know you had a mother."

Pinky gave him a wry glance. "Everyone has a mother—even me," she said dryly. "Did you give her the potion as instructed?"

"Yes."

The old Namdalarian mare staggered into the center of the crowded square. Foaming at the mouth and its coat covered with sweat, she pulled the heavy cart with Flanyanna and her four royal guards behind her. Arriving at the pyres, the Human Fairy driver pulled on the reins that cruelly cut the horse's mouth.

"Whoa."

With their swords, Tithoreus and the Tettigard guards cut the sisal twine that held the four royal guards.

"Get out." The Tettigards yanked them out of the cart and onto the ground.

The crowd was uneasy. They all knew Tettigards feasted on Human Fairy blood. It was even rumored that the Tettigards feasted on the blood of the prisoners of the Tower of the Forgotten—but to see Tettigards openly manhandle Human Fairies was something brand new. Convicted of treason, the four terrified guards walked up the wooden steps of the scaffold to the separate pyres. The executioner tied them to their stakes to be burned alive. Then, Tithoreus lifted Flanyanna from the cart with his appendages.

A somber hush fell over the crowd. Now, a royal was being handled by a Tettigard.

Queen Flanyanna's bearing never appeared more regal than at this moment. In her red dress she walked to where the executioner stood. He helped her up onto the scaffolding. Together they stepped up onto the highest step of the scaffold.

"Thank you," she said.

The executioner bowed.

She lifted her head facing her people. Her carriage and poise spoke that she was a queen, a good queen who the archives would record as among the truly Great Rulers of Kokakina. She would be counted among those who had raised the masses from the depths of the ignoble and offered hope of a better life.

"My beloved subjects. I say to you—do not be sad for me. If I've served well in my life, then I have not lived in vain, and I now die in peace and tranquility." The clear tones of Flanyanna's voice rang out in a brief reprieve from the effects of the potion.

The executioner took Flanyanna's delicate hand in his black leather gloved one and led her onto the center woodpile. Wrapping both her hands behind her, he tied her against the pole. With snake-like twine, he bound Flanyanna's torso and legs to the uncaring rod and stepped off the pyre and onto the steps, taking up the unlit torch. The sight of Kokakina's queen tied to a stake jolted a villager out of his inebriated trance.

"It's too cruel to burn her!" he shouted.

"Especially from a brother," a second spectator murmured.

"If she burns, she'll have no way to come back," cried out another.

The crowd turned ugly, pushing and shoving. The red libation that many had poured down their throats made for an angry mob. The Tettigards poked their spears at the Human Fairy villagers, pushing them back until they fell into a sullen silence.

Tithoreus waved his claw above his head to the executioner, signaling him to begin. The executioner lit the torch from a bucket of hot embers. He lit the four guards' bonfires first.

Their lit pyres started to flame. The royal bodyguards began coughing from the smoke. The executioner went to Flanyanna with his burning torch.

"Forgive me," he said.

"I forgive you," Flanyanna replied. "Perform your duty and be at peace. I can ask no less of you that I ask of myself."

Flanyanna's head drooped. The potion had taken its full effect. The wood snapped and blistered in the cold air. The crowd pulled back as the fire leaped higher.

Inhaling the fumes Flanyanna coughed. For a moment, she lifted her head up. Bleary-eyed, her head dropped again.

Doc Tikkum watched the flames surround Flanyanna. "Are you sure the potion will take effect and she will not suffer?" he asked, not caring who heard him.

Pinky did not respond and looked up at the empty sky.

"I fear I didn't do it right! She's going to go to oblivion— answer me!" Doc Tikkum said.

Suddenly, from nowhere, a sole black raven appeared. Cawing, he circled above Flanyanna.

Flanyanna heard flapping wings and looked up. "Husband, you've come for me," she cried.

The blackbird transformed into Petronero, who hovered above her as a Shadow Fairy.

"I'm ready now to come with you," she said.

Then—she rose.

As all watched, Flanyanna's etheric body separated from her burning physical one. She drifted up from the flames to join Petronero before the flames, licking at her physical body, consumed it in red-orange flames. But, she did not feel them.

Jolted out of their helpless dismay, the drunken crowd screamed in jubilation. Leaping about, they cried out in triumph and joy. Their Human Fairy queen had been saved from her brother's fiendish cruelty. Queen Flanyanna had died before the end of her three hundred years, but not from the flames. She would live the rest of her incarnation as a Shadow Fairy and be reborn, again.

"She's a Shadow Fairy with the promise to live again," the farmer shouted. He slapped a stunned and motionless Doc Tikkum on the back.

Flanyanna and Petronero hovered above the square. They twirled into an expanding blue energy before turning into two ravens.

"Look, Father! They turned into birds!" a child cried out.

"Nay, child. They're Shadow Fairies," his father explained.

He picked him up so he could see better.

"Queen Flanyanna will live the rest of her incarnation with her husband in the Shadow Fairy world," the boy's father shouted out for all to hear.

The resounding cheers of the crowd were deafening. Doc Tikkum watched the others in the crowd, adding his own shouts of joy to the din.

"I will miss her," Doc Tikkum said.

"Yes," Pinky replied.

"I need to know" he asked. "Was the potion poison?"

Pinky did not answer at first. "No. Of course not," she finally replied, her thoughts really somewhere else. She finally understood the full impact of the prophecy of the Rose Crystal that she had misinterpreted because of her love for her sister. Although she loved her sister very much she could not save her. Her mission really was to keep the princess safe from Markolous. At least Flanyanna went to the Shadow Fairy world rather than to the Lord of the Darkness.

But how am I going to save the princess from Markolous? If he doesn't already know that the princess lives—he soon will. He has spies everywhere. I have got to find my mother, she thought.

The mouse crawled from Doc Tikkum's pocket to his shoulder.

Everyone watched the birds disappear into the sky.

"I fear the land will never be the same. The Human Fairy queen is dead," Doc Tikkum said.

"King Markolous didn't even come to his own sister's burning," the farmer said in disgust.

There was a tug on Doc Tikkum's vest. He looked down to see Calisandra standing beside him.

"I've kept my side of the bargain, dearie. Now it's your turn," Calisandra said looking straight at Doc Tikkum.

"Excuse me. Do I know you?" he asked.

Calisandra's third eye stared at Doc Tikkum's shoulder where the magical mouse had climbed. Doc Tikkum shuddered. He realized that Calisandra was talking to Pinky in her mouse form, not to him.

"Not so fast. The princess has to reach safety before I deliver on my part," Pinky shot back through her third eye.

"Very well. But just remember, they gave you three days. You better get a move on, dearie. You're already well into your first day," came Calisandra's third eye response. With these words she lowered her head and dissolved into the crowd.

"Who was that?" Doc Tikkum asked.

"Oh, her? She's just a friend—a friend of my mother's. Let's go."

"A friend? Well, it didn't sound like a friendly conversation to me," he replied, "and what's this three-day business?"

"Oh, that's just the way she is. She gets irritated easily."

"Oh? Like you?"

Pinky's cheeks burned, but then her brow furrowed.

"Wait a minute. You can hear us, when we talk with our third eyes, can't you?"

"Yeah, so?"

Pinky slipped down Doc Tikkum's shoulder and into his vest. "Well, it's just that it's special. Something that a magical creature would do," she said. "A magical creature. You know, a unicorn."

"Oh, I see."

"Are all Tarragonians like you? Or, are you special?"

"Well—let's see….My children think I'm special all the time and sometimes, not often, mind you, but sometimes my wife thinks I'm special…."

"Okay. Okay. Never mind. Forget I ever asked. Nothing is what it appears to be," Pinky said, remembering what Calisandra had told her.

"Sometimes that's true. Now what?"

"Home. You're going home," Pinky said. "And we must hurry. When Markolous finds out I'm no longer in the Tower of the Forgotten and that I'm responsible for saving Flan from oblivion...."

"Say no more. Going home is the first good news I've heard since this business started." Doc Tikkum pushed through the drunken, dancing mob. He walked with the magical mouse in his vest pocket towards Happy Hollow.

Lord of the Darkness

A light breeze gently billowed the sheer curtains framing the window above the king's bed. Markolous tossed and turned in his sleep. The fake Rose Crystal necklace dangled in the canopy over his head. A jug of red wine next to the bed had tipped over spilling its contents all over the crystal floor.

A fog-like ether crept under the door into the bedchamber and moved slowly towards Markolous. Reaching the ornately carved bedposts, the ether slowly spread up and covered the king's bed. A dark specter rose and hovered over him.

An all-encompassing night sky and the endless ocean blend together. Incessant, hungry waves crash onto the tar-black beach. Coming out of the darkness, in tight-fitting black leather breeches and tunic, Markolous fights a stiff headwind.

"How did I get here?"

The sound of reverberating wings assaults his eardrums. Frightened, he turns and looks up. The dark sky is pulsating.

Thousands upon thousands of Shadow Fairy ravens fly towards him. The implacable black birds cover the moody, throbbing, cloudy night sky.

The swarming ravens dart back and forth. Their wings flap ever louder as they draw closer in the brooding firmament. In hopes of releasing himself from his bad dream, Markolous clasps his hands over his ears to protect his bursting eardrums.

"The shadow power is stronger here than in my awake state."

He runs down the beach, desperate to escape the birds. They dive down and attack him. They puncture his clothing and pierce his flesh with their pitiless, jabbing beaks. The battering wings slash his face, cutting his cheek.

Losing traction, Markolous stumbles in the soft sand. He scrabbles forward on his hands and knees toward the firmer, wet sand, closer to the sound of the ocean. Rising up, he sprints madly down the murky beach.

In the shadowy mist a ghostly figure dressed in a flowing red dress emerges and floats in the air above him. Her raven black hair sticks straight up.

On her forehead, the specter wears the symbol of the Shadow Fairies, a glowing crest of the moon.

He recognizes the royal, red satin dress that he gave Flanyanna to wear to maintain appearances on her burning pyre more than he does the figure's unsubstantial being, for he could see right through her.

"Get away from me. You're not real. You're a horrible nightmare."

Markolous stumbles, slipping to his knees. "I sent you to oblivion, to the Lord of the Darkness." He scrambles up and races across the wet sand into the dark night.

Exhausted and not able to run anymore, he stops, panting heavily. "It's not possible. How can my sister seek revenge if she's in oblivion?"

"Markolous." Flanyanna's whispering voice beckons him into the pounding breakers. Her voice turns into the turbulent waves.

Suddenly, a wild swell surges up from the ocean's depths and hits him hard. Its savage embrace pulls, sucking him down into the seething cauldron of its murky waters.

"Markolous!" The voice is everywhere now, breaking in on his growing madness.

The hands of death grip him. Only his haunting, terrifying torment remains. His sister has captured him in the Shadow Fairy world. He twists and rolls over himself. Somersaulting, he tumbles into the black, endless abyss.

Without warning, the crashing wave spits him out, back onto the beach. Salty fluid spasms out of his lungs. Clawing with his hands and feet to gain traction, he crawls out of the surf and rolls over. Battered and beaten, Markolous turns his head and looks up from the sand into the dark night sky.

The ravens are gone.

An ominous, lightless vapor leaks out of the sky and coalesces into a shadowy, looming figure. Markolous scrambles to his knees, bowing down to the ground. He understands why the Shadow Fairies left.

"Master." He prostrates himself on the sand.

The phantom raises a skeletal hand and points at Markolous.

"You were to bring me the White Fairy queen."

"I did, Master. I did bring her to you."

"Silence!"

The specter thrust his skeletal finger up towards the top of the White Cliffs. A tremendous lightning bolt strikes a huge rowan tree with red berries on the cliff just above Markolous. It crashes down, just missing him.

"You have failed me."

"Master, my sister, the White Fairy queen, she was sacrificed on the pyre to you," Markolous protests.

"You fool. Your sister escaped to the Shadow Fairy world."

"What? How is that possible?"

"Because you let your other sister live."

"Pinky? She's locked up in the Tower of the Forgotten."

"Silence." The Lord of the Darkness raises his bony hand again from the darkness that surrounds him and extends his index finger at Markolous, ready to destroy him with another lightning bolt. "We had a bargain."

"No. Wait. Please. Please. I'll do anything." Markolous covers his third eye.

The Lord of the Darkness lowers his hand.

"Then bring me her baby."

"Master, I cannot. My sister's child is dead."

"You imbecile! She lives!"

"But, I ate her heart the night of the Blood Moon."

"Bring me the White Fairy baby to feast on her pure, innocent light, or I will feast on you."

The Lord of the Darkness disappears into the black night. Markolous stands alone on the empty beach.

A chambermaid, no more than thirteen, in a white apron with a long black skirt, shook Markolous' thrashing body.

"Get away from me!" he screamed, confused by the return to his physical body.

"Your Majesty—wake up!" she cried.

Markolous' ethereal body reentered his physical form. Still caught in the frightening illusion of his dream he jolted awake. Hunched over and crouched in one corner of the kingly bed, he felt warm piss trickle down his inner thigh. He had sold his etheric body to the Lord of the Darkness to win the throne and he had misjudged the cost.

"Sire, you had a nightmare." The young maid's eyes widened as she saw the dampness on the front of her liege's nightshirt.

Noticing the direction of her gaze, a humiliated Markolous snatched the bed sheet and wrapped it around his lower half.

"Are you all right, Sire?"

"All right? All right? Of course, I'm all right. Guards!" he yelled. Tithoreus and the guards on duty burst into the bedchamber. "What's she doing in my bedchamber?" Markolous demanded, clutching at the sheet that hid his shame.

The guards and Tithoreus looked perplexed. Chambermaids had spent a great deal of time in Markolous' bedroom and left in the next morning—if they were still alive.

"Sire, I need to tell you that your sister went to…," Tithoreus said.

"Be quiet! You think I don't know? I know everything! I am your king! Seize her!" Markolous pointed at the chambermaid.

Tithoreus' insect appendages doubled in length and reached out. They excreted a sticky slime that snagged and engulfed the terrified chambermaid.

The stunned Human Fairies guards did not move. The king had given a Human Fairy to a Tettigard!

"Go back to your posts," Markolous ordered, still holding the sheet about his soiled nightshirt.

The guards dashed out the door, fearing they would be next.

"Sire, be careful. You can't just—" Tithoreus said.

"I can do anything I want to do. Do you understand? Get rid of them," Markolous said, cutting Tithoreus off. "And get rid of her."

Tithoreus bowed and turned to leave with the chambermaid.

"No, wait." Markolous jumped up on his bed, snatching the Rose Crystal necklace that dangled in the canopy. He rummaged under his bed for his britches and his boots. "I'll make Pinky read for me," he muttered darkly. Putting on his britches and his boots, he started for the door.

"But, Sire, she's been in the Tower of the Forgotten for over six months. For all we know—she's dead," Tithoreus said.

"Shut up! Shut up! It's her, all right. Petronero wasn't smart enough to pull this off while he was alive let alone from the Shadow Fairy world. I'm going to make her read this queen's necklace and tell me where the princess is."

"The princess?

"The princess lives, you idiot. And if I don't deliver the child to him, he'll feast on me." Markolous stormed out the door.

"Sire. Where are you going?"

Markolous strode through the halls towards the dungeon. At the end of a hallway, he felt along the wall and found the crystal that opened a secret passage to the Tower of the Forgotten dungeon. Echoed by the talking walls as he approached Pinky's cell the crystal floors of the dungeon resounded to the heavy cadence of Markolous' shiny, black leather boots.

"Open the door," he ordered the guards.

Terrified, the Peccarey guard with the skeleton keys pulled them out of his pocket—fumbling for the right one.

Entering the dark and dank cell, Markolous' eyes slowly adjusted until he could see Pinky's effigy hanging above the floor, suspended by chains. Clutching the darkened Rose Crystal necklace, he slowly and cautiously moved closer. He reached out— grabbed her dangling hair—and yanked her head up.

"I want to talk to you."

Blank, lifeless eyes.

He dropped the effigy's head in anger and stormed out of the cell. He did not know how she had done it, but Pinky had escaped the Tower of the Forgotten—something no one had ever done before. All these years, he thought Flanyanna was his greatest danger. Now, he saw that, despite being disinherited at birth, Pinky posed the greatest threat. "Pinky!" he screamed.

"Pinky!" The walls echoed back.

Markolous entered the Throne Room with Tithoreus. Evila and the assembled advisors bowed as he pulled out the Rose Crystal necklace. It was dark in his hand as he raised it to the streaming light that the leaded glass, arched windows allowed into the room. He handed it to Evila.

"Look into the queen's necklace and tell me where Pinky is," he ordered—knowing if he found Pinky, he would find the princess.

Evila greedily clutched the necklace. Strangely, it did not glow in her hands. "It's a fake," she cried out.

"What? That's impossible. I took it from Flanyanna's neck."

"I tell you, it's a fake. There is no living luminance in this crystal. The one you handed me yesterday here in the Throne Room—it was real, but this one is a fake. Someone has stolen my necklace." As Markolous snatched the necklace from her, she snarled, "You have been duped."

Markolous dashed the amulet to the floor. Rather than shattering into pieces, it vanished into thin air with a 'poof'.

"You kept the real amulet from me, from my seeing eye—and now Pinky has stolen it right from under your nose," Evila accused.

"Be quiet."

"It's mine. I'm to be your queen, not her. You must make her pay with her life for stealing my necklace," she said.

Markolous stared at Evila, "My dear, jealousy—becomes you...."

The inexorable, percussive beating of Namdalarian and Tettigard wings shattered the day's tranquility. Markolous on Calamtheus, with a half a dozen Human Fairy soldiers, flew swiftly towards the Lost Forest. Tithoreus flew in the back with his Tettigard soldiers, a distance away from the Human Fairies.

The armed party passed over the ancient stone bridge near Pinky's home as the flying horses and giant insects dropped from the sky to descend below the trees. The passage of their wings stirred the stream's placid surface as they passed over and landed in the clearing next to the cottage.

Markolous motioned to the soldiers to proceed cautiously. Although apprehensive about the Pink Fairy's magical power, the squad moved in closer at Markolous' command and surrounded Pinky's meager hut.

"Rosecenilla," he called out, "give yourself up. We know you have the princess."

No response from inside.

Markolous nodded to Tithoreus.

The sharp spines on Tithoreus' arms bristled as he beckoned to several of the Human Fairy soldiers to dismount and approach the cottage. As they drew near the door, a wall of yellow-pink crystal sprang up and blocked them. They dropped to the ground, unconscious.

"It's guarded by magic!" Markolous exclaimed.

The winged horses snorted and pranced, shifting skittishly.

They could feel the fear of their Human Fairy riders.

Markolous pulled his sword from its sheath. Spinning it counterclockwise three times, he thrust it towards the cottage, invoking a counter spell.

He nodded to another Human Fairy soldier. The soldier dismounted and dragged his two bewitched comrades away.

"Kick the door down, but don't kill them. Bring them to me alive," Markolous ordered.

With several hard thrusts from his boot, the soldier smashed the door open. On their mounts two soldiers stormed in. After a moment they came back out, shaking their heads.

"She's not here, Sire," one called out.

"Burn it down." Markolous pulled on Calamtheus' reins.

The soldiers picked up twigs, piling them around the outside of the bungalow. One pulled moss from crevices on the bridge to make a torch and ran back to the cottage.

"Give me that." Markolous extended his hand. With a focus from his third eye, he lit it and rode over to Pinky's home. Igniting the kindling his soldiers had gathered, he then tossed the burning torch on the thatched roof. The roof and the rest of the cottage were quickly consumed by the flames.

"So, now what do we do?" Tithoreus said coming up from the behind with his soldiers. "How do we find them?"

"I don't know. But I have to find the princess and kill her to ensure my rule." More than that, Markolous feared he would be the one consumed by the Lord of the Darkness if he didn't produce her.

"Sire?"

"Yes. We'll kill all girl babies born near the Blood Moon."

"But, will Human Fairies kill their own young?"

"If any soldiers blanch at my order, kill them."

"But, aren't you concerned about what they'll think?" Tithoreus nodded towards the Human Fairy soldiers.

"You heard me," Markolous said. "Gather up every female Human Fairy child below the age of one year born around the Blood Moon."

"Sire, let me get more of my brethren. They'll have no qualms about killing your kind's young. I'll go back to the palace and summon more Tettigards."

"Good idea, Tithoreus. I'll meet you at the edge of the forest."

Tithoreus nodded and took off to return to the Crystal Palace for Tettigard reinforcements.

"Follow me," Markolous told the soldiers. He urged Calamtheus to go airborne.

Leaving Pinky's burning cottage, the soldiers took up formation behind their king. They rose in the sky with their wings outstretched, covering the sky in dread and gloom.

In a hazy mist the cleansing began.

Markolous' soldiers swept through the villages and the countryside to fulfill their grim and horrifying task. They went to each Human Fairy's house with the intent of abducting all female babies under the age of one year.

The soldiers would demand female babies under one year without any explanation other than it was ordered by the king. If the parents resisted disclosing the child's identity, they were told all their children would suffer the same fate if they did not comply, forcing the parents to choose who would live and who would die.

Innocent girl babies were torn from their mother's breast, carried into the street, and tossed into a wooden cart with other baby girls. Screams of agony and sorrow beyond endurance rang throughout the night. Mothers and fathers pleaded, but to no avail. Their protests fell on uncaring alien, insect ears. The girl babies were found and ripped from their families.

In the manic insanity of it all, many Human Fairies tried to flee the giant insects with their babies in hand, only to be slain, their baby girls still taken. Tettigard marauders burned the homes of those from whom the babies had to be taken by force.

The night went by. Markolous did not rest easy until every girl baby was found. As the night wore on, the odious stench of fear and burning infant flesh grew in the land. The babies were sacrificed to the Lord of the Darkness who greedily sucked up their innocent light.

When it was done, the silence came. The abominable purge to assure Markolous' survival and his rule had run its course. The Human Fairies wept silently behind closed doors, shocked by the stark cruelty of the world in which they now lived. There were no more baby girls below the age of one in any Human Fairy house on Kokakina. Although the babies were burned on a pyre in the town square, the princess was not found among them.

The Raven Cottage

Deep in the Lost Forest, Lunamilla's thatched roof cottage nestled in a dense grove of evergreens. Tiny treasures taken from nature filled every nook and cranny of the quaint bungalow. On top of her rough-hewn, whitewashed kitchen table sat—a bird's nest with robin-blue eggs, a pile of uncut ruby crystals, and a multitude of ribboned conch shells from the seashore. Standing in front of the table, Lunamilla poured boiling water into a chipped, brown ceramic mug over a bed of milk thistle for her liver. On her wrinkled and sagging neck, she wore her latest treasure—the queen's Rose Crystal necklace. She had worn it many times before, when she was Kokakina's Pink Fairy seer and—remembering her magical presence—it glowed brightly.

Humming, she shuffled on her aching, swollen feet over the scuffed, wide-planked wooden floor painted in a black and white checkerboard pattern over to the outer hearth. She put her dented and scratched kettle back on the crane in the fire chamber. The fire had burned down to smoldering embers; she added more dry twigs from the pile on the floor to relight it. To her satisfaction she felt the fire warming and flushing her face as it reignited. Her gnarled hands crackled and popped when she opened a ceramic crock sitting on top of the mantle above the blackened stone outer hearth. She pulled out a tall straw and placed one end of it in the fire. It quickly burst into flames and she used it to light a beeswax candle sitting in the center of the table. Taking the queen's necklace from her neck, she gently swung it over the candle. Long experience had taught her that the motion of the necklace over the candle's light and heat would aid her to see into the heart matrix of the Rose Crystal.

A loud knock at the door resounded through the tiny cottage.

Startled, Lunamilla flapped her arms like raven wings, and she flew up into the air. She was not used to visitors at any hour.

"Ow!" she exclaimed, hitting her head on the center beam of the cottage.

Rubbing her head with her raven's claw, she peered out the small round window next to the door with the darting, robotic head movement of a bird. Twitching, she snatched the Rose Crystal necklace off the table with her bird claw. Clutching it to her heart, she frantically looked for a hiding place.

The visitor struck the door once again, this time even harder.

With a clang Lunamilla dropped the necklace onto the floor.

"Yes, yes. I'm coming—I'm coming. Hold your Namdalarians, for fairy's sake."

She waved her claw at the mantle. The lid of a biscuit tin sitting on it rose up. Lifting up off the floor, the necklace floated over to the open tin and settled in. The lid then put itself back in place. Satisfied, Lunamilla bird-hopped to the front door and—with her gnarled claw—unlatched and opened it.

"Well, look what the wind blew in," she said sarcastically, stepping aside.

"Hello, Mom," Pinky said as she entered. "How've you been?" She glanced around the minuscule confines of her childhood home and immediately felt less tense. She sighed with relief seeing nothing had changed. In the corner of the cottage next to the outer hearth, she saw her miniature bed, a present from her father when she was born. It featured carved rose water lilies on the headboard inlaid with rose crystals. The four carved legs were those of a dragon whose clawed feet spread out onto the floor. It sat on the hard-packed dirt skirting the checkerboard wooden floor in the cottage's center. She knew she had not spent much time with her mother as of late. After Pinky's father died, the rift that eventually became the civil war developed in the royal family. Pinky became preoccupied with helping Flanyanna stay in power as the Human Fairy queen to keep balance and harmony in the land.

"Terrible, if you really must know. But, you haven't been around much lately," Lunamilla said.

"Mom, you know why....."

"You're one to talk. You don't look so good yourself. In fact, you look awful, but I'm glad you got out of the dungeon."

"Mom, you never told me you had a sister."

"You never asked."

"Okay. Mom, do you have a sister?"

"This isn't the time to talk about skeletons in the family closet."

"Mom, that's not much of an answer."

"Well, that's all the answer you're gonna get." Lunamilla had never told Pinky about her family and her past.

"All right, Mom, have it your way."

"You may look like me and not your father, but you definitely have his temperament."

Pinky knew her mother was right. She was born with her mother's pale pink skin, and she inherited the magical talent of the Pink Fairies, but she did have her father's temperament. Like him, she was fair and just in her relations with others, but they both could make mistakes. One of her father's mistakes was not marrying Lunamilla and recognizing Pinky as one of his children. Her mother never forgave him for that.

But, Lunamilla was in awe of her daughter. Pinky's magical powers were truly spectacular, even for a Pink Fairy. She was proud to be Pinky's mother, but she never told Pinky. Lunamilla softened. "Let me have a look at you. Just as I suspected. They fed you only enough to keep you alive in that dreadful Tower of the Forgotten. Markolous is just like his mother." She shook her head.

"I'm hungry, Mother. I haven't eaten all day and, you're right. They didn't feed me very well in the Tower of the Forgotten." Pinky did not want to fight. She remembered how her mother was so critical of her when she was a child. It seemed to Pinky that nothing she ever did was quite good enough. Her mother expected perfection. Over the years, to handle her childhood wounding, Pinky spent less and less time with her mother.

Elfman shyly entered the cottage, bending his muscular body to fit through the door.

"Hello, Lunamilla," he said. His ten-point antlers brushed the ceiling. He looked around, remembering the cottage. He had often played here with Pinky when he was a Human Fairy child. "The place looks the same."

"What'd you bring him for?" Lunamilla snarled. "If you don't mind, I need to talk to my daughter—alone."

"I'm sorry, but it *is* my mother's house," Pinky said. She was ashamed of how her mother had treated Elfman all these years. "Please wait outside. I'll be there in a minute."

He lowered his head in acquiescence. "Sure. No problem. I'll be right outside, if you need me."

Pinky closed the door behind him.

"Mom, why do you insist on being so mean to Elfman?"

Lunamilla shrugged her shoulders, glancing at the tin on the mantle. "Because he's just not good enough for you."

"Mom—"

"Pinky—he's an animal now." Lunamilla turned her head away quickly, for she did not want Pinky to have the chance to use her third eye to discover that the queen's necklace was inside the tin. "All these years wasted. Why you love that enchanted buck more than anything else." Lunamilla shook you head in disapproval. "You've always let everything in the whole forest into the house. Why should I expect you to be any different."

She got a wooden bowl and spoon and went over to a cast iron cauldron sitting on the heated stones at the back of the hearth. Once there, she scooped out some still warm vegetable, root and herb goulash—leftovers from last night's supper.

"Mom, it doesn't matter what I do. You'll ever be happy with me," Pinky said in pained resignation as she sat down to eat the stew.

"What a strange thing to say."

"Well, it's true, isn't it?"

"Is that what you think? I accepted a secondary place in the king's life as his mistress in hopes of securing a better life for you—and this is all the thanks I get?"

"I'm not here to talk about that."

"A distant cousin to the king, rather than acknowledging you as his real daughter. On the throne you would have ruled with your heart...." Lunamilla cut herself off, gritting her teeth.

"I'm sorry. I won't bother you again, but...," Pinky retorted painfully, her face turning bright pink, the old wound festering.

"Was that really the best your father could do for you?"

"Mom—I need—oh, never mind."

"I now see how much you are my daughter...," Lunamilla said pointing her clawed finger at Pinky. "Expecting nothing and getting nothing. No. He didn't choose me. He stayed with his barren wife rather than be with his fertile mistress."

"Mom, I'm sorry he didn't choose you, but he was the king."

"Oh, and let's not forget that he married that dreadful, despicable Casafala whose bloodline is suspect— making all my babies illegitimate—my creations, worthless." Lunamilla went over to the tin containing Flanyanna's Rose Crystal necklace. Opening it up, she pulled out the queen's necklace by its 24-karat soft gold chain and dangled it in front of her daughter.

"Mom, the queen's necklace?"

"You know, families are overrated, especially royal families, but the jewelry, that's another story...."

"How did you ever get it?" Pinky asked incredulously, her hunger totally forgotten.

Lunamilla sat down next to Pinky on the wooden plank bench at the kitchen table. In the presence of the two Pink Fairies, the Rose Crystal necklace glowed brilliantly.

"It doesn't matter. It belongs to you now that Flanyanna is gone," Lunamilla said, placing the necklace around her daughter's neck.

"Oh, Mom, how could you.....You stole the Rose Crystal necklace from Markolous, didn't you?"

"What good is it to him? Don't worry. I left a fake in its place."

Pinky touched the necklace around her neck. Having worn it in service as the seer to her land, it felt very familiar. "Then, you know that Flanyanna's baby lives?"

"Of course, I do."
"Then you know that the Rose Crystal's prophecy is that the princess is to rule Kokakina?"

"And how can a baby that is not yet in our reality rule our kingdom?"

"Mom!"

"Don't you see? The Rose Crystal wants you to be the ruler until Flanyanna's baby is grown. You're the firstborn. It's what your father wants for you too now...."

Pinky removed the necklace from her neck.

"There are other seers in the land, you know," Lunamilla said.

"Mom, that's not why you stole it!"

"You really think you're the only one who can read the Rose Crystal?" Lunamilla retorted, looking Pinky in her third eye.

Pinky clutched the chain of the amulet in her hand knowing what her mother was telling her was true.

"He'd never have figured it out, but that Evila...," Lunamilla said.

"Evila?" Pinky remembered Evila. There were times Evila was at court when Pinky went to visit her father. She recalled her as being exotically beautiful—but very manipulative.

"Oh, you don't know? Markolous is going to marry Evila, that Blue Fairy trollop whose parents sold her to him."

"Markolous is going to marry Evila?"

"She's a seer, isn't she? He can't read the feminine heart matrix. The necklace is worthless to him without a seer."

Pinky held the Rose Crystal pendant in her hand, feeling its pulsating power.

"If I hadn't stolen this necklace, how'd you expect to keep the princess safe from him? By now, Evila surely would have read the crystal of our land's heart matrix—and Markolous would know exactly where to find the princess."

Lunamilla took the necklace back from Pinky and dangled it in front of her third eye, with the candle on the table shining through it. "Just look!"

The Tikkum children play with the princess in their home.

"All the sacrifices for those expensive tutors...." Pinky's mother's rolled her eyes. "Those teachers cost so much and obviously taught you nothing." She laid the necklace on the kitchen table.

"They didn't cost you anything!" Pinky retorted.

"All right! Never mind. For fairies' sakes, child, that Tarragonian won't be able to keep Flanyanna's daughter safe for long," Lunamilla said.

"You're right—never mind," Pinky admitted ruefully.

Lunamilla was taken aback. "So you agree?" She hadn't expected Pinky to concede so easily.

"Well, I'm here, aren't I? Tell me the truth. What happened to my brothers and sisters?" Pinky asked.

"I don't know what you're talking about?"

"Don't play games. Too much is at stake. I know you didn't kill them like everyone said."

Lunamilla froze for a moment before answering. "Well, I didn't use herbs to get rid of them. If that's what you mean," she shot back.

"Mother, I know you didn't do that. I was even told you drowned them."

"Who told you that? Casafala?" Lunamilla snapped.

Pinky nodded. "Please. Tell me. What did you do with them?"

Lunamilla's raven claws picked up a tiny, spotted suede gold and brown bag. She spat three times. "Casafala, Casafala, Casafala!"

"Stop with Casafala—it's over—it's over."

"Really? Foolish girl! Is that what you think? " Lunamilla put two ceramic cups in the sack.

"Mom, please, we don't have much time," Pinky said. "We need to save the princess! What did you do with my brothers and sisters?"

"Finally, you understand what it means to have a child who needs protection and to be saved—and you—you don't know what to do."

"Then, you do know where the princess can go and be safe—don't you?" Pinky asked.

"Of course I do. Why do you think I stole the queen's necklace from Markolous?"

"MOTHER—"

"Well, it's complicated. All right, I stole it for more than one reason. Okay?"

The water in the kettle hissed as Lunamilla poured it out on the fire to extinguish the flames.

Pinky got up from the bench. "I have known ever since I was a little girl—I knew my brothers and sisters were alive. Even though you never talked about them."

"I never mentioned them. Never. I was afraid Casafala—she'd have killed them if she knew they were alive. It was all I could do to keep you safe." Lunamilla leaned over and removed the blanket from Pinky's small bed with her clawed hands.

"Mother, you must tell me. Where—where did you take my brothers and sisters?"

Lunamilla sat down wearily on the bench with the magical bag on her lap. "I sent your brothers and sisters to Earth." Her eyes teared up as she folded Pinky's baby blanket and placed it in the magical bag.

"You mean they're living among Humans on Earth?" Pinky asked incredulously. All these years she had felt separated and isolated and now she realized not only did her siblings not get to live in the Lost Forest with their mother, they were also put on another planet, and not told who they really were.

"That's what I'm telling you. White Fairies have been passing as Humans on Earth for centuries. We best be going...." Lunamilla slowly raised herself up from the kitchen table.

"The princess will be raised by Humans?" Pinky gasped.

Lunamilla nodded. "It was good enough for your siblings."

"That's *awful!*"

Lunamilla moved around the cottage, stuffing things into the small, magical satchel that accepted objects far too big for its apparent size. "Do you have a better idea?"

Pinky did not. As much as she did not want to send the princess into exile, never knowing who she really was, she could not think of any other way to save her.

"Okay—how did you get them to Earth?"

"Didn't those tutors teach you anything—during the Blood Moon—that's when the ancient portal to Earth opens."

"You mean the ancient portal our ancestors used to get here from Earth?" Pinky asked, remembering the Human Fairy folklore handed down from generation to generation which she learned from Bessalina on her summers at the Faireye Manor.

Lunamilla nodded as she took the biscuit tin from the mantle and pushed it into the magical bag.

"And you—you still remember how to get there—right?" Pinky asked.

"I still remember. I haven't lost my senses—yet!"

"Of course, I didn't mean that!"

"Only a few thousand lightyears separate Earth and Kokakina—a walk in the park." Lunamilla raised her eyebrows as she studied her daughter. "Are you all right?"

"It's just that I-I didn't realize the princess must go to Earth."

"I know it's hard. It's hard to let go…," Lunamilla said.

"She won't be with her own kind. Never mind. How do we —I—get her to Earth?"

"You need to go the largest of the three islands off the coast near the Faireye Manor."

"The three islands?"

"Yes. There's a blue glacier on one of them."

"I remember it when I was a child at the manor....Go on."

"Well, it's nothing, really. Go to the top of the mountain."

"That's it? Go to the top of the mountain?"

"Well, not exactly."

"Mother—not exactly? What does that mean *not exactly*?"

"Those royal tutors....The Fey Portal is in the blue glacier and will open at the time of the Blood Moon. And that's how the princess will travel between the two planets in the creamy Milky Way. Yes, and, of course, you'll need to go with her."

"Of course...."

"It's amazing, really. You cut through time and space effortlessly. Don't worry, you'll have plenty of time to come back after you find her a suitable home for her among the Humans."

"Right. But, wait a minute. We just had a Blood Moon. I thought only happen once every sixteen years."

"Your astronomy taught by those expensive tutors is correct and incorrect," Lunamilla said.

"Meaning...?"

"Meaning—that's usually true."

"Well, then, this will never work. What am I going to do with the princess for sixteen years?"

"Now hold your Namdalarians," Lunamilla said with a twinkle in her eye. "It's rare to be sure, but Blood Moons can come again sooner, sometimes within a few days."

"You mean...?"

"We're having another Blood Moon in two days!"

Pinky remembered Calisandra's words to her the day before, that once the princess was born, she had three days before she had to give her heart to the Shadow Fairies. "There's enough time to get the princess to Earth. But, we need to go now, Mom, before Markolous figures out where to find her."

"What do you think I've been packing this bag for?"

"Mom—thank you. I'll never doubt you again."

Pinky's whole body felt a rush of relief as she rushed towards the door. Until this moment, she had been acting on blind faith, as had all readers of the crystals for eons. She realized the crystals hid the second coming of the Blood Moon to protect the princess. The heart of the matrix knew of the evil to which Markolous had succumbed in his service to the Lord of the Darkness.

"Wait! You're forgetting something." Lunamilla picked up the Rose Crystal necklace off the table and handed it to Pinky. "You're going to need this."

"You keep it for now," Pinky said.

"Very well, I wish you would make up your mind. You're just like your father," Lunamilla said, rolling her eyes and snatching back the amulet with her claw fingers.

"My father? I don't think so. I think I learned that from you." Pinky smiled.

"What are you talking about? Your father could never make up his mind."

"Now, I don't think we can completely blame him for that, Mother."

"You always did side with your father." Placing the necklace around her neck and happy to be wearing it, Lunamilla started towards the door. She stopped abruptly and looked back at Pinky. Mother and daughter stared into each other's third eyes, knowing a dark time was upon Kokakina.

"I should have turned Markolous into a toad the day he was born. It would still be more than he deserves," Lunamilla groused.

"Mom, let's go." Pinky hoped she would be able to take the princess and get her to Earth before the Shadow Fairies took her heart. But, her mother knew the way back to Earth. If Pinky could not take the princess, Lunamilla knew the way.

Lunamilla, now as a raven, hopped out the door with the necklace in her beak. Pinky grabbed the magical bag that Lunamilla left on the table and followed her outside.

"Mother, wait. You forgot your magic pouch." She picked up her mother's shawl from its peg by the door and ran after her. "And you forgot your shawl too. It'll be cold."

"Thank you, dear."

"Mom…." Pinky looked at the starry sky.

"What?"

Pinky wanted tell her mother about the deal she had made with the Shadow Fairies but it was not the right time.

"Nothing. Nothing that can't wait."

"Remember, the mind can only conjure fear."

"Yes, I know."

"*You're a Pink Fairy.* Your strength is to feel everything through your heart and then think. Always trust your heart and you'll know what to do."

"My heart…."

The raven was longer listening to Pinky. Her beady eyes stared at the magical pouch in Pinky's hand. It floated onto Elfman's antlers where he was standing next to Pinky.

"Here, take my bag and be useful for a change," she said to Elfman before turning back to her.

Without warning, the necklace lit up and flashed brilliantly, lighting up the night like it was daytime.

Pinky looked into the crystal and drew in a sharp intake of breath.

"What is it?" Elfman asked.

"Markolous! They know where I hid the princess. He's on his way to the Tarragonian village to kill her."

"We've got to stop him…," Elfman said.

Without a word, the raven reached down, picked up the queen's necklace in her beak. Then, spreading her wings, she flew up into the midnight blue, cloudless sky.

"Mother, wait."

"Pinky…," Elfman said in an aside, shaking his head to readjust the bag's weight, "I don't think your mother likes me."

"What? What are you talking about? Of course, she likes you. She's just lived in the forest a long time," Pinky replied.

"No, I don't think so."

"Elfman, I have to go with my mother. Meet us at Doc Tikkum's house with her bag." Pinky changed into a raven and flew off after her mother.

Elfman looked up.

Two moving black dots glided in the clear night sky. Angling their sleek, blue-black bodies to catch the wind in their outstretched, feathered wings, the wind's current guided them, and Lunamilla, carrying the Rose Crystal necklace, dropped into a steep, death defying spiral.

"No, she doesn't like me." He jumped into the bushes.

The Fairy Jig

Carrying the queen's necklace in her raven beak, Lunamilla landed on the stone bridge leading to the Tarragonian village. It dropped from her mouth when she reverted back to her Human Fairy form. Stooping down, she picked it up again and placed it around her neck.

"Well, that was a bit of a rough landing." With her clawed hands she brushed the red dust from her shoulders and the black feathers on her dress. She shuddered. "Pinky was right. It's a bit chilly." Pulling her shawl out of the ethers, she placed it over her shoulders. In the far distance a dusty cloud from the hooves of galloping winged steeds billowed down the country road.

"Mom, they're coming," Pinky said, landing and changing into her Human Fairy form.

"Of course, they're coming. What are you doing here? I thought you went with your buck?"

"No. I wanted to come with you."

"Well, that's nice—for a change." Her mother smoothed her hair. She ran her claws through the strands. "You know Markolous brought his Tettigards...."

"Yes. I'm sorry to say he isn't who he used to be," Pinky said.

Lunamilla shook her head. "Whatever. You always had a soft spot for him. Of course, you'd bring anything home and take care of it!"

"Mom, can we talk about this later?"

"Okay. How about those blood-sucking Tettigards? You can smell their blood lust a mile away."

"Mom, they don't have much of a smell...."

"Stop interrupting me. You're destroying my concentration."

"Okay, Mom. Just hurry up."

"Let's see. What do I have to do...."

"Maybe I can help you. How about the—" Pinky said.

"—the double-blind spell—" Lunamilla interrupted. "—it was your father's favorite."

"Mom, are you okay?"

"Of course I'm okay. What kind of question is that?"

"I don't know. I just wanted to make sure...."

"Would you stop interfering with my concentration?"

"Okay, I'll go get the princess."

"Good idea. Do that," Lunamilla said, with an edge in her voice.

"Mom?"

"Now what?"

"I just want you to know—how much I appreciate you—you know—raising me in the Lost Forest by yourself."

Lunamilla shook her head. "Daughter, don't butter me up."

"You know what Markolous will do to the Tarragonians."

"Lizard boots?"

"That's right. I can't just leave them behind...."

"The prophecy didn't say anything about saving those Tarragonians. We have to save *her*."

"But, don't you see? Doc Tikkum saved the princess from Markolous that night. He risked everything."

"That's nice, but they have no magic. I see no value in taking them."

"That's just it. They have no magic to protect themselves. And why are you wearing the Rose Crystal necklace? Somebody could be watching?" Pinky asked.

Lunamilla took off the necklace and held it in her raven's claw. "Okay. We'll take the fat scaly guy, he might be of help. But his family will just get in the way."

"Mother, Just do the spell. We're taking the entire Tikkum family—and that's final."

"Okay, okay, have it your way."

Pinky transformed herself back into a raven. "After you take care of Markolous, I want you to take the Rose Crystal necklace to the Còrcair Mountains. We'll meet you there." Following the stream, she flew towards Doc Tikkum's house.

"All right. All right. Be that way. Just like her father. I do like working alone. I can finally concentrate."

A shadowy figure appeared and hovered over the bridge.

"Easy for you to say," Lunamilla said like she was still talking to someone. "No, no—that's not it. I know they're almost here."

"Would you stop interrupting me? First our daughter and now you! Why does everyone keep interrupting me?"

She smoothed her hair. Running her claw fingers through her silver and black strands, she walked off the bridge and now stood on the Tarragonian side of the stream. "That's it—I remember now."

The Rose Crystal necklace lifted from her clawed hand. It glowed in front of her. She pointed one of her claw fingers at the necklace and then pointed at the bridge, circling it in the air three times clockwise—nothing happened.

"I wish you would stop interrupting me," she said, putting a claw to her mouth, tapping it, still trying to remember the spell. "Okay, I've got it this time," she said, talking to the late king. She smiled and her green eyes twinkled. "Well, I'm glad to see you like it as much as I do. At least we like one thing in common—besides our daughter and our other children."

Lunamilla swirled around and flicked at the necklace dangling in the air with her claw fingers and then towards the stone bridge. Another bridge appeared, an exact replica of the first one.

"See? I told you I could remember that spell." Lunamilla smiled, pleased with her creation. "What are you talking about? Once they cross the phony bridge, they'll be going in the wrong direction for miles before they know they've been tricked."

Suddenly, she fell down the creek embankment like somebody had pushed her. The necklace, floating in mid-air, followed and dropped next to her.

Markolous and his henchmen lurched around the bend in the road. Lunamilla raised up and pointed her claws towards one of the bridges. She then pointed them at the other bridge.

"Which bridge is the real one? Are you sure? I don't think so. I think it's the other one. I am hurrying, for fairy's sake—and stop telling me what to do—I can't remember with you always interrupting me."

Dust trailed behind the sweating, panting Namdalarians. Markolous and a company of Namdalarian riders raced towards the two bridges at a breakneck pace. Tithoreus and a squad of Tettigards flew behind, close to the ground.

Sweat dripped down Markolous' forehead, blurring his vision. He blinked. In front of him, he thought he saw two bridges. Suddenly, huge lilac bushes with purple flowers sprang up in front of the bridge that led toward the Tarragonian village and Doc Tikkum's house. He blinked again, for his sweat now mixed with the red dust from Calamtheus' galloping hooves.

The Namdalarians and their riders swerved away from the real bridge and galloped onto the fake one, Tithoreus and the Tettigards following closely behind. In a flash, they all disappeared into Lunamilla's illusion.

"I just love the smell of lilacs in the spring." Lunamilla closed her eyes and took in a deep breath, enjoying the strong fragrance. Now on the other side of the stream, she broke into a lively Human Fairy jig. Then she abruptly stopped, putting her hands on her hips. "Why can't I enjoy myself? Markolous is trapped in my spell. All right, all right. Have it your way." Lunamilla shook her head and started down the worn path by the stream that led to Doc Tikkum's house.

She stopped to look back at the bridge. "Where do you think I'm going—to help our little girl. She needs me. Glendorf, aren't you coming?" She motioned to his shadowy figure still on the bridge. "What are you talking about? We have plenty of time to get to the rebel camp. You know, the trouble with you and our daughter is that neither one of you knows how to have fun."

The Rose Crystal necklace rose up from the embankment. It floated towards her and dropped around her neck. She smiled.

Suddenly, she threw up her arms in disgust more than defeat and turned back. "Okay, have it your way. I won't wear the necklace." She took off the necklace and placed it in her mouth.

She and Glendorf turned into ravens. With the necklace, they took off and flew towards the Còrcair Mountains to the rebel camp.

The worn shutters of the Tikkum cottage were closed. A curl of smoke rose from the mud and rock chimney. A raven quietly knocked on the front door with its beak, hoping to gain entrance without disturbing the neighbors. But, no one answered the door.

"I think they're all still asleep. Why don't you go through the window," Elfman's voice suggested.

"Elfman—you startled me!" Pinky saw that the window off to the side of the door was slightly ajar.

The buck jumped out of the cone-shaped shrubs next to the Tikkum cottage, his passage rustling their lime-colored foliage. Lunamilla's magical bag still dangled from his antlers.

"Did I? Sorry."

"You're probably right. I don't want to startle the children. They'll wake up the whole neighborhood," she said.

The raven hopped up onto the ledge of the cottage window, knowing that as a bird, she would be less conspicuous to any Tarragonian neighbors who might be getting up. She pressed on the window with her raven's beak to open it more.

Suddenly, the window flew opened and a small, green-clawed hand snatched a very surprised Pinky. With ruffled feathers Pinky let out a loud—squawk—and disappeared inside the cottage.

Inside the mud and weed cottage, Pinky morphed back into her Human Fairy form.

Little Tither stood there, her stubby little legs planted firmly on the dirt floor. Her clawed green-blue hands clenched and unclenched. Her red tongue flicked in and out and her tail swished about below her rumpled muslin nightgown.

"What'ta you doing here?" Tither asked the shimmering Pink Fairy.

Pinky could see the princess asleep in her hammock next to the warm outer hearth and was flooded with relief. She was safe, for the moment.

"You're here for my little sister, aren't you?" Tither accused.

"Could you wake up your parents and tell them I'm here, please?"

"How do I know you won't hurt her?" Tither asked, her eyes narrowing in suspicion.

"I would never hurt her. I'm her aunt."

"You could be somethin' you're not," Tither said.

"Well, I'm not. I'm here to help. Would you please wake up your parents?"

"She doesn't want to go with you," Tither said defiantly. Her eyes narrowing even more, she kicked Pinky in the shin.

"Ow! " Pinky jumped in pain.

"Mom! Dad!" Tither screamed. She puffed herself out, looking like a baby red dragon. Her swollen and extended body made her quite formidable. Her long tail contrasted with the roundish head on her muscular neck. "She's tryin' to steal my sister!" Tither screamed at the top of her lungs.

"Shhhhhh. You'll wake up the whole neighborhood," Pinky said.

The whole household went into turmoil. All the other Tarragonian children jumped out of bed and crawled down to the cottage floor. They encircled Pinky, huffing and puffing. Black smoke poured from their nostrils.

"No, wait. Stop! You don't understand," Pinky said, coughing from the black smoke filling the small cottage and her lungs.

Tither scaled up to her parents' bed. She pushed at her father's back with her stout, curved, and pointed claws. "Daddy, wake up!"

"Scratch more to the right," Doc Tikkum muttered in his sleep.

"Wake up—that Pink Fairy is here again. She wants to take away my baby sister." Tither pulled down the sheet cover, revealing Doc Tikkum and Mother Tikkum in their muslin night shirts that covered them completely except for their green clawed feet. Reflexively, both her parents' feet contracted, the claws pulling back over the cushioning pads that covered the base of their toes and the balls of their feet.

A startled Mother Tikkum blinked open her eyes. "What's going on down there?"

"I've been tryin' to tell you—the mean Pink Fairy is trying to take my sister. Daddy, do somethin'," Tither said.

Mother Tikkum looked down. "Oh dear, what will become of us?" She pushed and shoved on Doc Tikkum. "Husband, wake up."

"Why do babies always have to be born in the middle of the night?" a groggy Doc Tikkum mumbled.

"Husband—" Mother Tikkum screamed in his ear. "It's the Pink Fairy."

Doc Tikkum jumped, hitting his head on the low beam. "Ow!"

Hearing Doc Tikkum's voice, Pinky looked up. "Tell your family to gather their things—we have to leave immediately," she said, still coughing from the black smoke.

"I'm not going anywhere in the middle of the night," Mother Tikkum protested, folding her arms in defiance across her chest and looking down at the smoke filled cottage.

"Markolous and his soldiers are near and they're coming here," Pinky said, still choking on the smoke.

"Children!" Mother Tikkum screamed at the top of her lungs. "Gather up your things."

"Mother," Doc Tikkum admonished his wife, "calm yourself. You'll scare the children." He knew their lives were never going to be the same again. Markolous surely knew by now that he had taken the princess out of the Tower of the Forgotten, but he thought it best not to say anything about that to his now hysterical wife.

"That wretched Human Fairy who calls himself King of Kokakina," fretted Mother Tikkum. She jumped from her bed and slithered down the wall to her kitchen where she gathered up pots and pans hanging on wooden pegs next to the outer hearth and slammed them on the table. She grabbed their eating utensils, wooden spoons, knives, and forks. On the outer hearth, a few loaves of bread were warming for breakfast. She folded everything into the spider-spun tablecloth on the kitchen table and lifted it up, using it to hold all its contents.

"You heard your mother," Doc Tikkum affirmed. "Gather your clothes and wrap up your blankets to make knapsacks— we're going on an adventure—a Tikkum adventure."

Immediately, the children released their prisoner, and scrambled up the wall to throw on their clothes. They scrounged about for their favorite toys and possessions. One small Tikkum took a special rock from the creek bed with embedded crystals. Another grabbed a cherished storybook. Tither's favorite was her beloved handmade doll with green button eyes.

Everyone moved at a feverish pace, gathering up their belongings and stuffing them in their homemade knapsacks. Their lives were at stake and the children responded to their parents' urgency.

Pinky picked up the princess and held her close. The little Human Fairy baby held Pinky's finger tightly and smiled up into her jade-green eyes. "Hi, there," Pinky said.

"Is that really the Pink Fairy, Father?" Abra asked, seeing her for the first time. He had been asleep both when Pinky came to get Doc Tikkum when Flanyanna was ready to give birth and when she came back with the potion for Flanyanna.

Doc Tikkum looked at Pinky, who was removing the princess' hammock from its hook. "Yes—that's her."

"How come I didn't see her either?" Frodora asked, admiring the iridescent Pink Fairy.

"You were asleep," Doc Tikkum said.

"Are we going to the Tower of the Forgotten, Father?" Abra asked. "You can tell me."

"No! Of course not. I told you—we're going on an adventure." Doc Tikkum did not elaborate further, for he did not know where they were going. He finished putting on his breeches and vest and went over to where Pinky was standing with the princess.

Pinky gently placed the princess on the kitchen table. She re-wrapped the child in the Tikkum's homespun tablecloth and tied it around her own shoulders, knotting it like a sling to fit better around her.

"Pinky, where're we going?" Doc Tikkum asked.

"I'll tell you later," Pinky reassured him. "We must go now. Markolous could get here at any moment."

Doc Tikkum went over to Mother Tikkum who was gathering herbs that were hanging to dry next to the outer hearth and placing them in her improvised satchel.

"Mother. It's time to go."

"Hurry, children!" she screamed.

Tither tugged on her father's vest. He picked her up.

"Father, where're we goin'?" Tither asked, clinging to her doll.

"Why, I thought you liked surprises." Doc Tikkum threw her up into the air to distract her because he had no idea where they could possibly go on Kokakina to hide from Markolous.

"Children, put your coats on," he calmly instructed. Setting Tither down, he picked up his spectacles from the carved wood mantle and slipped them into his vest pocket.

Gathering up his medical bag from the peg next to the front door, he slung it over his shoulder. The children took their coats from the wooden pegs all in a row and put them on. Doc Tikkum looked around his cottage for the last time and picked Tither back up. Safely in her father's arms, Tither clutched her meager belongings close to her chest.

"Boldness and adventure—that's the Tikkum way," Doc Tikkum said.

"Boldness and adventure! That's the Tikkum way!" the children cheered with their father as he opened the front door.

Pinky left the cottage with the princess in her improvised sling. Not understanding the gravity of the situation, the children happily jumped and leapfrogged as they went outside. "Boldness and adventure! Boldness and adventure!" they chanted as one-by-one they went out the door.

"Button your coats. It's still chilly out there. The sun hasn't risen yet. My nerves, my poor nerves," a thoroughly distraught Mother Tikkum groaned as she looked about her cottage, knowing it might be for the last time.

"Mother—" Doc Tikkum invited, holding the front door for her.

"Will I ever see my beautiful home again?" she asked.

"I'll make you a better one," he promised as they went out the door.

Doc Tikkum went outside with Mother Tikkum and closed the door behind them.

Elfman rose from his hiding place in the green foliage under the rowan trees. He shook his legs' massive muscles to relieve the stiffness and followed after them down to the creek embankment.

They were all risking their lives on the princess' behalf and she was too young to understand the danger in which she put everyone. Pinky didn't know what else to do but move forward believing the prophecy that the princess would someday rule. All she could do at the moment was to get everybody to the rebels' camp in the Còrcair Mountains.

Hopefully, Mom stealing the queen's necklace will buy us enough time. The Blue Fairy, Evila, is a powerful sorceress and will eventually find the princess in her own crystals, she thought.

"Nothing is what it appears to be." Pinky spoke so quietly no one else could hear her remembering Calisandra's incantation in the Tower of the Forgotten as she and Elfman pushed their way down to the creek embankment.

The Lost Forest

In the dark, blue-black night, long before the first morning glimmers lit the sky, Pinky led the way out of the Tarragonian village. Closely following her, fourteen serpentine tails and one buck tail swished along the narrow path by the creek. Pinky carried the princess across her shoulders in her makeshift sling.

The party quickly scampered through the patches of tightly closed cattails that covered the embankment. Reaching up ten feet the tall flowering spikes with their flat blade-like leaves hid them.

After a time the cattails became lower in height and no longer hid the adults. Only the children were covered. The group waded through shallows. The cattails reverted to a taller height and all of them, including the adults, were once again hidden from sight.

"I don't suppose you could tell me where we're going?" Doc Tikkum asked.

"To the Lost Forest," Pinky answered.

"Oh—but I-I...." He looked in the opposite direction. "I would swear the Lost Forest is in that direction?"

"Yes, it is."

"Then why're we going towards the Human Fairy village, not directly to the Lost Forest?"

"We're going this way because I don't want us to go through the open farm fields. We could be seen by Markolous' spies."

"Oh," Doc Tikkum said. "I don't suppose you know what that horrible smell is?"

"I didn't want to say anything to you in front of your family. Markolous has killed and sacrificed all female Human Fairy babies to the Lord of the Darkness in the hopes of eliminating the princess."

"Diabolical monster!" A thoroughly shaken Doc Tikkum took in a deep breath. "Thank you for saying nothing in front of my wife and children."

In front of them, the old stone bridge between the Tarragonian village and the Human Fairy village stood empty.

Pinky was very much relieved. "Now if I can only get everyone to the Còrcair Mountains in time—before the next Blood Moon," she whispered to herself. "Are all your children in good health?" She turned back to Doc Tikkum.

"Of course," Doc Tikkum said, puffing out his chest with pride.

"Good. That will help."

Suddenly, the unmistakable sound of the four-beat gait of galloping Namdalarian hooves coming rapidly towards them broke the silence.

"Markolous is coming! Quickly, hide your children under the bridge," Pinky said.

With not one moment to lose, the limber-legged Tarragonians leaped into the air, landing under the bridge. The chameleon-like creatures fearfully huddled together.

"Where's Tither?" Mother Tikkum asked.

"Daddy."

Doc Tikkum stretched his neck up from under the stone bridge and saw Tither standing on top of it.

"Daddy, look what I did," the small tot exclaimed proudly from her perch on the bridge, not realizing she had just put herself and everyone in deadly danger. "I jumped all by myself all the way to the top of the bridge."

Instantly, Doc Tikkum leaped from under the bridge and landed next to his daughter. He smelled the distinct odor of lilac bushes mixed with that of Tettigards. Tither knew from her father's tense posture that something was terribly wrong. She started to whimper. There was no time for them to join the rest of their family under the bridge.

"You must be quiet and brave. Can you do that for me?"

Her eyes growing as big as saucers, Tither nodded solemnly and became silent. Doc Tikkum placed himself over her and blended into the side of the bridge.

The lilac bushes from Lunamilla's spell hiding the bridge exploded open. Markolous, the Human Fairy soldiers on their Namdalarians, and the Tettigards flying behind them sped across the bridge.

"Children, change your color to match the bridge," Mother Tikkum spoke softly.

The children underneath the bridge obeyed and the chameleon creatures changed their appearance. They attached themselves to the stone wall covered with blue-green moss. They blended in perfectly with their surroundings. Twelve sets of eyes peered out of the rock and gleamed in the moonlight.

"Close your eyes until I tell you it's okay to open them," Mother Tikkum said. The eyes closed and disappeared.

Up on the road, Markolous raised his hand. The careening Namdalarians and their riders halted. The Tettigards hovered in space. "Back to the bridge." They turned around and followed their leader back to the empty bridge.

Underneath the bridge, Pinky felt his probing. She held the princess in her arms, knowing she could not hide her with a magic spell.

"Elfman—hide in the bushes," she whispered.

"What are we going to do?" Elfman asked.

"Don't worry. I have a plan."

Elfman leaped into the cattails and disappeared from sight.

The only sound was the cattails' swish in the wind and the creek gurgling under the bridge. Markolous sat on Calamtheus and looked about. "I feel the presence of a magical being." He jumped off his Namdalarian and slid down the slope.

Mother Tikkum's eyes popped open and reappeared. "Give her to me." Taking the baby princess from Pinky Mother Tikkum covered the infant with her body and changed back to match the rock.

Pinky disappeared in a 'poof'.

Markolous peered under the bridge. "Nothing," he muttered in exasperation. Disgruntled, he climbed back up and remounted Calamtheus, who snorted and smacked the stone bridge with his hoof for he could smell the Tarragonians.

"Sire, what is it?" Tithoreus asked.

"Nothing. I thought I sensed her—let's get to the Tarragonian's house," Markolous replied.

He and his soldiers raced away at a blistering pace on their Namdalarians towards Doc Tikkum's home.

The Tettigards flew behind in a close order military-style formation. This new ability was one that distinguished them from their ancestors on Earth, who only traveled in a dense, mindless swarm.

Pinky reappeared on top of the bridge. "Doc Tikkum, quick —get your family together."

One of the stones moved. A pair of eyes blinked at her.

"They're going to your house," she said.

"You saved my family. I don't know how to thank you," Doc Tikkum said dropping his camouflage.

"I don't think so…." Pinky felt badly, that she had not handled the bridge incident very well. "I think you and your wife saved your family and the princess too. All I did was disappear."

"No, if you hadn't warned me and my family, Markolous would surely have…," he trailed off. Still holding Tither in his arms he didn't want to say the unspeakable in front of her.

"Forget it. Maybe we're even," Pinky said.

"Maybe we are…," Doc Tikkum said, hugging Tither even more tightly.

"Are you sure your kind isn't magical?" Pinky asked him.

"All that we do has been passed down to us. We're chameleon creatures which gave us specific concealing abilities on our planet before its destruction That's how we have protected ourselves for centuries. Why do you ask?" Doc Tikkum asked.

"Oh, I don't know. It's just strange that you can morph into something else and you and your children breathe smoke out of your nostrils—sometimes." More and more, she was impressed with this mutant creature's abilities.

Tarragonians were highly evolved for survival. Over time, Doc Tikkum's kind had learned to adapt to first their own planet's harsh environment and now to Kokakina's never thinking they were once magical creatures.

"True, that is true to be sure. I don't know. To tell you the truth it just never came up until now. We just adapt to our environment—that's all."

Pinky skimmed down the embankment as Elfman left his hiding place in the cattails. She took the princess from Mother Tikkum under the bridge. "Thank you....we'd best be going," she said, starting in the opposite direction Markolous and his soldiers went. "We need to go at a faster pace. Do you think your family can do that?" she asked Mother Tikkum.

"Don't worry about us. We can keep up. Right, children?"

The children nodded.

"We're Tarragonians. We can leapfrog and cover ground far faster than a Human Fairy on foot can," Mother Tikkum said.

"This way then." Pinky pointed to the opposite side of the creek where the cattails were the tallest and would hide them, glad that she did not have the queen's necklace to worry about. "We'd best not cross the bridge. It's too high. We might be seen."

Elfman leaped across the stream with Lunamilla's bag flapping on his antlers like a loose sail. All the Tikkum children but Tither effortlessly leaped across the water to join Elfman on the other side.

"Daddy, I don't like this Tikkum adventure. I want to go home," Tither whimpered from on top of the bridge.

"What's this—complaining when there are bugs to eat!" Doc Tikkum put her on his shoulders. As they left the top of the bridge, he spied an iridescent, yellow, orange, and red dragonfly. His long red tongue flicked out and caught it. Offering it to his small daughter, he climbed back down the embankment to the creek where Pinky still waited.

Pinky extended her etheric wings, revealing their elegant, gossamer span to give her more lift and balance as she waded with the princess through the cold water to the other side.

"Daddy, they look like butterfly wings!" Beaticella exclaimed.

The Tikkum children jumped about in their delight. Doc Tikkum waded across the stream with Tither, her little arms clasped tightly around his neck.

"You and all your children can see my wings? I was never told this about your species." Pinky folded her wings back into her back.

"Well, nobody ever asked us," Doc Tikkum said.

This awareness went against all teaching of Pinky's culture. Only Human Fairies could see each other's wings, for they were magical. "Can all Tarragonians see Human Fairy wings?" she asked, confused that this creature who was supposed to be inferior to Human Fairies could see her etheric wings.

"Yes, all of us ordinary Tarragonians can," Doc Tikkum said as he slithered up the slope on the opposite bank with Tither on his shoulder.

As a doctor, he was a man of science, studying herbs, plants, animals, and other sentient species. He had studied many things over the years and knew that sometimes there was no explanation that one could understand.

"Well, I'm beginning to think that there is nothing at all ordinary about your species," Pinky said.

"Father, look!" cried Abra, pointing back across the creek.

A huge plume of ominous smoke billowed into the late night sky from the direction of Doc Tikkum's house. The cloud of smoke obscured the stars and seemed to almost touch the setting moon. The flames could be seen for miles.

"Father, are they burning our house?" asked a frightened Frodora.

"Yes," Doc Tikkum said, "but we're all safe and we're all together. That's all that matters."

"Doc Tikkum, can your species store water in your bodies?"

"Yes, we can....we shrink our nasal passages to trap more moisture when we both inhale and exhale. We can also eat the vegetation and get water that way."

"Everyone take a good drink from the creek before we go any farther," Pinky said.

After drinking their fill, Pinky led the way into the Lost Forest. Elfman fell in beside her.

"Children, single file and follow your father." Mother Tikkum sniffed down her tears so as not to upset her children. She dearly loved her cottage with all its family memories. "And don't dally," she added as she rewrapped her wool shawl around her shoulders and leaped next to one of her little ones who had stopped moving. "Move along now, dearest," she instructed a laggard child, pushing him along the path. "Leap like Daddy taught you." The child obediently leaped forward and followed his siblings. All the Tarragonians changed to the moss green color of the foliage in the forest meadow.

Looking into the dark, shadowy woods ahead of them, Mother Tikkum shuddered.

Dawn soon came. Pinky set a blistering pace that challenged the small Tarragonian legs. They labored through the tall blue-green grasses in the meadows in the Lost Forest, feeling the moist ground under their clawed feet. The dim daylight filtered through the overhanging trees. The children's leaps and jumps grew smaller and more listless as the day wore on.

"My children need to rest," Doc Tikkum said.

Noticing that their progress had slowed to a snail's pace, Pinky was forced to agree. "Very well. We'll stop here." She would have preferred that they keep moving, but the children's fatigue dictated otherwise for they had traveled for hours without pause.

Everyone put down their belongings and collapsed to the floor of the forest.

Doc Tikkum turned to his oldest son who was sitting on a boulder resting his tired feet. "Abra, would you please stand watch?" Doc Tikkum asked.

Abra puffed out his chest, and turned red. He nodded, "Of course—I will—Father," he said with pride for the responsibility he had just been given. Under the canopy of trees that hid the mid-morning sun, the other children and Mother Tikkum soon fell into an exhausted slumber.

Doc Tikkum reached for a piece of wood.

"No fire," Pinky said.

"It's just that it's getting cold—and surely a little fire would do no harm and lift our spirits?" Doc Tikkum asked.

"On the contrary it'll be visible and seen for miles," Pinky warned. "Markolous has spies everywhere. Even in the magical Lost Forest there are traitors who would sell their neighbors for a few crystals."

"Of course. I'm sorry. I wasn't thinking," Doc Tikkum conceded, kneeling down to stretch his calves. "How much longer to the rebel camp?"

"I don't know. That all depends on how fast we move. I'd say a few hours to cross the desert...."

"Desert? What desert? I thought you said we were going somewhere in the Lost Forest?"

"I said that to confuse any seers who might be watching, especially Evila."

"Evila? Who's Evila?"

"Markolous' new seer from the nomads in the north. He's planning on marrying her."

"Oh, I see. Didn't he ask you to marry him a long time ago?"

"Yes, a long time ago. We were silly children."

"Oh, I see—childhood sweethearts."

"Not really, It's not the time....It's more complicated."

"Okay....you're right. So where are you taking us?"

"To the Còrcair Mountains."

"The Còrcair Mountains?"

"Yes, we're going to the frontier," she replied.

"But, that's where murderers and thieves hide. Surely, you can't expect me to take my wife and children there?"

"That's just Markolous' propaganda. Flanyanna's faithful subjects have gathered there to fight him and put the princess on the throne."

"Well, I don't like this one bit."

"Neither do I, but that's the way it is. For now, anyway."

"Well, that's not very reassuring."

"I promise you—your family will be under the protection of the rebels." Saying no more she rose up to her feet.

"Wait a minute, you're not telling me everything? Something doesn't feel quite right...."

Pinky turned and stared hard at Doc Tikkum. "Of course, I'm telling you everything—you worry too much."

"Pinky, my wife worries and every time somebody tells me not to worry, I know I need to worry," Doc Tikkum said skeptically, turning red.

"It's time to wake up your children."

Doc Tikkum rose to his sore blistered red feet and roused his very tired family.

The morning sun's rays provided dim light for their way through the very dense foliage of this wild and untamed part of the Lost Forest. By midday, a vast flat, barren, semi-arid desert lay before them. Not a true desert, it was a steppe—a milder version of a desert with more rainfall and grasses to eat along the way.

"Daddy, I'm hungry," Tither said.

He gently put her down. "Mother—what have you got to eat?"

"All I have left is a few dragonfly cakes."

"Mother, divide the cakes up evenly between the children...."

"What about you? Aren't you going to eat?"

"I'm not hungry, Mother."

"Surely...." She stopped abruptly and said nothing further, knowing he would not eat if there were not enough food for both him and the children. "How about a drink of honey water?"

"I'm all right, Mother—really I am. Save it for the children." Doc Tikkum scanned the horizon. The steppe appeared to stretch to infinity.

"I'm not sure my family can take much more," he said, looking out over the waving grass occasionally dotted with gnarly sagebrush shrubs.

Pinky looked at his very tired Tarragonian children.

"How far behind us is that monster who sits on the throne?" Doc Tikkum asked.

Pinky probed the ethers with her third eye....

"Pinky?" Elfman nudged her cheek after a moment with his cold nose to rouse her from her trance.

"We can't rest anymore. Markolous is close," Pinky said as she awoke from her vision.

"But what about the days's heat?" Doc Tikkum asked. "It'd be easier to cross in the night's coolness, don't you think?"

"It would but we don't have that luxury. Markolous is only a few hours behind us. How much water does your family have left?" Pinky asked.

"My children have exhausted the water in their bodies. We have only a goatskin of honey water left...."

"Didn't you say you can munch on the grasses to stay hydrated?"

"Yes...."

"If Elfman, the princess and I drink the water from the goatskin and your family eats the grasses for moisture, I believe we'll be able to cross now."

"We can do that."

"Good. Let's get started."

"Pinky, you're forgetting something," Elfman said.

"What is it?"

"I can eat the grasses for my water source too."

"Right. I keep forgetting that." Even after all these years, Pinky had difficulty accepting that Elfman was a buck who ate grass and no longer a Human Fairy.

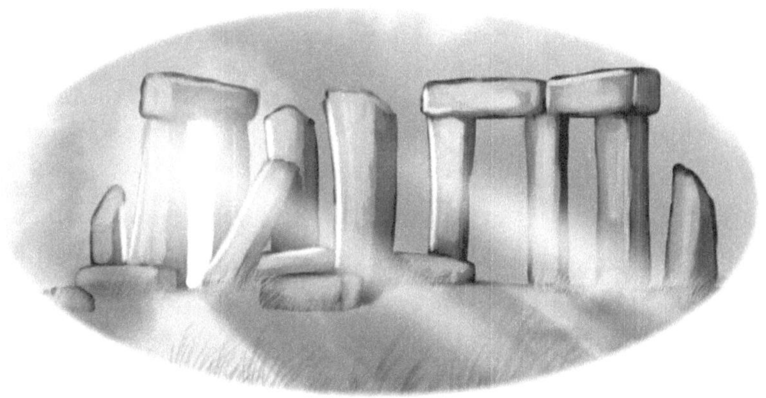

The Ancient Temple

Pinky, Elfman, and the Tikkums began their trek through the desert. The heat sapped their energy, but knowing that Markolous was breathing down their necks kept them moving at a scorching pace.

Finally, the weary travelers reached the far edge of the desert as night began to fall. A multi-voiced raven call pierced their ears. A large group of armed Human Fairies on foot and on horseback emerged from the oak and rowan woods that met the desert's edge and rushed towards them. The Human Fairies waved swords, shields, spears, and torches.

Doc Tikkum stiffened and changed to a bright orange-red, puffing out his throat and chest. Abra did the same. Mother Tikkum screamed in terror and gathered her children closer to her, afraid that the fierce warriors were out to do them harm.

"It's okay. They're friends," Pinky said.

"Don't worry, Mother and children, these are the queen's followers. They're here to help us," Doc Tikkum said.

The deceased Human Fairy queen's supporters cheered even louder as Pinky, carrying the princess across her shoulder in the makeshift sling, lifted her for all to see.

Carrying the queen's necklace in her hand, Lunamilla stepped out of the massed partisans. Pinky was very relieved to see she wasn't wearing it.

Seeing Pinky with the baby in her sling, Lunamilla felt a deep pang of loss. Even after all these years, she mourned for her other children whom she never knew. She knew the fate of the princess would be no different than theirs. The child's only chance was to go to Earth and live with the Human race. Except this time the need was not to be saved from Casafala's vile scheming, but from that of Casafala's son, Markolous, who would surely kill her.

Lunamilla embraced Pinky. She had no doubts that she had done the right thing when she stole the necklace to give to her daughter. Stealing the queen's necklace from Casafala's son gave Lunamilla great satisfaction. Somehow her long standing resentment towards Casafala had been healed. She released Pinky and put the necklace on her.

Lunamilla was heartened when everyone cheered as she put it on Pinky. *You see? You must wear the necklace. The princess won't be able to rule for another sixteen years, until she returns from Earth to Kokakina, and—don't forget—she may never come back,* Lunamilla said with her third eye to Pinky knowing none of her children returned. *With the Rose Crystal necklace, you can take the princess to Earth.* She patted Pinky's shoulder.

"Thank you, Mother." Pinky lowered her head as if in homage, but what she was really doing was hiding her third eye from her mother. She was tired and had very little energy to deceive anyone. She wanted to tell her mother about the Shadow Fairy deal, but how could she? She did not know how to explain how it all happened—selling her heart to the Shadow Fairies.

"Here, let me have her," Lunamilla said taking the princess. She cradled her in her arms.

"Pinky, would you please take your mother's magic bag off of my antlers?" Elfman asked.

"Oh, sorry, Elfman. Of course, you must be tired." Pinky took Lunamilla's bag off of his high chandelier antlers.

"I'm going lie down in some green, moist grass for a nap." As soon as she removed the bag, Elfman bounded away.

"Elfman? Wait!" Pinky was afraid she would not see him before she left for the three islands.

"Leave him be," Lunamilla said. "You must let him be his natural self. Besides, you have more important things that need your attention."

Pinky did not respond for maybe it was best that Elfman left to take care of himself. She did not know how to tell him that she sold her heart to the Shadow Fairies to save her sister and Kokakina. He and everyone else would know soon enough.

"Say something—anything will do," Lunamilla whispered quietly into Pinky's ear, still hoping Pinky would lead the rebels. "They're all half-drunk anyway."

Pinky took the princess from her mother and offered her to Doc Tikkum.

"Are you sure?" he asked before taking up the baby.

"Yes, I'm sure…," Pinky replied.

He reached out his clawed hands and received the princess.

"Stop! She'll change color," shouted an outraged rebel.

"That's a myth created to separate us from this magnificent species," Pinky shouted back.

"Daughter, what are you doing?" Lunamilla asked aghast. "This is neither the time nor the place for you to expound on your ridiculous idea that all creatures are equal."

There was a low buzz in the throng of rebels. Pinky stared into the crowd. The rebels were busily whispering among themselves for the princess' skin had not changed color from the touch a Tarragonian.

Pinky said nothing, for she knew her kind's prejudicial belief that they were superior to other species was very strong. "I'm sorry, Doc Tikkum, for my species' ignorance." She lifted the necklace from her own neck and placed it around the princess' neck. Taking the child from Doc Tikkum, she lifted her high for all to see.

"I give you the rightful heir of Queen Flanyanna, the true ruler of Kokakina."

The crowd bowed their heads and fell into a reverential silence. Kneeling before the princess, they were overcome by the sight of the royal Human Fairy heir wearing their culture's greatest talisman.

Lunamilla reluctantly bowed her head as well. She did not like it, but she knew her daughter had put the welfare of the princess before her own, as she had always done with Flanyanna. Pinky chose what she had always chosen—what was best for Kokakina.

The only sound was the cold wind from the night's drop in temperature thrashing and snapping at the tattered rags of clothing everyone wore, clothing that barely protected their chaffed and blistered skin.

"We are engaged in an epic struggle for our freedom from the oppression Markolous would inflict upon us...," Pinky stated, scanning the hopeful faces of the young and old.

The beleaguered crowd hung on to her every word.

"It will challenge us. It will call on all to sacrifice what we hold most dear," she proclaimed. "But we will prevail over Markolous and his evil master—the Lord of the Darkness."

Pinky lifted the princess with the queen's necklace around her neck high over her head. The Rose Crystal blazed brightly like a star in the night sky.

"I give you our true prophesied ruler."

Latching on to Pinky's stirring words, the crowd beat their swords wildly on their shields in clamorous support and chanted more of their resonating raven cries.

"Well, that was quite a show, daughter. Unfortunately, the princess is going to Earth for sixteen years and we have no one except you to replace Flanyanna during that time. Follow me," said Lunamilla, not at all happy with her daughter and not understanding her unwillingness to take on the leadership role.

They followed her away from the shouting rebels.

In an open, cleared space near the forest, Lunamilla led them toward hundreds of billowing tents that rippled in the night breeze. The tents were simply two pieces of cloth, open on the ends, that were attached to form two sides and were held up by two upright cut tree limbs. Although not substantial in structure, the tents gave the rebels some shelter and protection from the harsh elements in the Còrcair mountains.

"Tarragonians, that tent over there is for you." Lunamilla pointed to a tent a few feet across from where she stood.

Sensing the prejudice behind Lunamilla's words, Doc Tikkum's face turned a beet red.

"Please take the princess with your family to your tent. I'll be there, momentarily," Pinky said to him.

Doc Tikkum nodded and obliged, leaving Pinky alone with Lunamilla.

"Mom, why did you do that? Doc Tikkum and his family are *my* friends and they have jeopardized their lives for the princess."

"Well—so did I," Lunamilla said. "But I didn't steal that necklace just for the princess, I stole it for you, too!"

"I appreciate what you have done. I know now that I couldn't have begun to save the princess without it."

Lunamilla puffed up with pride.

"But Mom, please," Pinky said. "I would appreciate it, if you could somehow contain your disdain of the Tarragonians. Without them we couldn't have saved the princess."

Lunamilla and Pinky turned to enter a large tent.

"Umph. Very well. However, I am curious how a baby who still lives in the etheric realm, and not yet in the Human Fairy realm, is going to have any use for the powers of the queen's necklace?"

"Mother, you know as well as I do. The necklace belongs to the true ruler of Kokakina. And that's not me."

"Don't be a fool," Lunamilla protested. "She won't come into her power for sixteen years. The Rose Crystal wants you to lead at least until she comes back from Earth!"

"Possibly." Pinky went over to her tent's entrance. "But I'm giving the queen's necklace to a baby who has lost both her parents and is now being exiled to a hostile planet."

"You can't do that!"

"If I don't give it to her, she'll have no connection to us...."

"You can't do that!"

"She won't know who she really is—and stop telling me what I can or can't do! I need to get some rest before I go."

"Well, I'm not about to babysit a bunch of slithering Tarragonians while you're gone."

"Okay, Mother. Why don't you take her to Earth and I'll babysit the Tarragonians."

"...send your poor mother back to Earth...."

"You've been there before. You know the way better than I do. I think it's a very good idea," Pinky said.

"You don't see it, do you? This is your opportunity to rule. You're Glendorf 's firstborn child. Come back the hero who saved the heir to the throne and they'll follow you anywhere."

"Mom, I'm not to be the ruler of Kokakina. I'm the seer."

"Of course you're not. Why would I expect anything else from you? You always let them make you small when you were better."

"Mom, that's not fair!"

"Have it your way, but just remember the necklace is a divining rod that'll get you back to Kokakina. Without it, you'll be stuck on Earth just like your brothers and sisters!" Lunamilla stormed out, passing Tither who had sneaked in and witnessed the argument.

"You're taking my little sister away."

"Yes, to protect and save her. You wouldn't want anything bad to happen to her, now would you?" Pinky asked.

Tither shook her head.

Pinky picked up Tither and held her close. "I love her, too. Now, I'll tell you what. You go get your father and tell him he has to come with me and watch over your little sister for you. Would that make you happy?"

Tither nodded. "Okay. I'll go get Daddy."

No sooner had she scampered out the flap of the tent than Lunamilla burst back inside, panting.

"Somebody's stolen the necklace!" she exclaimed.

"What? You didn't say anything about it to Dad, did you?"

"Well, I might have mentioned something to Glendorf. I don't remember really...."

"Where is he?"

"He's at the ancient temple with all the other Shadow Fairies."

Pink rushed out of the tent.

"He'll never give it to you!"

The yellow moon's almost full illumination was framed by the pale stars. Doc Tikkum held his wife close to him.

"Husband, come back soon," Mother Tikkum said, kissing him and lifting the medical bag holding the princess to kiss her on her cheek. "And here, take this," she blubbered out between sobs, handing him a satchel Beaticella was holding for her. "If she cries she's either hungry or needs her nappy changed...."

"Yes, yes, I know. I've been through this process with you twelve times," he assured his wife.

"They're honey sweets for the journey and a brew of nectar wine," she sniffled, "and don't let anybody harm that reptilian skin of yours."

"I can assure you I am as attached to my reptilian skin as you are," Doc Tikkum said gently, laying a comforting hand on her shoulder. "I'll be back in two days for supper."

Mother Tikkum nestled into his shoulder. "I'll be all nerves and jitters while you're gone."

"Abra," Doc Tikkum said.

"Yes, Father."

"Abra, you're the oldest. Take care of your mother. I expect you to act as the provider and protector until I'm back."

Abra nodded solemnly, aware and proud of the trust placed in him. "Yes, Father."

"I'll see you all soon," Doc Tikkum assured his family, looking at all the sad faces. "You be good while I'm gone and remember about your mother's nerves." He winked at the children. The younger ones giggled.

Tither reached up and tugged at her father's waistcoat. "Will I ever see my little sister again?"

"Of course you will. When you're both grown up." Tither hugged her father's leg.

Doc Tikkum bent down and kissed her.

"If we're all grown up, how'll I recognize her?"

"She'll have those magical jade-green eyes."

"But how'll she recognize me?"

"Tither, you're not one that is easily forgotten."

Tither smiled.

"Goodbye, good wife, I'll miss you." He kissed Mother Tikkum on the cheek. He picked up the burlap sack containing the supplies and placed it over his other shoulder.

"You'll miss my cooking more than me, I suspect." A jittery Mother Tikkum waved her handkerchief. "Oh, I almost forgot. When the Blood Moon is full, you must blow me a kiss."

Grateful for the note of levity Mother Tikkum had chosen to inject into their departure, Doc Tikkum winked at Tither who giggled. "I shall be sure to blow you a kiss, Mother Tikkum, when the Blood Moon's full."

"We best be going," Pinky said, not telling Doc Tikkum they had to go to the Shadow Fairy temple to get the queen's necklace.

"Without my children, we'll travel much faster…," he said.

They soon disappeared out of the Tikkum family's sight and into the trees that covered the Còrcair Mountains' slopes.

"I'm confused. I must be turned around. I thought the ocean was the other way," Doc Tikkum said, looking back over his shoulder.

"Well, we will be going that way eventually. We have to do something first."

"What could possibly be so important that we delay?"

"Just follow me. It won't take long."

"Why are we making this detour? We only have twenty-four more hours before the Blood Moon."

"If you really must know, I'm going to an ancient temple where the Shadow Fairies live—to get the Rose Crystal necklace back from my father—who stole it from my mother."

"What?" Doc Tikkum said as Pinky moved resolutely on the path she had chosen. "Surely this can wait?" he asked.

"No, unfortunately, it can't…."

"…and why not?"

"Why does everybody have to know everything. Can't somebody have a little trust that everything is going to work out okay?"

"I was just asking a question, a logical question. Why do we need to go get the stolen necklace now?"

"All right. If you really need to know, not that it's going to make any difference, we can't take the princess to Earth without it!"

"Oh, I see. Very well, lead on."

Dense fog concealed Markolous and his mounted soldiers at the edge of a sacred oak tree grove near the ancient temple. Haunting, fierce sounds and eerie noises frightened both the soldiers and the horses. Even more than their riders, the Namdalarians knew that Shadow Fairies lurked in the vast gloominess.

Markolous leaned down from Calamtheus, listening to a dingy brown-gray rat crouched on a gray boulder. He was the perfect nocturnal spy for Markolous. His hearing was excellent and his eyes were finely adapted to seeing in the dark.

"They'll come this way," The rodent spy chittered, licking his yellowed, scummy and ever-growing incisors.

"Pay him—pay this disgusting snitch." Markolous handed a pouch of precious crystals to Tithoreus.

Tithoreus threw the rat the pouch full of crystals.

Snatching his reward in his grubby paws the rat retreated into the haunted woods.

"Get rid of the rat. I don't like my spies to be so self-serving. Besides I want my crystals back."

At that moment, a deafening roar of flapping wings assaulted their eardrums.

"Steady." Markolous pulled the reins tight on Calamtheus who was ready to bolt.

Hordes of ravens descended upon them. The moonlit night undulated with an ominous, pitch-black throbbing curtain that rapidly darkened the sky.

"This place is haunted with Shadow Fairies," Tithoreus cried as he glanced about.

"Run!" Markolous cried out.

Their nostrils flaring, the Namdalarians became as possessed. Twisting and turning, they reared up. The soldiers madly strove to restrain them. Despite their best efforts, the soldiers could not control the horses and were bucked off.

Terrified, the Namdalarians broke free from the soldiers' grasps and flew off from the tormenting ravens. The Human Fairy soldiers fled the attacking Shadow Fairies on foot, running into the feared, haunted Shadow Fairy forest.

Pinky and Doc Tikkum with the princess entered the sacred red oak grove. As they penetrated deeper into the grove, an eerie mist descended and shrouded them. In the distance stood the abandoned and spooky ruin of the ancient temple the Human Fairies' ancestors had built. The crystal pillars still stood high up on a raised platform two feet off the ground, seven of them on the short sides and thirteen on the long ones. The wooden beams spanning the pillars had collapsed years ago. The roof no longer existed. Only the triangular pediments high in the air at each end still remained in position.

Pinky motioned for Doc Tikkum to stay close. With her leading the way, they went single file through the overgrown and now entangling tree branches closer to the temple.

"Is this the Shadow Fairy temple?" Doc Tikkum felt queasy. His serpentine eyes swiveled, taking in the ancient ruins. His skin broke out in goosebumps. The Shadow Fairies were so misunderstood by everyone, even by Human Fairies. A creature of another species would have even more of a problem understanding them.

"Yes, this is where they live."

Looking up, a few black birds silhouetted against white clouds in the night sky flew past. Their cawing broke the silence.

"Are those Shadow Fairies?" Doc Tikkum asked, gulping hard and, feeling the night's chill, he ducked his head into his neck. "Do you think they saw us?"

"I don't think so. We're pretty well hidden by all the vegetation. They seem to be distracted by something."

"Good."

"Shhhhh—we must be quiet—very quiet," Pinky whispered ever so softly. "Stay here...." She motioned for Doc Tikkum to stand still until the ravens had passed over them.

Doc Tikkum froze and blended into the tree's green foliage. The Shadow Fairies' wings flapped slower and slower as they approached the temple on their return after attacking Markolous. They descended and disappeared inside not noticing the newest trespassers on their land.

"Ummm, Pinky, did you get along with your father?"

"Well, sorta. I hadn't really had anything to do with him since I was child."

"Oh, I see. Because of your stepmother?"

"Yeah."

The princess slept in Doc Tikkum's medical bag across his shoulder as Pinky pushed herself through the thicket of underbrush that led up to the Shadow Fairy temple.

She held up her hand to let Doc Tikkum know that she sensed something near. She motioned him to come closer and he readily complied. "We don't have much time to get the necklace from my father," Pinky whispered.

"I thought your father lived out his incarnation?" Doc Tikkum asked. "Aren't Shadow Fairies Human Fairies who died a violent, premature death?"

"You never cease to amaze me...Doc Tikkum. My father almost—lived out his incarnation."

"Almost? What do you mean?"

"I mean that somebody wanted to end his reign early," Pinky said grimly.

"You mean—Markolous?" Doc Tikkum whispered.

"Yes. Markolous—and his mother, Casafala. They could see they were losing our father's favor."

"So how did they do it?'

"They poisoned Father's food ever so slowly so no one would notice it."

"You mean...? Someone in the royal kitchen was a traitor to the royal household?"

"Markolous and Casafala hoped to get Father out of the way while Markolous was still the heir to the throne."

"Elfman's father did it?"

"NO—his father was fired long before...after Markolous turned Elfman into a buck."

"Oh, I see. Then who did it?"

"They never found out who did it. Poor Father. He realized he had made a mistake, and on his deathbed named Flanyanna his successor."

"Why doesn't anyone know about this?" Doc Tikkum asked.

"Those who knew were sworn to secrecy with bribery or threats of death," she explained. At the sound of branches snapping, Pinky stopped, not sure where it was.

"Look. Over there." Doc Tikkum pointed to a clearing in front of the ancient edifice. A shiny object lay on the ground. "Isn't that…?"

"Yes."

"But how did the queen's necklace get there?"

Without answering, Pinky straddled a moss-covered fallen oak tree in her path. "You stay here with the princess. I'll be right back—with a little bit of luck."

"Wait—it could be a trap," Doc Tikkum cautioned.

"Shhhh…." Pinky crawled over the ancient oak trunk moving slowly towards the glistening rose crystal pendant on the ground.

"But what if you don't come back?" he asked anxiously. "What do I do then?"

"If I don't come back, return to the rebel camp," Pinky instructed as she balanced on the log. "Find my mother, give her the necklace, and tell her to take the princess to Earth—do you understand?"

Doc Tikkum nodded and took a step back, holding the princess tightly against his chest. He lowered himself into the vegetation behind the log and turned green to conceal himself and the princess.

Pinky regarded the two eyes in the green foliage blinking at her. "Close your eyes," she said, softly. "I can still see you!"

Doc Tikkum covered the princess' eyes with his hand. When he closed his eyes, they both totally disappeared.

Pinky looked about cautiously. She transformed herself into a raven and swooped down, snatching the necklace in her beak. A clawed raven hand reached out and grabbed her.

"Caw—caw!" Pinky squawked, turning back into her Human Fairy form.

"Mother! What are you doing? It's me—Pinky!"

"For fairy's sake, what took you so long? I thought you'd never get here. Well, don't just stand there. Help me up!"

"Mother, I told you that I was going to get it!" Pinky steadied her mother with both hands to help her to her feet.

"No way. He wouldn't have given it to you. Old family patterns die hard, you know. So, I thought it best I paid your father a little visit," Lunamilla whispered with a gleam in her eye.

"Then—he gave it to you?"

"Well not exactly. He didn't want to, but the strangest thing happened. All of a sudden, he left with all the other Shadow Fairies. And, then, it was easy—I just took it." She placed the necklace in Pinky's palm.

"But why are you lying on the ground?"

"Because they came back and I didn't have a chance to think of any magic spell to hide. They don't come that easily anymore. I must be losing it."

"Let's get out of here. The place is crawling with Shadow Fairies. Can you walk?"

"Yes, of course I can walk. I didn't say I was feeble. Let's hurry. I don't want to see your father again and I'm not sure which one he is. Ravens all look alike, you know...."

Pinky and Lunamilla reach Doc Tikkum and the princess.

"Doc Tikkum, you take the necklace for now and I'll take my mother."

"What's he doing here?" Lunamilla asked.

Pinky firmly took her mother's hand and led her out of the oak grove. Doc Tikkum quickly followed behind with the princess and the queen's necklace. Lunamilla stopped abruptly.

"What is it, Mother?"

"Well, I don't know exactly how to get back. I went west, then I walked to the ancient blue stones, climbed up a rowan tree, then crossed back down behind their backs. No, we can't go that way."

"Why not? That's the shortest way, isn't it?" Pinky asked.

"Sometimes the shortest way isn't the best way. Markolous is in front of you if you go this way. But if you go this other way, he's behind you."

"How do you know that?"

"Didn't those teachers teach you anything? I know because the Shadow Fairies went that way."

"Oh, that makes sense," Doc Tikkum said.

"Of course, it does." Lunamilla looked him up and down. "Well, I'll be leaving you now and don't let your feelings get in the way again...."

"Mom, are you sure you don't want to go with us?" Pinky asked.

"I'm too old now to go through the Fey Portal to Earth."

"All right, Mom," Pinky said, disappointed Lunamilla was not coming.

"Oh, I almost forgot to tell you something I didn't tell you before."

"What is it?"

"Are you sure I can talk with—" Lunamilla looked at Doc Tikkum.

"Mother!"

"All right. I hope you know what you're doing. I didn't tell you about the role the Rose Crystal necklace plays in our world."

"Okay, I'm listening."

"The queen's necklace is the divining rod that connects Earth to Kokakina during the Super Blood Moon...."

"Mom, you already told me that."

"Now, let me finish. Remember how upset I was with you when you told me you were going to leave the Rose Crystal necklace with the princess?"

"Yeah?"

"Well, you can't do that! You see, the Rose Crystal connects us to Earth at all times...."

"What?"

"Of course—It's perfectly understandable, don't you see? We're Earth beings. How do you think we've survived here all these centuries away from Mother Earth?"

"You mean...?"

"Mother Earth is our source. We can't survive without her."

Pinky's thoughts went back to Calisandra who told her to remember that nothing was what it appeared to be. Calisandra also told her that the Shadow Fairies were going to use her heart to keep the connection between them and the Human Fairy world, but this was the first she had heard of this primal connection to Earth through the Rose Crystals.

"You mean, all this time? We've been connected to Earth, the Mother planet?"

"Yes."

"And we need this connection to survive?"

"Actually, I'm not sure."

"What do you mean you're not sure?"

"Well, we've always been connected, haven't we? I don't know what would happen if it was broken. No, that's never happened before. We have been connected since our ancestors came to Kokakina."

Pinky's decision to send the queen's necklace back to Earth with the princess now weighed heavily on her. She knew now by sending the necklace away she might be exposing her planet to destruction. But if she didn't do it, Kokakina would go into total darkness for Markolous had sold them all to the Lord of the Darkness....

"Anyway, I'm sorry I can't go with you, but you'll be all right," Lunamilla said.

"Yes, I'm sure of it," Pinky said, hoping it was true even though she had her doubts.

"Well, I guess I'll see you in two days then...."

"Yes...."

"Pinky, are you all right?" Lunamilla asked.

"Yes. I'm fine. Mom, just tell me—how do I get around Markolous and get to the Fey Portal?"

Lunamilla looked at Doc Tikkum.

"Mom, I told you. It's all right. He's a friend."

"All right. Go north through the woods for a ways, and then at the biggest oak tree in the center of a small meadow, go east a bit—you'll get around that no-good scum."

"Thank you, Mother. I'm sorry I was short-tempered with you before," Pinky said.

"Don't worry about it. We're family." Lunamilla took Pinky's hand. "I love you." She patted it as she said the words she needed to say.

"I love you too, Mom," Pinky said as Lunamilla released her hand and hobbled toward the rebel's camp.

"Mom, why didn't you send me to Earth, too?" Pinky asked.

Lunamilla paused and did not look back. "You were pink. You never would have blended in with the Humans." She walked on. "Your sisters and brothers, you see, they took after your father and have his pale White Fairy skin. They can pass as Humans."

"Mom, I just want you to know that you did just fine as a parent. Really, you did," Pinky said sincerely. Lunamilla smiled to herself and disappeared into forest of the ancient Rowan trees.

Pinky lifted the princess from Doc Tikkum's clawed hands. "I guess it's just us now," she said.

"Your mother is right. She's too old to make the trip now," Doc Tikkum stated matter-of-factly.

"Yes, I suppose she is."

"I can see you're disappointed she's not coming with us."

"Ummm—it would have been easier."

"Well, she has a lot of confidence that you'll have no problem getting the princess to Earth."

"Yes, she does—doesn't she...?"

Together, they made their way into the dense Shadow Fairy woods—going north, to escape Markolous.

In a meadow in the Còrcair Mountains, the winged horses, no longer frightened, gently grazed on the hight desert green grasses and settled down for the night.

In their midst Elfman knelt fast asleep, dreaming of his Pinky.

The Three Islands

fter leaving the temple ruins, Pinky and Doc Tikkum walked all night. They knew it was only a matter of time before Markolous figured out where they were going. They took advantage of the natural cover offered by the trees in the higher altitudes near the Còrcair Mountains. The prominent oak trees that covered the countryside lower down concealed them until they reached the coastal mountains.

Shrouded in a dense, purplish fog, they climbed in silence. Mostly on all fours, they scaled down onto the White Cliffs.

"It's too bad these cliffs are not broken by ravines," Doc Tikkum said, his breathing labored from his exertions.

"Why...?"

"We would have easier access to the beach."

"Just keep going. We're almost there. Do you want me to take her?" Pinky asked.

"No, she's light as a feather, she is. It's a good thing we're now on the rainy side and have all this protection," he said remembering how barren and rocky the other side had been.

Doc Tikkum's hands and feet were well out to either side of his reptilian body as he flexed his elbows and knees to pull himself through the hillside's thick, pungent, green foliage with the princess in the burlap medical bag on his back. His strong, supple spine swayed from side to side as they descended.

As she labored, Pinky stopped for a moment and wiped the sweat from her brow with her blistered fingertips, so it would not sting her eyes. A spectrum of rainbow light filtered through the fog and told her dawn was fast approaching.

"I'm not sure we're going to make it," she said, panting. "The Super Blood Moon is tonight."

Doc Tikkum looked back at his haggard new friend. "I can go faster. Can you?"

"I'll try," she said, out of breath.

As they neared the bluff's edge, the sound of waves crashing on the rocky beach assaulted their ears.

"Did you hear that?" Pinky cocked her head listening to the turbulent ocean throw another wave onto the nearby coastline.

"Oh—it sounds good to my ears. I wonder if the fishing is good in these parts?"

Pinky scrambled to the cliff's lip and stretched up, feeling the sea air on her skin. She felt her pores open and expand as the oxygen coursed freely throughout her body. "The sea air feels so good!"

"Aye, there's nothing like it," Doc Tikkum agreed.

Pinky flung out her arms, twisting and turning. The negative ion saturated air permeated her lungs and invigorated her.

"I've had the taste of the sea's brine in my nose these past hours," Doc Tikkum said, licking his parched, cracked lips, greedily tasting the tang of the salty air.

The fog had risen enough to expose a wide, pale, pink beach framed by massive, teal-speckled crystal rocks.

"Look down here. You can see the beach. The ocean has ground down these crystals for centuries," Pinky said.

"Well, actually, I'm not looking at the scenery—I'm too hungry. I'm still thinking about that kelp I've been smelling." Doc Tikkum's stomach rumbled. "Do you think I have time to catch a fish or two?"

The princess started to cry. He wearily removed the now wide-awake infant from his bag and placed her on a large, flat lichen-covered rock. "I see you're hungry too." He squatted next to her, stretching out his cramped limbs as he fumbled for her nectar juice.

"Here we go, little one." He picked her up and fed her some nectar from the goat udder used for all his children. He looked at her and smiled. "I don't think my hands and feet have ever hurt this much," he said, looking at his inflamed and blistered green-clawed feet.

The baby smiled at him. He turned and saw Pinky standing at the very edge of the White Cliffs, looking down. He had not noticed it before, but in the way she stood he saw great similarities between Pinky and the queen. The way she carried herself—the angle of her head, the lift in her shoulders—their postures were identical.

"A fine queen she was...," he ruminated, looking down at the princess. "Your mother? She was a good queen and I dare say you'll be as good if not better. So I'm told by your aunt—and I believe you will be too!"

"Look—I can see the three islands!" Pinky cried, pointing towards the horizon. A whipping wind billowed Pinky's skirt around her legs.

Off on the horizon, three islands poked out of the fog. Pinky raised her right hand straight out in front of her, slid it to the left and then down. Then, she took it across her body to the right and reversed to do a full clockwise circle before she slid down the hill.

"That *is* good news. But how are we supposed to get to those islands?" Doc Tikkum asked. "I don't suppose you can swim that far?" He paused from feeding the princess and sniffed the air. His body stiffened and he turned beet red. "Pinky! Tettigards! I smell Tettigards!"

Doc Tikkum lifted the princess from the rock, and put her back in his medical bag.

"Pinky—where are you? Wait for us," Doc Tikkum shouted. He slithered down the hill with a bouncing gait. As he reached the bottom, he saw a small, weathered rowboat with two hand-carved oars rocking on the shore.

"This is a fine boat," he said, pushing the boat into the agitated surf. "Is it real?"

"Well, for now it is." Holding onto the skiff's side, Pinky rolled over the gunwale. "Hand me the princess," she said.

Doc Tikkum removed his medical bag and handed it over to Pinky. "I guess there's just one way to find out!" He leaped in. Clutching the oars, he pulled away from the shore. He could smell the distinct odor of Tettigards even more.

The fog crept up the side of the cliff and covered the summit in a purple veil as they pulled away.

"Can you get us out to sea?" Pinky asked.

"I would like to do nothing more, madam."

Pinky stared up at the top of the cliff, as Doc Tikkum rowed. She knew only too well why the Tettigards were there. They would like nothing better than to feast on the sweet royal Human Fairy blood that they had coveted since their evolution on Kokakina.

Markolous and the Tettigards slowly lowered themselves onto the White Cliffs overlooking the Mara Sea. They looked down. The fog had dissipated on the ocean.

"I don't see anything?"

"There they are, Sire," Tithoreus shouted over the pounding surf, pointing out to sea.

The boat was a speck on a vast blue background. Markolous unfurled his etheric wings to fly after them.

"Sire, you can't fly from the White Cliffs. It's too dangerous."

"Shut up."

"These are still the White Cliffs. They're no different here than at the Faireye Manor," Tithoreus said, holding Markolous back with his arm appendages.

Suddenly, Elfman leaped out of nowhere and knocked Markolous to the ground.

Tithoreus pulled out his sword to strike Elfman.

"Leave him—he's mine." Markolous gritted his teeth. "What better revenge than to kill the one she loves most." He pulled out his silver dagger and assumed a low crouching defensive position.

Elfman butted Markolous with his antlers, throwing him again onto the ground. Stunned, Markolous dropped his dagger.

They rolled over each other, grunting and groaning, closer and closer to the cliff's edge. Markolous seized Elfman's antlers and thrust him over the side of the cliff. Losing his balance, Markolous tumbled off of the edge with him.

"Sire!" Tithoreus screamed.

Markolous felt the cliff's updraft sucking at him as he fell. He released Elfman's antlers and extended his etheric wings to buffer his descent. Elfman smashed onto the beach.

The air currents smacked Markolous up against the side of the White Cliffs slowing his descent. Then, he fell to the sandy beach where he lay motionless.

"Sire, are you all right?" Tithoreus asked.

Markolous groaned and painfully raised himself off the sand. Closing his etheric wings, he held his bruised ribcage. He stumbled over towards Elfman. The wind whipped over Elfman's body, ruffling his soft, blood-stained fur. Markolous kicked Elfman's flank.

Elfman heaved out a labored breath.

"He's still alive. Throw down my bow and the enchanted arrow," Markolous said, looking up to Tithoreus. His bow and the enchanted arrow drifted down in the turbulent White Cliffs air current and finally landed on the beach.

Markolous looked down at Elfman.

"Pinky loved me—not you," Elfman said, softly.

"I should have killed you a long time ago. It would have made my life so much easier." Markolous went over, picked up the bow and arrow and aimed at Elfman's heart at close range. He didn't know why, but his hands shook. "It's a shame to waste a magical arrow on you, but I did make you an enchanted beast, didn't I?"

Elfman saw Markolous' hands shaking. "She never loved you the way you wanted her to, did she?"

"Enchanted beasts must be killed with enchanted arrows," Markolous said, his hands shaking even more.

Elfman's eyes looked out at sea wanting to see Pinky one last time.

Markolous pulled back the bowstring and let loose the enchanted arrow, which flew true, straight into the buck's heart.

"Pinky," Elfman said his last word. It was barely audible.

Elfman, a handsome male Human Fairy with clear green eyes and honey-colored hair, rolled in the waves—dead. Crimson blood trickled from the corner of his mouth and dripped down, mixing with the wet pink sand.

The Tettigards used their finely articulating appendages to scuttle down the White Cliffs.

"May we feast?" Tithoreus asked Markolous.

Markolous nodded.

"Will you feast with us, Sire?"

Markolous looked strangely at Tithoreus. "You know I only drink the blood of females." He turned and looked out at the tiny dot that was the boat going to the three islands.

Pinky jumped up, holding the princess in her arms. "Elfman!" she screamed, staring back at the beach. The enchanted arrow stabbed deeply into her now broken heart.

"Pinky, You must sit down. You'll tip us over," Doc Tikkum yelled over the roar of the ocean.

The boat rocked alarmingly, and it nearly capsized as she unfurled her etheric wings. "You go to the three islands with the princess," she said. "I'll meet you there later. I promise."

"I said sit down. You can't help Elfman. He's dead." The boat pitched back and forth, almost flipping over. "He's dead," he yelled, "and we'll *all* be dead at the bottom of the sea—if you don't sit down."

Slowly, Pinky lowered herself on the center thwart holding the princess in her arms. "Elfman," she sobbed.

Doc Tikkum negotiated the pounding waves that threatened to spill out the boat's precious contents. "You best put her in the bottom of the boat," he said over the rough seas.

Pinky hesitated. Doc Tikkum softened. "It's the safest place for her now. Put her down—I say."

Pinky placed the princess under the center thwart, on the bottom boards, the deepest part of the undulating craft.

"I don't know if I will ever again see my wife and children. But I do know that the only one we can help at this moment is this little girl," Doc Tikkum said.

Bracing his strong, stout, muscular frame, Doc Tikkum thrust the oars deeper into the water, propelling the boat to the three islands with all his might. "Elfman gave his life for us. Now tell me, which island has the Fey Portal?" he asked.

"The biggest island, the one in the middle," Pinky said, pointing through the fog bank that surrounded the islands. Her third eye showed her which way to go. They rowed in silence.

Doc Tikkum turned and strained his bulging, reptilian eyes to pierce through the hovering film that lay low on the ocean as they moved closer to the big island. He thought about his dear wife and family, which gave him more courage and strength to move on as he pushed through the turbulent surf to the big island. With the water lapping on the sides of the dinghy, Doc Tikkum maneuvered the boat into an inlet on the largest island.

The islands occupied the wettest region on the planet. They were covered with temperate rain forests similar to ones found at Earth's North American Pacific Northwest region. On the shore red maples adorned with clinging, gray-green Spanish mosses on their branches swayed in the breeze. A few exotic red and yellow birds screeched and called to each other.

The trees began at the back edge of the pink sand and crawled all the way to the mountain. Diving into the water, Doc Tikkum guided the boat to shore. Carrying the princess in her tablecloth sling, Pinky climbed out of the boat and stepped onto the cold, pale, pink crystal sand.

In the orange sunset Pinky and Doc Tikkum looked upward through the billowing clouds to the glittering summit of the single, snow-capped mountain rising in the island's center.

"That must be it—yes?" Doc Tikkum asked as he pulled the dinghy up out of the water.

"Yes. The portal is in the glacier." With trepidation, Doc Tikkum gazed back at the waves and the purple mist that crept over the water. His keen extraterrestrial eyes scanned the sky and spotted flying dots that could only be Markolous and his Tettigards.

"You go ahead," he said. "I'll stay behind and hide the boat. I'll be along shortly."

He knew staying behind to delay Markolous and his soldiers would mean his death, yet he was willing to do so to save the princess who he dearly loved. His desire now was to make sure she and his own children would live in a free land and not be enslaved by Markolous, his Tettigards, and their master, the feared Lord of the Darkness.

"Don't be absurd...," Pinky countered in exasperation.

"No—really—I thought about it—a lot—I'll stay here," he insisted, his skin turning bright red and his double chin and chest exploding outward, forming the powerful and intimidating presence that Tarragonians made when they were ready to fight.

"Oh no you don't! You're coming with us, and that's final." She stretched out her hand, and the dinghy disappeared. "See? Now you don't need to hide the boat anymore."

Doc Tikkum shook his head. "Has anyone ever told you that you can be very…irritating?"

Pinky paused for a moment, the beginning of a slight smile playing at her lips. "You know, I think people thought it, but no one had the courage to tell me until now." She looked up. The full yellow moon was already visible. "Let's go. We only have a few more hours before the Blood Moon…."

"I just want to know one thing," Doc Tikkum interrupted. "If we miss this Blood Moon, when is the next one?"

"I don't know for sure. My mother would know. Blood Moons are random, so I don't know exactly when the next one will happen. But I do know that in sixteen years, there'll be another one."

"Because that's when you'll will bring the princess back to Kokakina from Earth. That's a long time to leave her there," Doc Tikkum said.

"Yes…it is a long time. But, she'll be safe on Earth."

"With who?"

"Very well, if you must know. I have relatives there."

He looked up the blue crystal mountain again and saw a path twisting back and forth along the escarpment to the snow-capped peak. "You look tired. I'll take her."

"No. I'll manage. You can take her later," Pinky said. They disappeared into the temperate rainforest as the faint buzzing vibration of the Tettigards wings grew louder.

Pinky and Doc Tikkum had labored up some thousands of feet along the precipitous escarpment. They hurried single file up the steep, treacherous rocky path with the princess. A few loose rocks tumbled down the steep cliff as they positioned their feet to continue their climb.

"The temperature is dropping fast," Pinky said, holding the princess in the thinning air as they climbed up towards the blue, glacial top. "Are you having problems breathing?"

"I'm fine. Here, let me take her." Doc Tikkum took the princess from Pinky, thinking it best to save Pinky's strength since she was the one who would be taking her to Earth. He folded the tablecloth sling more tightly to protect the infant from the icy cold air and placed her in his burlap medical bag.

Pinky looked down. Markolous with his Tettigards were flying high above the rain forest.

"They're flying...," she said.

"I thought they couldn't fly in cold weather?"

"Well, they can fly here...." Her heart sank. She quickened her pace up the hill despite the thinning air higher up. All she could do was have faith in the Rose Crystal prophecy.

The sweet odor of the Human Fairy royal line funneled down the steep incline and drove the giant, carnivorous insects to frenzied efforts, to a warp speed up the mountain towards their prey. The keen sense of smell in the pursuers' antennae pointed them directly towards Pinky and the princess.

Suddenly, the night took on an eerie glow. Pinky looked up at the moon. Although it was still yellow, it was now much higher in the night sky.

"The eclipse has begun. We must get to the top before the Super Blood Moon is at its closest point to Kokakina," she said.

Doc Tikkum's keen ears caught the unmistakable sound of the beating of the Tettigards' wings. It was a dreaded drone that all Human Fairies had learned to fear. It was the sound the Tettigards made before attacking their intended victims.

Doc Tikkum looked down at their pursuers. "You best go on with the princess. It's our best chance to save her."

"No. We must keep moving together. Besides, Markolous will make lizard boots out of you," she said, using her mother's words.

"Aye. Better he makes lizard boots out of me than he makes them out of my children."

"You know my sister was right about you. You're a brave and honorable creature. May I call you friend?"

"I would be honored, madam, and the best thing I can do for you and the little one is slow them down so that you can get to the Fey Portal in time."

"Persistence. I'm adding persistence to my list of your appealing traits."

"I can assure you—I have a selfish motive."

"Do you now? And what is it?"

"So my children will someday see the princess as queen on the throne—and be free."

"Ahhh, yes. Well, then, I didn't exactly tell you how the princess will get to Earth."

"No you didn't, but I do know that sending a newborn baby through time and space is preposterous. I don't care what the crystals say. It's the most idiotic thing I have ever heard in my entire life," Doc Tikkum said. "In fact, it's insane. I mean, do you know anybody who's ever done it?"

"Well, actually, I do."

"You do? Well that's a relief anyway. Who?"

"My mother."

"Your mother?" Doc Tikkum exclaimed in astonishment, throwing his arms up. He raised his torso up and turned red. "You asked me to sacrifice so much on something your mother said?"

"Yes, my mother."

"You're risking our lives and that of the princess because of something your mother told you? Why she spends more time as a bird than as a Human Fairy."

"I know my mother doesn't have the best of reputation and I know it seems far-fetched...."

"But you believe her anyway? You're crazy!"

"My ancestors came through this Fey Portal to get here from Earth."

"So you believe in your Human Fairy Tale folklore?"

"Yes, I do."

"This is preposterous! You're asking me to believe in a fairy tale."

Look, do *you* have of another plan to save her?"

Doc Tikkum bent his head down, feeling a mixture of sadness and shame for being doubtful. "All right. Let's assume your mother is right. You're saying it's the same Fey Portal that Human Fairies used to get to Kokakina from Earth thousands of years ago?" he asked.

"Yes, that's what I'm saying. The same portal."

"You're telling that the Human Fairy myth is real?" Doc Tikkum asked.

"All I know is my mother took my brothers and sisters to Earth and came back," Pinky replied.

"And you believe her?"

"Yes, I do."

"But why? Why do you believe her?"

"Because my mother wouldn't kill her own children."

"But what proof do you have?" Doc Tikkum raised an eyebrow.

"Me. She didn't kill me. If it's true that she would kill her children, why didn't she kill me, too?"

"That's a good question."

"Exactly. My mother raised me in humiliation and poverty because she knew I couldn't pass as a Human. My skin is too pink to pass on Earth."

"You know, that's a good, strong, and logical argument." Doc Tikkum was impressed by Pinky's reasoning as to why Lunamilla had not killed her. "Well, what have we got to lose?" he said, looking back at Markolous and the Tettigards. "I might as well believe in something. You can get us out of this, can't you? I mean after the princess goes to Earth?"

"Of course I can, friend."

The start of a red shadow on the right side of the yellow moon slowly crept into sight.

"It's beginning...," Pinky said, looking up at the summit and the reddish cast of the lunar eclipse without answering. The pearlescent radiance that the full moon normally cast on Kokakina dimmed as a red-hued light cascaded down on the glacier, bathing the peak in a reddish haze.

The Super Blood Moon

A faint buzzing sound came from the approaching Tettigards. In a collective swarm formation they were ready for the kill.

"Listen, my species can climb fast on this type of terrain. I'll climb the mountain with the princess, and you fly behind us," Doc Tikkum said.

"That's a great idea. Get going," Pinky said.

"We're in this together—right?"

"Right. We're in this together."

Pinky looked down at the magical Rose Quartz on the princess' neck, which dazzled in the reddish moonlight. She lifted it up. "Don't you find—I mean it's amazing—the necklace is a divining rod to get to Earth and back?"

"Yes—amazing—come on—let's go."

Doc Tikkum turned and climbed up the mountain with the princess.

"It not only guides you to Earth—it guides you back to Kokakina." She looked at Doc Tikkum and the princess higher up on the glacier.

"What—exactly is going on here?" Doc Tikkum stopped in his tracks and looked back at Pinky who was now a good fifteen feet below him for he was still climbing.

"It will guide you there and then back to Kokakina," she said.

The buzzing of the Tettigards' wings was so loud it hurt their ears and they could not hear each other.

"Why are you still down there. You're supposed to be flying behind us?" Doc Tikkum asked shouting.

"I'll be there shortly—I promise," Pinky beamed to him through her third eye speaking with him that way because she knew even though he did not know it yet, he was a magical being and was receptive to that form of communication.

"You know, I thought my wife was bad. But you? You're the most difficult, infuriating creature I've encountered in all my years," Doc Tikkum shouted angrily as he turned to resume the climb, scrambling over some boulders to get to the top.

The Tettigards were so close now they could hear the humming of the individual Tettigards' wings.

"What kind of a Tarragonian am I? I can't just leave her...." Doc Tikkum turned and saw Pinky standing twenty-five feet below him on the trail.

"Are you afraid of snakes, Doc Tikkum?" she called through her third eye to him, with a gleam in her eyes that was almost wicked.

"Now, what are you talking about—I'm a homeothermic reptile. Snakes are just lizards without feet, for fairy's sake," Doc

Tikkum shouted looking down the side of the mountain at Pinky, understanding everything she said to him through her third eye. He could smell Elfman's blood in the faint stink of the Tettigards and he knew his friend could as well. "What are you waiting for—FLY—FLY!" he yelled.

Pinky began to morph into something quite large. A gigantic, two-headed snake close to seventy-five long writhed on the trail. Without warning, the serpent lunged up and entwined Doc Tikkum, who was clutching the princess in his arms. He closed his eyes as he felt the squeeze of the snake's embrace. "Wait—no—what are you doing?" he asked. The snake undulated its body and threw them high into the air.

"PINKY—" Doc Tikkum bellowed. "I'm afraid of heights!"

The princess joined in, hollering at the top of her lungs, "Aaaah!" as they flew through the air toward the top of the glacier.

Then, the swaying, undulating coral-pink two-headed snake focused her slit-pupil eyes on the mountainside next to her and a legion of writhing, venomous, two-headed snakes slithered out of the crystal ice-covered rock.

Just then, Markolous, Tithoreus and the Tettigards arrived. Markolous and Tithoreus pulled their swords from their sheaths and slashed at the two-headed snakes.

Snapping and hissing, the serpents swayed back and forth. The two-headed vipers struck and snatched the Tettigards out of the air with their razor sharp teeth. The Tettigards attacked back with the deadly pointed rostra on their heads. But the two-headed snakes coiled their muscular bodies around the Tettigards, squeezing and suffocating them. Then, the snakes tossed the mangled insect bodies down the slope to their deaths. Soon—all the Tettigard soldiers had been obliterated. Now the only ones left, Markolous and Tithoreus, stood back-to-back, fighting the two-headed snakes.

"Tithoreus...," Markolous shouted.

Tithoreus turned.

"Don't look in their eyes—Pinky *is* trying to enchant us."

One of the two-headed snakes seized Tithoreus in its jaws. Wrapping its body around the Tettigard captain, it started to crush Tithoreus' exoskeleton as he struggled to escape. The two-headed serpent thrashed him back and forth and threw Tithoreus against the mountainside. His body lay motionless.

A familiar scent of Rosa Centifolia wafted into Markolous' nostrils. The jade-green eyes of the snake that had defeated Tithoreus bored into him. Using his shield, he blocked the enchanted snake as she snapped at him with her razor-sharp teeth. "I should have killed you in the Tower of the Forgotten when I had the chance...," he snarled, knowing it was Pinky. With a cry of vicious hatred, he jumped onto the serpent's back and thrust his sword into her neck.

The remaining conjured snakes arched and twisted into a shocking pink vapor, leaving only the one that was Pinky. The surviving enchanted snake's tongues flicked out between her four rows of teeth. There was no love left between her and Markolous. He had killed Elfman and Flanyanna—the two Human Fairies she loved the most. Gathering up her hatred, she struck.

Markolous raised up his shield and a vicious thrust of his sword lodged in her throat. Mortally wounded, the two-headed serpent collapsed. It writhed and coiled on the ground, transforming back into Pinky. Blood trickled from her mouth. Looking up, the sky around the eclipsing moon turned black.

A constable of thousands of ravens flew over the moon in a close order formation, regularly arranged—so close together their wingtips were practically touching. The formation hovered above Pinky, as Markolous raised his sword.

The caw of a sole raven broke the stillness as its shadow passed across Pinky's face. "Nothing is what it appears to be," she said, spitting out the blood in her throat onto the crystal, blue-white snow.

A pulsing pink beam shot upwards from her and twirled in the air.

Markolous plunged his blade into her breast. He thrust his hand into her chest cavity, reaching for her heart, to eat it to gain her power. His eyes widened in disbelief—Pinky's heart was gone!

Pinky's etheric body rose. It was no longer invisible. She was composed of fine points of light resembling icy particles painted on a window by the winter's frost. It looked like an outline of her physical body, but translucent.

Markolous dropped to his knees and lifted Pinky's still warm body into his arms. His face contorted. He had killed the only one he ever felt love for.

Pinky's lifeless physical body transformed into Calisandra. Disgusted, Markolous dropped her on the snow and crawled away for he was holding the corpse of the three hundred year old Dungeon Witch.

Pinky's shadow form turned and looked at him.

The constable of ravens swooped down.

Pinky morphed into a white raven and the congregated Shadow Fairies slowly raised themselves—their wings flapping in unison. Lifting off in a symmetrical V-shaped formation, they flew into the night sky over the almost total lunar eclipse with Pinky in the lead.

Tithoreus lifted himself up on one of his insect exoskeleton arms and pointed up the blue glacier. "Sire, the princess and the Tarragonian—they're getting away...." He fell back onto the ground having exhausted what little strength he had.

The cold glacier wind whipped at Markolous who stood still on the mountain. His skull began to change and shift and his lower face expanded to accommodate even larger canines.

In the coppery red moonlight, he unfurled his etheric wings, but, they were no longer sheer. They were now thick, leathery, and tainted tar black. A thickened membrane of skin and muscle stretched from the now dramatically lengthened clawed ring finger on his hands. His dark wings extended along the sides of his body, down to his ankles. His vampiric bat wings propelled him menacingly up the mountainside.

The moon was becoming blood. Markolous had transformed. He was no longer a Human Fairy. He had been consumed by the Lord of the Darkness. There was no turning back.

The Fey Portal

Stunned by the impact with the snowbank where he had landed, Doc Tikkum slowly got up. Somehow, he had managed to hold onto the princess. In her sling across his shoulder, she smiled and gurgled at him. His heart pounded faster, and his eyes widened in alarm for she was no longer wearing the queen's necklace. Panicking, he looked desperately about and was blinded by brilliant light flaring in the snow—the queen's necklace. He snatched it up and put it back around the princess' neck.

He went to the edge of the snowbank and looked down. He strained his eyes in the red moonlight reflecting off the glacier. A dark, sinister monster with flapping, membranous wings flew up the mountain towards him and the princess.

"Pinky!" he called out in hopeless desperation, but he knew she would not be coming. "I can't take her to Earth. I'm not magical."

In a frenzy he jumped back and turned to the mountain. The glacial ice before him shimmered. Moving as fast as he could, he ran towards the blue crystal glacier, looking for the entrance to the Fey Portal. He rubbed at the blue-tinged snow on the glacier with his hands. An iridescent reddish light came from inside the crystal mountain. The snow tumbled down, revealing a hole at the bottom. He dropped on all fours and, shoveling the snow away with his clawed fingers, he looked in.

A low growl emanated from the hole. He drew back, holding the princess behind him to protect her.

An arrow whizzed past and bounced off of the mountainside, just missing the princess. Doc Tikkum dropped onto his knees and scrambled inside the bored out hole, carrying the princess with one arm in front of him.

Magically, the glacier mountain pulled back to accommodate his size. He no longer had to squat for passage. The rigid, dense ice formation liquified as he walked through it. Now standing upright, he carried the princess through the frozen glacier. As soon as they passed through the glacial ice it solidified behind them.

Then, Doc Tikkum tumbled down into darkness. Instinctively, he curled into a ball around the princess and rolled down an incline, eventually stopping in growing light.

Standing upright, he looked about him in awe. They were in a vast catacomb with a vaulted ceiling that glistened with a multitude of humming colored crystals, ranging from three to twenty feet in length.

"Grrrrr...."

Doc Tikkum and the princess were not alone.

A pack of Hokkaido wolves paced back and forth in the cave. Above their shoulder blades, their dorsal capes and neck fur stood straight up. One wolf slowly moved forward toward Doc Tikkum. Moving his head, the wolf looked at the side of the cavern.

"What is it? What are you trying to tell me—Alpha Wolf?" Doc Tikkum asked, knowing that these wolves were sacred to Human Fairies.

The Alpha Male lowered his front legs and paws down and pushed his rear hips towards the back of the glacier until his body made an inverted 'V.' He bowed. Focused on Doc Tikkum, his stare was unflinching. He tossed his head in a slow, subtle movement and his muzzle pointed straight up as if he was going to howl. Instead, he gave a choppy bark, "Woof—woof."

"I don't understand...," Doc Tikkum said. "What are you trying to tell me?"

The agitated wolf's ears flattened back slightly as he stared hard at Doc Tikkum, his lips pursed together....

"Oof—oof," he emitted a soft, rapid, puffing sound.

"Oof—oof," the other wolves joined in with their muzzles lifted.

The vocalizations harmonized with the vibration of the crystals in the cavern.

Slowly, the back of the glacier slid open, revealing the now waxing Blood Moon and the vast panorama of dense stars in the Milky Way galaxy.

The wolves moved from the back of the cavern.

Hidden behind them, an underground stream flowed, with a small island in the middle. The water lapped its sides. Now bathed in red, it glowed in the red moon light.

The Alpha Male motioned with his body and his head for Doc Tikkum to follow him towards the island.

"The island?" Doc Tikkum cried. "Is that the Fey Portal?"

The light of the Super Blood Moon was so bright it nearly blinded him. He plunged into the red water with the princess high overhead. Wading towards the small—now pulsating—island, he could feel an electric energy running through his veins as he reached it.

Suddenly, the princess was ripped from his grasp.

Doc Tikkum turned to see a huge, winged, black vampire bat holding her in his hands. The vampire creature dropped to the ground and ran across the cavern floor in a bounding gait. Putting the princess down, he revealed his large protruding canines ready to drink her blood. He bent over the princess.

"NOOOO—" Doc Tikkum screamed, raising himself out of the water in a rage.

Markolous turned and let out a deep, unearthly roar.

Doc Tikkum ran across the cavern and grabbed the Markolous' throat, choking him. Markolous spun about, and, breaking Doc Tikkum's grip, tossed him across the cavern.

"The princess!" Doc Tikkum bellowed.

Markolous emitted another unnerving shriek and turned back towards the princess.

"Get away from her!" Doc Tikkum raised his battered body up, smoke streaming from his nostrils. Then, Doc Tikkum's scales became more pronounced—pentagonal-like teardrops. He started to move, but searing pain in his back stopped him. Wings that had been hidden for centuries popped out of his broad shoulders and down his back. He opened his mouth and fire belched out.

Markolous turned. Across the cavern stood a mythical creature out of ancient legend—a dragon.

"I said get away from her." Doc Tikkum's voice boomed out, strong and powerful.

Forgetting his fear of heights, Doc Tikkum flew across the chamber and grabbed Markolous. He dragged Markolous into the water. Markolous struggled but was unable to free himself from Doc Tikkum's massive clawed hands that throttled him, pushing him down into the water. After a time, Markolous' resistance ceased. He floated face down in the water.

Doc Tikkum pulled himself out of the water and, going over to the princess, picked her up. The island was now bathed in the Super Blood Moon's beams. It glowed red—pulsing and throbbing—each vibration held longer and deeper than the last. He carried the princess onto the platform and lifted himself up onto it. Steps leading up into the sky appeared.

Suddenly, a massive hand grabbed Doc Tikkum's tough, scaly neck and flung him back into the water. Markolous raised Doc Tikkum in his demonic hands and threw him into the side of the cave.

Markolous shot over to where Doc Tikkum lay—stunned. He drove his enormous canines deep into Doc Tikkum's throat. Doc Tikkum screamed in agony.

The magical steps to the Fey Portal started to disappear. The Alpha Male wolf leaped onto Markolous' back—biting into his neck forcing Markolous to release Doc Tikkum.

Doc Tikkum slowly raised himself up. The princess lay at the bottom of the steps to the Fey Portal playing with her foot as she watched the steps fade away. He extended his battered wings and flew across the cavern. He scooped up the princess and followed the disappearing steps that led into the Blood Moon.

A horrible yelp filled the cavern. The Alpha Male, the sacred guardian to the Human Fairy world, fell to the ground, his lacerated neck bleeding from puncture wounds.

Her belly hugging the floor, his mate, the Alpha Female, crawled over and lay down next to him howling to the Super Blood Moon.

Gathering himself up, Markolous extended his wings and flew after Doc Tikkum and the princess.

Now at the very top of the staircase that was about to vanish, Doc Tikkum lifted the necklace off the princess' neck and raised it towards the enlarged Super Blood Moon. With a sustained, hellacious roar that filled the cavern, a hole opened in the Blood Moon. With no hesitation Doc Tikkum jumped in with the princess. It closed immediately.

The mighty blast of the Fey Portal closing threw Markolous back into the cave, slamming him against one of the walls.

"No matter where you go," he screamed—rising up from the floor, "I will find you."

The Super Blood Moon was over. Kokakina, the land of the Human Fairies, went into total cloaked darkness.

Doc Tikkum and the princess fell into a suspended liquid space of dazzling light and plummeted through billions of pale, celestial bodies. The cosmic travelers plunged through the Fey Portal and slipped through time and space towards Earth.

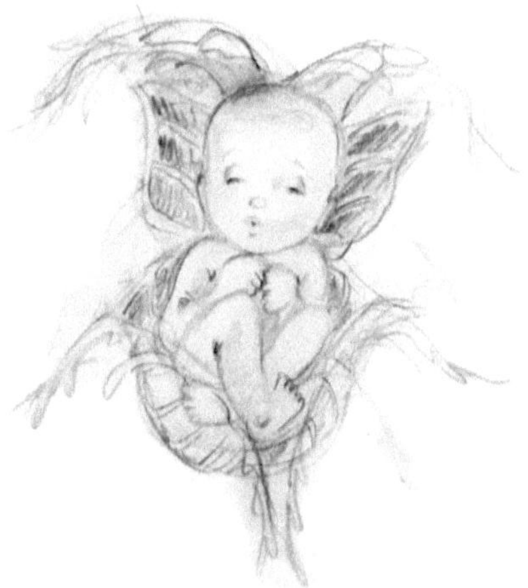

Earth

Although dark, the sky was cobalt blue. Flat, crew-cut, carrot-top mountains loomed as Doc Tikkum and the princess fell. An agave cactus, found only in a small area in the American Southwest, rose up high into the sky and pinpointed their destination. The purple lupine and Mexican gold poppies gently danced the rumba to the night crickets' beat—awaiting Doc Tikkum's and the princess' arrival.

Far below them, on the dusty red desert floor, rustling through some dry sage shrubs, a hungry coyote stalked his next meal. His rumbling digestion and keen instincts to hunt made his emaciated frame alert and his mind cunning. His large, erect ears framed his face showcasing a long, pointed nose with black nostrils and somewhat sad, though wild, green eyes. Crouching, he listened for sounds that would betray the hiding place of his next meal.

The luminous full moon provided bright light as the coyote's eyes scanned the red, dusty terrain. His light-brown and white fur blended with his surroundings. Suddenly, sniffing a strange and new scent, he stopped and glanced upward.

A mysterious shadow crossed over the moon. Cloaked in blackness, a three-dimensional object traveled through the Blood Moon, almost as if suspended in liquid space. Weaving out of control, the plunging object came straight toward the coyote. Frozen in terror, the poor, cringing creature flattened himself onto the ground like a pancake in a skillet, seeking some kind of protection.

Fortunately for the coyote, the falling object flew over him and landed elsewhere on the red desert plateau. If the coyote had blinked, he would have missed its dazzling arrival. Accompanying the night's orchestra of crickets blasting out a desert sonata, he unleashed a haunting howl.

With nostrils now flared at the Blood Moon, the coyote again picked up the puzzling, unusual scent. He darted his head in different directions licking his drooling chops, hungry for the unknown beasts he had never encountered before....

Tumbling, Doc Tikkum folded up like a ball, protecting the princess as he rolled in the red desert dust. He poked his head out of the loose, protective skin on his neck. Glancing about, his eyes rotated separately of each other like computerized lenses. He regarded the ancient red rocks. Bending down, he carefully took off his medical bag. He had resumed his original form.

He scanned the pink-hued moonlit horizon, smelling the sweet tang of sage as he examined the lay of the land, listening for any sounds of another creature. Lit by red light waves cascading down from the Blood Moon that had just transported them through the Fey Portal, he spied a sandstone canyon with an abandoned Anasazi village clinging to its edge. Hollow and empty, the only sound was the chirping of night crickets.

On the massive canyon walls were three infinity circles. Each displayed five circles, one inside another. For a moment, his protruding eyes studied them, and he understood their meaning. They were ancient Human Fairy symbols.

Slumping with exhaustion and satisfied that they were in no immediate danger, Doc Tikkum caught his breath and heaved a sigh of relief. There was no time to lose, though. He must accomplish his task quickly or he would be stuck on Earth and never see his dear wife and twelve children again.

Squaring his shoulders with renewed resolve, he cast his eyes about to determine his next move. The princess gurgled and cooed in his arms. She smiled because she knew him. Her eyes twinkled, and her baby Human Fairy wings, so light and iridescent, rustled in the desert wind.

"It appears your relatives have moved. No worries. We'll find them."

He wrapped her back in her warm tablecloth and put her in his medical bag. In the soft hue of the Blood Moon, through a sliver-like peek in the flap, the princess warily took in the unfamiliar red canyon surroundings. Her ability to comprehend with her five senses was more developed than those of a human baby, and she discerned danger.

With renewed courage, the hungry coyote rose up from his crouched position. Licking his watering mouth, he took in their scent. He had never smelled their exotic body odors before. His wild eyes seemed to penetrate into them.

His nostrils flared. He hadn't eaten in days and was quite willing to try something new. He howled at the Blood Moon as a dark, dense cloud drifted over it it. The coyote's nose told him where to go in the shadows. He ran full-throttle toward the new strangers in the desert. His broken, rotting cuspids chomped down in anticipation.

Rigid terror engulfed Doc Tikkum as he inhaled the stench of the filthy beast. He fled in the opposite direction with the princess. Ahead, he saw a campfire in the distance and smell the night air. "Humans...."

He clawed his way through the now heavy sagebrush that slashed his skin through his clothes, knowing the coyote was not far behind. He scaled the rugged red rocks. Now a hunted, tired creature, he slithered through the vast desert plain.

A deep gully yawned in front of him.

Scrambling his way down the embankment, he gasped, trying to get across the great divide before the pursuer caught up. His hands managed to dig into the soft red earth, getting a better hold as he scrambled over and ascended the far side.

"Aaagh!" He cried out, coming to an immediate halt.

A giant saguaro cactus towered in front of him, its arms raised, ready to vanquish opponents with its enormous fists. In the half-light, rows of saguaro sentinels emerged behind the first, all seemingly ready to kill them.

Doc Tikkum barreled through the field of cactus soldiers with his infant charge. The saguaro lashed out at him, cutting his clothing and puncturing his skin.

The coyote pursued in the red moonlight, drooling into the dirt as he ran. His eyes penetrated the darkness with radar-like precision. He notched his pursuit up to top speed.

Doc Tikkum raced across the desert flatlands toward the fire in hopes of finding humans with whom he could leave the princess. The red sandstone canyon and Anasazi ruins were no longer in sight.

The coyote stopped running and hunched behind a silhouetted, skeletal sage bush. Lowering his head, he examined the meal he had been chasing. The chase, bringing down his prey, ripping at its flesh and eating the entrails were all his birthright.

The cold desert wind picked up and clouds drifted over the Blood Moon. Shifting the backpack, Doc Tikkum picked up the coyote's foul stink again, and—as he did so—his color returned to dark red.

He had heard legends of strange, monstrous creatures on Earth. He had hoped not to encounter any. He wished he would instead find Human Fairies that had stayed behind or at least a friendly Mermaid or Merman to raise the princess. The Tarragonian sighed, wiping his brow with a fine, silk handkerchief made from spider-silk thread. Glancing up, he saw the clouds obscuring the moon begin to break up.

He knew he had to survive at all costs. The bundle he carried was far too precious and, therefore, he could not fight the pursuing creature.

The coyote sniffed, caught a fresh scent, and stopped in his tracks. Humans. He did not wish to enter the world of Humans. He knew they carried stiff snakes that belched fire and death. Frustrated, with his tail between his legs, he turned and pounced with his two front paws, grabbing something in his teeth.

Doc Tikkum didn't have his spectacles and without them he really couldn't see all that well. He had thought it best to leave them safe with his wife and now regretted his decision. In the newly emerged bright moonlight, he squinted and saw the coyote—the source of the stench—dancing a jig with an unknown partner—a consolation prize that would probably prefer not to be dancing with him—a poisonous snake.

Doc Tikkum huddled with the princess behind some sage. In front of the fire danced a female Human and a male Human. The male's hair was as long as the female's. Behind them sat a rusted, age-worn, hand-painted, pea-green Volkswagen bus.

The man handed his partner a pipe. "This is good shit...."

"You're not kidding!"

Doc Tikkum felt the burlap satchel on his back begin to move in a somewhat agitated fashion.

"Shhhh—my little princess."

He slowly crept towards the bus. Seeing an opening with a strange wheel in the front, he sat the princess on a cushy seat and slipped away, hoping to get back to see his good wife and family.

Suddenly, he realized he couldn't get back without the Rose Crystal necklace. He crept back to the princess and slipped the necklace from around her neck.

"I'm sorry, princess, but I need this. It's the only way I can get back to Kokakina. Don't worry. I'll be back. I promise, in sixteen years for you."

Looking around to make sure no one was watching, he transformed back into a dragon and slipped away into the darkness, flying back as fast as he could to the Anasazi ruins and the Fey Portal.

The End

Author

C. Jill Hefte is an award-winning filmmaker who was living in the red rock vortexes of Sedona, Arizona when she got the idea to write about Human Fairies. One night, after viewing the Blood Moon, she was awakened to a little girl's voice. When Jill asked who it was, she said her name was Clarissa Hedgestone, and that she was a Human Fairy. It has taken Ms. Hefte four years to create the five-part chronicle. Clarissa Hedgestone and the Blood Moon is the first of her series.

C. Jill Hefte lives in a fey cottage in Carmel by the Sea, California with her beloved fairy dog. Read more at AHumanFairytale.com. Follow author at https://twitter.com/CHedgestone.

Portrait of C. Jill Hefte by Vaughn Greditzer